Happy bi Sheila x

McGunker

Regards Michael

Michael Conaty

TRAFFORD
USA • Canada • UK • Ireland

Some of the characters portrayed in **McGunker** are purely fictitious and any resemblance to persons alive or dead is purely coincidental.

© Copyright 2005 Michael Conaty.

All rights reserved. No part of this publication may be reproduced, stored in a retrieval system, or transmitted, in any form or by any means, electronic, mechanical, photocopying, recording, or otherwise, without the written prior permission of the author.

Note for Librarians: A cataloguing record for this book is available from Library and Archives Canada at www.collectionscanada.ca/amicus/index-e.html
ISBN 1-4120-6196-2

Printed in Victoria, BC, Canada. Printed on paper with minimum 30% recycled fibre. Trafford's print shop runs on "green energy" from solar, wind and other environmentally-friendly power sources.

TRAFFORD

Offices in Canada, USA, Ireland and UK
This book was published *on-demand* in cooperation with Trafford Publishing. On-demand publishing is a unique process and service of making a book available for retail sale to the public taking advantage of on-demand manufacturing and Internet marketing. On-demand publishing includes promotions, retail sales, manufacturing, order fulfilment, accounting and collecting royalties on behalf of the author.

Book sales for North America and International:
Trafford Publishing, 6E–2333 Government St.,
Victoria, BC v8t 4p4 CANADA
phone 250 383 6864 (toll-free 1 888 232 4444)
fax 250 383 6804; email to orders@trafford.com
Book sales in Europe:
Trafford Publishing (UK) Limited, 9 Park End Street, 2nd Floor
Oxford, UK ox1 1hh UNITED KINGDOM
phone 44 (0)1865 722 113 (local rate 0845 230 9601)
facsimile 44 (0)1865 722 868; info.uk@trafford.com
Order online at:
trafford.com/05-1097

10 9 8 7 6 5 4

DEDICATION

Anyway this book is dedicated to the memory of those we lost along the way; our Dad Jimmy or "Jem" Conaty, our Grandparents Elizabeth and Mick Brady and Tommy and Annie Conaty, Uncle Jack and his wife Agnes, Kathleen and Katie Conaty, Uncle Benny, Baby Tracey; Anna Mae and Tony Hughes and their grandson Niall Lavelle, Jimmy and Mary Ellen Delaney, Finbar Delaney, Eilish Delaney, Ned and Pat Delaney, Paddy Smith, Séamus Cullen, Edward and Simon O'Hanlon, Gerard O'Reilly from Crubany and Darren Argue from Drung.

It's also dedicated to the memory of the wee ones that never quite made it.

May they all rest in peace.

It's for Phyllis our mother and for all she did for us and it also goes out to our brother Dermot and sister Anne cos they missed most of it anyway.

A special word of thanks to Mairéad Conaty and Tony O'Brien. I owe yous!

An apology to my good friend Tom Coyle. Tom advised me not to include bad language. Impossible Tom, not in the house we grew up.

Fond memories of Bruno.

Finally it's with love to my wife Martina and our childer, Niamh, Niall, Diarmaid, Muireann and Éadaoinn…

Bestest friends!

Chapter 1

Anyway Ned's brae is a tight one. From the moment you begin climbing it's an uphill battle, get as far as Mary Margaret's gate and you're entitled to a breather. Then the final stone-ridden bit of an ascent. Gawk round and it's an overwhelming feeling, look out at Corratubber, Fairtown, Heney and in the distance, Corranure. It's exactly 1638 of my steps from the top of Ned's brae down to McGunker's house. I know cos I counted them. It was the start of September 1973 and we came down that brae, Sean Reilly and myself, on an old cross-barred bicycle. Sean's on autopilot and there's me on the bar gripping the silver rim between the handlebars. Death-defying stuntmanship; one loose pebble, one stray cat or even one of Mary Margaret's two tethered goats and it was all over! Down that brae on the width of a worn tyre bedded into a rusty bicycle wheel with brakes squeaking like a rabbit caught in a snare. We flew past McGunkers, into the corner and out again. Flat road ahead. Survival.

A whole new world was opening up to me and the rest of us Conartys. We'd just returned from exile in Drumalee, near Cavan Town. Exiled through party politics. When there's war, innocents suffer. We'd been the refugees caught up in the crossfire between some angry key players: Nanna our Gran, Phyllis and Jimmy our Mum and Dad, Lizzie our Aunt and Fr. Eddie our Uncle.

There were six of us in it so far. James was the eldest with long legs, brown hair and freckles on his face. Michael, that's me, was next with shorter legs, blond hair and blue eyes and no freckles on me face. "The next priest" according to the old fogies. Even at ten years of age I knew the expectations were high. Sure hadn't there been a priest in the family for the past five generations and hadn't John Brady even been ordained first Catholic Bishop of Perth in Australia in 1845, as it said on his monument in Castletara graveyard. I knew I had to study hard, get serious, finish Castletara N.S. and go to St. Pat's. From there onto Maynooth to become Fr. Michael and then get out and go and serve God's people somewhere.

In the middle of the boys was Tommy. He hadn't long legs either but had jet-black hair to compensate for this and he wore thick-rimmed glasses to help the cast in his eye. Tommy also had a wart on his right thumb. Fourth down was Eddie or Ned as we sometimes called him after his uncle the priest. Eddie hadn't long legs but was built like a tank and questioned things intelligently. He could be quiet and sullen sometimes and didn't lose his temper too often, but when he did, he was worth watching. He'd curl his tongue between his teeth, bite on it and let fly. Next was Harry. Now Harry, like James, had long legs and like me, had blond hair. He was gangly, even at six years of age and being the youngest of the first five boys, quickly learned that the only way to be heard was to shout loud and often: "Why this, why that and why the other?" was all we ever heard from Harry.

Philomena was born in 1968. We called her the princess cos she was a girl, the first-born daughter to Jimmy and Phyllis. We woke up that October morning and searched everywhere for Mammy. All the gardens, the orchard, the hay-shed, even Packie Brady's rocks across the road. We felt lost, confused, cheated. Our mother was gone and we didn't know where. Was she dead? Would she come back to us?

Was it our fault? Were we ould-fashioned? All we had to do was ask Nanna but headless chickens don't stop to think, ever.

It was windy and wet. "Here's Daddy home" shouted James. "He'll know". Sure enough Dad did know and with a big smile on his face informed us that we had a new baby sister. Her name would be Philomena and Mammy was with her in the hospital. Nanna shook hands with Dad and told us she'd put on boiled eggs for breakfast and to come in soon. "Why have we a sister?" asked Harry as we headed down behind the hayshed and searched through the nettles for a ball. "Why is Mammy in hostipal?" came next and then "Where do babies come from?"

Dad was bringing in the cows and shouted "yous better go in......have manners and ate what yous get and thank your grandmother".

James landed the ball over the hayshed and led us in.

Anyway, I'm sure it had all kicked off from the word go, back in the early sixties. Mum was the youngest of four, Anna Mae the eldest and sandwiched in between was Eddie and Lizzie.

Their Dad, our grandfather Mick Brady, had died when they were all quite young and they'd lived in the shadow of Uncle and Canon John Brady P.P. Templeport, Cavan. By all accounts, he was a toughie; strong-minded, uncompromising and bossy. He commanded, even demanded respect. His visits to his home place of Corratubber were of royal proportions. He blew the horn of his Ford car and neighbours were supposed to jump to attention, open gates, bow the knee and then slink away in fear of eternal damnation. Not so, one Ellen Fargie Reilly, who once famously roared, "Kiss me arse, Father".

I'm sure Fr. John meant well but he had a funny way of showing it. I'm sure too that he was well intentioned with regard to the welfare of his nephew and three nieces. But then why? Why would he dissuade Eddie from becoming "Fr. Eddie" and send him up the

Civil Service road and then casually remind him that there were three farms of land in Corratubber and Fairtown to be nurtured and more importantly that the Brady name be maintained for generations to come. Poor Ned! His only crime was being the only son. A younger sibling had been stillborn. Perhaps he would've made a difference. Anna Mae, the eldest girl was easily the people's choice. A fighter of injustice, a giver, a mad hatter and one hell of a dancer. She saw shit, didn't like it and therefore fought it. She'd be accused of having attitude. Lizzie was next. Then came our Mum. Phyllis was the Cinderella of the family, minus the ugly sisters so to speak. She couldn't remember her Dad visually but told us of bouncing on his knee and him playing the fiddle to entertain them on the floor. I'm sure they'd had a special relationship. If only he had survived longer for her sake. McGunker always said that he'd been a great worker and a very genuine and daecent man.

Mick Brady was a peacekeeper trying to balance the erratic mood swings of a wife and those of a widowed sister of his, …not easy! Phyllis was two when he died.

Allied to this I'm sure, our grandfather lived in the shadow of the Canon, his brother and a few McEvoy gunmen to boot. The McEvoy brothers-in-law were tough Crosserlough republican gunslingers. Fighting a totally different type of oppression. Mick Brady looked out for the needs of his widowed sister and her family. He died a young father and left our Nanna to rear their family of four. This she would've managed admirably had it not been for outside interference. It was the start of a lesson for us all. Don't cause shite but don't take it either. On the whole the neighbours were good and helped out it would seem. Nanna was a thrifty woman, gathered the eggs, sold them and invested the proceeds in a rainy day account in Cavan Post Office. Tuesday was town day, Ned the donkey was tackled up and the journey undertaken. Eggs were sold and groceries bought. She only had the three girls to feed now as Uncle Eddie had been taken under the wing of the Canon to be educated. Anna

Mae would soon commence her apprenticeship to the clothing trade leaving Lizzie and Phyllis at home. When the Canon came knocking, offering to take another sibling into care, Phyllis lost out, not surprisingly.

Anyway she spent two miserable years in a place called Kilnavart near Templeport in West Cavan. Mary was the housekeeper, car mechanic, farmer, gardener and nurse all rolled into one. She was about sixty, a tough woman who nonetheless remained loyal to the Canon and stuck up for him when the need arose. Mary reckoned that our Mum would be educated by the Canon and then enter the teaching profession. Her Gaeilge was more than good. Nanna, however, felt that her daughter was merely an apprentice to Mary and would one day fill her shoes. She was powerless to do anything about it. Phyllis had been taken from Castletara and was now being educated by Master Lane in Currin N.S. He in turn surely felt pressurised when it came to the academic welfare of the Canon's niece. All in all, the end product was a two-year sentence of misery. Phyllis went to school, came home, helped with the chores and was then summoned to the parlour to face an educational interrogation from the Canon himself. She cried herself to sleep most nights and yearned to get home to Corratubber.

Salvation came in the form of big sister, Anna-Mae, who informed her uncle by post that Phyllis would not be returning after the Halloween break of 1946. The Canon took it but not on the chin! Diplomatic relations were broken off for about five years following receipt by Nanna of a stinking letter. The Canon was not impressed.

Phyllis returned home to resume her primary education in St. Clare's convent in Cavan. It was known as the Poor Clare's because of all the orphans in the care of the nuns there. A sound neighbour, Peter Rooney, would carry her to school on the bar of his bike. Peter was employed as a tradesman and was involved in the rebuilding of the Poor Clare convent following a tragic fire there in which many innocent orphans had perished: he was to play a huge role in Mum's future well being.

By this time Uncle Eddie was receiving his tutorage in U.C.D. and found himself in digs with a great Cavan footballer, PJ Duke. Anna Mae was working away in John Brady's drapery and footwear and would, now and again, treat her kid sister to tea and buns in the Milseáin Breifne snack shop at lunchtime in Cavan town. Lizzie studied away at the local tech.

By all accounts, Corratubber was an open house. Neighbours gathered in at nighttime; the Costelloes, Boylans, Cahills, Clarkes, Bradys, Mineys and Jemmy Dunne. Card games were played and everyone suppered on tea with currant bread and jam. Time passed, war and its rationing was over and a whole new era dawned. Anna Mae had migrated to the neighbouring town of Bailieboro and cycled the twenty odd miles home on her half-day. She'd do the hair, stick on some make-up, a nice dress, maybe one of Lizzie's, and dance the night away in Killygarry or Butlersbridge. She fell in love with a youthful and handsome Jimmy Greenan.

Lizzie was now working in the drapery section of Provider's Store in Cavan and Mother commenced her secretarial career in Smith's Garage at the top of the town in 1954. Eddie studied away in Dublin. Then out of the blue the Canon died. Seemingly, he'd always prayed that he'd die in a chapel and he got his wish at another priest's funeral in Killeshandra.

Anyway this opened the gates for Uncle Eddie to pursue his chosen clerical career, albeit at a mature student stage. He moved to Blacklion in Cavan to prepare himself for life with the White Fathers as an African missionary. He made his decision, Mum told us, on the wee hill at the back of Corratubber. It was a mixed blessing for Nanna. She liked the idea of Eddie being a priest but why head to Africa?

Meanwhile Anna Mae moved to Moate in Co. Westmeath, converted the front room of her new house into a shop and married a gas character called Tony Hughes. Lizzie married Sean Rehill. Phyllis grew up and graduated as secretary to the O'Hanlon family in the local Anglo-Celt press in Cavan town's Church Street. She was happy now and once Nanna could be appeased everyone else should be happy too.

Anyway, our Dad, Jimmy Conarty ran a bicycle shop at the top of Connolly St. with his brother Tommy. The Conarty boys came from Corriga near a village called Crosskeys. They, along with our other uncles, Patsy, Jack, Benny, Tommy and Harry were hardy men and could look after themselves. Dad, it was said, could easily pass as half-Italian. He was tall, bronzed and dark-haired. The fact that he was also one of the fighting Conartys no doubt enhanced his reputation. Anyway, through Peter Rooney, they found each other and married in 1960. Dad was now running his own meal store and shop on the outskirts of Crosskeys. It was the early sixties; Neil Armstrong was nowhere near the moon and JFK was alive and well. The troubles in Northern Ireland were almost a decade away, yet "one man one vote" had its own special meaning in Corratubber. From the word go our Dad was up against it. He was very much his own man and wanted it that way. He was genuinely in love with Mum, we knew that much. It was the constant interference he couldn't handle. Looking back, it's fair to say he was a victim of circumstance. He had married Phyllis Brady and with Mum came her mother, the home place at Corratubber and two outlying farms, one up the road called Ellens and the other down the way in Fairtown. Times had changed. Mick Brady was long dead. This was 1960's Ireland.

Anna Mae didn't give a toss. She was her own woman with no chip on her shoulder and had now purchased, with Tony, a lounge bar in Northgate Street in Athlone. The sign outside read "Hughes Bar and Lounge". Eddie studied away and was happy. Herself wasn't. She wanted her freedom and yet couldn't let go of Nanna. Fr. Eddie in turn had offered the ranch to her and Anna Mae. Both declined for differing reasons. He then gave it to Phyllis and with it tonnes of baggage and grief. Civil war and its unrest were about to erupt.

Chapter 2

Drumalee could've been a million miles away, it was only four. Different people, different culture and none of the kids wore wellies. We must've caused a stir. James, Michael, Tommy, Eddie, Harry and the long awaited kid sister Philomena. We picked up very much where we'd left off in Corratubber. A sloping garden up the back meant we could carry on with our agricultural activities; building farms in the clay and using long sticks as make-believe cows and horses. Though odd to the neighbours it certainly helped us to acclimatise and forget the troubles of the past. We lived second left in a row of four houses, on the way to Cavan town. Then again it could be said we lived third right in a row of four houses on the way to Castletara. Entry to the front door was via eight steep steps. Upstairs there were three bedrooms, a bathroom and a landing for building farms on with burnt matchsticks on wet days. Downstairs we had a kitchen of fair size with a jubilee cooker, a back scullery or kitchenette as some would call it, a box room off the kitchen and a big sitting room to the front. It was all new to us as we tore about excitedly, exploring our new environs.

Anyway the last few months had been decidedly dodgy in Corratubber. I remember seeing Dad standing in the hayshed as it poured rain one Monday morning. "Go on in, there's a good lad" he encouraged me. I beckoned at him to come in too. "Herself is céilying, I'll be in when she's gone", he replied. Herself left eventually, but the harm was done. Nanna gave out to Mammy about Daddy drinking with McGunker and Francie Kelly the night before in Eddie Gorman's pub. The mood was set for the day and weeks ahead. There always seemed to be tension when Herself was coming on a visit, while she was there and more especially when she'd gone. It filtered through to us kids. I'd look at Mum and feel sorry for her. She had a countenance of anxiety etched on her brow and her black rimmed glasses couldn't hide the tears. I hated when she cried. Nanna, now thoroughly wound up, could go days and weeks without speaking to Dad. She'd sit behind the newspaper and mutter away every time someone passed. I felt sorry for her too. She was old and frail. Her speckled blue pinafore concealed a lifetime of hassle and misery. Now and again she'd dip her fingers into a pocket and slowly withdraw a silvermint. Her false teeth had a small bit of cabbage stuck in the top row and the lenses of her glasses were perfectly circular. Her fingers were long and boney and she wore her hair in a bun, carefully roofed with a net cap. Most of all, she was or had the capacity to be, a kind and loving woman. She'd squeeze your hand now and again and we knew that deep down she loved us. If we fell, she'd pick us up, dust us down and miraculously find her last smartie.

A peace treaty in 1968 had split the old house in Corratubber in two. Tensions were high that summer, plenty of interfering and giving out. In the end a line was drawn and Nanna was left with the kitchen and scullery and back bedroom behind the range. The refugees didn't fare too badly. We were given the upstairs minus Fr. Eddie's room. Our kitchen cum sitting room would be the old stately parlour now stripped of its Last Supper paintings and other serene artefacts. Water was drawn by bucket round the house from the scullery and left beneath the table, which nestled on one side of our kitchen cabinet. The main door of this press, when not covering up the bric-a-brac could be slid down and used as a surface on which to

McGunker

butter bread. I watched Mum one day through the parlour window as she tried to balance her bucket of water and pick her steps on that mucky pathway. Suddenly she slipped and fell on one of Fr. Eddie's cabbage ridges. When I got round to her she was laughing. It had started to rain again and she looked up at me and said "Michael, in life sometimes you might as well laugh as cry, never forget that son". I helped her to her feet and watched as she wiped away the slimy muck from her tights. Between the daily living quarters of the now segregated house lay a hallway. Under the stairs Dad had installed a big white bucket to save his boys running round to the bathroom and consequently avoiding conflict. Each day the piss bucket was emptied of its contents across the ditch and returned to its spot. Once when Mam had us on a tonic, it turned to a limey green colour and Harry thought we'd all die from some rare disease or other. The door from the hall into our old kitchen was now locked tight though not sound proof. Often Nanna had visitors, usually Herself or Rose Costello or maybe even the priest or sometimes some of Fr. Eddie's student friends. On days like these we knew to be quiet and not to be poking around. Once I was sent round in my Holy Communion suit. I was given the strictest instructions not to overstay my welcome as the domestic climate was hotting up. Nanna brought me in and thought I looked lovely in my black jacket, festooned with white handkerchief, and short trousers. I joined my hands and clasped my Communion booklet and rosary beads. She gave me a silvermint and slipped a ten-shilling note into my pocket. "I'd better go now Nanna" I said, "cos Mammy said not to stay too long in case you were in bad humour". "Well galang with you so, you ungrateful pup", she replied as she ushered me unceremoniously out the back half-door onto the stony street. I didn't know whether to laugh or cry or whether I should give the big red ten-shilling note back or not. Moments like these, I later learned, were called own-goals. The harm was done. What was Nanna to think now?

Anyway Castletara National School remained our only contact

with the past and helped us to maintain the link with Corratubber. Bean Uí Fiaich was a tall, strong woman with white bushy hair. She'd been teaching a lifetime there and had provided us with transport in her KID 934 Mini Minor any morning that we managed to dodge the CIE bus heading from town out to Cootehill. Mum filled the big blue flask and dropped it into the black homemade holdall and that would do us all at lunchtime with a few bread and butter and sugar or bread and jam "sangwidches". Castletara School was grand, a two-roomer and nobody mentioned Drumalee. Each room was heated with a pot-bellied stove and we'd watch the big ones gather whins on Pe Smith's rocks every evening at half-past two. We were still part of the gang, accepted unconditionally by girls and boys alike. "Built 1891" it said on a stone on the outside wall. Mrs. Fay taught the juniors and Mrs. Sexton, the newly arrived Principal, had the senior room. I found myself in second class helping the wee ones to count with Guinness bottle caps. Gaeilge was important to Bean Uí Fiaich as was catechism and republicanism and the plight of the black babies in Africa and that of the travellers in their new tigíns on Cavan's Fair-Green. She was strictly teetotal and God-fearing and yet, had us all belting out the strains of "Armoured Cars and Tanks and Guns" at a time when things were hotting up miles away below in Belfast. We hadn't a clue but sure sang along anyway. At lunchtime we'd weed the garden plot at the gable of the school and throw grass down each other's backs and wait for the big boney fist to rap the glass pane and warn us to be careful. Mrs. Sexton's big ones kicked ball at the back of the school and I marvelled at the way Frank Coyle put power into his shots with his black boots. If only I could graduate along with Sean and Oliver Reilly and Andy Traynor and make a name for myself on that back pitch. After all, I was a fully-fledged Liverpool supporter by now and it was only a matter of time before I'd link up with Kevin Keegan and Steve Heighway and John Toshack at Anfield. We'd gone to the Santa party that Christmas of '71. Dad wasn't working that day. Someone else could fill the petrol at Smith's

Garage. Tickets would come through the school, pink for the girls and blue for the boys and this became for us an annual pilgrimage. "C'mon are yous right there now?" Dad roared, looking at his watch. "Wash your face you" he beckoned at Tommy " and no rooting any of yous, or acting the bollox when we get there". The six of us sat into the back seat of our A40, IID 414.

The village square was thronging. There was a buzz of anticipation every time we looked down the big hill towards the Protestant church. Sooner or later Santy would come round that corner and be in full view of the masses, neatly perched in the back box attached to a Massey Ferguson tractor borrowed from the Agricultural College in Ballyhaze. Still we waited and waited.

"Where is he? the stupid cunt", I heard one irate father of a young clan mutter. It got darker and the snow began to fall, first a trickle and then enough to mat your hair and shoulders. We shuffled our feet and reversed with the flow back to the steps of Pat and Hughie Brady's Annalee Lounge and Bar. My heel got wedged against the granite step and I couldn't budge. The only way was back as the crowd was pressing with an almighty heave. I felt squeezed and panicky and helpless all at the same time. I leaned backwards and went down…then I saw it…a Leeds United player definitely…in a white jersey…it was Peter Lorimer. "Possesses the hardest shot in Division 1", I got as far as when a big redheaded fella of about fourteen grabbed it from me and gave me an earful. I tried to explain but by now he and his fellow hards were deeply engrossed in conversation about Peter Osgood and Charlie Cooke.

"Blue is the colour, football is the game, we're all together and …" some of them were now chanting much to my father's annoyance.

"Yous and your ould soccer" he grunted in their direction. "Don't support Leeds or Chelsea either" said a voice in my ear. It was Aiden, Lizzie's eldest son and a cousin of ours. He was someone I'd always thought was a lot younger than he actually was. He had loads of freckles and a silly, mischievous grin.

"Look, Michael, support Liverpool, they're the up and coming team and they've got some great players. I've a few posters at home and I'll give them to ya". "Thanks Aid…" The crowd surged forward and there was an almighty cheer… Santa was in sight. The heaving and squeezing reminded me of cattle penned together in Cavan Mart. I could hear Dad in the distance "Stay together, Stay together…Phyllis, have you the wee one?" After what seemed an eternity our end of the queue reached a red-faced, whisky reeking Santy and we all shook hands. We got our customary "B" for boy brown bag containing a plastic tractor or farm set. With five of us fellas in it, one of us was bound to get a ball and sure enough Eddie did. It was bright yellow with DERBY, the manufacturer's name, blazoned across the front of it

Good, I thought to myself, he can't play it by himself and besides the old one had recently come a cropper under the big wheels of the black CIE delivery lorry at Drumalee crossroads. I told Eddie all about Brian Clough's mighty Derby team in the back seat of the car and gave a specific mention to a striker they had by the name of Kevin Hector. Ned was won over and the Baseball ground had a new fan.

On the way home nothing'd do Dad but that we'd go for a Christmas drink. Out the Dublin road we went to John Costelloe's MEADOW VI-W IN-. I'd begun to notice Dad's likeness for a Crested Ten and water. We always knew he went for a jar especially on a Sunday night with McGunker and for a short time had owned his own bar in Bridge St. Cavan. He'd bring Mammy home a small greenish coloured bottle with BABYCHAM written on the label. His drinking didn't mean we suffered, though. I'm sure Mam worried about him. As young as we were we knew he could hold his drink, we'd heard Peter Rooney say it about him and he was always good-humoured with the few jars. Mum would always seize this opportune moment and suggest doing something domestically that a normally sober Jem Conarty mightn't agree to.

"Wouldn't it be great if we painted the scullery", she'd suggest… "Sure I'll start the fecking thing now" he'd reply with a smile. It could be one or two in the morning but once agreed, the deal was done. And sure enough Mam would get cracking the next day.

Anyway John Costelloe's lounge was full and seated at the end of the bar was Jackie Fitch from Corratubber. Jackie was small in stature and like Dad, wore Brylcream in his hair. He served petrol at the pumps in Tractamotors at the top of the town. Like Dad, he too had migrated into Corratubber. He was married to Annie Miney and they had a young son, Paul, the same age as our Philomena. Their house sat on the very crossroads at Corratubber. In bygone days it had been a schoolhouse and then a shop and a home to the Miney family who'd been "well to do people" Mammy had told us.

Anyway Jackie enjoyed his pint and lilted "diddly oil dill diddly dee" his trademark tune. In the corner, waiting on her hot whiskey, sat his thin and bespectacled wife Annie. Paul drank water from a mineral glass. Outside in their red mini minor car sat Bonzo, the strangest looking goat of a dog you ever did see.

We gawked round at the glittering tinsel draped over the mirrors and thumb tacked to the ceiling were numerous multi-coloured balloons. Tommy had in his possession a Santy rifle with two sucker arrows. Wet the sucker and pull the trigger, it was that simple. I dared him to take a pot shot at one of the balloons dangling from the ceiling. He smiled but knew better. We decided to join the hard men at the bar.

John Costelloe was his usual good-humoured self washing a glass in a sinkful of soapy water. We got our feet on to the step of one of the bar stools and with elbows on the seats set about negotiating our way up. Suddenly BANG! The gun discharged under pressure and the arrow had hit its target and now stood stuck to a Hennessey brandy bottle on the dispenser attached to the wall behind the bar.

Dad roared but we'd long dismounted and gone. We were the only two to see where the sucker-bullet was and yet were helpless to retrieve it. John Costelloe dried his beer glasses and talked about football in Kerry.

We sat down. I thought of Castletara School…

"There was an ould woman
and she lived in the woods
Weelia Weelia Wallia
There was an ould woman
And she lived in the woods
Down by the river Saile"

We laughed again.

Chapter 3

Anyway we headed home to Drumalee late that night but still in time for Dad to nip back into Sean Boylans . He took his four eldest sons with him.

Sean Boylan's bar and lounge was located directly across the street from the surgical hospital with its tall imposing statue of a blue Virgin Mary. Heaven only knows what she thought of the carry-on there. It was a town pub frequented by country boys and the whiskey flowed freely. Sean and his wife Gretta ran a good house. Sean had hailed from Corratubber and had a close affinity with Mum's family. Sure weren't Mary, his sister and Phyllis best friends after all. Mary had gone stateside as a young girl, having had the traditional wake and hadn't Francie Kelly chipped in with "From this valley they say you are leaving".

All the neighbours left bawling. Gretta and Mam had worked together as secretaries in the Anglo Celt newspaper.

Anyway Sean was a fine big red-faced man. Battle weary and with a worn look on his brow he'd been brought up the hard way and according to McGunker went working on the roads at fourteen years of age. He had, like Dad, big, full, fattened hands. He'd been to England in the 60's and had returned home to run the Poor Clare's farm above on the Cock Hill. He and Gretta bought the pub and it became a focal point. There we were, us boys, our Dad and Eugene Reilly the huntsman. The place was stuffed and the banter lively at the bar. Dad always seemed to be engrossed in conversation; rich man, poor man it didn't matter a damn. If the Pope himself had walked in, sure Jem Conarty would've called a bottle of stout and a Crested Ten for him. James, myself, Tommy and Eddie sat at a round table munching our Tayto and swigging away at a bottle of red lemonade that Gretta had blown us. We'd pretend the red lemonade was whiskey and engage in the "one for the road" and "good health to ya" routine. "Cheers". Boylans bar was also frequented by many of the boys from the local Drumalee G.F.C. They were a sound bunch known to us; the O'Briens, O'Keefes and McCabes but one young gun, a guy called Capper fancied his chances against our Dad. Big mistake. Huge in fact. He loitered with intent amidst the Sweet Afton smoke and every now and again had something smart to say to Jimmy Conarty's gasuns. We didn't rise to the bait however and the young Capper became increasingly frustrated.

"See your ould fella over there at the bar, think he's great don't ya?" he slobbered. Our silent munching was picked up by Dad and a raised eyebrow enquired if all was ok.

"Yous think he's great alright; I'd bate him with one fist…Are you listening four-eyes?"

Tommy was wearing his thick rimmed, double paned glasses and the four-eyes jab was a step too far.

I saw Dad's hand on his right shoulder and young Capper was invited and then unceremoniously forced through the door and out onto the main street. Dad threw off his jacket and Sean O'Brien caught hold of it. He rolled up his white sleeves and I could see the y of his gallises tighten into his back. I knew he meant business.

Eugene Reilly ushered the four of us young ones into the back of the A40 and promptly closed the passenger door. He stooped forward, adjusted the mirror and began watching proceedings. I couldn't believe it. "Get out quick and help him" I roared trying to squeeze between the two front seats. By this stage a good crowd had spilled out onto the street and by my reckoning Dad was outnumbered by about forty to one!

Sean Boylan tried but to no avail. "Call one of my boys four-eyes Capper? Bate me with one fist would ya? " Dad roared.

"Quick, get out Eugene" we all screamed now. Any more laid back and Eugene Reilly would definitely have been horizontal McGunker used to say.

"Ahh in damn it, I think he can look after himself" he droned, "I've seen him before aye…". Left, right, left, precision strikes all on target. Through the back window Capper seemed air-borne for all of three seconds, then he rolled over the bonnet of a black ford Anglia and came to rest on the footpath in front of the Drumalee boys. Knock out. Lights out. Guards coming! Sean O'Brien threw Dad his jacket or tag-coat, as he was fond of calling it.

"Anyone else want it?" Dad enquired. No takers. Into the car and down Ashe Street and out the Cootehill road for home. Not a word spoken till we came to Lismagratty. "Four eyes, not the gasun's fault he's short-sighted" muttered Dad. "Goodnight Jem", "Goodnight Jane".

Back at Drumalee we climbed the wet steps. "Not a word to your mother now and don't forget your prayers, boys" Dad reminded us. A light tap on the doorknocker and we were in. Mum had the kettle boiling on the range and the white dot remained lit on our black and white telly. She'd been reading the Evening Press and the purply-red square in the top left-hand corner had been smudged by a wet dishcloth. Philomena's bottle lay half-empty on the sofa and Dad poured its creamy contents into a wee orange saucepan and left it on the cooker for morning. Outside the odd car spluttered past. We all hopped into the big bed, two up, two down. It was a socks on night. "Did you see that?" enthused Eddie. "Gawd, I can't wait till I'm forty-three and anyone that gives me shite, I'll down him alright", he continued. "Don't forget to throw off your jacket", laughed James. The floorboards creaked on the landing and Mum whispered "Goodnight, boys". The two younger ones, Harry and Philomena were out for the count next door. "Prayers said, boys?" enquired Dad. "Yeah" we chorused. He sat on the edge of the bed and told us he didn't give a damn what we did in life so long as we had manners and said our prayers.

"John F. Kennedy was no angel and neither am I," he told us. "But one thing they say about him was that he never said his prayers in bed. He always knelt on the floor. Prayers in bed don't count. So boys, if it was good enough for the President of America, it's good enough for us, out yous get".

Night Offering, Our Father, Hail Mary, The Creed, an O Mary My Mother My Hope, a Dear Sacred Heart Of Jesus and an O Angel of God. Then an Our Father and 3 Hail Marys for our two grandfathers Tommy and Mick and the souls in Purgatory. Knees and toes stiffened as we got up and hopped in, dodging the broken spring that stuck up like a compass in the middle of the mattress. We knew its exact location. "Goodnight boys, yous are good gasuns".

Anyway that night I dreamt like never before. We were back out in Corratubber and Nanna was on the back street surrounded by her multitude of Rhode Island Reds. "Chucky, Chucky, Chucky" she invited them, scattering meal from her apron. She smiled.

Later, Jane Cusack arrived from Lavey to look at his cattle and gave us a lift down the bull's field. The bales of hay helped to cushion the bumps as we passed through the gaps. "Do you own our farm now?" I enquired having to raise my voice above the spluttering of a busted exhaust on his Massey Ferguson 35 tractor. "Only when your father doesn't want it, like now" replied Jane. "I have it let for a while," he continued. We didn't know what "let" meant and didn't bother asking. The red whiteheads gathered round and munched greedily on the golden crisp hay Jane was scattering among the whin bushes. It started to spit sleet and the muck squelched beneath the back tractor wheels as we climbed the hills for home. A biting north-easterly wind left fingertips burning. We jumped off at the bull's field gate and headed over to the hayshed. The ball clattered against the corrugated iron as Jane's 35 meandered its way across Shantemon Pass.

Chapter 4

Someone had once painted "One man, one vote" on the wall of the Cootehill road and I often wondered why. The news was all about the troubles in Belfast but we were too busy with our soccer. Each of us now had our own team. James with West Ham, me with Liverpool, Tommy with Arsenal, Eddie with Derby and Harry had latched on to Man Utd. We had games to play, goals to score and celebrations to imitate. I wondered how players dribbled the ball past each other and what people meant when they roared "Mark up, mark up".

We loved our Saturdays. Plenty of action on telly, soccer previews and results and in between plenty of "rastling". Big Daddy and Giant Haystacks and Mick McManus. Our UTV was fuzzy. We threw all the fake boxes and body slammed each other on the creaky sofa. Mum would go the short distance to town and spend most of Dad's hard-earned money from Smith's garage. She always managed to squeeze a few bob from somewhere and invested heavily in comics for us. They'd come home rolled tightly together by someone in Foster's newsagents. Shoot, Goal, Roy of the Rovers, The Dandy, Sparky, Beano and Bunty for the princess. We simply gorged on soccer. Hotshot Hamish came from the Scottish Highlands and had even far more power in his boots than big Frank Coyle. Melchester

McGunker

Rovers had Roy leading them. Even if they were ten-nil down they'd come back and win eleven-ten. We loved Shoot best of all as it kept us in constant touch with events across the water. It had a "focus on" each week and players informed us of their very own favourite players, food and music. It even had "hopes for the future". Best of all were the feature writers like Alan Ball, Bobby Moore and the wayward Frank Worthington. Soon they'd sign up Kevin Keegan, I told myself, and give him proper acknowledgement of his genius status.

"Match of the Day" kicked off around 9.40 on a Saturday night on BBC1. We'd know the results from earlier in the evening having watched them come through on the tele-printer with Dickie Davis. Our treat was a bottle of Club Orange and a six-pack of finger-licking Chipsticks. Jimmy Hill of the long chin and the magical theme tune of Saturday nights. It showed Kevin Keegan turning to salute the Kop having scored another great goal in his number 7 shirt.

Clyde Best was a big black man playing up front for West Ham United. He was Jamaican and unusual. Unusual in that there weren't that many coloured players around in Division 1. Moore, Peters, Brooking. West Ham played stylish football and the Upton Park crowd, when not singing about blowing bubbles, applauded every decent pass. Dad might peep in and ask "How's Best doing?"

Which one? Was it big Clyde from Jamaica or little Georgie from Belfast. "Georgie Best, superstar, he walks like a woman and he wears a bra", we thought that hilarious. Best of the black flowing locks and magical dribble...why did he have to play for United though? We hated United, all of us, except Harry. We hated their fans because they were loud and proud even when they were losing. We liked Georgie though. He was always in trouble, disappearing between matches, not turning up for training, being found drunk with Miss World. Besides all that, he was world class. We read all about him in the Irish Independent and Sunday Press and Evening Press, Dad's newspapers from work. Best of all for Georgie was that he was Oirish, Norn Oirish. "Sure we're all Irish except that Georgie plays for Norn Ireland" explained James. "Why's that? enquired Eddie. "I dunno, something to do with one man one vote, now shaddup and listen will yous?"

Mum poured us all another sup of orange and went back to the kitchen to peel spuds for Sunday's dinner. "Are the Charlton boys on yet?" she wondered closing the door. Poor Mam. We looked at each other and laughed. We had her indoctrinated. Who'd ever forget the day she came running out to tell us that Best had been sent off for throwing muck at the referee. We tore in to witness Georgie exit Windsor Park in his all green Oirish jersey.

"Hall into Keegan, Keegan skips past Billy Bremner, plays a one-two with Peter Cormack, Keegan's through…Keegan scores!" Heaven! My mate Kev raced to the Kop end at Anfield Road and was mobbed by Toshack, Heighway, Callaghan and Hughes. Even little Brian Hall joined in as the crowd went mental. Then we saw it again in slow motion. The adrenalin pumped inside me. Mighty Mouse was unstoppable. "The best part about Stevie Heighway is that he's Oirish as well" I enthused. "Is he Norn Oirish?" asked Tommy. "Shaddup will yous and watch" roared James.

I hated Arsenal, Tommy's team. I knew they'd beaten us in the 1971 F.A. Cup final, a match I didn't see. I had however seen pictures of an outstretched Charlie George lying prostrate in the summer's sun at Wembley Stadium. I'd seen Stevie Heighway's goal on telly a few times. He cut in from the left wing and fired one in at the near post beating the great Bob Wilson. Arsenal equalised through either Eddie Kelly or George Graham and then Charlie George fired in the winner. He had long fine hair like a teenage girl and the papers once said that he was a bit of a playboy. I knew also that Kevin Keegan had been there that day. Our boss Bill Shankly, a Scotsman, had bought him from Scunthorpe United for £35,000. Things could only get better. Arsenal had big Frank McClintock and Pat Rice and Bob McNab at the back. They had another striker called John Radford.

God I hated them. They, along with Leeds, threatened our predicted supremacy and Derby Co. too.

Derby County had a good team. They were Eddie's team and played stylish football in their all white strip. We wondered what happened when they met Leeds. How could the ref tell the players apart? Then Aiden Rehill explained to us that the team away from home played in a different strip, their away strip. It had to be a different colour. How can a fat guy like Francis Lee score goals like that? we wondered. Kevin Hector was good too and they had a bald defender called Terry Hennessey. Dad said he must have Irish blood in him from somewhere. Chipsticks gone, fingers licked and Club Orange burbed, we crinkled up our bags then blew into them and banged with our fists. United were playing at home in Old Trafford in their red shirts. Things weren't going well. It poured rain and Bobby Charlton flicked a wisp of blond hair across the top of his bald head. Willie Morgan got fouled and Denis Law missed an open goal. Alex Stepney was their keeper and he took some of their penalties. The crowd sang "Glory, Glory Man Utd.", yet they were having a bad season. We didn't care "Georgie Best superstar…What's a superstar?" asked Harry leaving the room. No one answered.

Anyway we ate our cornflakes doused with hot milk in the kitchen and headed for bed. I brought a pencil and copybook with me. I tore out the centre pages and proceeded to write,

"Dear Mr. Shankly, my name is Michael Conarty and I'm now ten years old. I live in Drumalee in Co. Cavan in Ireland. I think you're a great manager and a very nice man. I love watching Liverpool on the telly and I pray hard for you and the team before each game. I don't want to be cheeky or anything but I've noticed that Ian Callaghan isn't as quick as he used to be. I'm sure he's a nice man too. Sooner or later you'll need someone to help out in midfield and I know I can do it for you when I'm older. Me and Stevie Heighway would get on well cos he's oirish too. Could you write back

to me and offer me a contract. I'm very fast and I've scored lots of goals against the big ones at Castletara School. I'll talk to Mammy and Daddy about it.
Thank you Mr. Shankly
Michael Conarty
Aged 10
P.S. Mr. Shankly, please don't tell Ian Callaghan I wrote to you. Thanks.

Next morning before Mass I scoured the house for an envelope. I couldn't tell anyone what I wanted and this vexed Dad. "What the hell is he looking for now?" he shouted, brushing the collar of his tag-coat. "You'll be late for Mass if yous don't smarten yourselves".

We went to Mass in Castletara. Fr. Woods was the priest and Mammy called for Nanna. She was waiting at the gate holding her crooked brown walking stick and sucking a silvermint. I felt sorry for her. We'd kept her waiting and it was all my fault. I felt for my letter to Bill Shankly in my trousers pocket. Good, it was still there.

I looked at the wizened skin stretched across Nanna's boney hands. I knew she washed then in Sunlight soap in a basin at the end of the table. She wore a big hat like a tea-cosy and said "Hello childer". Sure maybe one day we'll all be back in Corratubber and live happily ever after... I mused to myself, as Mum slowed, meeting Eddie Fitzsummons with his tractor and trailer load of creamery cans on the pass. Eddie, like Bobby Charlton, was going bald too, only he wore a cap to hide it. He bit his nails when not smoking his pipe. Nanna was excited this morning as she flapped open the air-mail envelope for Mum's attention on Tommy Tully's hill. We knew it was from Fr. Eddie. He always wrote on par-avion light blue paper in big print. "So he'll be here in a month" said Nanna, "Isn't it grand? Lizzie's excited". We all were. Tanzania was a million miles away and Fr. Eddie always took home slide-shots with him to show us, reflecting them on to a big white bed sheet draped from a wall in one of the bedrooms at Corratubber. He was an affable man. Tall and extremely thin, with oil-moistened curlish hair. An academic, a self-made one at that and a bit of an enigma. He'd been spoilt rotten, had it all and more and yet chose to walk away and help the poor downtrodden black people of East Africa. He wore thick glasses to protect his poor eyesight brought on by malnourishment. A man to be in awe of and yet very simplistic. He constantly read and experimented. He had a head for figures and dates. "On this day in 1937......"

Anyway, me and Oliver Reilly and Martin Smith were serving Mass. We had to kneel at the back of the altar with Fr. Woods standing in front of us facing the crowd. It was warm and sticky. We moved round for the consecration, trying not to look at each other in case we'd laugh. Kneeling down again I noticed a piece of paper right inside the rails on the worn floorboards. Oh no! My letter to Bill Shankly. Please God, don't let anyone find it, I begged. I peeped across every few minutes and wondered how I'd get to it. Then Martin swung but there was no gong! He missed the bell completely and fell over. Oliver laughed! Suddenly Pe Smith vaulted the gates at the rails realising, unlike us, that his son had fainted in the hazy morning heat of that sunlit altar. I moved, pretending to help him and knowing also it was a chance for salvation. Pe lifted his son. I lifted my letter. Together we carried a sweating and feverish young Martin into the vestry at the side of the altar. Martin came round on the priest's chair and looked at his father still dazed. "Go back out son, go back" whispered Pe. I stuffed the letter back inside my trousers pocket beneath the black and white sootan and rejoined Ollie on the steps. A collie dog came into the chapel and barked and then ran out again. Ollie looked at me with raised eyebrows. Fr. Woods continued, unnerved. The crowd lined up and I held the gold coloured plate beneath each chin. "The Body o' Christ"; "Amen".

After Mass, I raced outside. People were asking about Martin Smith. "What happened, did he get sick? Did Pe bring him home?" In the distance I spotted PJ Lynch. I knew he'd know what I wanted.

The Lynches were from Castletara and were big into soccer. We knew Sean and Tony and PJ and the youngest, Joe. They played Gaelic too but not with Ballyhaze anymore. They were dead handy all of them and should be playing for the County according to McGunker. Imagine all them brothers playing for Drung. PJ had bushy hair and was growing a moustache. "Where's Liverpool?" I asked him. "It's in England" he replied. "I know, but how would you get a letter there?" I continued. "You'd have to post it, " laughed PJ. John Coyle smiled. "I know, but where to?" I pleaded. Mammy and Nanna and the boys were waiting in the car. Across the road the older men lay against McCormack's front wall lighting up their pipes and smoking fags. They chattered away.

"Look, who are ya writing to, young Conarty?" beamed PJ sensing my impatience. "I want to know the address of the Liverpool team," I explained. "Just send it to Anfield, Liverpool, England" smiled PJ. "That should get it alright". I thanked PJ and leapt across the street heading towards the car. Mam got out and lifted her front seat letting me in. "What kept ya?" she snapped. I stood on Eddie's foot and he roared. "Will yous whisht in the back of the car and have manners at the chapel" shouted Nanna. I knew it was all my fault. Later that day I found an envelope and wrote on the cover: To Mr. Bill Shankly, Manager, Liverpool Soccer Team, Anfield, Liverpool, England.

Before licking the lid, I added another p.s. apologising for the fact that my letter was all crinkled up now and requesting again that Bill not mention anything to Ian Callaghan. Mam posted my letter without looking at it the very next day in Cavan Post Office. I know cos I was there with her getting the childer's allowance.

I wondered what Mrs. Fay would think.

"She had a baby
six months old
weelia weelia wallia

McGunker

She had a baby
Six months old
Down by the river Saile"

Chapter 5

Anyway, we enjoyed Fr. Eddie. Dad said he was drole. He liked him too and had once christened him Alex because of his eccentricities. Dad told us not to underestimate him. He was a gifted man and a great priest. He read and read and read. We saw some of his books. They were about Greek heroes like Perses. Dad said he could cock hay on a boiling hot day and nobody could keep up with him. He got up very early in the mornings, anytime before five like he'd been used to in Tanzania. A goldy coloured Morris Minor arrived from Mick Murphy's garage one day. It had no wheels on it and was propped up on four concrete blocks. Fr. Eddie laboured at its engine stopping occasionally to read from a manual. Inside, the roof was covered in cobwebs and mildew. He could've walked for Ireland Dad reckoned, big long slaps of steps that kept us panting alongside him trying to keep up. When we'd tell him something, good or bad, he'd say "Ah so, very nice, very good, so that's really nice". He'd stretch his bony fingers across his mouth and stifle a yawn. He ate nothing but cabbage and chicken and the odd slice of brown bread. He liked his fruit too and expertly peeled his apples, usually red ones, and sliced them right down to the core. People came to see him and gave him offerings to say Masses for special intentions. Dad said every penny went to the missions. He dressed in second hand clothes and wore odd-looking sneakers or sandals. He wore a watch on his skeletal wrist but we could never see the time as the clock face was always on the other side with the strap showing to the front. He'd go and see people-people in hospital, people that were old, people with new babies, people who'd sent for him. He had a Renault van this summer. It belonged to the White Fathers and Dad said, "Trust them to give him a hape of shite". The gear stick stuck out from the dashboard like a long hand brake. It cringed now and again especially when he changed going up hills. He collected mite-boxes in it and emptied their proceeds into a black bag. It weighed a tonne. Once he went to Granard and brought me and Eddie with him. He bought us chocolate cones and headed to general Headquarters as he called it in Longford. "Very nice, very good, so that's really very good" he hummed as he drove along. The older people told us that he'd worked his way right up to the Office of Town Clerk in Cavan in the fifties. He hated red tape and always tried to help out those who needed it most. He had a simple approach to life. "If it's not broken, then don't fix it" he'd say.

Outta the blue he'd close his eyes and nod off right in front of ya. You could be talking to him at the time. His legs would cross and he'd tap his shoes together. Once when Harry cut his knee badly and hobbled into the kitchen, screaming like a cut cat, Uncle Eddie stood with his back to the range and said, "Very good, very nice, so Harry that's really good". Totally oblivious.

Anyway he took us over that year to Corranure and showed us the tracks of the bull's feet imprinted in a flat rock alongside Kevin Reilly's lane. "Cos an tSearraigh, an old Irish word for bull, foot of the bull. It then became Caisleán Tarbh, Castletara", he said. Isn't Caisleán a castle I kinda thought to myself but chickened out of asking. "Some say Searrach is an old word for a horse," Uncle Eddie continued. "Why would a bull or a horse do that?" asked James. "Do what?" replied his uncle. "Leave their tracks in that stone" said James, scratching his head.

The sun went in behind the clouds and a light breeze whipped up. Aussie Kelly was coming towards us on his Ferguson tractor with its big silver milk tanker in tow. He waved and went on towards McCollums. We could see his son, Jude, standing by his side. Jude waved and smiled. "You see, the bull or the horse or whatever it was, was owned by the priest", Fr. Eddie continued, shielding his face from the light dust now blowing up off the road. "Anyway the tinkers came one night to steal it. It was a fine, strong creature, as big as the brown bull of Cooley". "What's Cooley?" asked Eddie Junior.

"Do you not know your history?" laughed Fr. Eddie who then proceeded to enlighten us with tales of Queen Maebh and Ailill and Cúchulainn and Ferdia and the battle at the ford. "Yeh, yeh I know that one" James exclaimed excitedly, "but what happened to the bull and the tinkers?" Tommy and Harry picked bilberries in the moss-covered ditch. "The bull or maybe even the horse leapt up in the still of the night as they walked along and killed them both stone dead. He left his hoof mark in that very stone and that's how Castletara got its name" Uncle Eddie replied. Cos an tSearraigh? Cos an tarbh? Foot of the bull or was it a horse? No mention of a castle at all, at all, I mused to myself.

We doddled our way back over the road past Philip Bradys and down the hill round be Jackie and Annies. "Sure look at Corratubber" Fr. Eddie began. "Tobair is a well and cor is a path, path to the well, the well that is across the road from the house". "Do yous watch Match of the Day in Africa?" Harry blurted out. Fr. Eddie smiled as we headed in the laneway for Nannas. Evening came. Lighting a Sweet Afton in the A40 as we headed for Drumalee, Dad was fuming. "Hypocrites, bloody hypocrites the lot of them". We looked at each other in the back sensing domestic strife. But no. It was Lord Widgery's unfair statement issued that day about Bloody Sunday. He'd praised the British Army for showing restraint and Dad would have flattened him with a box there and then. "That's British justice for yous boys, Rule Britannia my arse. Faulkner, Willie Whitelaw,

Paisley, the whole effing lot of them, all the Queen's boys. Sure they wouldn't know their arses from their elbows" he muttered. We knew not to argue. Mam adjusted her glasses and looked straight ahead. "Imagine having a name like Willie Whitelaw" laughed Eddie. We all laughed and then told Mam and Dad about the Castletara horse and the priest and the tinkers. Going past Lismagratty bog at the foot of Reilly's farm, where the council were now dumping rubbish, a gull swooped from nowhere and shit on the windscreen. "Shite for ya" roared Dad, as the mess slid its way down in front of him. "Shite, shite, shite" echoed Philomena on Mammy's lap. We all laughed. "I was talking to Cusack" said Dad, " and he's happy enough with the rent". He pulled the car in under the wall at Drumalee and we sat for a minute. "At least it'll be a few bob for the fall and we'll bring them down to Leddy's of the 'Bridge and tog them out for the winter" replied Mum. "Daecent people the Cusacks" said Dad. "Always were. He lets me know what's going on. He said to watch Peggy Dearg, she has it in for us. Wasn't he lucky she broke it off with him?" he laughed. "All because he liked a few whiskeys. The prick she married'll never give her any problems in that department" he finished. It was coded but we knew they were talking about some of Nanna's neighbours. We climbed the steps and headed in. After the porridge we raced the stairs and pulled the curtains. It was raining now and cars sploshed past on the road outside. Keegan plays it wide to Conarty, filling in for the injured Heighway, Conarty heads down the wing. The Kop rise……..

Chapter 6

The early morning traffic on the main road to Cavan always served as our alarm clock. We'd come down and root around for a slice of bread or maybe even a cream-cracker. Then we'd head outside, maybe up the back garden, all the time remembering our real home and fields out in Corratubber. We longed to get back there. Often, during the holidays, when Mam would go out to look after her Mum, we'd go for the spin and mess about outside while she administered the tablets to Nanna. Nanna took a pill for her heart, we knew that, and now and again she'd have what Mum called a wee turn. Dr. Lorigan would come and see her. Then she'd be fine again. She'd ask us to pull the curtains or maybe fix the bedspread for her. When she'd be having one of her turns she looked smaller and frailer than usual. Aunt Lizzie would be coming later in the morning and so we'd head back to Drumalee. I hated us leaving her like this in such a big old house all by herself, weak and vulnerable. I knew it went hard on Mam too and often witnessed her sob, though she'd always try and conceal both her tears and hurt from us. I knew the situation was both unfair and unavoidable and the feeling of helplessness gnawed away at me. A bitterness grew within me.

The neighbours didn't seem to notice the wellies so much when it rained. We could almost justify the wearing of them on days like these. Besides you could trap a ball and control it with the curve of a welly just as well as anything else on the market. Mrs. Galligan lived next door to us and was a walking saint of a woman. She was tall, thin, old, good looking and always graced us with a benevolent smile. She thought the world of the Conarty boys and gave us sugary sweets for every occasion. Out of respect or maybe by just being cute, we seemed to reserve our best behaviour for when she was around. She saw no wrong in us, with our wellies and snotty faces and sweaty shirts. There were no barriers for Mrs. G. She had in her house three lodgers and she called them "her boys". John West and Joe Leavy both worked in the department Dad said. They parked their meticulously kept cars at the front of her house. The third lodger was younger and more carefree and he too worked for the department. We chased poor Enda McGowan for his autograph every time we saw him simply because he played football for the county. Besides he had longish hair just like Keegan and Best and seemed to come and go at all hours. We mauled him at times in Mrs. Galligan's well-kept front garden, which was separated from ours, luckily for her, by a thick privet hedge. Her garden was well-maintained and tall wallflowers added brightness and colour. Ours was a jungle and when it rained, welly- induced sliding tackles were the order of the day. Now and again Mam would set a flower or two but they always seemed to wither and die. We had plenty of dandelions though and a rose bush someone had given Mam in good faith. Poor Rose! Poor Phyllis! Our back yard was accessed by a path running alongside Mrs. G's gable and turning at a right angle with the wall of her back yard. The back garden, as we called it, came flush to the top of a wall, which had been built back into the bank. A set of steps in the corner led us up to this back garden. Next door to us on the opposite side were the Timoneys. Pat was a vet and he and his wife had one son called Paul. Had all single boys in a family of one been christened Paul? I often wondered to myself thinking of Paul Fitch out in Corratubber. Anyway there were 527 of my steps between our back door and Sean Reilly, the Coalman's shop, at the Cross. I know cos I counted them.

A footpath, narrow in places, ran under Mrs. Smith's big two-storey residence with bright red roses, on past Brady the Auctioneer, past four ESB poles in total and up by the Texaco pumps. Reilly's house was huge. It had to be. It was a big grocery shop and home to Sean and Ita Reilly and their large, young family. We knew the two eldest boys best, Myles and John Pat. Myles was a big hitter in every sense of the word; John Pat was somewhat quieter and more reserved. We were seen as country ploughboys and therefore fair game for the lads our ages and older in Drumalee. Maybe they'd heard of our Dad's reputation and fancied their chances against Jimmy's young guns. Perhaps also because we enjoyed our own company and always travelled together in a pack of five, we seemed to attract more attention. They'd watch us playing farms with imaginary cows, building huts, throwing stones at low flying crows or using the handrail at the steps as a slide.

Anyway we crossed the road that day and headed towards a neat bungalow down what we called the narrow road.

The lawn was well kept and the apple trees carefully pruned. The curved wall on the porch of the house gave it an added dimension. The Caffreys or McCaffreys as we called them were quiet, decent folk. We knew there were boys there of our age and we had nothing to lose by sussing them out. Laurence was tall and well built for a boy of his age. He lay on his belly on a patch of lawn alongside the stream which ebbed past their home. He held a book to his face and read away to his heart's content. Inside we found Aiden, about my age and even skinnier. He was colouring on the kitchen floor. Mrs. Caffrey was chopping cabbage at the sink. She was a tall, refined looking lady and Mam had once told us she was a nurse. We weren't conscious of this but would be glad of her presence later on in the day. Aiden seemed quiet and studious and acted indifferently to the five lads gawking at him and his crayon work. Mrs. Caffrey

McGunker

poured orange juice for us and Aiden excused himself to go to the bathroom. Now we'd never do that. Besides back home we simply called the bathroom the toilet. I bent down and saw that he'd been working on a Jumbo book, a combination of colouring and join the dots which ended on page 612. He'd left a ruler as a marker on the page he'd been engrossed in. We slurped our orange juice and Mrs. Caffrey smiled. Aiden returned but politely declined our offer of a game of soccer. We left. Outside it had started to drizzle through the sunshine. We stuck on our wellies and headed back up. James, Eddie and Harry went to Reilly's shop for six Black Jacks, funded no doubt by Mrs. G's latest donation to the cause. Tommy and I lingered outside Caffrey's ornamental gates for a while and then doddled across the narrow road. The drizzle had by now turned to a heavier shower and we stood on the ditch to gain shelter under the whitethorn bushes. The ESB pole clearly warned us of danger but sure we swung on it anyway. Wellies don't grip so well on slopey embankments. Tommy slipped, let go off the pole and in the process fell right out in front of Paddy Reilly's oncoming brown Austin 1100. I saw it happen in front of me and felt powerless to react. I froze as he was pegged almost slow motioned through the air and then landed on the road again like a wet bag of coal. I screamed, convinced he was dead and guilty therefore by association, of his murder. I stooped down. His eyes rolled backwards. Paddy Reilly opened his door and stood there speechless and shocked. We looked at each other. My heart heaved and my lungs got ready to burst as I ran up the hill, my legs on autopilot. Out of breath I raced through the back yard into the scullery and negotiated the steam of Mam's frying pan. "Where's the boys?" Phyllis enquired. "Tell them their tea is ready" as she pulled another KP peanut from her shop-coat pocket. "Go on Michael, get them, there's a good lad and sure maybe you'll throw out a few knives and forks and a bit of red sauce and …"

"Mum, Tommy's been hit by Paddy Reilly's car and, and …" I spluttered.

"What? What are you talking about?" she interrogated as she ushered me out through the back yard, stooping to go under the clothes line and rushing me on down the path-way alongside Mrs. G's gable. I felt her boney knuckles and her ring dig intently into my fingers. She wasn't letting me go. "What, what…?" she sobbed. Her glasses were steamed up now in the heat and confusion as we ran along the slimy, green footpath. "It's ok Mammy" I tried to reassure her. "It's only the tip of his little finger" I lied. "I promise, I promise" I reassured her. Please Jesus, please God, please Mary, don't let him die. Mum's pace slowed and she squeezed my hand tightly once more.

She seemed more trusting. Thanks God! She won't have a heart attack now and we'll not be left half-orphans and there won't be a double funeral of mother and son in Castletara Chapel. Down on the main road there was pandemonium; traffic chaos ensued as the little white ambulance sirened and shunted its way to the scene of the carnage. "O Glory be to God, Michael, you said it was only the tip of his little finger" panted my mother.

"Please God, please God don't let there be blood and guts and goo everywhere and above all else don't let him die, or Daddy'll kill me and then Mammy'll surely have a heart attack and then there'll be a triple funeral of Mother and two sons in Castletara Chapel!" The onlookers parted, having recognised the little lad's mother, and I could see the ambulance doors about to close. I recognised the lady inside, it was Mrs. Caffrey. She had spotted Mam and proceeded to pull her up the step and into the emergency zone. I stood there watching the blue-lit ambulance trundle its way down that narrow road. Guilt ridden, I tried to cry and couldn't. My stomach tightened. I picked up his cracked glasses and turned around to see my other brothers. "What happened? What happened?" James roared, his lips spewing blackjack saliva. I just looked at him. "Poor gasuns" I heard a woman say. "Where's their father?, I thought someone went for him". Someone had gone for Dad, gone all the way up past Pat

McGovern's shop with its Tango Orange sign and across the road to the pumps. They'd now obviously gone straight to the surgical hospital across the road from Sean Boylan's pub.

Inside, the rashers had been burnt black and there was a stench of despair. "Sit down now boys and don't frighten the wee one," implored Mrs. G. We could see a tear in her eye as she tried to reassure us. Philomena sucked a bottle of cold tea in the playpen and fingered the blond curly hair of her half-dressed doll. "If only, if only…" I thought to myself.

Dad arrived back at news time. Tommy wasn't dead, wasn't maimed, wasn't bleeding and wasn't getting home for a few days. "He's got a big bump on his temple" said Dad. "Where's that?" enquired Harry, " and a bad wrap to his arm, otherwise he's as sound as a pound".

Dad always spoke truthfully so we now knew the score. Mrs. Galligan put on the kettle and we headed outside for the obligatory game of soccer. Keegan shoots, Keegan scores!

The neighbours called in the days ahead with seven-up and tayto and someone even brought caramel sweets. Tommy arrived home enjoying his newfound hero status. Gerry Maguire, manager of Smith's garage called with a bottle of Powers Gold Label.

"Can we drink this Lucozade?" enquired Eddie. Gerry laughed. He wore a nice blue suit and with his tanned looks and short hair could easily have passed as Dad's brother. He always smiled. He drove a company car and James said he had a touch of dyeabitix whatever that was. It didn't matter to us. We liked Gerry Maguire's gentleness and he always made us feed good. He and Dad pulled well, Mum always said. We were happy again.

"She had a penknife long and sharp
Weelia, weelia, wallia
She had a penknife long and sharp
Down by the river Saile".

Chapter 7

Anyway next day after dinner dathlones arrived; Anna Mae and Tony and our cousins Lorna and Derek. They'd left the bigger ones, Eamonn and Declan and Aidey at home to help with the pub. Anna Mae had an aura about her. You immediately felt good in her company and she reminded me a little of Nanna. She liked us we could tell. "My God, the height of ye all" she exclaimed as we lined up like steps of a stairs in front of them in our kitchen. They always said "ye". Mammy stuck on the kettle and Tony teased us. "James is so tall and wiry and look at Michael now with his white hair turning grey, haa haa, and what about Tommy surviving a big crash like that…and Eddie and Harry, you'd swear they were twins; yeh twin girls" he laughed.

"And don't forget wee Philomena" said Anna Mae, picking her up and wiping the remains of a Marietta biscuit from her chin. "God help ya with all these big brothers to contend with".

The princess had nothing to worry about. She'd soon find her niche and would adopt a can't beat them might as well join them approach to life. Anyway the doorknocker clunked and Dad went out through the hall. He called back "Phyllis, Phyllis, come here a minute". We knew it was someone important as Mum always fixed her hair with her hands at a time like this. "Some of yous wet a drop of tae and James, take out them fig rolls I told you about" she whispered.

Anna Mae ushered her out. We had a cream jubilee cooker in our kitchen and Mam had left some spuds simmering on a pot of hot water. James took cups, mugs and anything else he could get his hands on down from the press and Tony sat down with the Irish Independent from Smith's garage. He was balding and bronzed and his brown crombie coat provided perfect colour co-ordination. "Would you like a spud?" I enquired of Anna Mae. "Do you know something? I'd murder one" she replied. She stripped off the already pealing spud skin and sliced through its flouriness, nicked a little piece of butter and sprinkled a dash of salt. "Mmm, gorgeous" she smiled. Dressed like a film star with oodles of jewellery, Anna Mae could still be ordinary and that's what appealed to us most. Lorna and Derek sat impassively amidst the din. Derek was about nine and had a mischievous grin and shoulder length, goldy coloured hair. He looked like an Osmond in his matching pants and jacket. We liked him. He supported Wolves and talked about Derek Dougan. James told him about Dougan playing alongside Georgie Best for Norn Ireland too.

Lorna was a couple of years older and was gorgeous looking. She had shiny, shoulder length dark hair and a full set of beautiful white teeth. She wasn't too keen on us, her cousins however, and looked incessantly at her silver watch doubtless wondering when she'd get out of here.

Mam called out from the front room "Tommy, Tommy, come here a minute, I want ya". This was a cue for us all to go and, wanted or not, we traipsed out through the hallway. All for one, one for all. Besides there could be something going. It was Paddy Reilly the driver of the car. We all shook hands with him. He was a very nice and gentle looking man who'd taken the accident to heart and was now profusely apologetic. A very genuine man Dad had always said and we could sense this ourselves now. Paddy had sweets and treats and a big bottle of Cavan Cola, not just for Tommy, but for his loyal comrades as well. This man just stood there looking so gracious that I immediately began exonerating him from any notion of attempted murder. After all we'd been told not to be swinging from poles, sure hadn't the ESB even stuck up signs and anyway the day was wet and we should have gone on with James and the boys. And sure it would have been all my fault if there had been a triple funeral in Castletara and, and, and…

"It's alright now boys, say thanks to Paddy" said Dad " and tip on outside for a while, there's the good gasuns".

"Thanks Paddy" we chorused as we legged it outside almost running over Mrs. Yorkman, our posh neighbour from two doors up, who got as far as "How's little…?". Seeing Paddy Reilly at the front door, Mrs. Yorkman u-turned and noticing the Westmeath registration of Dathlones hastened her step back up home.

"Mind our good walls," she pointed as a Johnny Giles-like thunderbolt struck a concrete post and spun up into the hawthorn hedge.

We had a long stick that we kept in hiding for occasions like this and James duly went off to get it. With his added height it'd be down in no time. "Bet ya can't name the Liverpool team" beamed Derek up at me. "Bet ya I can; Clemence in goals, Lawler and Lindsay, Tommy Smith and Emlyn Hughes, Larry Lloyd, Keegan, Cormack, Heighway, John Toshack and Ian Callaghan or sometimes Peter Thompson or even Brian Hall."

"Wow" said Derek. By now I knew my stuff alright and began to feel increasingly more confident about my chances of signing up at Anfield. Surely even Bill Shankly would be astounded by my knowledge of L.F.C. I could tell him for instance that Peter Cormack had cost a massive £110,000 from Nottingham Forest and that he had originally played for Hibernian in Scotland and that Stevie Heighway had a university degree in something or other and that he hadn't lived in Ireland since he was a child. I couldn't help but wonder why he hadn't written back to me yet though. Surely he'd gotten my letter ages ago. Maybe he'd sent one of his scouts over to watch me playing on the narrow road or even beyond at Castletara school. They'd report back to him and then he'd write offering me terms, wouldn't he?

Later, Dathlones left, prompted in no small measure by Lorna's impatience and went on out to Corratubber to see Nanna. Anna Mae left a big box of goodies. She always did. It was a tea chest and Tony lifted it carefully from the boot of his car before slamming the lid down and saying, "Right says he, but she never wrote". Dad laughed and we waved them goodbye. It was a good feeling having it to say that we had well to do relations like Anna Mae and Tony. Inside, the box was quickly opened and its contents revealed. Plenty of clothes. Polo-necked jumpers and big collared shirts from America that Eamonn and Deckie and Adie had rejected no doubt. We were new fangled with the sneakers or "gutties" as James called them and tore into them searching for the right sizes. Now we had something between good shoes and wellies, something to trap a ball a bit better with. Keegan shoots and scores.

Anna Mae and Tony would end up in Ballyhaze in Austin Brady's bar and lounge with Lizzie and Sean. We knew that and we knew that Mum and Dad would be joining them later. It was protocol. Lorna and Derek would sleep over in Rehills. We finished our tea and bread and jam and headed for bed. Mammy soothed a hot and cranky Philomena and got her to sleep. Out in the bathroom, stripped to the waist and shaving, Dad could be heard talking and humming away to himself. He always did this at shaving time; "Is the priest at home boy or may he be seen?"

Then he'd break into a song;

"Many young men of twenty said goodbye
All that long day from break of dawn, till the sun was high
Many young men of twenty said goodbye
My boy Jimmy went too that day

On the big ship, sailed away
Sailed…"

"Will you whisht Jimmy" we heard Mum say on the landing, "God knows the wee one's not well, she's very hot and I don't know if I should go at all"

"She'll be grand," replied Dad fixing his galasses and trying to comb his hair at the same time. "Boys, say your prayers and be good," he instructed from the doorway.

"Many young men of twenty…"

Chapter 8

Anyway we threw off whatever clothes we'd worn that day and headed for the hay, as Dad called it, in our tee shirts. No fancy pyjamas. The five of us slept in the one room and after the customary bit of rustling, settled down for the night. We heard the knocker of the door rebound as it closed and the A40 rev up beneath the streetlight. Time for another bit of kickboxing until someone got hurt or something got broke. James and I knew the score. We'd wait till the rest were asleep and then head back down stairs for a while.

We could smell the woodbines through the banisters as we tiptoed the stairs. Opening the kitchen door we could see Murphy as he popped open a bottle of stout. "Ahh me sound men, what about ye?" he enquired. Eddie Murphy hailed from Co. Monaghan but had lived near us at home in Corratubber with his now deceased sister Mrs. Tully, her husband Patsy and their family of four. Murphy was great craic. He had a wrinkly face and twitchy eyes. His silvery grey, oiled hair slinked back in the fashion of the day and he winked his left eye incessantly when reinforcing his point of view. His Monaghan drawl intrigued us and he told us countless tales from home with plenty of reference to the McGittericks whoever they were. Anyway everyone in Monaghan seemed to live in the lane before, after or just right opposite the McGittericks, and we were supposed to know them all.

Murphy drank his stout, wiping away its creamy moustache. James offered him some of Gerry Maguire's whiskey and poured some water from the cold tap into the "Black and White" enamel jug that someone had once nicked at a wedding in the White Horse hotel in Cootehill. "Where's the rest of the wee uns?" Murphy enquired. "They're all asleep", we answered simultaneously. Eddie gave us the remains of a packet of wine gums he had in his pocket. The first few tasted of fag smoke but we chewed away regardless. James then buttered two heels of Pat the Baker's sliced pan. I got the strawberry jam and we poured two mugs of milk, draining the carton in the process. Murphy told us a story about ten IRA men hiding in a bog somewhere in Co. Monaghan more than likely near the McGittericks. Anyway these boys were stuck in mucky, boggy, freezing water ready to free Ireland from British oppression some of these days.

"Do you like West Ham?" asked James as he tongued the red jam from the corner of his mouth.

"Oul soccer, oul soccer, oul British soccer" snarled Murphy " and ten men lying in wait, cold and famished with the hunger up the road from McGitterick's lane". We looked at each other and laughed and then took out the cards to play a game of Ould-Maid. It was all that we knew. By now it was gone two in the morning and the streetlights shone brightly as I peeped out the curtain of the front room. No sign of them. After ten minutes or so all James had to do was pick the right card to match up his pair and leave Murphy with the Queen and title of Ould-Maid. He duly obliged and Murphy snarled again. We laughed. "I might as well be an ould maid as an ould bachelor," he roared banging the table and lighting up another Woodbine. He cracked open another bottle of stout and flicked the cork with his middle finger off the table and across the floor into our coal-bucket. "Yous boys better get to bed, it's near three o'clock in the morning," said Murphy. "Ah that clock's an hour fast" chanced James. I could picture Mam trying to get them all out of Bradys. No doubt Nanna would hear tomorrow of their escapades and our

Dad would be blamed. Eventually we heard the soft drone of IID 414 pulling in and we legged it upstairs. "What about ye?" enquired Murphy at the door. Dad left him home and Mum peeped in. Sensing we were awake she edged her way towards the bed. "Were yous good? Did Philomena waken?" she whispered in the still of the room as her three younger sons lay sound asleep. "God knows I'm worried about her, she had a high temperature and the clothes were stuck to her back this evening with sweat". Mam looked uptight and lost. I looked up from beneath the blankets and felt sorry for her. I knew she worried too much for her own good. Worried about Nanna, about us, about Dad, about Lizzie, about what people thought and now about her sickly daughter. I knew she was guilt-ridden too. She'd left her mother alone in Corratubber though not by choice. She'd gone to Austin Brady's. There would have been bad humour if she'd stayed at home with her sick child. It was a no-win situation and I could see the heartache in her face. "Don't worry Mammy, everything'll be alright" encouraged James letting go off her hand as we heard Dad close the kitchen door. The speckled wallpaper patterns criss-crossed before me and then he switched off the landing light.

"Go on son, you can do it" encouraged Shanks as I warmed up along the touchline. The fans were singing my name and generously applauding Brian Hall off the field at the same time. It was one all versus Leeds with time running out. K.K. had equalised Alan Clarke's clearly offside effort before half time. We desperately needed those two points to stay in the championship race. Anfield rocked in expectation. A Leeds attack was broken up on the edge of our square with Peter Lorimer screaming for a free kick. He always did that. Crazy horse, that's Emlyn Hughes, hoofed it out of defence and Kevin took it down and controlled it, all in one movement. Spotting Stevie loose on the left wing, he fed him the perfect ball and Heighway headed for the corner flag and sent over one of his inch perfect crosses. I'd timed my run to perfection and noticing Toshack about to rise, screamed, "Leave it John". I threw myself at it full frontal and headed it past David Harvey in the Leeds goal. The momentum of my run and diving header left me lying in the net looking up at a sea of red scarves. Big Tommy Smith picked me up in his granite-like hands and the boys gathered around and squeezed me to death. "The boy wonder does it again" I heard the BBC commentator roar into his microphone. "Magic, absolute magic" beamed Kevin into my face. "Great ball Stevie" I smiled as Heighway ruffled my hair. The whistle blew and the crowd, still on their feet from my goal, erupted into a crescendo of "champions, champions". Shanks raced off the touchline to protect me from fans and cameramen alike. Back home I could see them excitedly viewing events on T.V. "Well done son" whispered Johnny Giles as he patted my back. "I'll see that you'll soon get a game with the Republic, up front with Don Givens, how would you like that?" I smiled and nodded appreciatively. Heading down the tunnel between the policemen and stewards, Shanks turned and looking at me and Kevin said, "Boys, some people think football's a matter of life and death but us three know it's far more important than that. Atta boy young Conarty, we're still in contention". Kevin looked at me and winked.

Anyway the younger ones were up before us next morning and I could smell the toast warming in the kitchen below. Hearing Mrs. Galligan's soft voice we sensed something was wrong. We jumped into our trousers and ran barefoot down the stairs. In the kitchen Mrs. G smiled. "Ah James, Michael come on and sit down" she cajoled. She'd set the table, something we'd never do and had buttered and jammed a neat pyramid of toast which was being dug into by Tommy and Eddie and Harry. James grabbed a slice and asked, between crunchy mouthfuls, what was wrong? He stood there needing an answer. "Please James" she pleaded, "just eat up, there's a good boy, let me through here now and I'll pour you young men strong cups of tea, your mother and father will be home soon enough". As if on cue, the doorknocker rapped and we all crammed out into the hallway. I knew by Mam's face she'd been crying. The glasses were steamed up and her normally pale cheeks were now rosy red.

"It's alright now, it's alright, c'mon here, come in" said Mrs. G as she embraced her. We shunted along into the kitchen and circled Mammy as she pulled out the steel chair with the ripped plastic seat cover. She gave us a black jack each and we thumbed them open not daring to take our eyes off her.

"Is she alright Phyllis?" asked Mrs. Galligan. "She's fine, she's fine," stuttered Mum. "Jimmy'll be home soon". She wiped her runny nose into an already wet and crumpled hankie and looked round at us, her five boys. "Poor Philomena was very sick during the night boys, and, and …" She started to cry again and we knew it was serious.

"C'mon boys, why don't ye make your beds and find something to do and I'll make your Mam a fresh cup of tea," Mrs. Gallligan chided. I lay on the top of the bed. I could hear the kitchen door close tightly and I choked back the tears. James was fixing the wallpaper on the landing with white cellotape. Tommy and Eddie bounced a ball in the backyard and the dustbin lid clattered annoyingly. Harry whistled on the steps out the front. He was the youngest of us boys and closest to our only sister. After all she always stuck up for him and God knows he needed protecting. Though tall for his age, Harry was boney and awkward and always seemed to say the wrong thing at the wrong time. He was also master of the hit and run tactic. He'd stir it and then leg it and tant from a distance. When his cover was blown and revenge imminent it was always Philomena he'd seek refuge behind. "Don't hit him, don't hit him," she'd shout. I pictured her stumpy little hairy legs and the way she held her left middle finger in the grasp of her right hand. She was a bubbly little lassie and we'd just gotten used to her doll- playing and housekeeping role imitation. Best of all was when she joined her big brothers, standing in goal and shouting "Don't blast it, don't blast it" when one of us teed up a volley.

She'd left in a hurry, I could tell. Her cloth and one-legged doll were caught in the rails of the cot.

"It must be serious," agreed James, "she never goes anywhere without that wee cloth". My eyes scanned her little bedroom and a tear rolled down my cheek and onto the speckly pink dots of her black linoed floor. Please God, please God, don't let her die, I moaned from within. "I'll give up my dream of playing at Anfield" I promised, "just don't let her die".

Downstairs Mum busied herself sweeping and fixing. St. Martin de Porres had a candle lit before him on the kitchen table. It was that serious. Philomena had convulsions, whatever they were. She'd had a high temperature and luckily Mam and Dad had checked her late into the night. She was frothing and fitting and her eyes had rolled backwards into her head. Dad grabbed her from her cot and Mam alerted Pat Timoney from next door. They immediately raced to the hospital in Pat's Vauxhall Viva charging through a Garda checkpoint on the way. Pat was left at the Surgical door to explain as Dad raced with his wee girl, stretched motionless across his arms, screaming for help.

A doctor was found. He began immediately to battle the temperature. A young nurse cold bathed Philomena. Her temperature was reduced though she'd have to stay in awhile for observation. It had been a close call.

It was a defining moment in all of our lives. We became more aware of the preciousness of this gift of life and how it could be taken from any one of us in an instant. O Angel of God my guardian dear, to whom God's love commits us here, Ever this day be at my side, To light and guard, to rule and guide, Amen.

"No matter where yous go in life say your prayers and have manners," he would tell us. "Say Hello to everyone by their name, none of this Howya business, respect people but be afraid of no-one at the same time. Remember you're above no one and beneath no one either, oh, and six be two'll do us all".

I reflected on the pact I'd made with God. I'd given up my dream and he'd saved my little sister. I knew Kevin would understand.

"She stuck the knife in the baby's heart
Weelia Weelia Wallia
She stuck the knife in the baby's heart
Down by the river Saile"

Chapter 9

Anyway I always liked to write and in my imaginary world believe that things could be better. I didn't like it though when the boys called me "John Boy" sometimes and even suggested that I should be stuck on Shantemon Mountain just like he was on Walton. I understood John Boy however and he knew that he was only keeping a record of things so that he or none of the rest of the young Waltons would ever forget their roots.

I'd watch Mammy peeling the smallest spuds out in the back kitchenette perhaps only getting two chips per spud and yet sticking with it through the sweat until she'd get a fryer full. We feasted on those homemade chips with a pinch of salt and a dabble of red of brown sauce, all washed down with mugs of milk. I'd never forget these days I promised myself.

Bean Uí Fiaich liked the past too. She liked her history and took us from Fionn Mac Cumhaill and the exploits of the Red Branch Knights right up to Padraig Pearse and his mates in the blazing G.P.O. of 1916. "Our past moulds our present and dictates our future," she once told us. Anyway there was a wee hole in the school roof and two snowflakes dropped in and gently nestled on the shoulder of Andy Traynor's jumper. Andy came from a huge family of sixteen or seventeen. His father was a postman and his mother probably peeled small spuds too. She was an avid knitter and kitted them all out in blue, green and yellow jumpers. I saw her carrying two buckets of water from the well on the Corfeyhone road one evening that we went there to play with Andy and Brendan, his older brother. Then she made a big plate load of corn-beef sandwiches for us all. Leeds United were on the telly and their fans were fighting with the other crowd from Europe. Part of me felt sorry for the Traynors and more of me admired the way they got on with life and made the most of what they had. There were older brothers and sisters away in Dublin and England and other places. Maybe they helped out. We knew Phyllis and Carmel and Geraldine and now they had a new baby brother.

Anyway Bean Uí Fiaich talked one evening about the kind old doctor that lived on Farnham St. in Cavan that looked after everyone and never charged the poor for his services. Now he was dead and gone and they were knocking his old house down because it was a falling wreck and considered a danger to society. We shouldn't forget this good man we were told and to mark the momentous occasion of the knocking down of his home and surgery, Bean Uí Fiaich decided to fill her mini-minor and take us into Cavan Town to witness the event. We'd say a decade of the rosary on the spot for the poor man's soul and then go up to the big cathedral across the street and light candles for him.

. That night I couldn't sleep. I shuddered at the thought of lighting a candle and kept getting flashbacks to our First Holy Communion. We'd all been told to bring in a sixpence to Castletara Chapel to light a candle for the Holy Souls on the day we made our First Confession. Everything was grand on the day and Fr. Comey the P.P. couldn't have been nicer. Fr. Woods, his Curate, was there too. We liked him best. Anyway we lined up on the aisle to light our candles, first Margaret, then Hazel, then Oliver and me and Sean.

Michael Conaty

Did ya ever shove your hands into your pockets and root around discreetly for something you knew wasn't there? That was me on that fateful morning. The sun shone through the back window of Castletara Chapel, eclipsed only by our Lord himself, standing on a big blue ball.

I knew he wouldn't mind but what about the priests and Bean Uí Fiaich? There'd be war, I knew rightly. "How could ya forget your sixpence on such a special day? It's throttled ya should be", they'd say.

I daren't let on and yet the moment of truth was fast approaching. I sweated like hell as Margaret's sixpence clunked at the bottom of the silver box marked "candles 6d each". Hazel was next, clunk! She lit her candle slowly and then it went out. It bought me time. "Please God, please God, I need a miracle here" I whispered. Looking up at him, through his beard, I could see a smile.

Outta the blue I unearthed a bicycle wheel-washer in the lining of my pocket that Harry had been messing with at dinnertime the previous day. I'd taken it off him and there had been a roaring match. I could feel it now and knew it might be my salvation. Hazel got her candle going and Oliver clunked his sixpence. "Bless me Father for I am about to sin just after having made my first Confessions, please help me and I'll pay you back the sixpence, I promise", I whispered to him. He smiled down on me. Concealing the washer between me thumb and finger and hoping it wouldn't jam in the slot, I closed my eyes and hoped for the best. My clunk was louder than the rest of them as it hit its target. I pushed my 6d candle down and lit it for the Holy Souls.

Anyway we piled into the car that evening and headed for town and prayed the rosary for the black babies of Africa and the itinerants in their new tigíns on the Cock Hill overlooking Cavan. Did ya ever pray the rosary at seventy miles per hour in a small mini-minor for people you didn't even know and wonder why?

We pulled up at the wall outside the Protestant church on Farnham St. that Protestants went to in their gleaming suits on a Sunday morning. Why did they call their chapel a church and why did they go to service and not Mass like the rest of us, I wondered, but daren't ask. John Tynan went flying past in his red mini-minor that sounded like a rally sports car, IID 321. I waved but he didn't notice us.

We walked up through the pathway and in the distance saw the big lead ball swing over and back thumping the life out of the old house. I couldn't see the point in it. This was a good man, why flatten his home?

We lit our candles in the big cathedral using proper sixpences and headed for home.

"Mary Margaret, Kathleen Clarke, Kathleen of the shop, Mrs. Edgeworth, Roseanne Brady, Phyllis Conaty, Mrs. Tully…"

Bean Uí Fiaich handed out the monthly edition of Caritas and we gleefully grabbed what was ours for delivery. Sometimes it was the Far East, sometimes Africa, sometimes The Messenger, today it was Caritas. Then the clock struck twelve, "D'Angel o d'Lord declared unto Mary".

We finished the Angeleus and I took out the blue Catechism book that Bernie Tully had given James a few years previously in readiness for "Who is the Creator of the World?"

After lunchtime Bean Uí Fiaich pushed the tuning fork through her white, bushy hair and told us we were all going to write stories about what we'd seen the previous evening and that if they were good, she'd post them off and maybe if they were really good, Caritas might even publish them. The big ones came out to do their knitting and I watched Anne Costello fixing her hair. James and Martin Brady knitted one and purled one and looked at each other and laughed. I knew how John-boy felt now but kept my head down and wrote like the clappers.

On the way home from school, Martin and James were sniggering and laughing about something. We were going home to Nanna this evening and Mammy and the rest of them were coming out after. It's exactly 685 of my steps from the school down to Edgeworth's shop at the foot of the chapel brae. I know cos I counted them. Mrs. Edgeworth gave us a penny bar each even though we only had enough for two of them. Then we set off up the hill. The boys were still laughing as we stopped again by the disused quarry at the butt of Shantemon Mountain on the Castletara side.

Now Felim Dunne was in sixth class and a fully-grown man as far as I was concerned. The boys didn't like him and I sensed that the feeling was quite mutual. Felim and I got on grand however. Sure didn't he often buy me an ice-lolly in the shop and we'd slurp them as he pushed his Uncle Jemmie's big cross-barred bike up the hill past the chapel. No harm in Felim, a grand fella I thought, but then why didn't he buy ice-lollies for James and Martin too?

Anyway he'd been kept in this evening for messing about with Jimmy Greenan's Tayto crisps that lunchtime. James took from his trousers pocket a butt of white chalk and the pair of boys knelt down on the road and printed "SHIT FOR DUNN". I couldn't believe it. Not only had he left out the E in Dunne but had obviously also forgotten that Felim travelled by bike and would, if he saw it, quickly catch up with us and exact his revenge. James soloed his burst, orange football up the hill towards the plantin as the older folks called it.

John Tully sat on the bonnet of his blue Vauxhall car beside Kettoes bush. We knew he'd been looking at his cattle and slowed our pace to speak to him. James picked up his ball. "You boys are in a hurry this evening, are the British Army chasing yous?" he laughed. John Tully intrigued us. He'd been in Dáil Eireann with Clann somebody or other, we knew that, but we could never understand or daren't ask why he was missing three fingers. He stuck on his black hat and told us the story of Kettoe's bush, a hawthorn tree that stood on its own across from Hughie Smith's lane. It was alive alright but never grew leaves. "Legend has it" said John, "that the poor oul widow woman, having seen off the last of her children during the famine and now left all alone in the world, had sat beneath it and cried". He paused.

McGunker

"Next morning she was found dead on that very spot and from that day till this no leaves grow on that bush".

"How do you know it's alive then?" piped up James.

"Good question" answered John taking a penknife from his breast pocket. We watched as he made a slit in one of the branches. "Look" he enthused, "plenty of sap there and yet she never sprouts leaves or yields fruit".

Our local history lesson over and conscious of the passing time, we bid John good luck and quickened our step over the mountain pass, down Sailor's hill, past Finn Mac Cool's fingerstones signpost, down Ned's brae, past McGunkers and on for McKiernan's lane.

Martin had passed his own turn-off above Mary Margaret's, taking the scenic route home with us as he and James giggled away. They exchanged passes practising their back heels and I got an odd kick myself.

Like a bird of prey Felim Dunne swooped up behind us on his big, black bike, grabbing James' orange ball. In a flash he was gone again with the ball on his carrier back up the very hill we'd just come down.

It was a hot, sweaty time of the evening despite the cloud cover and James paused for a second. And then he was off. The faster he ran the harder Felim pedalled, looking behind occasionally and laughing aloud. Back up Ned's brae with James in pursuit, Felim soon disappeared out of view. Martin looked at me and I knew what he was thinking. Should we stay or should we go? Go on home or go after them even? We sat on the ditch and pulled a shoot of grass each. A big fuzzy bee floated on the honeysuckle nearby and the sun momentarily came out from behind the clouds and then disappeared again.

"James isn't stupid," snapped Martin. "Surely he knows the more he runs the further Dunne'll cycle". I called out his name but to no avail. I knew James wasn't stupid either but that ball was ours and must be fought for. Guilt set in. Maybe if I'd run then my friend

Felim could've been pacified. I spat out green spit and Martin looked at his watch. Twenty-three minutes past four, way behind schedule. I looked at Martin and felt sorry for him too. He was the youngest of a big family and his father was dead quite a while. He never discussed him and neither did we. His older brothers Michael and Benny were hardy goers. They had tractors and diggers and a bulldozer too. We knew Mammy's people and them had always been friends. Daecent people as Dad might say.

In the distance Felim veered off at the top of Ned's brae and short-cutted home Brady's lane. We could pick out his smirk of contentment. The sun came out again and one of McGovern's cows scratched herself against a rusty nail on the gatepost nearby. Tar bubbled on the road and I looked over at Corratubber knowing Nanna would be watching us home. A sticky situation in more ways than one. Casting my eyes back I could see the big beads of sweat on James' beetroot-red face as he ran toward us clutching his ball.

"I'll kill him when I'm older" he panted as he brushed past. We said nothing. Martin quietly parted and we jumped the ditch and headed across for our meadow. True to form Nanna stood at the end of the byre. "What kept yous? Are yous alright, my God, I thought something had happened" she frowned. We walked with her to the back door and went through the sky-blue scullery with its dripping tap and sat down at the kitchen table shuffling our school bags beneath.

On the cooker sat rust-colour fried spuds piled on the pan. We tucked into the cabbage and sausages and Nanna spread some butter on our spuds. James drank plenty of water.

"Hurry up with yous now and feed the hens for me when you're done" she prompted, as she gathered the skins to be mixed with layers mash. Bellies full, we headed out with the feed to the back street. "Come back for a treat when you're finished" Nanna called after us. The hens came running excitedly, then scattered sideways when the big red rooster appeared. They clucked in anticipation. We didn't like the rooster. Big and bold and bossy, one glare from him laid down the law. "Is that the room the McEvoys threw the gun from?" I enquired, pointing up to the window over the back street. "This isn't Crosserlough, that's where the IRA are," replied James as he scattered out the last of the feed. Suddenly and without warning the rooster attacked. James went down on his hunkers and losing his balance, the rooster was quickly in on top of him. He scrambled on his knees across the street. I picked up a stone and moved nervously towards the target and screamed. It was over as quickly as it had started. The blood froze in me. "What happened?" shouted Nanna. A squirt of blood trickled down James' neck and onto his shirt. He was still in shock as Nanna led us in covering his head with her hand. My heart thumped. I looked back at the rooster, now flexing his leg muscles alongside the gate and I vowed revenge for this some day soon. Inside, Nanna tenderly mopped where James had been pecked and then washed the blood from his neck. It was such a small wound and yet it took its time to stop bleeding. "Yous must have startled him," she explained as she handed us bowlfuls of custard and jelly. Later that evening, back in Drumalee, when the story had been told and retold, Dad looked at James and examining his head said "It's not those who can inflict the most, but those who can suffer the most, who will conquer". We looked at each other. We had conveniently forgotten to tell the Felim Dunne saga and explained our lateness, which Nanna had obviously complained about, by saying that we'd been helping John Tully with his cattle. "Say that again", said Harry to Dad. "Say what?" he replied. "I dunno, something about conkers". We all laughed and Harry, sensing that he'd said something funny, looked round amused; "what, what?"

Dad went on to tell us the story of Terence McSwiney who had died of starvation in a British jail in the 1920's. "Imagine no bread or jam or chips or tea or spuds for a whole day" beamed Eddie. "McSwiney did it for seventy three of them" said Dad. "Do yous not know your history at all?" he continued, "it's no wonder the ducks are barefooted," he laughed. He always said this at times like now and we never knew what he meant. He opened his Sweet Aftons, smiled and picked up the Evening Press.

Chapter 10

Later, Mam and Philomena left Dad into work. We waved goodbye from the slip road and carried on with our match. We played a game which involved scoring three and staying outfield. Once you had three in the bag you stayed out until the rest were eliminated. Last man on the field took over in goals. Tackles flew in as we all chased after the same ball. The trick was to play a one-two against the wall and dodge your opponents and score. The trouble was that after all your hard work, someone else could capitalise and nip in for glory. We called anyone who hung around waiting for the loose ball a line-watcher. Mum was back from town and called us in for a feed of rice laced with raisins. The cold milk sat on top and we all mixed and slurped away happily. Frank Coyle arrived. He and his family had left Castletara too, albeit in different circumstances, and moved to a nice two-storey house on Church St. Frank's dad, Charlie, and our Dad were good friends. He worked on the council and the two of them often enjoyed a drink in Boylans. Charlie had a huge garden to the rear of the house. He grew everything there; spuds, cabbage, lettuce, rhubarb, onions, leaks and even beetroot. It was surrounded by a high stone wall and the broken glass, bedded in cement on top, discouraged visitors. Mrs. Coyle had sent out a bundle of rhubarb with her son and Mum accepted it gratefully. It would do nicely with a bowlful of custard. It started to rain and we trudged out to the front room and fought over the sofa.

"How come youse haven't UTV?" asked Frank. "Is it broken or what?" We never had UTV, ever. It was just fuzzy and consequently we missed programmes like Benny Hill and more importantly all the midweek soccer coverage and the Big Match with Brian Moore on Sundays. We knew this from the other boys at school. "Dad's forgotten his sandwiches", Mum shouted in, "will some of youse dodge in with them to him, he has his flask and I can't leave cos Lizzie and Fidelma are calling" she explained.

James and myself, being the eldest elected to go. We stuck on our coats and skipped down the steps. Frank Coyle joined us. Off we set in the mizzly rain. James clutched the tin foil wrapped ham sandwiches and we hastened our pace. Up the town past Providers we went, crossing over the street to have a gawk at the farm sets in Connolly's toy shop. On again, soon reaching Pat McGovern's, where Mam did her Saturday shopping. Pat was sweeping at the door. Who comes out only Mrs. Sexton! She stopped and spoke to us and enquired after Philomena. We said goodbye. Across the street I spotted Tony Tully carrying a T.V. into G.T. Electric, a shop he ran with another man called Good. Tony was a son of John's of Clann na Poblachta and missing fingers fame. I had a moment of inspiration and figured that if anyone could fix our UTV, surely it'd be no bother to an electronics genius like Tony. I crossed the street and Tony smiled when I informed him of our plight with no Benny Hill or westerns or The Big Match on Sundays. "Sure I'll call in some evening on my way home, maybe today" he assured me as he rushed inside to take a phone call.

Up at the pumps Dad was talking to two men from Lavey. He loved hearing all the news from where he called home. "How's Sean Mac?" he enquired. "Wasn't he in McCauls all weekend" came the reply. "Are these your gasuns, Jem?" the taller of the two enquired as James handed over his lunch.

"Aw deedn't they are, and the big lad's a son of Charlie Coyle of Cullentra" he replied. "Ould fashioned boys I can tell ya" he smiled, winking at us. Smith's garage was busy and Benny Hannigan the taxi-man squeezed in through the sliding door of Dad's hut to sign the credit book. The whole talk was of the power cuts in England and Ted Heath and the oil crisis. The Lavey men left having arranged to meet Dad in Crosskeys at the weekend. A brand new, blue Princess car pulled up as we left. It was Jack Flood the hackney-man from Abbey St. and hearing us say goodbye again told us to hop in and he'd give us a lift. Sure wasn't he heading out to Cootehill. We marvelled at the plastic covered seats and the smell of newness. "Who'll win the Cup Final boys?" he enquired on the way up Farnham St. "wouldn't it be great if Leeds were bet be Sunderland?" he enthused. We dropped Frank off at the Cathedral and getting out of the car at Drumalee I asked Jack how much we owed him for the lift. "On the house, as your father would say" he laughed and drove off.

Inside voices were raised. Nanna wasn't well again and had taken a turn. Dr. Lorigan was worried about her well being and didn't like her being on her own in Corratubber. "Sure what can I do?" pleaded Mum. "You were the one that suggested we'd leave in the first place, it's not easy for me, I've Jimmy and the children to consider as well". Herself was ris looking and charged back, "Didn't you get three farms of land out there and what would Fr. Eddie say and it's all fine and well for you and I'm stranded with Himself away working every day and poor Mother…"

She handed us Crunchies and said we'd gotten taller and then closed the kitchen door out after us. We stood in the hall and listened as the racket about Nanna started all over again. How come she never calls to give out when Dad's here, I wondered to myself.

Outside we went and played a game of three and in. The Reilly and Smith and O'Brien boys went past. They were talking about the new family who'd moved in across the road from the shop. We knew the two boys, McGraths from America, Michael the eldest and

Stephen or Stevie whom we'd met on the road. "Hey cuchiecoo, who loves ya baby?" laughed Myles in an America accent. We liked Kojak the lollipop sucking cop but not Myles. We carried on playing and then Tony Tully pulled in. He climbed the steps behind us and we ushered him into the room. All he had was a red screwdriver. The din in the kitchen subsided. He rooted at the little black knobs and quick as a flash up came the UTV news. There'd been another bomb blast, this time in Londonderry according to the man looking out at us from the screen. "Where's Londonderry?" asked Harry. Tony smiled. "Michael, I'll kill you, I haven't a rex to give him" I heard Mam say out in the hallway when Tommy had told her the good news. Tony wasn't going to bill her, he laughed, as she rustled whatever few coins of new money she had in her shop coat pocket. She thanked him and enquired after his mother and father and as quick as he came in Tony was gone again. The boys were thrilled, sure even Dad would be happy when he'd get home I reassured myself as Sean car pulled up outside and waited till Lizzie and Fidelma made their exit down the steps. Looking at Mam I knew she'd been crying again and this served to spoil the return of UTV. I slammed the ball against the wall in time for Mrs. Yorkman to remind us that her little boy had gone down for a sleep and for us to move away as quickly and as quietly as possible.

I hated the tension caused by Herself's visits. I knew what it would lead to for Mum; more guilt, fear, frustration and bad humour too. It felt like a heavy cloud hanging over us all day and it spoilt our happiness. The only difference this time was that there seemed to be a consensus of opinion that a move back to Corratubber might be best for all, but there would have to be a few conditions attached. "No interference, no story-telling and no shit-stirring" I heard Dad say that night as he and Mum mulled over things in the kitchen. He'd always said that Nanna or Mrs. Brady as he called her, was the best in the world if only she was left alone. Sure hadn't he and her brothers got on famously. I sensed a willingness on Dad's part to move back. I knew deep down he'd like to grow a few spuds, have some cattle and be able to make cocks of hay just like everyone else. I told James what I'd heard and he too became excited but warned me not to say anything to the rest for fear of building up our expectations and then being let down. Anna Mae's visit the following Saturday evening helped to confirm our hopes. We just sensed something. There was an air of expectancy in the house. If only they'd call a press conference like they do on the telly I told myself. The hours passed. Nothing was said.

That night we met Sean Mac from Corriga for the first time. He arrived with Uncle Harry, Dad's youngest brother and a big favourite with us all. Harry was always jovial and messing and codding. Anyway they came from the pub, the two of them with Dad and the humour was good. Mam stuck a few chops on the pan and sliced up an onion. Sean Mac was full, I could just sense it in his eyes and his slurred speech and laughter were a dead giveaway. We knew Dad liked him. He had a bit of a reputation for the drink and this in Crosskeys country gave him status. We were down on our knees flicking the switches of our soccer stadium that Santy had kindly dropped off the previous Christmas. Red versus blue and a ball bearing made its way around the pitch. The goalie, when flicked properly, could make world-class saves. The reds no. 2 looked like our Chris Lawler and everytime the same coloured No. 7 got the ball at his feet, you were sure to pull the trigger and score. "Supper's ready" we heard Mum call the men. "Come on Mac" cajoled Dad. "Are ya a man or a mouse?". Getting to his feet and with John Power swaying in his head, Sean Mac stumbled and in an effort to save himself falling, promptly knelt in on top of our good soccer stadium. Of all the players on that damn pitch that he had to aim at, the one he succeeded in knobbling for life was our red No. 7. "C'mon you oul woman ya" laughed Dad helping Mac to his knees. "Sorry childer, sorry" he muttered as they made their way to the back kitchen and a greasy feed of chops and onions and bread all to be washed down with mugs of strong tae.

I knelt and looking at the carnage, thought of all the rough tackles that Kevin had taken in his time, from the likes of Bremner and Giles and Chopper Harris. Would ya look at him now? I gently tried to lever him sideways on his spring, back into the correct position, but it was no good. K.K. would never be the same again.

We went to bed. Eddie was singing.

"Two brave policemen came knocking on the door
Weelia weelia wallia
Two brave policemen came knocking on the door
Down by the river Saile!"

Chapter 11

Anyway I'd never been given a letter with my own name on it before in my life, ever. Steve, the postman, smiled and said "at least it hasn't got a window on it". We raced inside and upstairs to where Mam was making the beds. I flittered it open and the £1 postal order fell to the ground. Eddie quickly picked it up. In the excitement I could barely focus on the words of the letter addressed to me. Elbows and shoulders crowded me. I got the bones of it. Caritas had been impressed by the story and had decided to publish it.

The House Coming Down

Mrs. Fay took us to see the house being knocked down. It was once lived in by a kind doctor. He treated the poor people and didn't charge them too much. The big lead ball swung over and back and flattened the walls. The bricks dropped like leaves, falling off a tree in autumn. We felt sad going home that day.

There was mayhem. We all knew it was something good. Something great had happened in our lives, not just mine, but everybodys. All for one, one for all. We roared ecstatically and lost the run of ourselves. Eddie had his calculations done in seconds. "That's sixteen pence each for five of us and a twenty pence for Michael, after all he won it". No one objected and neither could I.

"That's some pile of blackjacks and gobstoppers and football stickers and…"piped up Harry. "Can we go to the shop?" he pleaded. "Maybe yous should wait till your father gets home" said Mum, "he'd like to see it, and Nanna too, it's only fair, isn't that right Michael?"

Again I couldn't object. I wanted Dad to see my earnings, to see the happiness, to see that everything is possible, to see that he was right. Hadn't he always preached to us about the importance of reading and writing and learning and using our imaginations. Hadn't he always reminded us of the chance we had in life and to go and use it. Sure look at John F. Kennedy himself. He was a dreamer too. Sure Dad often quoted him: "Some men see things as they are and say why? I dream things that never were and say why not?" They were some poet's words but he used them anyway. Sure hadn't Kennedy's people left Co. Wexford without a rex in their pockets during the famine. Look at how well they'd done in America. We knew their story. We felt connected somehow. We'd seen John F's smiling face on a blue plate hung up in the corner of Philip Brady's house in Corratubber and in the opposite one a much more serious looking Pope John the twenty-third. Had his family struggled too I often wondered. Didn't he make it good himself, probably against all the odds as well. Imagine being Pope of the whole world, I often thought. Imagine being as well known as JFK. Imagine having it to say that you were the Pope before the present one, Pope Paul the sixth. Imagine! Imagine if we were somehow related to the Kennedys. Sure they're bound to have heard of the McEvoys from Crosserlough and the Conatys from Corriga and of how Fr. Eddie had given up everything and gone to help the black babies in Tanzania….

Anna Mae and Tony had been to America and sure hadn't Tony a brother called Teddy Hughes and hadn't JFK a brother called Teddy too who'd survived a car-crash in which a woman had died, through no fault of his own, in a funny place called Chappaquidick.

Hadn't there been an awful lot of begrudery and ill will towards the Kennedys from the FBI and the CIA and J.Edgar Hoover and Jimmy Hoffa and Lyndon B. Johnson. Sure didn't they all conspire to have Kennedy shot dead and assassinated and all because he was Catholic and Irish and only wanted to help Martin Luther King and the blacks. Us Irish and the blacks of America have an awful lot in common, I'd firmly believed from a young age. We'd faced oppression and bullying and injustice just like them but our spirits were indomitable too and could never be crushed. We would never give up in the struggle either. Sure hadn't they shot Bobby Kennedy too, according to Dad. Shot to death and assassinated by Sirhan Sirhan in a hotel kitchen when he was about to get the Democratic nomination and be elected President of America just like his older brother. Didn't he leave ten childer behind him and his wife, Ethel, expecting another one. And he was Catholic and oirish and more than likely said his prayers, not in his bed, but on the floorboards, just like his brother, and no doubt wanted to help the black people too. He would've been in favour of Civil Rights and "one man one vote" and would've probably come to Norn Ireland and helped the poor Catholics there suffering from injustice and unemployment and begrudgery too, all at the hands of the British. Bobby liked Robert Frost's poetry Dad had once told us. "Promises to keep and miles to go before I sleep, and miles to go before I sleep". It was something to do with a fella on a horse travelling through a forest and Dad knew every word of it. And he hadn't even got an education. "Yous have a chance, take it, take it with both hands wide open, read, read, read" he lectured us.

Anyway Harry followed me around all day. "Will you be on television now Michael, will you be famous, will you tell them that you've got a brother called Harry, can I stand beside you?" he pleaded. I looked at my youngest brother with his tossled hair and blue eyes and trousers too short for him and felt good. I felt even better with James. He was my only big brother. I knew he felt good too, felt good about me doing something that gave everyone recognition. I knew he'd seen a lot in his time being the eldest and most sensitive of us all. I wanted to identify with him and give him hope. I wanted more than anything else for him to be proud of me and to stop calling me John-boy now in the same way that I was proud of him but couldn't say it or show it either. I wanted to connect.

"There you are son, stop asking silly questions and get writing and be famous like your older brother" Dad said to Harry. Harry looked at the huge hard-backed ledger that opened out like Mrs. Sexton's roll book and sifted through its heavy pages. He closed it again and struggled to carry it upstairs. It did indeed look like a roll book and Harry felt out of his depth and all because he was only going into first class and hadn't yet learnt enough big words to write a story. Eddie, the mathematician, came up with the ideal solution that night before we slept.

"If you can't write big words, then write figures instead, nobody's ever written down all the numbers before and I'll help you" Eddie promised him as he rummaged under the bed for a pencil. Off he went; one, two, three, four, five, six, seven, eight, nine, 10,11,12,13,14....

No need for commas in between, just a matter of writing figures and keeping going until he'd reached the end of the big book. On the front cover he neatly printed HARRY CONATY, NUMBERS, AGED SEVEN AND A BIT.

Anyway Sunderland bet the mighty Leeds United and Jim Montgomery their goalkeeper, couldn't be beaten that day and he pulled off save after save from Clarke and Lorimer and Giles and Bremner. Sure didn't he even get the woodwork to help him. Ian Porterfield scored their goal and Bob Stokoe, their manager, danced across the field in his overcoat and proved that even for second division football teams, dreams can come true. We were crossing the bridge over the Annalee river going to under twelve football training in the Flag and Meadow football pitch and some of the older Ballyhaze football boys with long wiry hair and Kung-Fu jumpers were spitting down into the river. Tom Quinn had red hair and studs in his shoes which clicked on the roadway. His denim jacket told me he was a member of the Hell's Angels and the smoke from his fag drifted off into the balmy air of that summer's evening. James was up ahead with Eddie Rehill, our cousin and one of the Ballyhaze lads. He was our link. We liked Eddie. In fact everyone did. "Mrs. Sexton is our teacher and we call her sexy" I informed Tom Quinn as he sucked on the butt of his cigarette through brown stained fingers. He flicked the butt skywards and it dived all the way down into the river and away under the bridge. "And is she?" Tom enquired blowing the last of his smoke into nice, neat circles that seemed to evaporate and disappear. "Is she what?" I replied. "Is your teacher sexy?" Tom asked looking at me with a smile.

"I dunno, but that's what we call her anyway" I said confused. We caught up with Felim Plunkett and Paudge Masterson and Barry Tierney and the other big lads from Ballyhaze. "This is young Conarty from Castletara and he's got a sexy teacher" smiled Tom as he introduced me to them. We crossed the garden beside Johnny Conaty's and Hubert, who was also one of the big boys, came out and vaulted the fence by the side of his house and joined up. I wondered if we were cousins but didn't like to ask. I hated Gaelic cos you couldn't dribble the ball on the ground and you had to be able to dig your foot in and hope you wouldn't fall over and that the ball would spin up into your hands. Then you had to solo. This was tricky especially since you had to run with the ball at the same time and hope you wouldn't take too many steps or drop it or get a clout from someone whose job it was to mark you. Also the ball was far too hard. It had O'Neills written on it and hurt like hell when you got it into the stomach or more especially when it bent back your fingers as you tried to catch it.

The bigger boys seemed to know what they were doing and I

envied them. They knew where the forty was and what a sideline ball was and could score points from a forty-five instead of simply taking a corner like we did in soccer. "Face the ball, face it," shouted Paddy Walshe from the sideline. He was smoking a cigarette and seemed like a nice man. He fiddled his cap over and back and then folded his arms. In the distance I could see Enda McGowan and Hughie Newman and Stevie Duggan. These were the senior players, the stars, the county men as they were called. I watched Stevie Duggan as he jinked his way through and slotted the ball to the net and then it whacked me! Right on the side of the face, that bloody O'Neills ball that us younger ones were meant to be training with. The sting was unbearable and the laughter hurt even more. Paddy Walshe picked me up and consoled me. He reprimanded those that were laughing and led me to the sideline where he picked up a bottle of water and dashed some into my face. "There you are, young Conarty, you're alright now" he comforted. "Just always remember to keep your eye on the ball". It stung and yet I felt better because Paddy had singled me out and made me feel good, even though the county men hadn't noticed. "Have you no proper boots?" he enquired, looking down at my runners. "Maybe there's a pair in our house that'll fit ya". He patted me on the shoulder and headed across the field.

We walked all the way home that evening, us Castletara boys, me and James and Martin Brady and Martin Lyons and Oliver and Sean Reilly and Sean Prior too, who lived halfway between. Mammy picked us up in Corratubber. Nanna was happier now, happier than I'd ever seen her before as she walked us across the grassy street to the car. She handed us sweets from a green Colleen bag and said we were good gasuns. Jackie Fitch blew the horn of his mini-minor as he sped up the brae beside us with Bonzo giving chase. Mam drove home. "What comes after 99?" Harry wanted to know but we were too busy watching a bunch of girls giving chase to Benny Hill between a cluster of trees at a very fast pace. The music made us laugh. Later on, before heading to bed, we saw a familiar sight on the BBC news. The remains of a bombed out car had smoke smouldering from it somewhere "in Co. Londonderry" according to the pretty newscaster. There had been "no warning and it was miraculous that no one had been killed or seriously maimed by these cowardly terrorists," said the serious looking RUC inspector into the camera. Eddie took shots with a lime green tennis ball out in the hallway with Tommy protecting the hall door goal nets. Dad arrived home and stuck his head in just as Elizabeth sat astride her majestic horse and the song implored God to save their gracious Queen. "Put that shite off, is that all yous know," he roared. Sheila Crotty's céilí with Mammy was over and she headed out the front door bidding us all Goodnight. Her blonde hair-bun sat perfectly still, tightly clipped against the night's draft as she headed down the steps and off again towards home.

"Now childer, yous better get to bed," chided Mum.

Chapter 12

Sure we'd often go out to Nanna on holidays, James and myself that is, and we knew the lie of the land fairly well so to speak. We knew Packie Brady's shop and kitchen and became regular visitors. Kathleen, Packie's wife, ran the show inside and out. Kathleen was a small red-haired woman of wirey dimensions and could, Mc-Gunker said, in her day, tackle a pony better that any man. They had one daughter, Eileen, who was five years older than James and wore glasses. She always had her friends Teresa Murphy and Bernie Tully call by and they engaged themselves in the music and fashion of the day. They teased us regularly about becoming their boyfriends. I was easily led but James being older and cuter knew better so we gave them a wide berth. Anyway Packie and Kathleen's shop was a thriving little country business. It was on the left of the hallway and people invariably crossed over into the kitchen on their way out for the obligatory cuppa tae. Their kitchen was powered by a jubilee cooker which thundered aloud and belted hot water around copper pipes which meandered their way behind a small wooden stair leading up to a one-bedroomed loft. Kathleen had rashers and sausages sizzling away. Packie sat in his chair by the window watching the world go by and cracked codes and completed crosswords on the daily papers. He was tall, very tall, well built and had been destined for a great career down in the Army Barracks in Athlone, according to Mum, until a kick from a pony left his brother Philip minus one kidney and Packie had to forsake the military and return home to run the family farm. We knew their people and ours went back a long way. We knew also that Packie had built, all by himself, their home incorporating the shop behind the ditch that ran parallel to the Cootehill Road way back in the fifties.

Sure wasn't Fr. Eddie his first customer. He purchased a box of Maguire and Patterson matches that morning and wished Packie every success with his new enterprise and hoped he'd have a multitude of customers in no time. "Sure if they all buy as much of me as you just did Eddie, I'll be a millionaire in no time" quipped Packie. A very intelligent and witty man and Fianna Fáil to the backbone. Packie had loads of theories, most of them involving conspiracies, and though often far-fetched and over the top in imaginativity, he enthralled us nonetheless. He tuned in his wireless for the regular news bulletins and this along with his constant reading of papers, magazines, Reader's Digest and Ireland's Own left him out on his own in terms of general knowledge. His kitchen and underground store to the back were regularly used for Fianna Fáil meetings and fund-raising bazaars.

Anyway we left the shop and Kathleen walked us across the road just as Jack Rahill's yellow bread van pulled in. Jack whistled. "I hear talk yous could be coming back," said Kathleen as we reached the big hayshed and double lean-to Packie was building on the far side of the road. We didn't answer. "Well?" came Kathleen again. "I don't know" replied James opening his blackjack bar, "we'll have to wait and see". We stood inside the roofless shed and when Kathleen had gone back over the road, headed our way up through Jim Costelloe's meadow. This saved us climbing the pass and Jim never minded. "How's the boys?" came his friendly voice as he lowered a galvanized bucket into the well on the far side of the pass under his house and threw some water into a half-barrel for his white-headed cows. We zigzagged our way up what we called Costelloe's brae shouting hello in at Mrs. Costelloe who was hanging towels on their whitethorn ditch. It's exactly 2615 of my steps from Nanna's gate to Packie's door. I know cos I counted them. Ray Reilly, the vet, went past us in his green Volkswagen car just as we reached our destination. He was lighting his pipe.

Back in the kitchen, Nanna busied herself tidying and futeering as she called it. She made a pot of tea and buttered some homemade soda bread for the pair of us. Outside the last of the hens headed in for the roost and she closed the door in behind them. She picked up the Anglo-Celt and read the Ballyhaze news. It was bright when we went to bed. We always slept upstairs in her room in the same bed, the three of us, with James lying upside down, to prevent any giggling and laughing. The problem was that we could still pull at each other's toes which caused consternation if we couldn't suppress our laughter especially during the rosary. We just couldn't help it . The bawling of one of Packie's cows out on the rock and the echoing distant bark of someone's dog were all that were to be heard. We turned over to sleep. Lying there I was struck by the enormity of things. This big old house and all its secrets. How on earth did Nanna manage on her own all these years? Had she never been afraid? Hadn't she lost out in life's unfair dealings? Hadn't we lost out too? Wouldn't it be great to get back home and make up for lost time, I thought to myself excitedly? Would there be trouble? Would there be rows? No, I had to be positive, I told myself. We'd move back and everyone would be happy. I just knew it. Still, I begged God, just in case, before nodding off into dreamland. I just loved wakening up in that room especially like now in the summer time. The yellow curtains failed to blind out the morning sunlight and outside all was still and quiet. We made our way down to where Nanna had lit up her range and a sombre sounding Charles Mitchell spun out the news from her wireless box neatly perched on a shelf on the kitchen wall. "C'mon boys, eat up some stirrabout" she smiled "and then go and have a wash and freshen up". The bathroom lay to the back of the kitchen and was separated from it by a scullery full of pots and pans and a cylinder of gas and bags of Layers mash for the hens and a couple of galvanised buckets. We washed ourselves with the bright yellowy sunlight soap and then headed for the back street. Here we heard Nanna's chirping; "Chucky, chucky, chucky". I stared at that rooster and a shudder ran down my spine remembering our previous encounter with him.

"Here gather them eggs and make yourselves useful boys" we heard Nanna call. I stared around those old buildings, the barn, the stable, the ould byre which went in a straight line beneath a galvanized roof running the length of the street. I remembered days of long ago. I flashbacked through what seemed an eternity now and heard the pigs squeal that we used to keep and saw the calves being let out on the lower back street to nibble at the docks and other weeds before being unleashed on the green fields proper. The yellow goo ran down my trousers leg as I tried to balance my batch of eggs. James laughed. We brought them into the kitchen and placed them in the big circular straw-woven basket that nestled in the deep windowsill, shaded in part by the heavy pushed back curtain Nanna had once made. James went out again to get a bucket of turf. "Yous are one short" said Nanna as she rearranged the golden brown eggs to her own satisfaction. "Sure maybe that ould wan has stopped laying altogether, maybe I'll bring her to Sheridan the fowl man, for all he'll give me". I was caught between guilt and confession and conveniently let it go as the news came on again to tell us that several IRA suspects had been picked up in early dawn raids across Belfast and were now being questioned by RUC detectives. "God help them," says Nanna, "they'll fairly get it them boys, innocent or guilty".

We headed back out and up to the orchard which could be accessed through a gap in the block wall facing the back half-door. It was like a tropical jungle up there. Lots of apple trees surrounded by briars and nettles and choked by the ivy that stuck to the trunks. There was a lovely pear tree in the corner and though its yield was never on the big side, we climbed it first anyway and bit into the hard cores, not much bigger than some of the sour crab apples we'd get at Mary Margaret's laneway. Scattered between and reaching to the sky stood numerous ash and oak trees and these helped to umbrella this enchanting place. Bees flitted hither and thither and birds chirped away in the darkened heights. We found a rusted penknife which cranked open and with it we carved "James and Michael summer 1973" into the thick bark of a tree which stood on the ditch and helped to shelter the back-street on lazy, sun soaked days like this one.

Bellies full, we headed round to the hayshed. We knew it had been built by Mick Brady our grandfather in hard times and its tall girders were now brown and rusted and the arched timbers holding the galvanize together, a join-the-dots of woodworm. The new byre was 19 of my footsteps across from the hayshed. I know cos I counted them. We opened its double doors and inside a maze of cobwebs clung to its corners and hung from its timbers. Flashback time. We had a very old cow that stood in the upper corner that James had christened "worownouldcow". Broken down it read "our own old cow". She was one that Dad had bought as a calf and stood next to the oxion cow, obviously one he had picked up at an auction. He had ten in total and they'd been sold when all the neighbours and dealers came on the day of our own auction before departing for Drumalee. We were kept inside that day and watched the small lorries and tractors and trailers mosey down the lane at the close of business. They took everything. All our cows and calves and heifers and bullocks and the mower and hay-shifter and even the shovels and forks and slash-hook. A Lavey man bought the hayshed full of loose hay, hay that had been nurtured and cut and turned and rowed and cocked and tied and drawn in. All gone. Time stood still. An old stout bottle that had once dosed a bullock or cow stood on one of the dividing walls and the ivy had found a crack in the upper corner and crawled its way in from the adjoining dairy. Some caked cowshit came away from the wall when James kicked it and a rat ran out from beneath some old furniture stacked in the corner. It ran down the group as Dad called it and out through the hole in the corner of the wooden door. We left too. The mizzly rain led us into the shelter of the garage across from the byre door. A garage that had been built for Fr. Eddie's car. The doors were gone now and the door jams formed a perfect set of goalposts. When it rained like now we simply belted a ball against the far gable wall, occasionally thundering it up against the chipboard ceiling that hid the galvanized roof. It had one broken window in its upper corner and sometimes we'd chip the ball from the street outside and try to squeeze it through. If you missed at least the ball rebounded for a second go. Then again you could throw the ball up on the roof and try to head in the dropping cross. If all else failed, the galvanized gable end of the hayshed provided ideal shooting practice. We'd play squash against it and try and return service regardless of where the ball had landed. Mam arrived with the rest of the gang and stacked in the boot of our A40 were neatly piled bedclothes and throw-overs that would normally only be taken down at the onset of winter. The signs were ominous.

> "Are you the woman that kilt the child
> Weelia weelia wallia
> Are you the woman that kilt the child
> Down by the river Saile".

Chapter 13

Anyway Dad arrived home that day in 1973 with a new fangled machine that added and subtracted and multiplied and did all sorts of magical things with numbers. He called it a calculator and we queued up eagerly behind each other on his shoulder to watch him operate the buttons. "Gimme a sum, any sum" he looked around at us.

"What number comes after 999?" piped up Harry. We all laughed. "Give him a chance," pleaded Dad as he switched his attention from the calculator to Harry's big ledger. Right enough, there they were, every single digit from one to nine hundred and ninety nine. Amazing. Dad shifted the calculator towards himself again and deleted all the zeroes Philomena had entered when she'd gotten his back turned. He smiled. She stood there with the red bow in her hair that Mum had attached earlier, knowing she wouldn't be given out to. "Now son, watch this," he said as he entered 999 and then, pushing the plus sign, added on one. "There you have it Harry, it's one thousand; one and three zeroes.

Harry copied it in with his butty pencil and then faced up to his next dilemma. "What comes after that?" he enquired. Again Dad picked up his magical number machine and proceeded to plus another one. Harry was away again, head down, writing frantically, aiming for his second thousand! He seemed totally oblivious to our laughter and sense of relief that this project was actually keeping him occupied and more importantly quiet!

"Leave him alone" cajoled Dad as he smiled. "Sure maybe one day with all these figures in his head he'll be an accountant or maybe work in the bank or the post office, or somewhere you'd never know".

Eddie wondered what would happen when he reached the end of the big ledger or even when there were no more numbers to write. "It's ok" James assured him; "Mrs. Sexton says numbers are infinite".

"What does that mean?" asked Harry raising an eyebrow to a conversation he wasn't meant to be hearing.

"Numbers go on forever, they don't end," replied James.

"Of course they do and I'll prove it," said Harry as he got stuck in again with a barely visible lead point.

It transpired that Dad had been given the calculator by one of the many salesmen who'd call by the pumps on a regular basis. People were good to him. He communicated well, endeared himself to people and like now, reaped the rewards.

He was heading up this evening to his home place of Corriga to see his mother Annie. Tommy and I volunteered to accompany him. Corriga was his native townland on the outskirts of a wee village called Crosskeys. He loved going up that road and pointing out the different farms and places he'd been to as a gasun himself. It was as if this was his Corratubber, his homeland and a place he too longed for. We enjoyed listening to him. Everyone up there seemed very neighbourly and close and most importantly of all, had to have a nickname. There was the doctor, the fat man, Sean Mac, Eonie the brat, Anthony Owney Andy, Mattie the pup, Dutcher and many many others. Our grandfather was known as Tommy the road, presumably because of the close proximity of the family homestead to the Corriga road. I wondered if people addressed each other by these names or merely used them when the relevant characters weren't listening. I couldn't imagine someone coming out with "Well Fatman, how are you today?" It just didn't seem right.

I even wondered if people knew these nicknames were attributed to them and resolved to find out sometime.

Uncle Harry was just finishing the milking when we pulled in on the street. His sons, our cousins, Mossie and Pat-Joe were with him. Young gasuns. We headed inside where Kathleen, Harry's wife was busy hand-washing clothes in the kitchen sink. Uncle Harry put the big silver kettle over on the hottest part of their black cooker. Annie Conaty was our other granny though we never called her Nanna. She was a tall lady with silver, wispy hair and sharply pointed facial features. Like our Nanna she had no husband. Our other grandfather, Tommy the road, had died in 1970 at the age of 98. He was a small man, very quiet according to Mum and we barely remembered ever seeing him.

The powers that be had dictated that visits to Corratubber be kept to a minimum and consequently we'd grown up not knowing these relations of ours. I wondered how Dad felt about this and often felt saddened for him. Surely he felt it.

Anyway like Nanna, Annie Conaty sat in an armchair and shook hands with us and remarked how tall we were getting. We stood there not knowing what to say and so when the grown-ups resumed their conversation we slipped out onto the street that sloped down towards their back door and started exploring. Across the way came the grunting of a large, hairy sow that lay in a crate as ten hungry piglets suckled away to their heart's content. In the passageway of this shed lay a carpet of empty Paul and Vincent sow and weaner meal bags. The mother appeared twitchedy and uncomfortable and tried to manoeuvre herself to a better lying position but her young ones were having none of it. Flies, about twenty of them, stuck to her eyes and flitted around the big red bulb that hovered over this family, dangling from the end of a baler twine that had been attached to one of the roof beams. Mother pig squealed and we turned to go. Outside a car had pulled up and strange faces were looking in at us now. We felt uncomfortable. Should we not know these people? Uncle Jack was wearing black trousers with gallises over a white shirt in much the same fashion as our Dad.

He shook hands with us. He was tall and thin, hardy-looking with jet black hair and I noticed that, like Dad, he tipped his cigarette on its end against the side of the box before lighting up. With him were the Boyle brothers, Pajoe and Harry, Dad's cousins and Sean and Tommy and James and Norbert, Jack's sons and our cousins.

Wasn't it strange the way names were passed down from one generation to another in Dad's family I thought to myself as the men poked away at that fresh hay that had just recently been deposited in Uncle Harry's shed. Names like James or Seamus and Tommy or Mossie and Pajoe and Harry. Names that appeared in every cousins household in that part of the world. Maybe that's why they all had nicknames around here. It would be impossible to distinguish between them otherwise.

Sure hadn't we a James and a Tommy and a Harry ourselves. Then again, Michael and Eddie and Philomena had obviously been sliced from Phyllis's side of the tree.

I rubbed some rust from an iron girder as we looked at these long lost cousins of ours. They looked at us too. These were farming men, our uncles, and their sons were steeped in a totally different tradition than us. It was almost cultural now, the difference. It made the move to Drumalee all the more poignant. We'd been starved of a truly agricultural upbringing and lacked experience now in front of these hardy looking country boys. Basically we'd become townies. They had freckly faces. We had soft-skinned hands. There was no point discussing soccer. This was Lavey, a place where people soloed the ball and gave each other dirty intentional shoulders. Nevertheless we felt connected. We could sense the respect these people had for Jem, our Dad, and the feeling was mutual. We knew that Jack and Dad were close. Sure hadn't they been to England together and, according to legend, fought alongside the Kanes and the Cusacks any of the Brits who fancied their chances. Yes, there was a connection alright and nobody on Mam's side of the family could ever sever it, I felt.

"Maybe these boys'll stay for a few days and we'll harden them up," laughed Uncle Harry as they headed towards the car. We looked at each other and I sensed Tommy was up for it. Dad gave me a fifty pence coin to be spent between us and warned us to have manners. Off they went up Corriga brae. We knew they'd pick up Sean Mac and go to McCaul's pub in Crosskeys. It was routine. Phyllis would sit up and wait no doubt in Drumalee.

We wandered about for a bit exploring the apple garden and spud field and then peeked in again at the pigs. Mother was asleep now and the young ones nestled tightly together under the warm rays of that red lamp. We went inside. It was darker than our house and the television wasn't roaring. Granny gave us a choice of stirrabout or colcannon for supper. Back home we called stirrabout porridge. We'd tasted colcannon before as Nanna had often made it for us out in Corratubber. It was a concoction of mashed spuds with butter, milk and onions. We thought this recipe was unique only to Nanna. Obviously not. In fact our two grannies had a lot more in common than they themselves might have realised. I looked at our Dad's mother. Though taller in stature she bore many resemblances to Nanna. She had the same wizened skin and boney knuckles and that unique elderly smell only grandmothers can have. She enquired after Mam and all the rest of them and then proceeded to give out to Tommy for getting knocked over by a car.

It was late now and we were shown to a room behind the cooker that had orange curtains and a blue lampshade which dangled precariously from a wooden ceiling. Kathleen had prepared a comfortable bed for us and we thanked her. Outside a cow bawled in the distance and I immediately thought of Packie Brady's rock across the pass in Corratubber. We didn't sleep for a long time trying to adjust to our new surrounds. A spider shuttled across the ceiling and I poked Tommy with a rigid elbow. He was out for the count. I still couldn't sleep. I tossed and turned in this cosy setting and then heard the banter and laughter and the clapping shut of a car door. It was Uncle Harry home from McCaul's pub. Outside the window, he hummed the same tune as Dad; "Many young men of twenty said Goodbye", as he fumbled at the door latch. He peeped up at us and seeing me awake, smiled. "I'll leave the kitchen light on and the door open for ya" he said as he switched off the lightbulb in our room. His face was red now and he had a happy countenance. I lay in the darkened room and heard him go back outside again and wondered why. In less than a minute our room light came on and Tommy sprung to attention mystified. "Quick boys, do youse want to see a sow pigging?" Uncle Harry wanted to know. We were up in a shot. Across the way the ninth pig was sliding its way through the muck and goo and slime of its mother's rear end and joining the rest of the pack. Harry lifted one or two of them towards the feeding area and then instructed us to manoeuvre the lamp across the way. The family next door were none too pleased at losing their little bit of luxury and Mother pig grunted her disgust. Quick as a flash Harry picked up the new arrivals one by one and proceeded to crack their teeth with a wee pair of pliers he'd taken from a shelf on the wall. I found this disgusting and was glad to be sent to make up a mash at the tap on the back street. This would be given to the new mother sow, part reward and part encouragement to allow her new offspring suckle.

"Now boys, yous can go home and tell McGunker Brady in Fairtown that yous had to come to Corriga to see a sow pigging" Harry laughed. Back inside he made us wash with Sunlight soap and then stuck on the kettle to make us a mug of tae. We sat on the sofa and watched as he stoked up the dying embers in the cooker. He lit a fag. We talked. He asked us about school and the like and then wanted to know how we felt about going back out to Corratubber. Our eyes lit up. So it was official then. It must be. Dad must have mentioned it to him. Now it was serious. We drank our tea and feasted on cream crackers and jam that Harry had hastily thrown together. "Do yous know this fella?" he asked taking from the mantelpiece a football sticker. We did of course. It was the heavily bearded Trevor Hockey from Sheffield United. We had cards like these at home, loads of them, bought for us by Mum in Pat McGovern's shop from her earnings in her new part-time job with Abbey printers. She'd go up the town on a Friday evening and get us a packet each as a reward for putting up with Dad's fried eggs, over baked beans and dry cakey spuds when she hadn't been around. I laughed and asked Harry what he was doing with a Trevor Hockey football sticker. He said he'd found it on the street. Maybe we'd dropped it or one of Jack's boys? I felt heartened that Harry had bothered to pick it up in the first place. We then talked about Best and Law and Charlton, he'd heard of them all. Of course he knew Keegan. Sure everybody did. It was well past four when we hit the sack for the second time. It had been an eventful night and now perhaps because of the hour we'd spent indulging in footballing talk I again found myself at Anfield. It's raining heavily and the crowd are waiting in anticipation. They seem fearful. So too does Jimmy Magee the commentator.

"I see it and yet I don't believe it, Kevin Keegan hands the ball to the young Conarty schoolboy, The Kop holds its breath, such an important kick in this UEFA Cup tie, it's do or die now......he scores, young Conarty scores and the crowd applaud his bravery. Borussia's players drop to their knees. A last minute penalty and Keegan puts his faith in the young schoolboy from Ireland, who surely has a big future in the game now".

We trudged off that mucky pitch, Kevin and I, shaking hands in consolation with our German opponents. Jimmy Magee stepped forward and requested an interview. Kev smiled.

"See ya back in the dressing room, Michael".

"Cheers, Kev".

Chapter 14

It was late the next morning when we woke, very late. The sunrays shone like laser beams through the gap between the curtains. I tried to move but it seemed as if the roof had caved in onto our bed during the night. The weight was almost unbearable. Over the blankets lay a multitude of boots, shoes, wellies and assorted women's footwear. Nestled on top were four old car tyres with rusty wires protruding. We knew it was Uncle Harry playing one of his jokes and the grin on his face up in the kitchen over a breakfast of boiled eggs and toast confirmed this. Later Sean Mac arrived on his Ferguson tractor to collect the milk. Harry rinsed out the cans and introduced us. He remembered us and thinking back to the night he'd fallen on our football stadium, we certainly wouldn't forget him. Harry was going to the mart in Ballyjamesduff with a lovely wee white-headed heifer calf. She bounced enthusiastically out of her straw bed and up into the little grey trailer. I felt sorry for that calf not knowing where it was going or where its life would end up. The adrenalin built up in my belly thinking we'd get a ride on the Massey Ferguson all the way to Ballyjamesduff but it was deemed too dangerous an expedition by Kathleen. Their four little ones, our cousins, played in a pile of sand that combed like a miniature beach up under a straight wall that ran from the pier of the gate back to the gable of the house. Built no doubt by Uncle Harry. Dad had said he was handy.

The postman reversed allowing Harry out onto the road. The calf bawled a farewell to us all. Later I found an old pair of clippers and feeling we should be earning our keep, began trimming the neat hedge that ran parallel to the other one out onto the road. Tommy went looking to see if any of the cows were a bulling at Kathleen's request. The sun shone through distant clouds any chance it could get and peeling off my jumper, nestled it on a hawthorn bush I'd just clipped. Did ya ever feel the urge to have a piddle and yet be too embarrassed to walk into someone's house and ask them to use their toilet? That's how I felt that morning. Stupid, awkward! It wasn't as if they'd deny me access or anything, I knew that. I couldn't help but feel I'd burst and yet tried to put it to the back of my mind by thinking of other things. I pictured Gilbert O'Sullivan sitting at his piano humming away and wondered what he'd do in a similar situation on Top of the Pops. I unzipped me trousers and proceeded to piddle against the back of the block pier when I suddenly became conscious of someone coming towards me from the house. It was Kathleen, with a shopping list. The pier helped to obscure the view. Tommy came running in the lane behind me shouting that none of their cows were a bulling. I had to stop half ways through and hope for the best. Distracted on both sides I felt the hot stingy piss or urine, as Mrs. Yorkman would call it, soak into the leg of my trousers. Tommy looked at me. Kathleen wanted groceries from the village. Harry had forgotten the list. The sun beamed down now as we made our way up that winding, hilly road and we were half-tempted to cast our jumpers aside and pick them up on the way back. What'd happen if a shower came on though? We compromised by tying them around our waists. Confessing that he too had been busting, Tommy joined me in relieving our bladders along the roadway all the while keeping a watchful eye for oncoming traffic.

We looked at the landscape and spotted the odd cluster of friesioned and short-horned cows enjoying their mid-morning break, chewing the cud of earlier eaten dewy grass. Their sighs reinforced their air of contentment as they lay there flicking their tails occasionally to scatter unwanted flies. Looking at the rocky shale in the gap-ways I couldn't help but think of Fr. Eddie and how he might link this townland of Corriga with Carraig the Irish word meaning rock or stone. I smiled and wondered to myself. Just then Tommy spotted some sloes on the ditch and we bit into their sour internals spitting out the stones as we doddled along. "Howya boys, are yous going to the fair?" laughed the man with a cap on his head as he dismounted his old cross-barred bike. His friendly, benevolent disposition suggested he knew us and sure why wouldn't he? It was Benny, yet another uncle of ours. We told him our names as he rummaged through his pockets eventually digging out a ten-penny coin. We thanked him. He enquired after Mam and the rest of the family. We'd heard of him before of course but couldn't recall meeting him. He was a quiet sort of man and I couldn't picture him sitting up all night drinking Crested Ten whiskey in McCauls bar or Boylans or anywhere else for that matter. He worked on the Council and lived with his wife Una and their family of five, one Seamus, our cousins, down the road on a farm in a place called Corraghoo. "Were yous ever in there before?" he asked pointing to a single storey building across the way. We followed him in. The wooden door hung on one hinge now and someone, probably boys of our own age, had busted the windows in a moment of idleness. Benny proceeded to tell us its history. It had been a shop in its day, a thriving one at that, with a meal store adjoining it and the young man that ran it had travelled the countryside one day a week selling cow meal and the like and buying eggs from the housewives. We walked over the splintered glass and peeped out the, as yet, intact back window. I lifted a notebook that dated back to an entry in 1958.

"Where is he now, that man?" enquired Tommy dusting a clingy cobweb from his shoulder. "Ahh, I dunno, some say he ran off and married a pretty woman down Castletara way and now years later, they've five boys and a wee girl. Maybe yous know them, the mother's name is Phyllis". Benny laughed as he lifted his cap and mopped the perspiration from his brow. We looked at each other in amazement. It was our Dad, Jem to them, Jimmy to us, he was talking about.

We remembered hearing about the shop and the meal store before but never knew its location. Here we were. Sure hadn't Dad often joked he should never have left Crosskeys in the first place? Benny bade us farewell and we set off again. I peeped back promising to have a closer look on the way home. In my fantasy world I imagined us all living here now and having unlimited access to Blackjacks and Long John chewing gums and the like. We'd never be stuck either for bickies if someone important dropped in. The great thing about poles along a roadway like this one, I'd learnt, was that if you walked between one set and ran between the next two, you were bound to shorten your journey. It was the same on the Castletara road down by Tommy Tully's house. The village of Crosskeys was quiet this morning. The odd Massey Ferguson or greyish coloured TVO scuttled through with a transport box echoing every bump in the roadway. We saw McCaul's pub and Shiels Lounge-bar and grocery next door to it. There wasn't much sign of life in McCauls now and the shut front doorway suggested the occupants were having a lie in. A young man, well dressed with greased back hair lit up a cigarette and nodded at us. "How's she cutting?" enquired Tommy. The young man laughed.

Inside, the old lady smiled as we handed over the list that had been tightly wrapped around the two pound notes. "Yous boys are strangers, do I know yous?" she muttered turning around to reach up for a box of Lyons Tea. "We're Conartys from Corratubber but we live in Drumalee now and we're hoping to go back to Castletara soon" Tommy informed her. "Our mammy is Phyllis and our daddy is Jimmy but people up here call him Jem," I added. She stopped and plucking a lollipop each for the two of us from a jar on the counter smiled into our faces. "Sure don't I know Jem well indeed and your mother, are yous stopping with Harry and Kathleen below in Corriga?" she enquired, reaching out a hand that had just been swiped in her apron. "Sure I heard that Jem and the boys were in McCauls only last night, they're gas men when they get going. Make sure yous tell him and your mother I was asking after them. I'm Mrs. Shiels, they'll know me", she continued as she cut a long slice of bacon in half and threw it on the scales to balance them up. It was the same set of scales with pounds and ounces and an arrow pointing upwards that Packie and Kathleen Brady had in their shop in Corratubber. "There we are now, a half pound of rashers, tell Kathleen I've no dettol today" the old lady said. She added up the bits and pieces on the white wrapping paper and locked the change tightly inside. Then, just like Packie Brady, she tightened all up in a wrapping of string, breaking it off with a flick of her wrist. She smiled again.

"Can we get a can of coke each?" Tommy enquired between sucks of his lolly. "We've our own money, Daddy gave it to us last night".

"Indeeden yous can young man" came the reply "and put your money back in your pocket this instant, this is my treat", she said, handing us two tins.

The Sweet Afton clock read twelve thirty now and the tingling of the bell over the doorway signalled the entrance of a plumpish lady with a brown coloured woven shopping basket.

Without stopping to think I asked her was she the Fat Man's wife. "Galang with ya now youl fashioned pup" came the swift reply. "God knows, childer these days", she continued making her way through the open door. Mrs. Shiels laughed. Outside the sun shone as strong as ever now as we clicked open our cokes and gurgled the fizzy black contents which bounced off the back of our throats and whizzed through our teeth bringing unimaginable relief. This was as good as things could ever get, I thought to myself, getting over the earlier rebuke. We missed them at home of course but loved the novelty of our newfound freedom and the goodwill that went with it. We scrunched up our coke tins as we made our way back inside Dad's old shop. A wasp loitered with intent near a solitary dog-rose bush that climbed its way down from the nearby ditch. Inside I stared at the old wooden shelving, most of it cracked now by the passing of time and worn down by layers of cobweb and dust. To think they were once stockpiled with all sorts of goodies. We made our exit just as a TVO tractor came across the brow of the hill. The young driver had a freckly face too and the redness of it allied to the beads of sweat that soaked his brow suggested he was a hardy goer. The older man wore a brown hat and seemed to be balancing himself in the transport box behind. "Woh, woh, give these boys a lift" he beckoned to his son. I noticed the feather in his cap as he hauled us aboard and quick as a flash the young driver revved up and tore on again.

We hung on for dear life and felt the relief of the wind in our faces at the same time. The older man codded us about girlfriends and the like and then asked us if there were many frogs about Castletara.

"Frogs?" I shouted aloud over the din of the smokey exhaust.

Just then the driver screeched to a halt at Harry's lane and we hopped out. He pulled the choke shutting down the engine at his father's request and seemed none too pleased at this unscheduled stop. He seemed to me to be a young man with plenty on his mind and it doubtless revolved around farm work. I could tell by his rolled up sleeves and his tightly laced boots. "Come on Da, them cattle'll be out" he chastised, looking at his white-faced watch.

"Take your time, do you not know these boys?" his father chided.

It turned out that this was yet another uncle of ours, Patsy, a tall, fine man, a good-looking man and guess what? His son's name was Tommy! Our cousin. Again we'd probably met Patsy before but couldn't recall. We'd heard Mam always speak kindly of him saying he was a perfect gentleman. He had another son, Andy, and an older daughter Maura who I remembered now talking to Dad one day in the town.

She was tall too and good-looking with short black hair and an impish smile. Harry's tractor came into view at the top of the hill and we stood one side to allow him access. Our little white-headed friend bawled in the back. The men talked and Harry moaned, "Sure you couldn't give them away". Our young cousin Tommy scratched his head and complained; "The ould feckin EEC, I thought things were supposed to get better".

I agreed with a "yeah" not having a clue what they were on about yet sensing the need to contribute something and not just stand there like a gom. "These boys are going to gather frogs down in McGunker Brady's bog in Fairtown and make their fortune", Patsy informed Harry. Harry laughed. "God knows they're worth a gathering" he said. Uncle Patsy informed us that the frog-man would call every second Thursday and pay the princely sum of thruppence per frog providing they were of a certain size and dimension. Thirty-three of them would almost make up a pound note. Better money than calves were making. We made our way inside where the aroma of Kathleen's chicken soup greeted us at the doorway. In the window ledge sat a small, dice-shaped, cardboard box with Mammy's familiar handwriting blazed across the front. "Michael and Tommy Conaty, c/o Harry and Kathleen Conaty, Corriga, Crosskeys, Cavan" it said. A white sticker on the reverse side and written by someone in Stradone Post Office informed all and sundry that it had been opened there in case it contained a bomb! Uncle Patsy laughed. A series of letter and parcel bombs across the border in Norn Ireland had been keeping everyone on their toes and some had been sent south in recent times. We'd become more aware of the Troubles, as they were called, since the bombings in Dublin and more especially Belturbet, a town not too far from us in Cavan, where two young innocent people had been blown to their deaths in December of 1972. Dad had said it was the Unionists, Paisley's crowd, bringing the war down south and showing the Free State they wanted nothing to do with us. We had no choice but listen to the News, either Charles Mitchell on the radio, or the UTV news or "our own station" as Dad called RTE. The papers were full of it; Sean Mac Stiofáins hunger strike intrigued us. He was leader of the Provisional IRA or the Provies as people called them. Then there was all this talk about Kenneth Littlejohn, some sort of a British spy who was going to kill all round him. I couldn't make head nor tail of it all, all these people shouting at each other; Gerry Fitt and Patrick Donegan and Brian Faulkner and Liam Ahern and Conor Cruise O'Brien and Erskine Childers and Lord Carrington and John Hume too. We'd grown accustomed to their faces in Dad's newspapers and their voices on the radio. It was all so confusing at times. Equally bewildering was the fact that someone up in Stradone Post Office had been prepared to risk life and limb before safely dispatching me and Tommy's post!

"I wonder if there's a bomb in that wee box?" I imagined the Postmistress saying. "Well there's only one way to find out and that's by opening it......Bang!"

Then again why anyone would want to parcel bomb Michael and Tommy Conaty in the first place? Sure, we were no angels and plenty had called us ould-fashioned pups in our time, but this would be taking things too far. On the way home in the car that night Jack Lynch was suggesting on the radio that the bombs in Dublin in December of the previous year were the work of British Intelligence agents. Daddy agreed with him.

"I am the woman that kilt the child
Weelia weelia wallia
I am the woman that kilt the child
Down by the river Saile".

Chapter 15

Anyway I found myself continually drifting between conflicting worlds of fantasy and reality. I loved reading and felt secure with Enid Blyton's Famous Five as they supped on ginger lemonade and feasted on homemade buttered scones before heading off to solve some mystery or other. I loved the anticipation. It was the same with anything I read. I became part of that world. A good-humoured or courageous book character left me feeling good-humoured or courageous. Likewise football, I modelled myself on Kev. I stuck up obstacles on the road and learned to dribble around them. I jumped in the air like Keegan and celebrated goals with the same aplomb. No one noticed. I didn't care. I felt secure in this fantasy world. It kept my mind nourished and envigorated. When boredom set in I felt bad. This caused hopelessness and that wasn't good. You gotta have hope, I learnt. Hopelessness led to worry and this caused fear. It was genetic of course and couldn't be avoided but sure I didn't know this. Mam had mentioned it. I worried what would happen if Mam or Dad died. How would we cope? How would we survive? Particularly if Mam died. Lots of children lose their Mams, I knew that. Sure hadn't Uncle Patsy lost his wife when the children were young. I pitied them when I heard this after coming home from Corriga. Maybe that's why Tommy, our cousin, was so hard-working and always rushing around-maybe it helped him keep his mind off things by being occupied all the time.

Still, this fear rooted itself deep in the pits of my stomach and caused my heart to race. I was in turmoil. I prayed and prayed and prayed begging God not to let anything bad happen and to keep everyone and everything as they were. God listened, I just knew he did. Like when we were measuring angles with our glass yokes; "Massey Fergusons" Oliver called these protractors. Anyway it was coming up to my turn and everyone else knew what they were doing and I just felt a right gom sitting there anxious and embarrassed at the same time. Suddenly the door opens and in pops Fr. Dolan diverting everyone's attention. I just knew God was listening. Sure he'd even orchestrated Fr. Dolan's visit in the first place, to get me off the hook at sums time. God, I hated Maths and envied Hazel and Martin and Eileen and the rest of them that were great with parallel lines and fractions and polygons and symmetry and even the indices.

God understood soccer too, I just knew it. He liked Liverpool, he had to. Sure look at how often he changed things when I prayed fervently, begging for a penalty or even a corner or anything to get us an equaliser. I knew that Bill Shankly had to take some of the credit. After all he had once said in Dad's Evening Press that "it might take you eighty minutes to win but don't get frustrated because ninety minutes is a long time". But still I wondered did he realise how many of our late, late goals were down to God's intervention. Liverpool were now playing in the UEFA Cup and we all sat on our sofa watching them playing Spurs in the semi-final. This was a game of two legs. James explained that this meant the teams played each other home and away and the scores were added up at the end. Gerald Sinstadt had a funny-sounding name but a great commentator's voice and he talked about "aggregate scores" and "away goals".

"What comes after 9,999?" shouted Harry from the back of the sofa. No one answered. We'd won the opening game 1-0 at Anfield but now Martin Peters had equalised at White Hart Lane and it wasn't looking good. Then "Keegan puts Heighway through and" pause, "he scores, Heighway scores!" My stomach muscles loosened. Pressure gone, hope again. Now all we had to do was hang on. Spurs needed two goals because of Heighway's "away" goal James explained to us. An equaliser was no good. They needed two. An away goal was worth double in the event of a draw.

Harry found out from Mam that it was 10,000 and got down to business once more only popping his head up to tant me when Martin Peters scored another one. "Please God, please God," I begged. Spurs were after our throats now. Perryman and Gilzean and Chivers and Peters. Funny names but classy players. All white playing kit. Martin Peters hit "the woodwork" as Gerald Sinstadt called it and then it was all over. I knew God had gotten us through.

Now we'd face the funny sounding Germans from Borussia Moenchengladbach in the UEFA Cup Final. They too had classy players like Gunter Netzer who wouldn't look out of place playing Gaelic football for Ballyhaze. But I didn't care. I just knew we'd win this European trophy because God would listen to my prayers and no matter how technically sounding this Moenchengladbach team were we'd beat them. Yes of course we would, me and Kev and Stevie Heighway and John Toshack with the Kop behind us singing, "You'll never walk alone". Still I worried. Like today. Oliver wasn't in and I went up to serve Mass on my own. It's approximately 1213 of my steps from Hennesey's old house to Castletara Chapel. I know cos I measured them. Approximately, not exactly, because I kept looking back in case anyone was watching from the school and think I was wasting time and trying to dodge sums class. Fr. Dolan's car had pulled in at the shop. I could see him inside talking to Mrs. Edgeworth. People said he was "an ojous nice man". I wondered whether to stop or not. Maybe Fr. Dolan might want to give me a lift, he always did that, he was good to us. If I kept on going he'd have to stall his car on the brae and this could be inconveniencing him. Then again, if I waited, presuming I'd get a lift, he might think I was a presumptious ould fashioned pup. Caught between two minds and having crossed 722 of my footsteps already, I decided to gamble and go. I met Eamonn McCormack coming down the hill on his tractor. I had to stop at 740 and pretend I was tying my shoelace. Eamonn smiled and waved. He hadn't noticed. On I went distracted only by the heaving of McCormack's cows as they panted in the morning sunshine awaiting their exit from the farmyard. So many friesians. Inside the old ladies sat huddled together, heads bent closely as they whispered away to each other. With Fr. Dolan late now, old Mrs. Maguire as we called her, had proceeded to get the altar ready. I liked her. She reminded me of Mrs. G. She never missed Mass a day in her life walking the long lane out past Martin Smiths, come sunshine or hail. Dad had said she was genuine and no Holy Joe like some of the other hypakrits as he called them. "Running to Mass, up to the front row and then cutting each other's throats," he said. He had no time for the Holy Joes. "So heavenly that they were no earthly good, full of pride and full of shite as well" he'd say "running to Knock thumping their craws, hypakrits the lot of them. I could tell yous a thing or two about them," he'd say. "Feck the begrudgers". Anyway there we were, meself and Mrs. Maguire. She had a soothing effect, a squeeze of your hand or a pat on the head that told ya it was ok and that even if you dropped the cruets of water and wine she'd mop the mess up and take the blame for it. Not that Fr. Dolan would pass any remarks anyway. Sure he wasn't like that at all. So everyone said. When Mass was over he cleared his throat from away deep down. The stench of doused candle smoke adorned the chapel as I left. Fr. Dolan thanked me. Yeh, I liked him and could see why others, even the older fogies as we called them, could like him too. He was young and friendly and approachable and even played full back with the Ballyhaze team. His jet-black hair was neatly groomed to one side and he had thickly set sideburns like Elvis Presley. You'd see him in the shop usually after

Mass. He'd pick up his paper and packet of milk chocolate goldgrain biscuits and he'd smile and head out humming a tune to himself. I could even visualise him sitting down watching a good game of soccer and enjoying it too and he'd probably be the sort of man that would see through the Holy Joes too but wouldn't say it. Anyway Mrs. Edgeworth handed me the teacher's paper and a penny bar for myself. I thanked her. She smiled. The stream rumbled down Johnny McCormack's field and under the road through a big pipe into Pe Smith's rocks. I thought of the old women whispering in the chapel before Mass began and could hear them say "Ah there's the wee Conarty gasun with the blond hair. Sure he'll surely be the next priest and then that'll be six generations, sure won't it be grand".

This bugged me. I liked God and he was good to me and I wouldn't mind helping him but this ould nonsense really embarrassed me. I was only ten years of age for God's sake, leave me alone and let me grow up normally and not be dictating my future for me. They were putting me off if only they knew it. Pe Smith's morris minor car rattled down the hill towards me. He honked the horn and smiled. I laughed. We liked Pe. Once when we met him in the shop and he was giving out about someone awkward and he said that they were built like a bull's arse and had a brain to match. He bought penny bars for us and Mrs. Edgeworth agreed with him that we were indeed good gasuns and not in the least bit ould-fashioned.

Anyway there we were playing against the big ones on the back street and them beating us and it getting hotter and stickier by the minute, especially for those of us wearing wellies. James and Martin Brady and Martin Lyons stroked the ball around playing possession football thinking they were Johnny Giles and his boys at Leeds United. If we hadn't the ball, we couldn't score and I resolved to get it no matter what. They were winding us up and I didn't like it. The harder I tried the easier it seemed to become for them and they laughed and I hated this and wanted Sean and Andy and Oliver and Martin to hate it too. But no! It's not nice, pig in the middle football. Now I liked Martin Lyons. The boys called him Curly Wurly because of his tight curlish hair and his likeness for the new chocolate bar. He was a lot shorter than "Big Jock" the name given to our James now and he had freckles on his face and arms. He was simply in the wrong place at the wrong time and I lashed out at him as I tried to regain possession. He flicked the ball to one side and laughed in that teasing kinda way that only serves to rub it in further. I saw red. Forgetting where I was and confused and thickened by the blazing sun and dehydrated and helpless and soakened to the skin because I hadn't taken time to take my jumper off like the rest of them, I lashed out again. Martin laughed and placed his hand on my head in order to distance himself from anything else that was coming his way. My head throbbed now. I'd gone too far. He swung me around and got me into a headlock leaving me totally helpless and with no moral high ground worth mentioning either. After all, I'd started it hadn't I? And now he was entitled to defend himself. He tightened his grip and my jawbones stiffened and teeth locked together. What really hurt now though was James, my only big brother James admonishing me for getting thick and ranting at me to cop on to myself. Yeah this really hurt. It got worse. His grip loosened. I sank my teeth into Martin's freckly wrist and he roared a scream of shock into my face. He let go in time as Mrs. Sexton came strolling round the corner. Grabbing both of us by our necks, she frogmarched us back into her room and gave us a right bollicking banning us in the process from any more football till the end of the month. The rest of them came in later and I sat there as thick as a ditch focussing intently on the ink-well in front of me not daring to make eye contact with anyone round me. I wanted to cry and couldn't. Ashamed and embarrassed and guilt-ridden and fearful I vowed I'd never sink so low again, especially not into anyone's arm. Anyway Mrs. Sexton had spent ages teaching us all about erosion and how our coastline was being constantly eaten away by the elements. Picking up a long cane she made her way across the floor and proceeded to point up at the big map of Ireland or Éire as it said on the top. "Can any of you tell me now why our Western coastline is so jagged and torn and full of inlets and bays and headlands?" she wanted to know.

All it took was one word, one powerful word; EROSION and I knew it but couldn't say it because of what had happened earlier and because I was still sulking and sitting there like a cursed dog not wanting to comply. "Well?" Mrs. Sexton enquired shifting her gaze across the room and spotting a hand that had sprung up in third class. It was our Tommy. "Please Miss, that side of the map you were just pointing at is all jagged and torn now cos there's a whole lot of little guts in and out".

The room erupted. Our teacher tried to conceal a smile. "I'll gut you in a minute if I go down to ya" she roared at him. Moments like this one were priceless. Even Mrs. Sexton could see the funny side of it and she'd spent days after all trying to get that seven-lettered word into our heads. "Erosion" she screamed for the very last time. I glanced across and caught Martin staring. Better humoured now we found it easier to exchange a grin, a grin that said everything was ok again and that the past was the past. Move on and pick up pieces time.

Then there was the time when Teacher called out "Tomás Ó Connachtaigh" and I responded with an "ASLATHER" cos he wasn't there to shout out "ANSHOOK" and her raised eyebrows enquired why and I said "please Miss, he's gone to Dublin with his eyes" and she retorted "well, he'd look damn funny going without them". The older ones collapsed in laughter. Anyway Tommy and Harry had been sent to a specialist in a Dublin hospital called "The Eye and Ear" because they each had a cast or turn in their eyeballs and the optician in the Clinic in Cavan wanted them rectified. They were away for a week or so and even though the house was ojous quiet we missed them. We worried for them too especially since Jude Kelly had told our Eddie that the process involved taking their eyeballs clean out of their heads and wiping them with a cloth before putting them back in again dead straight this time. The surgeon would have to wear special gloves and make sure not to drop either eyeball on the ground Jude had informed him. Anna Mae and Tony called to Drumalee on their way home from Monaghan Co-op where Tony had had a meeting with some of the "big boys" as he called them. He was trying to get a better cut on the milk he bought there before he and Deckie, our cousin and his son, dispensed it round the town of Athlone in a Volkswagen van. Anna Mae handed us Tayto crisps and warned us to keep two packets for our missing brothers. Mam made tea and Dad poured two whiskeys from a Crested Ten bottle and then laughed as he recounted the story to Tony. Anyway the nurse had handed Harry a plastic cup and told him to go to the bathroom and provide her with a sample of urine. Harry was back in a flash having filled the container from the tap. The nurse looked baffled but sure it was all her own fault. If she'd requested a cup of PISS instead of URINE then sure Harry would've had no problem in delivering. Tony laughed hysterically and Anna Mae tried not to. They got ready to go and Dad told us to hit the hay and say our prayers. "That's right" laughed Tony "and do whatever yous want in life but make sure none of yous ever come home a guard or a priest!"

Barely half an hour had gone when the referee had abandoned the first leg because of the heavy rain at Anfield. Moenchengladbach and Liverpool would have to do it all over again on a drier night. I went to bed not knowing whether to be relieved or disappointed. The following Wednesday night big John Toshack flicked a few balls in and Kev had us two up in no time. Larry Lloyd made it three and Ray Clemence even saved a peno. Liverpool would win easily now but could they survive ninety minutes out in Germany and not concede four goals. Gunter Netzer worried me in the second leg. He was all over the pitch. "World Class" the commentator called him. The Germans pulled two goals back and I sweated and prayed simultaneously. My guts were knotted and the whole second half was coming up. If they could score two in the first forty-five minutes then they were capable of hitting four in ninety. I emptied my bladder and went back to watch. As it happened God was listening and we went on to win our first European Cup, though not as big as the one United and Celtic had taken back in the sixties, James had pointed out. Still I felt good. It was a great achievement and I took personal pride in it. This was my team, I'd chosen it on Aiden Rehill's advice and now I was reaping the rewards. Better still United were struggling, Best was missing and Bobby Charlton was going to retire. "What comes after 10,999?" Harry shouted as I skipped out the back door and dodged under the clothesline. I was on my way to Reilly's shop for fish fingers. "Keegan's through, he's onside, Keegan shoots….he scores! Eye oh me addy oh, we've won the cup".

Chapter 16

I'll never forget that day in August of '73, never, ever, ever! The build up, the anticipation, the waiting, the expectation and above all else the packing. We were on the move; us Conartys.

Back to Corratubber, back to our spiritual home, back to a land that had been begrudged to us by some but ultimately back to freedom. Mam carefully packaged the last of the delph and whatever glasses we'd accumulated over the years in Anglo-Celt newspaper, and the tea-chests with the corrugated inside edging, were carefully placed in position at the back of an ould blue van with double doors that didn't shut flush and which had been given to Dad for the weekend by Gerry Maguire in Smith's garage.

Now, Aidey Hughes our cousin was the Harry of their family. He'd been up for a few days and found himself giving a hand and more often than not creating a nuisance. Like Harry, though much older, he was tall for his age and had the annoying habit of always being in the wrong place or saying the wrong thing at the wrong time. He bugged Dad, I just knew he did.

Aidey was about fifteen or sixteen and thrived on smart remarks. We liked him. Today he found himself perched between James and myself in the front as Dad tried to release the handbrake and head for Corratubber with our first big load.

A clatter at the back told us that something had fallen. This irked Dad who came out with one of his customary four-lettered expletives. "Hold on, hold on" shouts Aidey, "if there's going to be panic, at least let it be organised!"

We looked at each other and then glanced across at Dad who by now had that ballistic type frown on his forehead. We thought it funny but daren't laugh. We made our way out the Cootehill road turning right for the Corratubber pass, following Mum who'd gone ahead with the younger ones in the A40. It felt so good. The adrenalin pumped. Summer wasn't just over yet and we'd be making our way back to Castletara School in a fortnight's time with an address that read Corratubber, Cavan. The happiness stalled. I worried. I wondered how it would go. What would Nanna's reaction be? Would there be tension? What would Herself do? After all Nanna and Dad hadn't seen each other for the best part of four years. Would old antagonisms surface? For Dad it can't have been easy, I thought to myself, looking across at him and wondering what was going on in his head. Was he apprehensive or nervous? His poker face gave nothing away.

Deep down I knew he was capable of getting on with Nanna and if truth be told, actually liked her. He felt sorry for her. She too was a victim of circumstance. Sure hadn't he often defended her? "Mrs. Brady's a grand woman if only she was left alone" he'd said. He was prepared to gamble. And maybe the cards now were dealt slightly in his favour. He didn't take any joy in hearing that Nanna couldn't manage on her own now in that big, old house and no doubt dreaded anything ever happening to her, alone.

He knew Mum would pay the price then and didn't want this. With us back in Corratubber Nanna would have a greater sense of security and could freely call out for assistance if needed. This had to be the way now. Sure hadn't Dr. Lorigan warned them often enough that Nanna was incapable of fending for herself any longer and that without company she'd surely have to go to St. Felim's or "the home" as it was called by the grown-ups.

The key players, Fr. Eddie, Lizzie and Anna Mae also now realised that our homecoming was imperative. None of them could very well take on the responsibility of caring for their mother. This was their only outlet. Us back. But it had to be conditional as far as Jimmy Conarty was concerned. From now on there could be no shit-stirring or story-carrying. If he wanted to go out for a drink or two with Kelly or McGunker or Rooney or Murphy or indeed all four simultaneously, then that was his perogative. Everyone else would have to butt out and like it or lump it. And no more ould begrudgery either. The land was ours and that was that. He was no fool, our Dad, and knew exactly who'd been courting Nanna in our absence.

People like "Barnaby Jones" as he called him, a distant relation who thrived on being connected to the Bradys and the Bishop of Perth and who glorified in the five generations of priests that had been spawned in Corratubber. For him this house and lands were a holy grail. Anyway Barnaby Jones had been covertly visiting Nanna every Sunday night hauling with him hampers of food and fruit and home-made soup, most of which had made its way to Drumalee only for Dad to pour the soup or "Biddie's piss" as he called it, down the sink. He knew the story alright and the motive too. Sure hadn't they even made enquiries about the deeds of the place and whose names they were in and wondered could the will be contested. Gorman the auctioneer had tipped him off about loose talk in his public house on Main Street and warned him to watch his back. These were cunning people. Running to the top of the chapel of a Sunday morning as if butter wouldn't melt in their mouths, proud people petitioning Mother Mary on their knees at Knock Shrine in Co. Mayo and all the time concerned about everyone's seed, breed and generation. Watch them he'd have to!

We made our way through the walls and piers and up that little incline with the gable end of the rusty-red hayshed facing us. No balloons, no fanfare. Mam and Nanna were out on the street and Tommy, Eddie and Harry were already gone exploring their newfound freedom. It was like a big adventure to them and maybe they were better off not realising the implications. I stood and paused and wondered. And then it happened. The handshake that said it all. "Jimmy, how are ya?" Dad looked at her. "Mrs. Brady, how are you?" It was more than a handshake however. It was symbolic. It buried the past and welcomed the future. I looked at them now. Our Dad and our Nanna. Both were gracious. No one claimed moral victories. This was a new beginning and everyone should rejoice. Both sides were willing to try and from now on there could be no hidden agendas. The begrudgers could find someone else's door to knock on.

"Leave the stuff for a while Jimmy" said Nanna as he cranked open the back doors of the blue van. "I've the kettle on and a little something ready to eat". She turned to lead us inside and I noticed she wore her good black Sunday shoes with the little ripple of brown tights nestling on the shiny leather. Her brown walking stick had the look of being more leaned upon and her steps were laboured and more careful now. She looked older and frailer than at any other time I could remember. Still this was our Nanna smiling her benevolent smile and happy to entertain. She sat us down to a feed of rashers, sausages, fried eggs and dipped bread. I noticed how she pulled out a chair for Dad at the top of that wooden rectangular table which was covered in a flowery vinyl spread. Stuffed to the gills we headed outside prompted by Mam to chorus "Thanks Nanna" as we departed. We were like greyhounds exiting traps. The autumn sun shone brightly and tried to take the chill out of the light wind that blew from Packie's rocks.

Eddie took a ball from the back of the car and without pausing to take in the enormity of this moment we started a game, using the garage doorframe as goalposts. It was three and in.

The weeds we trod on had now had their day. This ground was being liberated. Over the coming weeks and months we'd grind them back into the ground they'd sprung from, never forsaking a chance morning or nightfall to have a kick around. Once when the ball got stuck in the egg-tree hedge, I paused to look at the drifting clouds and overwhelmed by the happiness within me, remembered that I'd forgotten to thank God for all this. He'd brought all this about, I just knew he had. He'd heard our prayers and answered our heart's desires. Thanks God. "James, Michael" we heard Mam call from the back door. In the kitchen we saw the strangest sight. There was Dad sitting by the cooker, with a cigarette nestling on a glass ashtray, being handed a glassful of Power's whiskey by our Nanna. She'd already placed the small delph jug containing cold water on a chair nearby. "There you are Jim, that's some of Tony Hughes' stuff, good health to you now". "And to you" raising his glass, "thanks Mrs. Brady" replied Dad.

Some things were still like Drumalee, like the way Mam listed what was needed from the shop on a scrap of paper and wrapped it round a pound note before handing all to James. Nanna rooted through her little black purse and finding a couple of coppers as she called them, told us to bring back penny bars for everyone. Skipping round by the back wall and heading for Packie's big meadow, we heard cousin Aidey lecture the younger ones on the importance of adhering to the offside rule. We looked at each other and smiled. Packie had left a plank of timber across the drain which took us back out on to the Corratubber pass. Jim Costello was bushing a gap having moved his cattle and we shouted Hello across at him. Down at the shop, Kathleen busied herself hanging clothes out on the whitethorn hedge to dry before coming in and rummaging through the wooden till under the counter for a fivepence. "Go on in, Packie's in the kitchen" she gestured before heading for the black coin-box in the corner of the hall. "Kathleen Clarke wants the bullman, I'm ringing him now, I'll be with yous in a minute or Packie'll get what yous want either" she continued. Inside Packie was reading about a place called Sunningdale. I saw it in his newspaper. It was something to do with the Irish and British governments and the Unionists and the SDLP and the power sharing. "Where'll it all end at all atall boys?" Packie wanted to know. We shrugged our shoulders. "Fianna Fáil out of power, the IRA bombing everything in sight and mark my words, dother crowd'll come down south again and blow us all to smithereens. Soon it won't be safe to go into Cavan town anymore". He folded his newspaper. We made our way across the hall to the shop. We could hear Kathleen on the phone. "Aye, aye good girl that's it and make sure he gets word, make sure it's Scobey, there's good calves after him, she wants Scobey up". We looked at each other. We were home alright!

Later that evening we headed for Fairtown.

Chapter 17

"Hard work's not aisy and dry bread's not graisy". So McGunker said. He was bringing in cocks of hay from the far meadow with Bob, his horse, pulling the shifter. We were sent over to help out and to have manners! McGunker lived at the foot of Ned's brae with his sister, Roseanne, who'd been to America for a few years and had returned to stay when their father died. He called her Sister and she called him Brother. Both had to be around the sixty mark we figured. No one rightly knew how the name McGunker came about. Sometimes he'd call us the McGunker Conartys and then close his eyes and laugh. We simply called him McGunker back. He was a tall, thin man and he wore a pair of black, thick-rimmed heavily glazed glasses. McGunker didn't carry an ounce of fat. First and foremost he was a bachelor farmer who freely admitted to having left school at a very early age to help run the small family farm. We knew from Mam that their mother had died a young woman leaving her husband to rear five offspring, McGunker and Roseanne and Maureen, another brother Philip who'd died quite young too and an older brother called John the Yankee because he resided in the States and who'd come home every so often laden with dollars and goodies. Roseanne had taken home with her some Yankee expressions which we found unusual and quaint. She referred to the footpath as the side-walk and frequently began her sentences with the phrase "Well, like I mean…" We liked Roseanne. She had ladylike qualities that appealed to us young boys. We respected her and knew, that like Mrs. Galligan in Drumalee, she had good time for us. Her smile was endearing whether she was dressed for a bit of farm work or decked out for a visit to Cavan town or a trip to Castletara Mass. McGunker himself was very much in touch with everyone and everything around him and expected us to know who he was talking about every time he regaled a story from the old days. He was outspoken too and had frequently fallen out with some of his neighbours over things like cattle thieving and dogs barking and young pups passing ould-fashioned remarks as he called them. He'd gotten on well with the older generation but didn't like the attitude of their offspring; "Jumped up whelp, pon my soul I remember a time when it was different with me and his father" we'd often hear him say. Once McGunker's mind was made up then that was that. He was a firm republican with a deep hatred and distrust for all things British and he'd listen intently to the big brown wireless box perched on its own shelf, to hear what "our boys" as he called them had done that day. He had pretty much the same likes and dislikes as our Dad and that's why, despite the age gap, they got on so well together. The sort of man that would sit up late at night to watch Muhammad Ali fighting and dancing in the ring and feel connected to him in some way cos he too had to battle oppression mainly because of his colour. "Sure didn't he walk into a fancy restaurant with his shiny Olympic medal dangling round his neck and they wouldn't serve him cos he was a nigger and didn't he then go and throw the damn thing into the Ohio river and wasn't he right not to have gone and fought in Vietnam yon time during that war the Yankees started and couldn't win, God I only wished I'd gone to Croke Park last year to see him fight Lewis and shake his hand and clap him on the back" he said and clenching his fist banged it on the kitchen table shaking the life and some of the sugar out of Roseanne's wee silver bowl.

Anyway their home was a simple three-roomed affair, exceptionally well kept both inside and out. The only door led you into the kitchen and it in turn had a bedroom on each side. There was a loft but we never saw it. A marble topped table on the right gave shelter to a galvanised bucket of water that was freshly drawn each day from the nearby well. Above that a kitchen dresser was home to all sorts of big delph plates and ornamental dishes and soda cakes were left out to cool on its front shelf each morning. A little white fridge filled the right hand corner and a perfectly square window on the back wall looked out onto Fairtown bog and to where Red John used to live and Ted Reilly's camogie hill and our fields too. The kitchen table housed the TV set which had a wire running from its rear out through the wall and up to an aerial that stood majestically on top of a big steel pole in the back garden. Alongside the wireless on its shelf stood the obligatory Sacred Heart lamp and next to it pictures of the Pope and John F. Kennedy. Sticks and turf lay neatly piled beside the black mistress cooker that nestled beneath the chimney breast with a browny gold tap that released hot water from a tank on its side. A long drape was hung inside the door and pulled over to keep out the draught from Halloween onwards.

Once when Roseanne had the flu and we'd gone up to her room uninvited to enquire after her welfare, we noticed a large, dark brown ornamental dresser protected by the covering of a white sheet. James lifted the cover and looking at Roseanne in the bed asked did it come from America and if so had it been taken over to Fairtown on the Titanic? Roseanne coughed, smiled, coughed again into a big white hanky and then gave us silvermint sweets.

Their front street was perfectly square and cement covered, surrounded by a thick combination of privet and eggtree which was intertwined by dog roses and other assorted wild flowers. Two heavy metal blue gates hung on thick piers directly parallel to the narrow roadway which ran past. To the left were three outhouses which, like the dwelling, were carefully whitewashed each May and these in turn were home to a pile of turf and sticks and bicycle wheels and harnesses and an old rusty wheelbarrow and other horse gear collected over the years. A pile of empty 10:10:20 fertiliser bags had been neatly bundled together and tied by baling twine and these sat awaiting further use in the corner. A pump in the dairy adjoining the house could be switched on by pressing a green button and this room was also home to a heavy copper sprayer and a barrel and a box of Dithane 945 which had been bought in Poles Creamery for the spud blight.

    McGunker's way of farming, though admirable, was slow and methodical and everything painstakingly done by hand. Not a wisp of hay went unaccounted for and every hedge about the place was kept neatly trimmed by a pair of wooden handled clippers which were sharpened by a side stone and greased regularly. It was the same with the scythe. Cutting rushes or stemmy grass McGunker would pause regularly and resharpen its edge with a swish of the side stone. Then with a flick of his cap and a spit in his hands he'd be off again. He'd twist ropes from the cocks of hay with an old rickety hand-twister and pull the butt anticlockwise from around the base with alarming ease. Their hayshed was open ended and the byre which housed five, fat, hand-milked cows, was built adjoining it with a wooden door in the middle of the wall, through which loose hay could be pulled morning and evening. A wooden, well greased, wheelbarrow deposited the night's takings in the wintertime each morning across to a dunkel in the adjoining garden. A narrow and curving cement path brought you back down on the far side of the byre to the dwelling house, with a pig-sty and pen on one side and four or five ridges of early spuds on the other. A little homemade wooden gate with its own black latch separated the domestic dwelling from the farmyard. Onto the gable end of their house lay another white-washed outhouse covered by black felt and battoned down by lengths of crooked timber. And that was it.

    McGunker's farm itself was to be found on either side of the roadway and each small field had for its protection a red-painted gate and chain.

Anyway there we were in late August, us boys and McGunker pitching hay into the shed when up arrives Roseanne with bottles of hot tea and slices of warm soda bread laced with blackcurrant jam. I pictured the Famous Five in my mind as we welcomed a breather from this hot and dusty affair. "We might be getting some cattle soon and a tractor" announced James "and if we get a tractor then we'll be able to get the hay in quicker and give poor oul Bob a rest". McGunker smiled. Bob munched on a scoopful of rolled barley he'd been thrown and after sipping from the water trough seemed to snort in agreement with James' earnest intentions. For a man that never went to school McGunker knew plenty. He wanted to know for instance how we felt about Juan Peron being re-elected President in faraway Argentina and did we know that the Perons and the Bradys were distant cousins. He closed his eyes and laughed. Roseanne gathered up the bits and pieces and threw the scraps to their collie dog. Having enquired for Mam and Dad and Nanna and us having thanked her, she set off on the short journey back to the house. A cool breeze blew up and provided relief and I couldn't help but sense Roseanne's contentment that here at last her brother had both help and company. McGunker pulled on the last of his Carrolls cigarette and casting the butt aside set about slowly winching the final cock of hay in the field. Bob staggered and then set off across the road before being reversed into the hayshed with McGunker cajoling him; "Eck a bit, eck a bit, eck, woah, Bob, woah". Tommy and Eddie had stayed in the field feasting on a cluster of blackberries they'd found in the corner. McGunker undid the twisted rope and rolled it up carefully before throwing it on the pile beneath the big rusty girder. He then plunged his pitchfork into the capping and proceeded to lob forkfuls of hay on to the bench where James stood and he in turn lobbed them back up to me. All I had to do was spread and tramp the hay around at the top occasionally clanging my sweaty and hayseed-ridden head against the galvanised roof.

The six o'clock Angeleus bell at Ballyhaze echoed in the distance and McGunker, taking off his cap, went down on one knee and crossed himself. He only lifted his head once and that was to beat his chest.

We thought it better to stop too and mutter a few prayers to ourselves, careful to avoid eye contact. Prayers over and cap back on, McGunker scraped up what was left on the ground and then announced "That's what we were looking for, as the cobbler said to his missus!"

"What were they looking for, the cobbler and his missus?" I ventured to ask.

"The last, the last" laughed McGunker. "That's the last of it thank God and thanks be to God for Jem Conarty's boys".

Tommy and Eddie arrived in with clear evidence of their feast smattered around their lips. We watched as Roseanne took the cows in and followed her as she treated them to bucketfuls of wet mash. Then grabbing two stools, she and McGunker sat down and pulling on hair clad teats, filled the white foamlike substance into buckets balanced between their ankles. Occasionally either would stop and strain what they'd collected into a big silver creamery can, which when near full would be taken down in the wheel barrow and left sitting to cool in a neatly painted red half-barrel of water by the pumphouse door.

Steam rose from the cows backs as they twitched their tails and waddled their way out the door and back up to the field. We watched again as Roseanne half-filled five buckets of creamy nourishment and proceeded to feed their young offspring at the garden gate. These plump white-headed calves then turned to feast on a bucket of meal McGunker had strewn across a wooden trough that nestled beneath the shelter of a big horsechestnut tree. Roseanne then took us inside and sat us down to bowlfuls of hot custard topped off with juicy portions of rhubarb. She then pulled James one side and whispering into his ear, handed him a list for the shop which was time enough the next day when the Celt would be out. McGunker insisted on us being paid two silver fifty pence coins between us and then walked us up to the gate before waving goodbye. We leapt the ditch and crossed the fields for home. By now Harry was on 27,104,

>They had a strong rope six feet long
>Weelia weelia wallia
>They had a strong rope six feet long
>Down by the river Saile

Chapter 18

Anyway Dad had bought five bullocks and a solitary heifer and the grass was so long you could hardly see them in the meadow. We were ecstatic. We'd run in and out every so often to see whether they were lying down, standing up, eating grass or simply scratching themselves.

Now we could call ourselves farmers. Nanna smiled. She still had her pile of hens outside and a couple of dozen young chicks she'd bought from Elmbank Hatcheries in Cavan which were housed and fed in the barn. Occasionally a ball would come across the galvanised roof and scatter all before it much to her chagrin. Then Dad would arrive home from work and hand her the Independent newspaper. She'd sit in the green office chair he'd managed to salvage from the scrap heap at Smith's garage and immediately focus on the deaths which were to be found on the second last page. Mam was kept busy too, getting the bits and pieces ready for us heading back to school. The big difference this September was James going to secondary level. He and the two Martins had enrolled in the Tech, much to the annoyance of some of the relations. Now he couldn't very well go to Loreto which was a college strictly for girls in wine-coloured uniforms but "why weren't they sending him to St. Pat's boys college?" Herself wanted to know.

After all her own boys went there and it was deemed fairly elitist. Sure any gobshite could go to the Tech. What would all those Brady priests of past generations think for God's sake?

They'd be fiercely disappointed but Dad maintained that the Tech was as good, if not better than anywhere else and James would do the best out of it. He was a bright lad, tall for his age and very capable Dad had said. Sure didn't he know that Buenos Aries was the capital city of Argentina years ago, when Mrs. Sexton was doing Geography outside in the yard on a hot summer's day with the big ones and him only in fourth class.

He'd managed to trip somewhere and leave a bullet-sized hole in the left knee of the brown trousers Mam had picked up for him when they'd taken us down to Leddys of Butlersbridge. I watched as she patched them for him with a darker shade of material that only drew attention to the fact that they'd been holed in the first place. Harry had suggested camouflaging the hole by having James colour his kneecap with a brown marker he'd gotten in a packet from Eithne Reilly and sure no one would notice the difference then. James gave him a clip and Harry bawled.

I loved going into fifth class now and joining Martin Smith and Nora Tully for History and Geography and Comhra Gaeilge. They were the big ones and we were with them.

"Oíche Shamhna a bhí ann. Cheannaigh Mamaí úlla, bairín breac, cnónna agus líomanaíd. Chroch Daidí úll sa chistin".

I marvelled at the way Tim McGillicuddy knew so much history and how he could record it for us in his Living in the Past textbooks. Like the way Strongbow did a deal with Diarmaid McMurrough and ended up getting all the land and marrying his pretty daughter Aoife. And how the Irish lived in crannogs and celebrated Lughnasa on the first day of August and hunted wild boar in the forests and then on cold wintry nights sat around a big fire and listened to the seanchaí telling exciting tales of the heroes from ages ago. Long before Kevin Keegan's time.

Michael Conaty

Dad had picked up a green van, JID 624, to replace the A40 which was well bet he'd said. It had two front doors and double doors on the back with no side windows and we'd sit on a couple of scaffolding planks he'd gotten from Frank Tracey and installed on either side. Mam dropped us four boys and our sister who'd just started, off in the mornings and call back for Philomena when the wee ones got out at two o'clock. This left us to walk and kick a ball our way home across Shantemon mountain. Sometimes we'd be joined by Oliver and Sean who'd join us in target practice at the disused quarry. It was usually an old beer bottle carefully erected on a big boulder and each gunslinger, starting with the eldest, fired five stones. We'd toss a stone with spit on one side to start, since Oliver and myself had been born barely ten minutes apart and we could never remember who came first.

They were first cousins, the Reillys and being the eldest now at school, I was allowed to go to either house when asked, usually on a Friday evening. Lisdunvis, where Oliver lived, enchanted me. It had been the rector's house in bygone days, an ojous lump of a building altogether, with steps leading up to the massive front doorway. McGunker had told us he remembered it twice as big, sure hadn't they knocked down the half of it years ago.

Their back door led out into a great big courtyard surrounded by numerous outhouses and stables. At the far end stood their byre, which like the rest of the stonework, was carefully whitewashed each spring. Kathleen was Oliver's mum and she and our Phyllis were great friends. We still referred to her as Kathleen Kelly, her maiden name. Oliver's father was Eddie, a farmer and a huntsman, who kept himself and everything around him neatly groomed and tidy. "Aye, me sound fella" he'd greet ya, no matter who you were. Over their byre which hosted a batch of seventeen fat Friesians at milking time, was a huge loft with a trap door, through which bales of hay could be dropped at foddering time. Lisdunvis had everything. Plenty of sticks for fires that crackled summer and winter and a frying pan for rashers or "graklins" as they called them and the big Halloween treat that was boxty. Boxty cakes were made by Dot, Kathleen's mother, and involved painstaking hours of hard work, pealing and kneading their own home grown spuds. Kathleen would send home a boxty cake with me and we'd feast like bloated frogs on these thick-crusted slices, which when fried on a greasy pan, were sumptuous. There was always an abundance, whether daffodils in their laneway in Spring or multi-coloured dahlias in their oval garden to the front in Summer or conkers and hazelnuts that drooped from big, elderly trees in the fall. Biscuits stockpiled like you'd never see in our house and bottles of minerals that reminded me of Sean Boylan's bar. Anyway their Massey Ferguson 35 tractor had FNI 10 painted neatly front and rear and served as both workhorse and family transport. Bags of groceries were neatly placed in the transport box at the back.

We liked Angela, the eldest of the three girls that came after Oliver, not just cos she had a heart condition which left her with a bluish face on cold days. She was the same age as our Tommy, a quiet, softly spoken girl with glasses who never complained. We looked out for her, especially at school and worried when she wasn't in and had probably been confined to bed by Dr. Lorigan. Then she'd be alright again and none of us passed any remarks. Their world was a million miles in distance from ours and I could never imagine any of them being warned to have manners and not to be ould-fashioned like we would. Or to be shouted at to stop roaring and galloping about like wild horses when the neighbour's funeral was going out the lane past our house or like the time when our Tommy had shouted "Well Gawky, do ya see enough?" when a young lady, climbing the hill, had dared to look up and watch our antics. Or even like the time when Benjy hadn't invited Mam and Dad to his wedding for fear of upsetting the neighbours and we'd gone instead to the Park House Hotel in Virginia to celebrate their wedding anniversary. Anyway when the chips had been eaten and the coke drunk we headed outside and proceeded to tramp like a herd of bullocks through the stately gardens uprooting every rose bush and shrub in sight till Mam and Dad had to shout at us and then make a hasty getaway in the van hoping no one had seen us. They had hounds, too, the Reillys, a big batch of them that were housed in a fenced-in yard and let loose with the other dogs from Owley and Lismagratty of a Sunday to scurry around Shantemon mountain or Fairtown bog in wanton pursuit of a fast moving hare.

    John Reilly was Sean's father and Oliver's uncle and wasn't his wife Bridgie a neighbour of Daddy's from Corriga and sure hadn't she the same maiden Conarty surname and we often wondered if we were related through Tommy the Road or the Fat Man or even the Doctor Conartys. They too kept hounds and Sean, like Oliver was an only son for years till he got a baby brother, Aiden, to join him and all his sisters, who played camogie for Castletara on Ted's hill. Anyway Sean's mother was a kindly woman and she tried to teach me how to milk a cow by hand one Saturday evening. She was a whole black cow with an ingrown horn and I kept one eye on the bucket she ate meal from to make sure she was happy. Twitchedy and nervous, she slapped me in the face with her wet, shitty tail before stepping forward and putting her big black hoof into the bucket. "Never mind" Mrs. Reilly consoled as she wiped the shit away and watched the small sup of milk I'd collected meander its way across the cement floor. "If at first you don't succeed......" she continued, reminding me of Bean Uí Fiaich who'd frequently use such sayings at opportune moments and who'd talk about "striking when the iron is hot, boys". They had a horse too, like McGunker and Sean's dad would draw the milk cans out the laneway in the slipe to be collected at the main road. Sometimes I yearned to be an only son like Oliver or Sean and be able to get whatever I wanted and to have the undivided attention of parents who could give me a jumper and football and money for my birthday or even just to have my own bicycle to go places on without having a brother on the carrier behind me and another balanced on the handlebars before me and two more running alongside roaring "wait for us, wait for us". It was like being shackled by constraints. Like that summer's morning when we all gathered at Castletara Cross waiting for Tommy Brady's bus to take us and Laragh school to Butlins on our tour. Mam had scraped and pinched for a few months and delegated James to take control of the five pounds which was to be divided amongst us when we got there, warning us not to lose any of it and not to get lost ourselves or sick or anything and above all else to have manners. I watched as Sean and Oliver unzipped purses containing a tenner apiece and wondered how we, with a hard found pound note each could compete. Butlins was great, a wide open theatre with plenty on offer and Mrs. Sexton had even allowed us the luxury of breaking up and going off in groups provided we had manners and came back to the bus on time. Sure we thought we were in Las Vegas or somewhere grand like you'd see on the telly. And then I saw it and knew Dad needed one, but with only thirty pence left, I couldn't afford that brown coated penknife whose little red sticker was clearly marked at fifty pence. Munching the last of my cheese and onion Tayto, I turned to follow the boys who wanted another last go on the bumping cars. It bugged me. I wanted that knife for him and turning on my heal headed back to the stall and enquired of the man there would there be any chance of me being able to post him on the missing twenty pence from Cavan. He smiled leaving me momentarily optimistic and then pointed to the small red sign which read strictly no credit. And then it happened. It was one of those moments you don't see coming and pointless in wishing for. Annie Miney took my three ten pences and adding two of her own instructed the man to give me the penknife. I looked at Annie through her circular glasses and thanked God she'd come that day to mind her son, wee Paul Fitzpatrick. Promising to pay her back I legged it through the crowds and the candy floss and the aroma of burgers and chips and joined up with the boys who'd finished ramming each other by now and were making their way back towards the bus. I held on for dear life to Dad's gift and pressed it down in my trousers pocket and climbed the steps to be greeted by a racket of gun caps cracking and whistles blowing and lucky bags popping. Mayhem. Now it's a well-known fact that hard men like our James and the two Martins sit on the back seat of every bus. It was no place for the likes of us and I hesitated as Martin Brady beckoned me, for fear of making a fool of myself and having to trudge all the way back up again. Martin wanted to see the knife and eager to impress I flicked it open. Tommy Brady got as far as "Are yous all…..?" when shutting the blade down, I sliced myself across the inside of my left thumb. The pain was instant and the spurt of blood confirmed my fears that it was deep. I bent my thumb inwards and headed back up the bus trying to focus on a newfound ideological approach that had worked for me in recent times. This ideology was simple enough. "Don't talk about it or look at it and it'll go away". Too late. "Please Miss, Michael Conarty just stabbed himself" chorused everyone from Castletara National School. The sweat ran down my back and my head steamed up. "Oh God, it looks bad" yelped two of the Laragh girls before turning away in disgust. Now that didn't help. "For Feck's sake go away and leave me alone!" I shouted at them.

Tommy Brady shut his engine down and stood up with Mrs. Sexton to examine this potentially fatal wound. "Looks like stitches" he muttered to her. I wasn't meant to hear this. "Oh God no, not stitches" I stammered, refusing to show anyone the thumb now. The thoughts of it made me weak at the knees. I'd never had a stitch before but presumed it involved the use of a thread and needle and suddenly on top of all the sweat and dizziness, I felt the urge to empty the contents of my stomach. Tommy Brady produced a plastic bag and I duly obliged. The whole bus, especially the Laragh ones, stood up gawking and relayed a running commentary to the ones behind them. "Oh God, he's going to faint, oh no, he's puked now and there's some on his jumper, it's disgusting, yeuk". This didn't help either. Embarrassed now and emotionally out of control I found myself being led towards the first-aid centre, where after a long wait, a young doctor in a white coat nodded his head and agreed with the earlier diagnosis; yes indeed a stitch would be needed. I pleaded with him. Telling him he was busy enough already and that I was sure he was needed by someone else in a greater predicament, I suggested just wrapping it in a hankey, not talking about it and then it would be sure to go away. Mrs. Sexton and Tommy Brady helped to restrain and encourage me. "Come on, there's a good lad, you'll be fine, nothing to it". I felt the needle come deep down inside my thumb and then I lashed out, knocking the contents of the silver trolley to the floor. A glass bottle cracked.

"Now cop on will ya and have manners". Fear and embarrassment got me through it and I emerged with me thumb swathed in a big bandage and a sling round me neck. We'd kept the others waiting for over an hour and they weren't impressed. I was left sitting at the front with the Laragh girls who kept asking me did I want to throw up and if so could I please use the plastic bag. A whisper in my ear informed me that the penknife was safe and sound in James' possession and that he'd give it to me when we got home to Castletara Cross. Pass no remarks!

The very next day I went up to Annie Mineys with twenty pence from the fifty p coin Nanna had given to me for getting me thumb cut. Later on we headed to Fairtown.

> They hung a rope around her neck
> Weelia weelia wallia
> They hung a rope around her neck
> Down by the river Saile

Chapter 19

Anyway McGunker had been to town and having consumed more than his fair share of whiskey and stout in Noel Bradys, was eventually left home by Charlie Breslin the hackney man. He had all the news home with him and thought it odd that he had to go the whole way to Cavan town to find out what was happening in the neighbourhood. He twisted his cap and laughed in that divil may care way the men did when they had a few jars in. He shoulda contacted the local correspondents RadioActiveKate and CharlieFarley Dad informed him. They called her RadioActiveKate because they reckoned she knew everything that was going on long before anyone else did and she, too, only went to town once a week. She knew who was pregnant, how they got pregnant and when they were due before the poor unfortunates had probably even figured it out for themselves. The men laughed. It was worse now that she had the phone in, as her network of fellow nosebags didn't have to wait to meet her in the doctor's surgery of a Friday anymore. It was different with CharleyFarley. He was more blatant. The sort of fella that'd just pull up with ya along the road and ask ya straight out exactly what ya'd had for your breakfast. We knew they were harmless ourselves, not in the least bit malicious and just two of the many characters in the neighbourhood we were getting used to.

The men drank tae and Harry informed Roseanne that he had now reached 90,905 in his quest to write down all the numbers known to man. She smiled and then buttered soda bread for us and asked about school. Eddie and Tommy told her all about Fr. Gilligan and the poem they had to learn. Roseanne stopped what she was doing and clearing her throat began:

"The old priest Peter Gilligan
Was weary night and day
For half his flock were in their beds
Or under green sods lay"

We looked at each other. Dad and McGunker stood up and edged their way towards the door. They were heading over to Kelly. We knew what that meant. We headed round by Fairtown bog and the shouting in the distance attracted our attention. The Castletara camogie girls and their trainer, Joe Hegarty, were just finishing up their practice session as we came across the top of the pass that led to Ted and Nell Reillys. We waited till the Callaghan and Smith and Reilly girls were all gone and then proceeded to have our own kickabout.

The great thing about Ted's camogie hill was that it had white lines marked out on it and the goalposts were solid. More importantly they had a crossbar attached.

It was a level field too and a cow and her calf grazed at the far end totally oblivious to us. It even had its own form of floodlighting, like you'd see at Anfield or Old Trafford, with 200 watt bulbs protected by a galvanised lid, perched at the top of light poles that stood slightly bent and contorted by the elements.

We knew they were 200 watt bulbs because we busted one with a stone to find out. Sure we were in Dreamland. Often times it was almost as exciting to hit the woodwork and join in the melee for the rebound as it was to actually score. When someone hit a post we called them "Don" after Don Givens the Irish and QPR striker who seemed to hit the woodwork on more than his fair share of occasions. Here on Ted's hill, we could be Hurst and Best and Hector and Keegan and Pat Jennings and there was no one to bother us at all, at all. It was getting darker now and the light misty rain dampened our hair as we jumped the ditch and headed down one of the three long fields we owned in Fairtown. At its far end were two fairly wide gardens where Dad said we'd set spuds come springtime. Then there was the bog-field, so called because it "mearned" the wet flatlands under the hill at the back of McGunkers. Above it was a big triangular garden that we named the three cornered field. The field above that lay below the big bull's field, so called cos Mick Brady, our grandfather, used keep a bull in it. We had no name for this one so we simply called it the field under the bull's field. To the right was Clarke's field and below that, three fields called Jack's land cos Dad had given the grazing of it to his brother when we were in Drumalee.

And that was it really except for the hill behind the back door and the far hill off the first one. The meadow sat square-shaped beneath the back doors of the byre and the rocks, as we called them, were whin covered and stretched all the way up to Jackie Fitches crossroads.

"Once while he nodded on a chair
At the moth hour of eve
Another poor man sent for him
And he began to grieve"

"What does W.B. stand for?" Eddie wanted to know. "Look, it says W.B. Yeats, he musta writ this poem". Mam explained the William Butler bit and told us he was a great Irish writer and poet and that he had obviously hung on to his mother's maiden name.

"From now on I'm going to be Eddie Brady Conarty," he announced between slurps of his cornflakes and cold milk. Mam smiled. The Traceys arrived just then. "Say hello to Baby and Frank" Mam instructed. We shook hands and they seemed to like us. They were friendly. Heading to bed Harry wanted to know how you could possibly call a woman baby? "Coochie-coo, who loves ya baby?" we laughed. James explained that her real name was Margaret and that being the youngest after all the boys in Dad's family, before the arrival of Uncle Harry, they called her Baby cos they couldn't say her proper name and so it stuck for life. It was the same for anyone called Cissy or Sonny or Molly or Dot. There was always a reason behind it. Baby was a tall and good looking and friendly woman and we knew her and Dad were close. Frank Tracey was a quiet man, short in stature and hardy looking and mad about Gaelic football in Lavey. Frank was a builder and farmer and he and Baby had had loads of babies themselves. In keeping with tradition, two of our Tracey cousins had been named Seamus and Tommy.

We chewed on the wine gums Baby had given us and James took out his big French book from school. He'd been trying for a few weeks to teach us some of this new-fangled stuff. We were more interested in acting the bollix.

Je swees
Tu ay
Ill ay
L ay
Noos sums
Voos ates
Ills sunt
Elles sunt

Chien is a dog and bonjour means hello or good-day and noir is black and oui is yes and non is no.

And that was that.

We still acted the bollix.

Eddie had Dad's Evening Press open and was reading about the Republic of Ireland football team.

Giles and Treacy, what would Frank think? And Conroy and Mulligan and Heighway of course. They had wee shamrocks on their jersies. James explained that they could play as international footballers as well as for their clubs over in England. He hated England and hoped Poland would bate them and then they wouldn't qualify for the World Cup. He then had to explain to Eddie that cheering for Kevin Hector in a Derby County shirt was one thing but he must never do it when Hector was playing for England. We were all puzzled now. I could never imagine myself booing Clemence or Hughes or especially not our Kevin.

"You don't have to boo them, just remember that England think they're great with their Rule Britannia shite and that they claim to have invented the game of soccer and Dad says there's not a country in the world but that they didn't invade and cause trouble and that they think they have a God-given right to everything going and sure look at the Queen and the whole lot of them" he explained.

"Ha-Ho" shouted Harry imitating Dad. It was all beginning to make sense now. Besides look what the British Government were doing to the poor Catholics in Norn Ireland. Not giving them jobs and driving them to throw bricks and stones and petrol bombs and clatter dustbin lids out on the streets. And on Bloody Sunday they shot dead all the innocent people for their civil rights and for shouting "Up the IRA". Sure it wasn't fair at all. And they locked up the Price sisters and stopped Colonel Gadaffi's boat from Libya and it only trying to bring in guns to help the IRA. I thought back to Bean Uí Fiaich.

"Armoured cars and tanks and guns
Came to take away our sons
But every man'll stand behind
The men behind the wire".

"Is the IRA good or bad?" asked Eddie. "They're trying to help the Irish get their Catholic civil rights and drive the soldiers out of

Belfast" Tommy responded. Harry kept on writing his figures. Eddie said that Sean Cahill had told him in the school that the IRA put bombs under peoples' cars and kill soldiers and would shoot the Queen and all belonging to her straight between the two eyes, if they got half a chance.

Harry stopped writing and wanted to know if Ian Paisley was a priest and if so was he in the IRA? He said he wore a collar. "No, he's in the UDA" James snapped. "What's the difference in the IRA and the UDA?" asked Eddie. No one answered.

On the back of the Evening Press was an article about three young Dublin lads; Brady, Stapleton and O'Leary who were not in the IRA or pegging stones at anyone either. They were about to make the big time at Highbury playing for Arsenal it said. The three of them had long wiry hair, like our James and were only a couple of years older than him.

"What comes after 99,999?" he shouted. We looked at each other.

"I have no joy nor rest nor peace
For people die and die
And after cried he God forgive
My body spake not I"

We went to sleep and Toshack nodded down Brian Hall's corner and Keegan half-volleyed to the net. But it was ok to cheer now as K.K. was wearing his no. 7 Liverpool shirt!

"He knelt and leaning on the chair
He prayed and fell asleep
And the moth hour went from the fields
And the stars began to peep"

During the night one of Packie Brady's calves ate a sponge handball out on the rocks and died. I know cos Kathleen told us the next morning when we went down for a batch and a pot of red jam.

Chapter 20

Anyway if McKiernan the tradesman had kept his mouth shut then things might've been different. He didn't and what followed was an ojous holy terror. There he was fixing a window for Annie and Jackie when he overheard Peggy Dearg shouting at us that we were only a crowd of tramps and bastards. He told Annie. Big mistake.

We called her Peggy Dearg cos Dad called her Peggy Dearg ó thiar na gleanna. We called her husband Prince Philip cos Dad said he walked around the place as if he had a hot poker stuck up his arse like Mr. Windsor himself. He had no earthly say in the world either. If it hadn't been the kittens it would've been something else doubtless. The relationship between the dominant parents, one male one female, our Dad being the former and Peggy Dearg being the latter, was akin to an IRA box of gelignite, primed and ready to explode at any moment. It was only a matter of time. For our part we were both ignorant and guilty. Ignorant of the fact that during our absence through exile in Drumalee, Peggy Dearg had come to prominence and proceeded to domineer the entire locality and had almost every man, woman and child shitless of her, with the few exceptions and McGunker was one of them. Grown men daren't answer back so what hope had poor ould Prince Philip?

Our crime was that we dared to stand up for our civil rights and confront her and to this end, Jem Conarty's boys were pronounced guilty.

It wasn't so much our civil rights as those of Peaney our grey, malnourished ex-stray cat who had unfortunately decided to give birth in their hayshed. We heard about it at school and on the way home pulled up and initially, politely requested that we might go and see the new additions. Our demand was rejected so we then sought an assurance that Peaney and her kittens would be kept safe and allowed home when the time was right. Standing rigid like an RUC inspector at a roadblock and with a sally rod in her hand as a baton, Peggy Dearg was in no mood for compromise. Not now, not ever. I listed our Peaney's rights and then she swung for me. The tirade which followed bet all as the ould ones'd say. We went home. A line had been drawn in the sand and there was no going back now.

Phyllis being Phyllis was mortified and blemt us for being ould-fashioned pups at first. Her embarrassment turned to anger for a while and then fear itself set in. Not so much terror of Peggy Dearg in itself but rather the sense of trepidation in Dad finding out and of the way he might handle things.

We were all made to swear solemnly not to utter a mouthful and assured by Mam that nature would take its course and that Peaney would very soon carry her offspring out of their hayshed and up through our whinny rocks and back to the promised land.

"The Quiet Way is the best way" she finished.

And so it would've been if McKiernan the tradesman hadn't told Annie Miney and she in turn hadn't told our Dad. Big mistake. Armed with an Oxford English dictionary and accompanied by me and Tommy and Eddie, Dad headed for Headquarters as he called it. Prince Philip stood by the doorway offering niceties. Dad wasn't interested and informed him that to date he'd never hit a woman in his life and he wasn't going to start now. Prince Philip looked bemused. And then it happened. Peggy Dearg clamoured for the high moral ground by labelling us ould-fashioned whelps and a bad influence on her own childer, who of late were now picking their noses and biting their nails and uttering all kinds of profanities. It was all our fault.

Dad kept his focus however and producing his dictionary invited Peggy Dearg to look up the definition of the word bastard. She declined and went on to rant and rage about the carry on of us, his pups. Prince Philip went white and then grey for a while and interjected with the odd "Ah now, ah now". No one listened.

"It means illegitimate, do ya hear me? You're suggesting that our boys are illegitimate, well they're our boys and they're no angels I'll admit, but they're still our boys and me and Phyllis can vouch for every one of them, so don't be calling them bastards, do ya hear me now?"

Annie Miney arrived as a prosecution witness. Prince Philip, fearing the worst, began a spiff about neighbours needing each other and that the jolly thing to do was to shake hands all round. "Ah shake hands me arse," roared Annie. "You're an oul snake in the grass and you want us to shake hands, whisht will ya?"

I looked across at Tommy and Eddie and sensing the seriousness of the situation begged each other not to laugh. "Why don't you be a man for once in your life and stand up to your Mrs and put manners on her?" she roared, pointing her boney finger into his face. Prince Philip stood there. We left.

Anyway that should've been that. The air had been cleared and nothing left unsaid by either party and both sides should've moved on and gotten on better and Peaney should've come with her kittens. She did eventually, alone. Though admiring on the one hand his audacity in having a go, McGunker was adamant that Jem Conarty had made a big mistake. Time would tell.

Nobody else in the neighbourhood had ever stood up to Peggy Dearg before. They either begged forgiveness or slinked away for fear of a rollicking or for the most part just turned a blind eye to the shenanigins of Peggy Dearg and her self-righteous gobshite of a husband.

We'd be boycotted, McGunker predicted. And do ya know what? He was right. We noticed it in the little things of ordinary everyday life. Like Benjy for example. Now Benjy was a young energetic farmer making his own way in the locality. We liked him and he liked us and he'd always be joking and codding. But now he guarded against been seen talking to us anymore if either of the Royal couple were close at hand.

He, like the others, distanced himself. If we were on the road with him and they came past, he'd be sure to turn and busy himself with a bit of rusty wire, turning his back on us and then waving profusely before bowing his knee at the passing motorcade. We'd wave too of course but to no avail. Prince Philip only waved back when Peggy Dearg wasn't with him. Otherwise he observed protocol. "Yous better be going on now" Benjy would say, no doubt embarrassed at being caught in such close proximity to Jem Conarty's boys. He was an ojous man for confession and would never miss a Saturday evening's appointment before the first Friday of the month. Anyway, there we were on one such evening, me and James. Straggling our way home and plotting a bit of divilment having been to Confession and getting our souls cleansed. Benjy had his mother with him in his Ford Anglia car and he hesitated before pulling up to give us a lift. We liked Benjy's mother. She was old now with wizened skin and years of toil had left her frail body slightly bent forwards. She enquired after Fr. Eddie's welfare and gave us a lemon sweet apiece. Benjy hopped questions. He liked doing that. And then he stopped suddenly telling us his handbrake wasn't working the best and maybe it'd be better if we got out now and saved him the bother of having to pull up at his own laneway further on. As young and naieve as we were, we weren't stupid, either of us. We knew rightly that the road was dead level and there was no need for a handbrake at all at all. The real problem for Benjy was the risk of Jem Conarty's boys being

McGunker

seen to alight from his car in full view of the Royal household. Now that wouldn't do. So we hopped out and thanked him nonetheless and James muttered "gobshite" as he closed in the door. "That's the ould bollocks," I added.

McGunker was right. Fear of Peggy Dearg led many of the neighbours to be seen to distance themselves from us. And yet some of them delighted in stirring things up any chance that they'd get on the sly.

Like yon evening in Packie's when Dad had gone in for a half pound of Killashandra butter and the Anglo-Celt.

Benjy was there with CharleyFarley and Batty, standing propped against the wall like awkward goms wondering what their next move should be. I sensed their insecurity. It was as if they'd just been talking about him and dreaded being found out. They scuffled their feet and harrumphed their throats. Dad handed me an ice-lolly as we headed out. "How's, how's…the neighbours?" Batty blurted as he tried to snigger and impress his fellow overgrown goms. "Why don't ya ask them?" Dad snarled back in his face, "I know I would but then that's the difference between me and you, I say things to people's faces; come on son, we're going". Outside the evening air was getting cooler now and a light breeze whipped up the dust and leaves off the street. A lone swallow swooped low signalling rainfall.

"Looks like more moisture now Jem", Batty continued trying to be sociable and undo his smart alec remark. He stood there in his tweed jacket with the sewn on leather elbow patches and informed Dad that him and the boys were going into the town. CharleyFarley stood there like an awkward teenager. Benjy shuffled his feet.

"Well, go on boys don't let me hould yous up, I've a family to rare so I won't be joining yous. And sure please God someday, before it's too late, yous'll get women of your own and then yous'll know what it's all about. Have yous tried advertising in the Farmers' Journal or the Ireland's Own?"

Dad looked at Packie and the two of them laughed. Benny Hannigan's minibus pulled up and the three boys headed off to the town. Packie was bent over in two with the laughter by now and signalled at Dad to come back. Dad lit up a fag and laughed aloud.

"Maybe we should help the three Casanovas" Packie suggested as he pulled two bottles of stout from under the dresser and taking a biro from his jacket pocket, proceeded to scribble. I licked the last of me ice-lolly and dropped the wet stick into their coal bucket and looked around at the array of delph plates and bric a brac that adorned their glass side-case. I fixed my attention on a picture of a showband propped up in the corner. It was a small postcard-like photo of Brian Coll and the Buckaroos and someone had scribbled "To Eileen, best wishes from Brian" in thick black marker across the front.

The men finished their stout and Packie left the bit of cardboard he'd been writing on in the window shelf. "I'll give it to them tomorrow" he laughed. Brady's big white cat slinked in as Dad opened the door to head out and I glanced over at the writing. It read:

"Wanted: Young woman from a distant county of sound seed, breed and generation. Apply Cavan farmer. Early 40's. Own farm and house and mother too. Must be aisy kept and willing to work.

Preference given to nurses!"

We drove across the Cootehill road and headed up the pass. Prince Philip was coming down in his brand new Vauxhall Viva. He smiled and saluted. He always did when Peggy Dearg wasn't with him. Dad laughed.

"Armoured cars and tanks and guns
Came to take away our sons......"

Chapter 21

Anyway Francie Kelly was a legend long before his time, according to himself, that was! He was a gas man. Tall, bald and very funny. He and Mam had known each other for years and sure hadn't he been part of the Castletara Moonlight Players drama outfit with Fr. Eddie and the rest of them in bygone days. Kelly liked a laugh and was seen as a bit of a character who'd do literally anything to have one. His catchphrase was "Bejeminey". Bejeminey this, bejeminey that and bejeminey the other. Everything revolved around Bejeminey. He lived and farmed and laughed on a hill at the back of Michael Reilly's of Corravarry and made sure to get out to Ballyhaze at least two nights a week for a few scoops as he called them. Dad liked Kelly and Kelly liked Dad. They drank and laughed and argued together and mightn't see each other for weeks but it'd still be the same when they met. We knew Kelly liked us Conarty gasuns too and sure hadn't he even stayed up with us on a few different nights in Drumalee when Mam and Dad had been out with Dathlones and Eddie Murphy being unavailable. Francie's stories always had a hero in them, usually himself. They enthralled us. Like the night he told us the one about going forty-seven rounds of bare-knuckle boxing with the big Englishman in Sharkey's hayshed. The Champ as they called him had bet all before him until Kelly was persuaded by the crowd to climb in and have a go!

Reluctantly and only because he was being egged on by his fans, Francie did so and the rest was history.

His stories were so vividly descriptive that he took you there as if you were facing the Champ himself and feeling every blow he had to throw at ya.

"The bigger they come, the harder they fall," he said and we'd laugh knowing that no matter how uphill the task, the outcome would always be the same.

"Would you bate Joe Frazier or Muhammad Ali?" we wanted to know. "The two of them together" he laughed. "Sure bejeminey that wouldn't be fair, only two of them against me, Francie Kelly, sure they wouldn't stand a chance bejeminey!"

Then there was the story about the rat, the biggest, dirtiest rat with maybe five or six legs on it that roamed through his house for years and couldn't be caught. He had an ojous pair of pink eyes according to Francie and he'd come out on the kitchen floor at night time and stare at Kelly as if to say "come on I dare ya!" He'd tried everything to get him. The strongest rat poison that he only seemed to thrive on, rat traps that he played with and three big, hairy, wild cats that he chewed up and spat out, according to Kelly. "Did ya kill him with your bare hands?" Eddie asked eagerly. "No, bejeminey, I thought of it alright gasun, but I decided to go one step better" Francie announced. He lit up a Carroll's cigarette and pulled on it slowly. We waited with baited breath.

"Bejeminey, I was watching John Wayne on that oul box one night and him out on a rocky mountain shooting red Indians like there was no tomorrow, so I sat down there at that very table and wrote to him when the film was over and asked could I borrow his rifle for a wee job I had to do meself, bejeminey". "Did he write back Francie?" we shouted. Kelly pulled on his fag and thought for a while. "Well now, bejeminey he didn't, but sure didn't he go one better. I waited and waited for a reply from Hollywood and sure couldn't understand why it wasn't forthcoming, gasuns. And then, bejeminey, I was coming in the lane one morning from the shop and this big float of a Yankee car pulled up beside me and the driver rolls down the window and asks am I Francie Kelly, bejeminey?"

He got up and poured more black tea into his mug and stubbed his cigarette butt into the top of the cooker.

"Was he delivering the gun to ya?" asked our Eddie. Kelly fixed his cap and sat down again.

"He wasn't, but bejeminey doesn't he open the back door of the car and who steps out only the bould John Wayne himself".

"Wow, John Wayne himself" we replied excitedly. James laughed aloud. "Bejeminey, it was and sure he stood up on the lane out there and stretching out a hand says, so you're the famous Francie Kelly, I've heard all about ya!"

It got better. John Wayne stayed for three nights with Kelly and warned him to keep his mouth shut for fear of attracting unwanted attention. Francie had agreed and up until this day had never mentioned it to a soul. He was only telling us cos he knew he could trust Jem Conarty's gasuns. The pair of boys sat up each night with the loaded shotgun and on the third night, the king rat appeared and John Wayne had him in his sights and pulled the trigger but didn't the frigging gun jam and up leapt the rat and sank his tiger-like teeth into his throat. Sure he squealed like a rat himself.

. "What did ya do Francie, what did ya do?" We all sat goggle-eyed.

"Bejeminey, sure I had to save the poor oul divil anyway and didn't I grab the rat with me bare hands and thrash him to bits against yon far wall". We all turned and looked around for some semblance of evidence. "And then what happened?" enquired Tommy.

"Sure what happened, what happened? Sure bejeminey poor oul Wayne sat there in shock for an hour and then we drank a bottle of whiskey apiece and the next morning the big car arrived back for him and he only left on condition that I'd come over to Hollywood sometime and make a movie alongside him bejeminey".

Only James doubted him now and he stood there sniggering at the rest of us. Francie smiled and put his head down.

"You're only codding us Francie," I said.

"Well, bejeminey, I might be but sure the next time yous are watching him on the telly, yous'll notice he always wears a red hankie or scarf round his neck and sure isn't that only there to hide the teeth marks he got from the rat's bite sitting there in yon very armchair."

And that was that. We went home convinced and never mentioned a word of it to anyone for fear of attracting any unwanted attention.

Anyway Francie would ceili now and again and you'd spot him a mile off tipping along the road with an overcoat thrown over his shoulder. He'd drop into McGunker for a chat and then short cut it across the fields to our house. Him and Nanna got on fine too. He'd always enquire after Uncle Eddie and Nanna knew that the pair of them had been great friends. She'd make tea in the kitchen and pass no remarks when he and Dad headed outside to look at a heifer or something knowing full well that they'd link up with McGunker and Peter Rooney eventually, and find themselves after hours in Sean Boylans or Gormans bar. It didn't matter now and sure Nanna often took out a bottle of Tony Hughes' whiskey and poured two drinks at the table before they'd even go.

"Bejeminey, I was in the town today and the boys were telling me I'd make a great politician but sure as I told them, that's all fine and well, but sure who'd strig the cows when I'd be away at all them big meetings above in Dublin?"

And strig the cows he did, morning and evening, and then run down with the two cans of milk to the bridge at the foot of the lane and leave them for collection. Then he'd stick on a boiled egg for himself, cut a few thick slices of batch, butter them thickly and then wash the whole lot down with a big mug of strong tea.

Kelly and McGunker had a lot in common. They were both confirmed bachelors but that didn't stop them tanting us about the girls. Like McGunker, he too had probably left school early enough but this hadn't prevented him from being knowledgeable either. He'd buy the paper from Mrs. Edgeworth and read it from cover to cover. And then there was his black and white telly. He'd watch the news and keep abreast of current affairs.

"Bernstein and Woodward, bejeminey they're the boys alright! Sure didn't they break into yon big Watergate building in Washington and show them democratic bucks up. Sure that Nixon boy is an ojous whelp altogether. Bejeminey, if I got me hands on him".

He'd watch Steptoe and Son and Hall's Pictorial Weekly and Benny Hill too and laugh himself hysterical. And football, even though he labelled it an ould foreign game. Still, if he'd gotten his way he'd have united Ireland, North and South, not just politically but sportingly as well and then we'd all see!

"Bejeminey, if ya had Giles and Best and Givens and Dougan in the wan team, you'd have some outfit and with Pat Jennings in the goals, they'd be hard bet". He liked Keegan too cos I asked him and sure hadn't he watched both legs of the EUFA Cup Final when Liverpool had beaten Moenchengladbach 3-2 and he called them yon German crowd and said it was no harm to see them bet after all the trouble Hitler had caused in his time.

"Bejeminey, Keegan's hard stopped for a fella so small, sure he's gone past them in the blink of an eye and even I couldn't catch him".

Francie had a Massey-Ferguson 35 tractor that seemed to spend most of its time in the hayshed and we wondered if he ever used it but daren't ask. He told us that he had a powerful motorbike one time but that he had heeled her upside down on the middle of the road one night when he was being chased by the British Army for fighting for Ireland's liberation and that he had to leave it behind him for fear of attracting unwanted attention.

"Bejeminey, whatever yous say gasuns, say nothing". Francie winked and then laughed out loud again.

Anyway we rushed home to the telly.

Chapter 22

"Goals pay the rent and Keegan scores his share," the commentator said and do ya know what? He was right. I'd been half nervous in the lead up to the Cup Final with Newcastle because of their big England centre forward, Malcolm McDonald. He'd been saying in the Evening Press that he'd destroy the Liverpool defence. And so I worried and prayed. There was no need. Sure, they had MacDonald and Tudor and McDermott but in the end it didn't matter. Mammy and Nanna were in the town shopping that Saturday and had called into McKennas for their customary treat. Nanna would insist on Mam having a hot whiskey and this couldn't be turned down for fear of causing offence. Poor Mam. She'd be dizzy and giddy the whole evening afterwards. Anyway we watched the game and Stevie Heighway got one and Kevin got two and then it was "all over bar the shouting" Dad said. The reds were singing "We shall not be moved, we shall not, we shall not be moved, just like a team that's won the FA cup, we shall not be moved".

Mam and Nanna came home and Mammy's glasses were steamed up and then she put on the frying pan. She couldn't have cared less who'd won the cup and had never heard tell of Malcolm MacDonald for that matter either. Later she felt sorry for me and asked did Bobby Charlton play well. We laughed.

Michael Conaty

Dad was more interested in getting things done outside. Saturday was the only day when we were all at home and the emphasis was put on cutting sticks, grubbing the spuds we'd set in Fairtown or dosing the cattle or bushing holes in ditches or even whitewashing. Anything was better than watching yon ould feckin soccer. We'd be sent out to scrape the street of all the muck and overgrowth that had accumulated over the years and then we'd fight over the brush or the wheelbarrow. Harry was cuter. He'd slip off unnoticed to somewhere quiet and continue with his numerical quest. Sometimes Gerry Flood would give a hand. We liked Gerry. He was a tallish, well-built, iron fisted man who lived on his own in a wee house in Fairtown. He rode an ould black cross-barred bicycle and was perceived by the people as being a bit odd. You could meet him on the road and speak to him and he'd turn his head the other way and mutter something into the ditch.

He was always tinkering at things, putting them together or taking them apart. Dad reckoned he was dead handy and highly intelligent. He'd take a notion and hop up on his bike and ride twenty miles away to an auction and maybe arrive home with a battered and rusty pair of vice-grips that no one else wanted. He'd have them functioning in no time at all. We enjoyed Flood as the men called him and we'd imitate him when he wasn't watching. "Aye in damn it aye, to be sure, oh aye" we'd say before clearing our throats and landing a big dirty spit somewhere. Dad reckoned he could ate spuds for Ireland and McGunker told us that when Gerry's father and mother had died, he'd made coffins himself for the both of them. Once he'd been dropping spuds with Jimmy Glancy and the other men at Red John's years before. It came to grub time and Red John's mother put on a saucepan load of boiled eggs and asked Gerry how he liked his, meaning hard or soft and he replied "Aye in damn it, with another one Mam". The men laughed. They said he was drole whatever that meant. We didn't care and we'd arrive home from school and see Gerry cutting the gardens out at the front with a scythe and we'd ask him would he like tae? Then we'd go and make it for him and bring out a big plate load of batch bread, buttered and jammed. He'd only be after having his dinner but he'd sit down again anyway and ate away to his heart's content. McGunker laughed when Dad told him.

He lay back on the ditch one day and smoked an oul, damp, Sweet Afton fag that Eddie had found in the hay shed. Then he told us about how he had tracked a big red cock-pheasant up on Shantemon Mountain for weeks before finally clocking him one day with the slash-hook he used for cutting branches. He took the head clean off with a single blow and brought him home where he plucked and cooked him and then made soup from his bones. Tommy felt sick. Then he told us that the Government above in Dublin had come down and given the people frig all for Shantemon and then proceeded to plant it with thousands of trees. They stuck a big wire fence around the whole lot to keep the likes of him out but Finn MacCool would come back someday and level all before him.

That very evening we climbed Shantemon and found the finger stones intact. Big lumps of rock standing there in the shape of a hand, reaching out to the sky and none of us could budge them. We tried. McGunker had land at the very top of the mountain and on it were the stony remains of an old house now laid bare to the winds and the rain. We climbed the crab apple tree and fired stones at the crows that flew overhead. McGunker had told us that there had been a shop there once and that the poor people from all over had come to it in hard times. They sold everything bar spuds because of the famine which had been caused by the British Royal Family indirectly. "Bad cess to them" he'd said.

Harry and Eddie went searching for forgotten about blackjacks. We laughed and told them to get us a can of coke apiece when they were at it.

And then it happened.

The loudest crack of thunder you ever heard in your life seemed to shake the mountain from side to side and sent Harry off screaming for his mother. The poor lad was terrified as we scurried for cover only for Tommy to roar at us to keep well out in the open. Peter Smith had always said to stay away from trees and cattle when there was thunder and lightning about. "What's, what's lightning?" stuttered Harry as we made our way down.

"Are we all going to die?"

His fear scared us all the more.

"Come on to hell quick, we'll head for Roseanne's" shouted James as we legged it across Ned's brae. And so we did, only stopping momentarily to catch our breaths and to fire a lock of stones at Mary Margaret's goats and dare them to attack. We were safe enough we knew, as the poor demented creatures were tethered together by a small blue rope and hadn't the intelligence to attack in the same direction. The air was sultry and calm now but the occasional distant rattle served to keep us on our toes. We were hardly five minutes in McGunkers when the downpour came. It washed the street like never before. McGunker sat in his armchair and cursed the electricity for going off in the middle of the news. Two rioters had been shot by the British Army and he wanted to know more.

Roseanne sprinkled holy water on us and shouted at Tommy and Eddie to keep away from the window. And then, as quickly as it had started, it stopped again and everything was still and the sun shone brightly, throwing out a dead heat over the land.

McGunker laughed when we told him where we had been and said it was surely the giant that had come back to scare Jem Conarty's boys off his mountain. We went up with Roseanne to see the clocking hen. She'd put a horseshoe in with her to protect the eggs during the storm. It was something our Nanna had told her to do. Phil Denning arrived in the shop van and they talked about the storm and he told them about the way the road had lit up before him beyond in Drung. He gave us ice-lollies and asked us our names and our ages. Harry was still trembling and looking skywards distrustingly. He pulled on

James' sleeve, muttering "come on, come on, we better go home, come on James please, I wanta see Mam in case we all die".

And so we set off, only meeting Prince Philip's car on the road but he didn't wave to us because Peggy Dearg was with him. Nanna was reading her paper in the front room when we came in and couldn't understand how we were bone dry and hadn't gotten an awful drowning altogether. Mam had the fire in the grate lit and the power came back on and "Coronation Street" flashed up on the telly. She was scrambling eggs for us in the saucepan with no handle and Harry held on tightly to her shop coat and worried about Dad getting home safely. Mam explained to him that the safest place to be in a storm was in a car because it was insulated and earthed against all types of thunder and lightning and besides there was nothing to worry about now since the power was back on and the storm had gone. He wasn't convinced. We sat on the sofa and in between mouthfuls of buttered toast and scrambled egg told Nanna about the mountain and Finn Mac Cool and what McGunker had said and about Roseanne putting the horseshoe in with her clocker. She smiled and put down the paper and said all this stormy talk reminded her of her old friend Cissy Thunder above in Crosserlough. She started telling us a story.

"Was that her real name?" laughed James. Nanna gave us one of her scornful looks so we knew to listen now and above all else not to snigger or laugh.

Anyway weren't Cissy Thunder and our Nanna the two fastest runners in the school and one day didn't the Master send them all out on the road and tell them to run for a mile to the one tree and then turn and come back. The first runner home would win a new pencil. So there they were neck and neck, beating everyone in sight, boys and all, at their ease. Nanna knew she had the beating of her and got ready to pull away and claim her prize, when who did she see lying on the road, having fallen a hundred or so yards from the start, only her little brother James. His two knees were cut and he was bawling for help. She ran past him and then turned to go back. Cissy Thunder ploughed on regardless and won the pencil. We couldn't believe it.

"Blood's thicker than water," Nanna informed us. We looked at each other. Philomena was colouring a picture and humming to herself. "Was your James one of the IRA men?" our James wanted to know.

"Indeedn't he was, the Lord rest him" Nanna replied, blessing herself. Harry looked up thinking there was more thunder.

"Sean Cahill and Jimmy Lyons says the IRA men blow up pubs and houses and cars with people in them and then the guards have to come and shovel up their guts off the road" Eddie blurted out.

"My brothers, the Lord have mercy on them, wouldn't agree with that carry on, I can tell yous. They fought the British Army years back and the only civilians ever killed were at the hands of them Black and Tan blackguards and in trotten they were some whelps, driving round the country, burning the hay and shooting cattle and searching the people's houses and torturing the poor divils. Sure someone had to fight back".

She crossed herself again and so did Harry, crawling back in behind the sofa and kneeling on Philomena's ankle in the process and causing her to yelp. We jumped.

"Tell us about the gun, tell us about the gun" James shouted excitedly. And so Nanna did.

Anyway it so happened that Peter and James McEvoy were on the run during the troubles and only appeared home once in a while and that was usually to have a feed and to pick up the creamery cheque and then tear off through the fields again to fight for Ireland's freedom. No car bombs in them days. And then the Black and Tans would pull up in a lorry and them half drunk and they'd jump out and search all the IRA houses in Crosserlough and McEvoys was sure to be one of them.

They'd rip the place apart and break all before them and laugh and our Nanna was only scared once and that was the time that someone had hidden a pistol in their loft and she knew that if it was found, then they'd all be arrested and tortured and every beast about the place would be shot stone dead. We sat stunned, wondering what happened next. Anyway didn't Nanna lift the pistol and make her way to the upstairs bedroom window and when no one was looking, throw it out and down into the trough full of pig swill her sister was mixing on the street. She paused…and then it happened again. The bang was louder than the one we'd heard on Shantemon and it shook all before it and put the lights out again pitching the place into darkness. The fire glowed warmly giving us some semblance of security as we scurried beneath her armchair.

"Is it the IRA, is it a bomb, is it Finn Mac Cool?" squeaked Harry. We all wanted to laugh and couldn't. Outside the evening sky lit up violently and we waited for the windows to blow in on top of us.

"Remember O Most Gracious Virgin Mary…"

The heavens rattled again and the lightning scorched.

"Are we dead Nanna, are we dead?" I asked feebly.

She held our heads together and soothed them gently. Mam had Philomena on her lap.

"Implored your help or sought your intercession …"

The bangs grew louder and closer. I wished that Dad would come home and prayed he'd be safe wherever he was.

"To thee do I come, before thee I kneel, sinful and sorrowful…"

I couldn't help thinking that maybe it was the end of the world and wondered how poor Dad would cope when he'd find us all huddled together stone dead in front of the fireplace.

"But in your clemency, graciously hear and answer me. Amen".

Nanna told us childer to bless ourselves again and soon after the skies opened once more and the rain hopped off the slates outside above us and washed the street like it had done a bit earlier beyond at McGunkers.

Mammy lit candles and we all sat waiting and waiting. Silence.

"I wonder what Willie Whitelaw is doing right now," said Eddie. We laughed and cheered knowing we were safe again. Harry wasn't convinced. Philomena had fallen asleep sucking her thumb and clinging to her wee knotted rag. Mam picked her up. Upstairs the candlelight flickered on the mantelpiece and we imitated Mam's hand movements as she silhouetted rabbits onto the wall facing Packie's rock. Dad arrived home safe and sound and called in to say the prayers. We knew by the aroma that he'd taken refuge in Sean Boylan's bar. Sure hadn't the guards and the fire brigade men told everyone to stay indoors for fear of being swept away in the floods that swamped Cavan town.

We felt secure now and Harry blabbed all out about Finn Mac Cool's finger stones and the famine shop and the Black and Tans above in Crosserlough. Dad stroked his fifth son's blonde hair and smiled. "Ah don't worry me son, the McEvoy boys were well fit for them".

"Daddy, daddy, do ya think Finn Mac Cool didn't like us boys up messing on his stones and is that why he rattled the mountain on us?"

"I'd say he did it alright me son but only because he doesn't like young gasuns pegging stones at Mary Margaret's goats".

We looked at each other. Dad laughed out loud and then made his way downstairs again. We could hear him;

"Is the priest at home boy?

Or may he be seen?"

That night all Roseanne's eggs, bar one, split right open and the clocker refused to go back to her nest. I know cos she told us the next day when me and James went over with the Celt and twenty fags for McGunker.

McGunker

"And that was the end of the woman in the woods
Weelia weelia wallia
And that was the end of the woman in the woods
Down by the river Saile!"

Chapter 23

Anyway on the day of the holidays we got out at half-twelve and sauntered off home up the road by the chapel. The ball we had was busted though still flighty enough to cross the ditch and land in the graveyard. We all went in. Most of the plots lay untended and the stemmy grass had turned to hay seed in places. Kieran McCabe had once informed us that the Government made people write R.I.P. on peoples graves and that it meant Rip them up if you don't believe they're dead but so far no one had dared. McCabe called each of us Harry even when we were all standing together in front of him.

It was sultry and wet at the same time, a bit like the weather in West Germany where the World Cup had been held. We were having our own tournament at the back of the hayshed when he arrived. He was black and white and very fast and could leap six foot in the air and take a ball down better than any of us. We looked at each other.

Nobody knew where that Collie dog had come from or cared, for that matter. Now he was ours. We called him Bruno and he became part of the family, literally. The months passed. He was definitely ours. Mam could tell the time every evening by the way he'd sit with his ears cocked momentarily and then spring to his feet and sprint up the pass to meet us coming home from school.

We'd open the back door and Bruno would tear off and resurrect the ball from where it had last been booted and sit panting by its side with a look in his eyes that urged us to have a game. We never let him down.

He got to know each one of us by name, I'm sure of that. He had this inbuilt mechanism that deciphered where a ball was going and more importantly what the recipient was likely to do with it. So when Tommy was in goals and ready to kick it out Bruno immediately ran to the back of the pack knowing full well he'd punt it out as far as possible. It was the same with Harry. Bruno made sure to head for the hayshed whenever Harry pulled the trigger knowing rightly he'd screw it a mile wide no matter how close he was to the goals.

We tried to teach him to chase the cattle or rustle out a few rabbits for us above on the rocks or even to try and kill the rooster one day that Nanna was away with Fr. Eddie, but it was all in vain. All he wanted was a ball and he'd sit waiting with one between his paws, occasionally nuzzling it with his nose or gnawing into it safe in the knowledge that it had already been busted by some of us.

Dad walked past him one day and muttered "Ah sure they have ya destroyed, you're not worth a shite, them and their ould soccer, they have ya addicted."

Anyway Poland qualified and England got left at home and we gorged on football. It was our first real World Cup though James claimed to remember seeing Pele and Jarzihino and Riveliniho and the save that Gordon Banks made in 1970. He was the eldest and so we didn't dispute.

Instead we marvelled at the Dutch side in their orange jersies playing their total football and focussed intently on one guy called Johann Cryuff in his number 14 shirt. Even his name sounded world class I thought. But then so too did those of Johnny Rep and Johann Neeskens and Rensenbrink and Van de Kerkhof.

Even McGunker telling us that William of Orange had come from Holland and cheated at the Battle of the Boyne above in Na-van and battered the poor Catholics, did nothing to dampen our admiration for Cryuff and co. "Sure isn't that why the buggers wear orange jerseys" he said "and wouldn't we be far better off cheering for Scotland cos they were Celts too, like us, and if they had any wit wouldn't they go and fight with a few stones and get their independence too". And so we cheered on Scotland who had Joe Jordan and Billy Bremner and Peter Lorimer and Willie Johnstone playing for them against a team from Africa that we never heard of before called Zaire. Anyway, Scotland beat them 2-0 but sure didn't Yugoslavia come along then and hammer the same Africans by nine goals. Then Scotland drew 0-0 with Brazil who weren't themselves at all, at all and James told us that their flair was gone.

"What comes after 189,999?" We looked at each other. Fr. Eddie and Lizzie arrived and we all had to stay quiet.

There was a man missing in Ballyhaze and the guards were out searching the river for him. "Clare to God, what's the world coming to?" Nanna wanted to know. Later, she was in bad humour retelling the story about the girl who refused to sit next to the lassie with cow-dung on her leg in Loreto College. Her parents had requested that their daughter be moved away from her.

"In trotten, mark my words and we'll see which of them lassies gets on the best, she'll not always be smelling of dung the poor wee divil".

Fr. Eddie poured more tea. "So, very nice, very good, that's really nice now" he assured all present.

And so it was. Except for the Scots of course.

They drew 1-1 with Yugoslavia and went home on goal difference.

Poland did fierce well though and we supported them cos they'd dumped the English out and James told us they were all Catholics in Poland and sure weren't they fighting for independence from Communist Russia and there was no point in blaming the Queen this time.

The German pitches were like Ted's hill. Wet and slippy after big teams of rain even though the sun shone during the games.

The Germans had classy name sounding players too like Breitner and Holzenbein and Muller and Bonhof. We watched every single game and yet on the day of the final between Holland and Germany, we were up in the orchard rooting at something and Eddie had to tear out and tell us it had started.

By the time we got in, Holland were a goal up. They'd been awarded a penalty by Taylor, the Englishman and Johann Neeskens smacked it past Sepp Maier in the German goal. The commentator said it was a sensational start and Eddie reckoned the Dutch would go on and win it by at least twelve clear goals now.

The orange shirts were all over the Germans but Dad told us they wouldn't give up too aisy.

Then, sure enough, they got a penalty for a foul on Holzenbein and Paul Breitner made it one apiece.

"McGunker says there's two Germanys, one in the west and one in the east and someone like Red John built a big wall between them and if you tried to cross it, you'd be shot stone dead by the IRA or someone else like them" Eddie informed us.

We looked at each other.

The Dutch piled on the pressure and had loads of chances but then the Germans took the lead through their chunky wee striker, Gerd Muller. James told us he was called Der Bomber back home in Germany. "Which one?" Eddie asked. No one answered.

Later Muller scored again but it was disallowed for offside. We willed Cryuff to score an equaliser but he couldn't. Harry kept writing his figures. And that was that. The whistle went and our first World Cup was over.

James was disappointed. He wanted Brazil to win but couldn't believe how dirty and awkward they were and wondered what poor oul Pele would think of them now.

"Is that soccer still on?" Mum would occasionally enquire not fully understanding that a big tournament like this could last the guts of a month. We didn't mind.

As long as she kept carting homemade chips and diluted orange or bowls of hot rice smothered in cool, clear milk, into us in the room, she could ask all the questions she wanted. Then we'd head outside to a vigilant Bruno and try to re-create a Cryuff twist or a Muller swivel and shot, or even a Sepp Maier flick over. Maier wore gloves and the TV people thought it strange. Tommy improvised by pulling on an old pair of socks. Anyway McGunker arrived dressed to the nines. Someone had died in Redhills and he wanted to get to the removal. Dad shaved in the bathroom and Mam wanted McGunker in for tae. He declined and lighting a fag came over to watch us. We showed him the cattle that stood chewing their cuds and flicking the flies beneath the meadow ditch.

In the distance we could hear Peggy Dearg reprimanding Prince Philip. "Boys o boys" went McGunker. He laughed. After they'd gone and with the long summer's evening ahead of us, we wandered aimlessly about wondering what to do. Then we saw him standing there, isolated. Nanna's big red rooster! He raised his head suspiciously and then headed for the gate. Game on!

We tore after him despite James' protestations. It was alright for him. He was getting away to football training with Dessie Reilly and the boys. This was a challenge we just couldn't resist. The further he ran the harder we chased. Now and again he'd rise a foot or two off the road dodging the hail of stones that followed him. It looked as if that rooster was an expert Irish dancer. We took him all the way to the crossroads whereupon he veered right and up into Annie and Jackie Fitches back garden. Big mistake. Bonzo sprung like an Indian tiger sending our estranged rooster skywards. He came down with an ojous thump,

readjusted himself and headed back down the pass for home. We turned our guns on Bonzo. How dare he attack our poor innocent rooster. The cheek of him. We connected once or twice and sent

Bonzo yelping for cover. Annie stuck her head out. "Ah Christ boys, what are yous doing to poor oul Bonzo?" We didn't wait to answer. Slowly but surely and a little nervously too, we cajoled our feathered friend fondly back down that road reassuring him occasionally that the past was the past and it was now time to get home. We could hear Nanna in the distance, "Chucky, chucky, chucky". The humming of Eddie Fitzsummons tractor coming into Costelloes brae drew more friendly gunfire. We had him this far and we couldn't afford any mistakes and sure the odd stone or two would only help to hurry him along. Mercifully he headed back through the gates and ultimate sanctuary. "I'm telling Nanna" yelped Harry as he headed towards her up in the garden. "Do and we'll fecking kill ya and rip your numbers book to bits" Tommy retorted.

We saw Nanna in the distance poking with her stick at a penny bar wrapper that nestled in the moistened grass. Harry had a change of heart and headed for the scullery. We explained what had happened and how the startled rooster had suddenly taken flight and how we'd gone to rescue him and how we'd been attacked by Bonzo in the process and how relieved we all were to get him home safely and especially now to see him heading up on the roost. She smiled and handed us a silvermint each and entrusted Eddie with one for Harry. Eddie smiled too.

Much later Dad arrived home and came up to tell us to stop acting the bollix and to get to sleep. We said the prayers and I told him how I'd begged God earlier that day to help Cryuff and Neeskens. "Begod yous are some boys alright, that's a first to be sure, good Catholic boys praying for a shower of Orangemen!"

I checked the curtains.

Outside Bruno lay with the ball in front of him, waiting. He cocked his ears momentarily. All was well.

The next morning Nanna told us to whisht as Charles Mitchell was trying to read the news. She dipped a Marietta biscuit into her tea.

Chapter 24

Anyway I went upstairs and leafed through the pages of Fr. Eddie's Greek book. This Cyclops was an ojous buck altogether, with his one eyeball and him as big, if not bigger, than Finn Mac Cool himself. Fear possessed me. A cold shudder ran down my spine, I shouldn't be in Fr. Eddie's room never mind reading his books.

Anyway along comes Odysseus and tells the Cyclops that his name is nobody and fills him with red wine. When he gets him half-jarred, Odysseus and his boys plant a big sharpened stick through his only eyeball and leave him with no sight at all, at all. Well the Cyclops goes clean mad and roars for his mates to help him, shouting all the while that he's being attacked by nobody. They don't answer his call thinking he's half mad in the head. The next morning Odysseus and the other Greek lads crawl out with the sheep when the Cyclops opens the cave and then they make straight for their ships. Exciting stuff alright.

"So, very nice, very good" I could hear Fr. Eddie outside. I dropped Odysseus and ran to the landing window. He was talking to a stoutish young boy with curly hair who kept replying "aye, oh aye, oh aye aye". They came inside. I ran downstairs and joined the rest of them gawking. It was our first meeting with Martin Breslin. We listened. Sure wasn't his mother, Annie, one of the Clarkes of

Corratubber and didn't she marry one of the Breslins and hadn't they moved up to Belfast years before. I wondered if he knew anyone in the IRA. His accent bet all. Temperamental and full of mischief at the same time, James nicknamed him the Belfast Bomber. We peppered him with questions about the IRA and the UDA and petrol bombs and the Queen of England and Gerry Fitt and even Willie Whitelaw, but all to no avail. The bomber hadn't a clue and couldn't care less anyway. He never shut his mouth.

"Georgie Best, Superstar
He walks like a woman and he wears a bra". We laughed.

He was that little bit spoilt, being the youngest, but we allowed for that. Sure wasn't his poor dad dead and with Martin and his mother and family living in Norn Ireland and having to duck bullets and stones, as we thought, life couldn't have been easy. His two older sisters, Kathleen and Anne, made sure he wanted for nothing. We didn't begrudge him this either. All the same, when things weren't going his way at the back of our hayshed, he'd storm off home to Auntie Kathleen and still be exchanging obscenities with us and him halfways up the brae.

We wouldn't see him for a few days and then he'd simply re-appear singing "Glory Glory Man United…" as if nothing had ever happened. We passed no remarks.

Now Eamonn Boylan was different. Dublin born and bred. Quiet and unassuming, he quickly melted into the Conarty pot and became part of our folklore. His dad, Seamus, was one of the Boylans and he'd started holidaying with his Uncle Matt in Corratubber that summer.

Eamonn supported Leeds and had plenty to shout about since their twenty odd games undefeated league run. Plus they had Johnny Giles from Dublin who was as oirish as any of us. Anyway the pair of boys became like adopted brothers of ours and when Mam shouted "Come on in boys", she meant all seven of us.

We'd tant and fight and kick lumps out of each other outside and then head for the kitchen for a feed of homemade chips or rice. Best of all was that we could now play three on three outfield with Tommy in goals. No offsides, no line watching and no penalties either. Anyway things couldn't get better. We hadn't intended any devilment that Sunday evening as we made our way across to Ted's hill. If we'd stuck to our usual route then it could've all been so different. We didn't. Instead we found ourselves lured into the Royal's oval-shaped orchard garden, with its over laden plum trees, begging to be plucked.

Despite the fact that our bellies were still only halfway through the digestive process of a pot of hot rice, this was an opportunity we just couldn't pass up. Besides, we knew we were safe enough. They went "up home" every Sunday evening and didn't return till milking time. We tore into it forgetting to leave someone on lookout duty. We were novices but we'd soon learn. Them plums hit the ground like stones being tipped off the back of one of Nulty's lorries. "Oh shite" roared James spotting Prince Philip coming out for the cows. "Quick, leg it boys".

And so we did. Not for the border with Mexico, like in the films, but for the ditch that lay between our fields and his. The swipe of his half-inch water pipe left bruising on the backs of our legs for three days afterwards. But we'd survived, all of us and lessons had been learnt.

In future, we'd carry out a little bit of surveillance work beforehand and have the lie of the land checked out. Above all else if someone was meant to be away ceilying, then we'd have to allow for them coming home early. That's where the lookout post became essential, we persuaded Harry.

The next time we got it right in spectacular fashion. Kerry were on the telly playing a Munster final when we hit Jemmy Joes that late summer's evening. It wasn't personal.

We liked Jemmy Joe and his wife, Mrs. Jemmy Joe. They were

good to us, always sure to buy a ticket whenever we called and hand over eclair sweets when the Far East was delivered. All the more reason not to get caught. James reckoned it was a soft target till I reminded him they had a sharp collie dog who'd smell us a mile away. We came across by the back of the old quarry and only started crawling on our bellies when we reached their big meadow. James and Eamonn Boylan headed along the whitethorn ditch that encompassed the farmhouse and quickly returned to inform us that there were two or three cars on the street and a lot of football shouting coming from the house. It meant they had company. Maybe Pete and Brendan Reilly and their mates. It left our job all the more high-risk. It could also be advantageous having them in there. After all, if they were shouting for Kerry to score, then their distraction created the opportunity to strike that we needed. We wriggled our way under the thorny wire only stopping once to untangle the Bomber's jumper. I felt like one of the IRA men Eddie Murphy had told us about stuck below in McGitterick's bog in Co. Monaghan. Adrenalin drove us on. Eddie accompanied Harry on sentry duty and knew to whistle if anyone appeared. We'd split and leg it home as arranged earlier. James had urged us not to forget the golden rule:" Don't get caught!"

If anyone was captured we were to sing dumb, but if we were being threatened with being bet to death with a stick, then we were to say we were out looking for a stray kitten.

They'd even left ladders out for us and there I stood perched two rungs from the top of one of them, shaking branches like the divil and all the while keeping an eye on their back door. The bomber and the boys scurried around gathering the loot. Old Mrs. Clerkin's appearance in her back garden to retrieve clothes from the line only added to the tension and sense of guilt at what we were doing. She was their neighbour, a kindly soul with plenty of wine gums.

The dog lay back in the evening sun none the wiser to our carry-on and seemed more preoccupied with his itchy back. So far so good. More roaring inside. We stockpiled our ill-gotten gains into a fertiliser bag Tommy had found at the butt of the ditch and made our exit. Those plums only needed the slightest squirt for the stones to pop out and the apples couldn't have been juicier. We devoured some and carried the rest. The revving of a car engine on Jemmy Joe's street diverted us away from our intended escape route and we found ourselves scurrying along the ditch at the back of Castletara chapel.

Knees trembled, adrenalin pumped and salty sweat poured as we waited for the car to come down McCormack's brae. It started to rain. Martin Breslin said we should take sanctuary in the chapel. We didn't know what sanctuary was but we legged inside regardless. The big heavy brown door clanked behind us and all was suddenly still and quiet now. We hopped the steps up into the gallery, a place we'd only ever see when singing hymns at Christmas time with Mrs. Sexton and Maura Hannigan. There was dust everywhere and years of cobwebs had blanketed themselves to the corner walls. The rain pattered outside on the roof. We sat in silence. A poster for the Vincent de Paul collection lay rolled up and discarded beneath a larger and more colourful one belonging to Fianna Fáil.

"Is there going to be thunder?" Harry whispered to me.

I squeezed his hand to reassure him. "I want Mam, I want Mam". The minutes passed and feeling a little more confident now, we stood up and stretched ourselves. James decided it was safe enough to come down.

"If anyone comes in, kneel down quick and pretend we're saying the rosary for the Holy Souls or the black babies or someone" he warned us. We tiptoed down and stood awestruck at the back of the chapel. The still silence was only interrupted by the quiet ticking of a clock that hung on for dear life to the front of the gallery. Feeling slightly more confident we manoeuvred about exploring our serene environment. Tommy and Eddie looked at the confession box. The stations read l,ll,lll,lV,V all the way round to XlV. James explained that these were Roman numerals and that they had to be used in

Catholic chapels like ours because the Pope lived in Rome and that Fr. Eddie had once told him that when in Rome you had to do what the Romans did.

We looked at each other.

He peeped out through the doorway and informed us that the coast was now clear. "I wanna go home, I wanna go home," Harry pleaded.

It was still raining and we had more exploring to do. Martin gonged the bell and the sound boomed all around us. We tittered. The plaque on the wall listed all those who'd donated new windows way back in 1951. It also said that 1067 dollars had come from the children of Castletara now living in New York. Tommy told Bomber Breslin that these poor children had to run away from Castletara during the time of the famine for the want of spuds that the Queen of England and her British servants had stolen and most probably pealed and fried into homemade chips for the Black and Tans that were coming to Ireland to capture the McEvoys above in Crosserlough. Eamonn Boylan laughed and tanted Martin about being British himself and told him that his passport in years to come would have U.K. citizen stamped all over it.

Martin got thick and stormed towards the door. It opened before him and we could see Mary Margaret as she took off her gloves. She came in. "Good evening", she beamed at us all as we dashed for our seats.

"Dow O Lord ill open our lips," shouted James but no one replied.

I scooted down off the altar and stared at Jesus being laid in the tomb. I stood my ground and decided to pray. And then I saw him looking down at me from the big window at the back of the altar and thought back to Jemmy Joe's orchard and Mrs. Clerkin at the clothesline. I felt sick. I knew he wasn't happy.

Anyway Mary Margaret bowed her knee and moved on to the next station. She whispered her prayers. Eddie nipped Harry. He squealed. The rest of us looked away. We were ould fashioned pups, there was no doubt about it now, I thought to myself. She'd probably tell the priest and he'd tell the bishop who'd then have no option but to write to the pope in Rome and what would he think of us then? He'd be sure to write back to Fr. Eddie and he'd tell Nanna and she'd call us whelps and then Daddy would surely break all of our necks. I reversed slowly and bent my knee onto the hard floor. If only I could make it to the back of the chapel and then we'd all leg it home and if Nanna was smiling, then that would be a sure sign that God had persuaded Mary Margaret not to open her gob and that all was forgiven. I could hear the twinkling of the beads as we stood back to back on the centre aisle. Mary Margaret stopped praying. "I think you're going the wrong way," she whispered into my ear. James and Eamonn Boylan burst out laughing and legged it. I excused myself and then tore out after the rest of them, nearly tripping as I tried to geneflect like we'd been taught to by Bean Uí Fiaich. I looked back. Mary Margaret smiled to herself and then she looked up to see Jesus Christ fall for the first time.

I didn't bother with the holy water. We made our way up through the old graveyard with its wonky headstones and funny writing. Some of the people had been here since 1760 and before. "This stone erected by Brian Brady in memory of his father Terence departed this life dec 1781". I pulled Harry along. Mick Brady was buried in the corner somewhere but we hadn't time to pray for him now.

The ground was bumpy and hollowed in places and Harry clung to me for dear life, fearful of falling into someone's grave and never been seen again. In the distance we could see Mary Margaret's dog sniffing at our loot. He scratched at the grass momentarily and then pissed unceremoniously on top of our bag of apples that nestled there beneath the ditch. Well, we cursed him sideways and fired stones after him. He legged it, yelping.

We'd suddenly lost our appetites now and no amount of pleading from Martin and Tommy could persuade us otherwise. "There's nothing more dangerous to humans than ripe apples pissed on by a dirty mutt of a dog" James announced. And so that was that.

We made our way across the top of the graveyard and out onto the road not bothered now by pursuing cars. We fired stones at the poles and pulled sloes from the bushes.

The blackberries on Hughie Smith's ditch were mushy after the rainfall and their only useful outlet now was that of dirty ammunition. We pelted each other. The Bomber took one across the butt of his lug and ran on ahead frothing obscenities.

We came to the flat of the road and in the distance a young couple made their way towards us. He was tall and bronzed and Yankee looking with his white shorts and buckled sandals. He wore no socks. She too had the look of a yank about her, what with her blonde pony tail and sparkling white teeth and gleaming pink cardigan that lay draped over her shoulders.

They were holding hands.

"Hi there, you guys, hiya doin?" he enquired.

We muttered hello.

She looked at us and smiled.

James enquired if they'd been to the mountain and the young man, pointing to the silver camera that hung round his neck, informed us that not only had they been up there, but that he'd taken some great shots of the finger stones for his college friends back home in the States.

The young lady took his camera as he lined the seven of us across the road. Taking it back he told us to smile and then he clicked. She looked on approvingly and then rubbing the tops of her brown arms, said, "C'mon honey, we best get goin". She smiled at us again.

"Well, so long you guys, so long" he beamed and putting his arm around her shoulder, turned to go. And then it happened.

The Bomber had been quiet and sullen up till this but just as we were about to depart, he blurted out:

"Did yous have sex up on the mountain?"

We looked at each other.

The young lady blushed and turned her head downwards to the road.

"Why you cheeky, no good, son of a bitching Northern Irish punk" he roared as we legged it for Ned's brae. We laughed as we ran, a nervous laugh, a laugh that told us we were all in trouble if the big Yankee fella gave chase. He didn't.

We doddled down Ned's brae.

McGunker was clipping the hedge.

Roseanne was with him moving the big, wooden steps a little further on, each time he descended.

"Boys oh boys, if it isn't the McGunker Conartys and the Dub and the IRA man" McGunker laughed.

We helped Roseanne gather up the thorny clippings and bundled them over the ditch into the shuch that lay behind.

Roseanne couldn't have been happier. Their nephew was home on vacation from the States. He had his fiancée with him. Surely we'd met them over the road? We looked at each other. Silence.

"What's sex?" Harry shouted.

They looked at each other. More silence. Roseanne gave us Colleen sweets and told us to be on our way before the rain came on again. We left our goodbyes. McGunker took off his cap and scratched his head.

"Glory, glory Man United…" The Bomber tore on ahead.

Eamonn stopped, bent over in two and laughed.

"There'll be some shit now" James remarked.

"The Yankee fella and his Mrs. will probably think we're all Conartys, it's alright for you and the Bomber". Eamonn laughed hysterically now.

We came up to Miney's crossroads. The boys turned left. We headed for home. It had been a bad day all round. Apples, sex and Yankees. James stood thinking. He laughed. We waited. Sure the photograph would clearly identify Breslin and exonerate the rest of us.

We all felt relieved. Besides the Yankee had already identified the Bomber's accent. We carried on. Not guilty!

If there was one thing us Conartys hated, then that was being blamed in the wrong.

Our spirits lifted even more when we saw Dad and Peter Rooney standing by the grey twenty tractor that had arrived in our absence. Its registration read KID 56. There'd be no holding us back now. We touched the gear stick and flicked some of the switches. There was no handbrake. Peter lit a Woodbine and smiled at us. We liked him. Everyone did. Mam's people, Dad's people, us.

The two of them got into the van.

Dad waved goodbye. We left the tractor alone.

Inside, Mam sat quietly in the corner. Nanna was making tea and Lizzie was talking.

She handed us our Crunchies and we thanked her. Mam smiled.

Nanna slapped the old tea leaves from the pot into her yellow basin.

From the upstairs window I could see the green van slowing down at McGunkers. My stomach turned.

I stood upright. Don't think about it and it'll go away. Flashback.

Jemmy Joes, Mrs. Clerkin, Mary Margaret, her dog, the Yankees...

I emptied all out on the landing floor. Some of it scited up on the wallpaper. The boys yelped their disgust. Looking for a towel, I vowed never to eat another apple the longest day I lived. Mam shouted up at us to have manners.

I went to sleep with a vomitty taste in my mouth. It was a terror.

Chapter 25

Anyway the next morning Fr. Eddie packed his bags and brought them into the kitchen. He wanted to leave early for the smoke as he called it, to continue studying for his master's degree in Belfield. We thought he was going to become a teacher. I overheard him and Mam talking. She was worried about Nanna. She'd been taking more of her turns and Dr. Lorigan had warned them to keep a tight eye on her. Mam wondered how she'd feel if James and I were posted to sleep in the same room as her. At least we'd be there if anything went wrong during the night and could quickly alert her and Dad. Fr. Eddie thought it was a good idea. He twisted his wrist and looked at his watch. He then checked the clock and looked at his watch again. His bus was going at eight. It was now quarter to.

Mam was leaving him in. "Very nice, very good, so that'll be very nice, give me a ring during the week, say Wednesday between 1.15 and 1.30, so that'll be really good". And then they left.

We'd never been out before together on our own at Halloween time. Ever. True, myself and James had gone the year previously with Martin Brady and Martin Lyons when we'd linked up with Brid and Mary Reilly and Sean and had learnt that you had to disguise yourself with a proper false face and sing a proper song before anyone gave you a penny. The dark night made it all the more exciting. We went to the Englishman's house. He was related to Martin Brady. His dog barked when the light came on. He was tall and balding and well to do looking. We sang armoured cars and tanks and guns. He smiled. We liked him. He knew a lot about soccer and had often talked to us at the chapel about the old days. He'd mention players like John Charles and Charlie Tully and Peter Doherty that we'd never heard of. Dad said he was daecent. And so he was. He gave us a fiftypence. We couldn't believe our luck. Normally twenty was the going rate, with maybe an apple or two or a fistful of nuts thrown in for good measure. We headed for the road. The Englishman followed. He enquired if Martin Brady was amongst us. Martin took off his false face. Then he gave him a fiftypence for himself. We looked at each other. Then we walked on. No one said anything. Martin put the fiftypence in his coat pocket. The rest of the cash rattled in the custard tin that Mary Reilly kept cuddled between her black gloves. Still no one said anything. We split the night's takings at Packie's shop and headed up the hill for home.

This year would be different. The five of us togged out heavily to counter the sharp frost that the weatherman and Mam had warned us about. We hit the locals first. Harry was apprehensive. He didn't know the words and he thought there might be thunder. Eddie told him to hum.

"Armoured cars and tanks and guns
Came to take away our sons
But every man will stand behind
The men behind the wire
Through the little streets of Belfast
In the dark of early morn
British soldiers came......"

Annie Miney gave us twenty-five pence. Paul was reading his comics.

Peggy Dearg had the lights off.

Roseanne made us tae.

Michael Conaty

"Did yous get up to any divilment yet?" McGunker wanted to know.

"It's a safe night to go acting the lad because it'll be blemt on the spirits and divils that go wandering the country at this time of year" he informed us. We looked at each other. Harry wanted to go home. Roseanne gave us ten pence each. She had it neatly stockpiled on the shelf beside the wireless.

McGunker poked more fun. Anyway, the stars shone like jewels in the night sky as we made our way around Castletara. The quicker we walked the warmer we'd get, James advised. Then we sweated heavily under warm layers of clothing and welcomed the break between houses to take off our masks. Householders all had the very same reaction to our armoured cars and tanks and guns. They'd look and laugh. Some tried to yank off our identity protection, though not too forcibly, before parting with the cash. We went to the protistent house. James told us to sing "Weelia, weelia, wallia". We did. Harry hummed the air of armoured cars. They didn't notice. We walked down the lane. McGunker had told James they were very daecent people and had done their best to help the Catholic people in penal times and had even hid the priest when the British were looking for him and them sure to hang him from a tree when they'd get their hands on him. Bless us and save us.

"Was Willie Whitelaw there?" Eddie asked. No one answered.

The temperature dropped still further and crusted tractor tracks formed by the side of the road. The younger ones were becoming tired and toes begged for a bit of heat. We headed for home. Dogs barked occasionally. Clouds shrouded the full moon now and again and the ditches became crisp and crunchlike. McGunker's light was still on and we could hear the telly. Mam made us tea and toast. James spilled the silver and copper out on the floor. Four pounds and seventy-six pence. Our feet warmed in no time and then we decided we'd go again, just the three big ones. Eddie and Harry protested.

Nanna had silvermints. They stayed. Whatever we'd make would go back into the pot with the earlier takings, we agreed. The moon shone brightly now and our cheeks turned cold.

Stones, small stones, that we'd usually kick ahead of us, were frozen solid on the brae that glistened before us. Mrs. John enquired for Fr. Eddie. So did Mrs. Lyons. We walked to Cahills and Coyles and Smiths and Tullys. Mrs. Coyle gave us a fistful of coins and the same again of sweets. The dog barked. We headed back towards Shantemon. James lowered his voice as we came up towards Dunnes. We stood on the road.

"If Felim is here, he'll be sure to get us so keep your eyes open," he whispered. Mrs. Dunne had a kindly smile. She insisted we'd come in out of the cold. She pointed to the steaming rhubarb tart on the table. The older men sat smoking. They spoke. We knew Phil and James well. Phil was Felim's father, a blocky man. James was his brother, a bachelor and Felim's uncle. Farming men. Nanna and Mam had always spoken very highly of them saying they were daecent neighbours. Sure hadn't James or Jemmy, as they called him, often helped out at home years back and never minded being called day or night. Nanna depended on him. Him and our Uncle Ned were great friends. I watched him now as he lit his pipe. We took our time with the hot chunks of rhubarb all the time casting our eyes around waiting for Felim to appear. He didn't. Mrs. Dunne talked about the school. I glanced at the photo on the wall. I knew Sean and Teresa and Susan, the older ones and Bernie and PJ. Felim had a smirk on his face. He was the youngest. Phil stoked up the fire and landed a big whitethorn stick in on top of the slack. Mrs. Dunne said we were great gasuns altogether. She enquired for Nanna and then gave James the money. We left. The dog lay on the doormat and we stepped over him. A collie like our Bruno. He barked an idle bark as if he felt he should be doing something and then he lay down again. He whined. We headed out the lane. Their chicken shed doors were wide open. Not a bird in sight. We'd seen Felim cleaning it out a few days before. Big, red, cone shaped drinkers that could be suspended from the roof inside, sat piled against the gable wall. We looked at each other. James lifted the first one. We looked back towards the house. Darkness. Then we lined them like traffic cones all the way back up the brae and over towards Lyons'.

No one appeared. We laughed. "He'll come home and have to clear the road," James said. Up and down we ran carrying two at a time. We laughed again all the while knowing Felim would see the funny side of it. "Sure he'd do it himself", James said. And then we legged it. Down McKiernan's brae, sticking tight to the ditch where our wellies gave us a better grip. We jumped the Royal ditch knowing we were safe and that Prince Philip couldn't see us trespassing. We slowed our pace coming round by the hayshed and swore not to open our mouths. The next morning me and Oliver served Mass.

"Lord wash me away my inikwidty and cleanse me from my sin".

Fr. Dolan bowed his head in acknowledgement and I returned the two glasses to the side table. Mrs. Maguire smiled. Some of the older women were looking at the notice board in the porch. Paint flaked on the damp wall. Oliver was talking about Queens Park Rangers. And then it happened. The biggest and hardest and sorest kick in the arse I'd ever got left me temporarily paralysed to the spot. I looked round. It was Felim. Shock.

"Pass that on ya little blonde fecker and tell the big fella it's only a matter of time". He sniggered and brushed past us.

Oliver looked at me. We walked out. I moved gingerly towards the car. I got thick. I knew we'd been found out, sure it had been too obvious anyway, I lamented in the back of the car. James laughed a nervous laugh. "Pass no remarks of Dunne, sure he'd do the same himself, don't worry we'll get him back next year", he consoled. The pain worsened with every bump. Dad wondered what we were muttering about. We said nothing.

Packie and Kathleen were watching "The Big Match" when we called that evening. "Them ould Liverpool feckers, I can't stand them", Kathleen goaded me. Heighway scored and the snow fell heavily over Anfield. The referee changed the ball for an orange one. It didn't make any difference for Tottenham. Toshack headed another one in just before the full time whistle. Brian Moore said we were well worth the two points. Bobby Moore got booked playing for Fulham.

Kathleen made tae and offered us slices of breac. Out in the shop, an old Anglo Celt lay spread across the counter, to be used as wrapping paper. The Kilnaleck news said that someone's beagle had been hit by a car. It was a fret. "Is Santy coming?" Packie asked as we ended our ceili and headed across the road for home. A bitterly cold, easterly wind cut through us and we hastened our step. Jem Costello had a bundle of hay on his back. His cattle roared their approval. We shouted hello.

Oliver Reilly was there when we got home. He wore his new duffle coat with its rim of hairy fur round the hood just like the eskimoes in our geography book. We headed outside and kicked ball for a while before deciding to go hunting with Bruno. We circled round Fairtown bog encouraging him with an odd "Hss, boy, hsss, hsss Bruno, kill!"

He looked at us bewildered.

Oliver explained how the core meadow worked. Nobody owned it really, at least not all of it. It was divided up with a spade mark here and yonder defining the borders. A bit for Ted, a bit for Mary Margaret, a bit for Gerry Flood and a bit for McGunker. "It's all in the wan," he said. We headed up by McGunkers rocks convincing ourselves we'd surely rise something on the mountain.

Bruno headed off towards McKiernan's brae. We changed our route and followed him. The big, moggy cat clung for dear life at the top of the old pear tree hissing away for all she was worth. Bruno barked like hell. "Hss, Bruno, hss, hss".

I fired the first stone and missed. There then followed the customary bombardment till the poor moggy decided to take a chance and leapt straight down into the bushes and then scurried along the briar-ridden shuck. Bruno couldn't get in. We laughed and fired more stones. But the moggy had made it and leapt to and fro across Brady's field. We stood looking round us. McKiernan's house was no longer lived in. Sure hadn't Petie packed up and gone in search of his fortune in Canada, leaving the farm behind him. The Dunnes had it let.

Anyway the front of the house had a big window either side of the hall door with a dozen neat panes of glass looking invitingly at us. The rules were simple. Nominate a pane of glass, hit it and get ten points. Someone else's pane and they get the bonus points. Bang, bang, bang. Great crack. Now and again we'd cease fire and go to the ditch to gather up more ammunition. I ruffled the dry clay with my welly and then looked up and saw him. I froze to the spot.

Jemmy Dunne sucked on his pipe and looked at me. Not a word was spoken. I turned and legged it down the hill past the boys. "C'mon quick", I panted. "Michael, Michael, take your time, come back, Michael, Michael", the boys roared.

Great, now he had a name and knowing we were Jem Conarty's gasuns was sure to inform him and then there'd be ructions altogether.

That night I twisted and turned and couldn't sleep. Felim Dunne smirked in my dreams. The days passed. Not a word was said. Daecent people the Dunnes. They passed no remarks.

At school we got ready for Confirmation. They were horrid fond of olive oil long, long ago. The Greek athletes rubbed it into their muscles to give them extra strength and each time God picked a new king for Israel, someone came along and poured a dollop of the stuff from a cow's horn in on top of him. The book said it was symbolic. Mrs. Sexton said it was to do with the anointing and talked about the three persons in the one God. God the Father: old man, long white hair and beard, God the son: young man, long brown hair and beard, who died for us all on Calvary, for our sins. Breaking windows and robbing orchards could be included in that. And then there was God the Holy Ghost. Now, he was a bit of a mystery cos none of us could ever visualise him. Nonetheless he would come upon us if we had manners and strengthen us as proper Christians for the long road that lay ahead of us. Then there was the pledge:

"I promise to abstain from alcoholic drink until I reach 18 years of age" it said on the card.

We'd have to pick a new name for ourselves and sign the card and then give it to his Lordship, the Bishop to sign and then he'd know who was going to go on to become an alcaholic and who wasn't.

Bean Uí Fiaich hated the drink. Mrs. Sexton pointed out that there was nothing wrong with it in moderation. Sure didn't our Lord himself have a few at the wedding feast of Cana? He didn't go home stocious drunk though. I thought of Sean Boylan's bar and lounge. Christmas came and went.

We'd never ever seen him cry till that morning, ever. The tears rolled down his cheeks. He stood there. "God, Jimmy I'm horrid sorry for ya, you know that". Nanna looked up into his face. There were tears in her eyes too. "I know that Mrs. Brady, I know, thanks". He rubbed the back of his hand across his cheek. His nose was runny too and he sniffled. We stood there knowing something was wrong and needing to be told.

Granny in Corriga had been found dead in bed. It was sudden, horrid sudden. We didn't know what to say or do. It was a terror. We stood there gawking at him. "How did she die?" Eddie wanted to know. "Is she definitely dead? Sometimes old people are just asleep and you'd swear they were dead, like Nanna in her armchair, but if you cough or make a noise, she jumps and wakes up and asks what's wrong?" Nanna didn't hear him. Dad closed his eyes. Mam sent us upstairs for clean clothes. I looked back. I felt sorry for him, my own father, and couldn't tell him so.

We knew he'd been close to his mother. Sure she'd told us herself above in Corriga. He'd always sent a few bob home from England when he was there with the Kanes and the Cusacks as a young fella. Now she was gone.

We went up to Corriga. All of us and Nanna. The place was eerie and quiet. Mam warned us to have manners. She didn't have to. Neighbours stood on the street smoking fags. The men moved forward and shook hands with Dad. "Sorry for your trouble Jem", they nodded. Mam told us not to be in the way. We shuffled sideways. Uncle Harry was crying. We shook hands with him. Not a word was said. The neighbour women busied themselves making tae and passing round the sangwidches. Kathleen boilt the kettle again. I looked round. All our uncles were there and Baby too. Patsy smiled at us. Jack and Benny and Dad were talking. Uncle Tommy gave us hot sweets. Baby cried.

The men smoked. More people called. The house was full. A cow roared outside. "Sorry for your trouble, sorry for your trouble". It was too bad, too bad. It was a fret. I could detect the faint scent of whiskey. The bigger ones went to the room. I picked up the little bit of palm like everyone else and sprinkled holy water on my Grandmother's forehead. I said a prayer. She lay there, quite still and very white looking. Everything was white. The bedclothes, the tablecloth and the sheets that covered the press. I thought of the soda bread and ginger cakes she used to bake. She had beads wrapped round her blue fingers. "The Lord a mercy on her", an old man whispered. His breath smelled of whiskey and fags. It got dark. Dad said we were going home so as he could come back up for the wake. No one protested. Philomena sucked the last drop of her bottle. On the way out the lane, he stopped the car and rolled down the window. The young man shook hands with him. "Sorry for your trouble Jem". The cow bawled again. Little specks of snow nestled on the young man's overcoat. Dad introduced him to Nanna. He already knew Phyllis. "Hello childer", he looked into the car.

Sure Nanna knew his father well.

She'd known Ned Sheils a lifetime, hadn't she come from beside him at home. Dad drove on. "C'mon, we'll go and see him, it'll only take a few minutes", he said. He turned up the road. Nanna said there was no need and that she didn't want to put him out.

He drove across the same hills that me and Tommy had walked yon summer's day and slowed to show Nanna the shop. He pulled in on the village green and helped her out onto the street. They went towards the bar. She picked her steps in the darkness of that evening and stopped once or twice to lean on her stick. Dad waited. The snowflakes fell heavier now and we became excited. The minutes passed. Then the young woman came out and told Mam to come in for Gawd's sake. "Ah, we better not, we'll stay here, we're grand thanks all the same", Mam insisted. We were bucking. The young woman got her way. We leapt out.

Inside the open fire blazed brightly and it felt more like Christmas than ever before. She poured us our cokes and presented the Tayto.

"What do yous say?" Dad reminded.

"Ah sure they're grand childer, leave them alone", the young woman replied.

Anyway the men at the bar were sorry for Jem's troubles too. Nanna and Ned Sheils sat in the corner. They talked about the old days and who was dead now and who was dying. It was a fret. It bet all.

The door opened. More men came in with snow on their caps and shoulders. They too were sorry for Jem's troubles. The Sweet Afton clock read quarter past nine. The car park was carpeted now. The tracks of the cars in front of us left parallel lines all the way home. Dad took his time and came down through Stradone. Nanna pointed out the doctor's place.

He went back for the wake.

Mam made porridge. Philomena slept on the sofa with a moustache of coke over her lip. Peter and Mrs. Rooney came in. They sat up to the fire and James took their coats. They said it was too bad.

"Poor Jem, it'll go hard on him". Peter shook his head. Mrs. Rooney clasped her hands.

We went upstairs to bed. No one wanted to act the bollix now, not on a night like this. We lay awake for a while whispering about all that had happened. Poor Granny. I felt sorry for her. My belly ached. She'd gone to sleep and hadn't woken up. Kathleen had found her. It was sudden alright.

I turned over. Though she was old, she was still our Dad's Mam. It must be hurting him badly.

"Will our Mam die some day too?" Harry wanted to know.

No one answered.

The kitchen door into the hall opened. It was Mam. "Whisht childer now and go to sleep, say a prayer for poor Granny, them's the good boys".

There was silence.

Then James said we wouldn't play football or watch the telly for a few days outta repect for Granny Conarty.

There was more silence.

The adults talked down in the kitchen.

"What comes after 249,999?"

"I'll tell ya tomorrow Harry, go to sleep", James urged. We all did.

Chapter 26

Anyway Spring came and Nanna was having more of her turns. Dr. Lorigan kept calling. We knew to stay quiet. She had to take capsule tablets, one half red and the other half grey. We found one of them on the floor once and opened it up. There was powdery stuff inside.

We knew to stay quiet especially when she wasn't well. We didn't have to be told. She liked to hear the news when we'd come in from school, what we'd done, who we'd met on the way home and what we'd learnt. She'd talk about De Valera and Dan Breen and Sean McKeown, dressed as a priest. She'd doze off now and again in her armchair and then suddenly wake up with a jolt, all the while pretending she was in control and hadn't been asleep at all at all. Then she'd rub her eyes beneath the spectacled frames and sometimes you'd see a tear or two. Was it moisture or had she been crying? I could never be sure. Once I'd heard the adults say that when you're old and getting closer to dying you begin to look back at your life and maybe have regrets and begin to feel lonely for those you knew and that are now gone before you. I couldn't help but pity her now if this was the case.

Then she picked up again and started going outside to her hens and even got a dozen day old chicks from Elmbank Hatchery. Tony and Anna Mae called. Derek and Lorna were with them. "Dathlones are here", Harry shouted. Anna Mae had clothes and biscuits and sweets and Tony gave Nanna a half bottle of Powers whiskey. We looked at each other.

Derek wanted to play football. We insisted on showing them the calves we'd bought very cheaply in Cavan Mart because the EEC had fecked the country up and now there was nothing. "Imagine the poor ould farmers queuing up begging for help and for someone to give them something, anything, for their calves", Tony said. The people couldn't get over it. It was a terror. We bought a Friesian heifer calf for fifty pence and called her Licker. Dad made up a pen in the byre and there Licker lay with the rest of them drinking milk replacer twice a day and picking at bits of hay. McGunker told us that Andy Hatter had once told him that if you lifted a calf once a day, every day, then you'd be able to lift her when she was a fully-grown cow. Lorna was disgusted. She said the smell was foul and vulgar and couldn't believe she was actually related to us. We laughed. She walked off smiling. We knew she didn't hate us really and we quite liked her cos she was one of Dathlones. We played ball for a while before they left for Ballyhaze. Mam said they shouldn't go to the wedding that coming weekend. To get someone in to mind the childer might only vex Nanna she felt. "She likes her independence and I daren't tell her we're afraid to leave her here on her own with them, she'd be insulted", Mam said. Dad listened.

Anyway they did go to the wedding and left us with Nanna but only after warning us not to act the brat and to go along with whatever she said and to do the jobs and mind the wee ones and they'd be home as early as they could. Mam wore Anna Mae's blue frock.

Nanna boilt eggs after the Angeleus. She said they'd keep us going till evening and then she'd make us a feed of colcannon. Eddie wondered about chips. Nanna looked at him sternly.

The younger ones didn't like their eggs and nibbled at the sliced brown bread instead. None of us sniggered. Suddenly Nanna whipped

Philomena's eggcup off the table and proceeded to empty its contents into a mug and mix it together with a dollop of butter.

"Trotten, when I was your age I'd ate it", she snapped before pushing the mug right over in front of her. Philomena sobbed quietly. I held her hand under the table.

The rest of us kept eating.

The rooster crowed outside reminding Nanna to feed the young chicks that ran around out in the barn. I went with her. They scurried about nibbling at the pellets she placed on the newspaper sheets on the floor. She got me to top up the saucers with water. The chicks were flighty. A strong burst of sunlight came through the little window and we left them. Anyway we lazed around for a while and made sure not to rise any ructions. Harry's pencil nib broke and to keep him quiet, James pared a fresh one.

Later on Lizzie and Fidelma arrived. The car drove off. I felt uneasy. We were kicking a ball against the inside garage wall. Lizzie told us to stop it. We ate our crunchies and only scattered when Fidelma came out with a basket of clothes for the line in the hayshed. The calves bawled in the byre. Tommy imitated them. She told us to have manners and not to be upsetting Granny or she'd deal with us.

"Her name's Nanna", I shouted, "no one calls her Granny".

She dropped the basket and reminded us that we were only ould-fashioned whelps and that it was a disgrace for our mother and father not to be raring us properly and not putting manners on us. We laughed.

The sight of McGunker down in the meadow lifted our spirits. "How's all the McGunker Conartys?" We ran to him. He'd come over to check on the cattle.

"Who's that lassie in the hayshed?" he asked. We told him.

We asked him in for tae. He declined. He walked round the stock and said they were doing the best.

"Is that bullock a bulling?" Eddie asked with some concern.

"No, gasun, no, he's not", McGunker replied, laughing. He unfolded his arms and stuck his hand into his pocket. We watched as he opened a fresh pack of twenty red Carrolls.

"Is Mrs. Brady alright?" he enquired.

James assured him that Nanna was the best. He pulled on his fag. Turning to leave he told us not to bother saying he was over. He declined Harry's offer of a game of soccer by saying he was busy and that he had to go and see a man about a dog. "Good luck gasuns; mind yourselves". He walked away laughing quietly.

We ate the colcannon after they'd gone. None of us touched the tractor. Philomena sucked her thumb and pined for Mam.

The boys were playing ball at the back of the hayshed when I went up to Ned's room.

It was the first room at the top of the stairs, a long narrow room with wooden floorboards and a ceiling that stretched back out to the far wall of the house.

It had always been known as Ned's room, Fr. Eddie had told us, because of Ned Smith from Crosserlough who'd come to help work the land for Nanna when Mick Brady had died.

Above it in the loft lived the McBreegans, an imaginary clan who couldn't sleep at night time if childer below them were acting the brat and making noise. Or so Uncle Ned had said.

I flicked on the light switch.

Ned's room was full of bits and pieces not being used anymore and still deemed too good to be thrown out.

I saw a bar stool and thought it must've come from Dad's old pub in Bridge St. or maybe Sean Boylans or maybe even Dathlones had given it to Nanna. Old curtains with rusty hooks lay piled in the corner and someone had neatly folded a pair of blankets and left them sitting against the hot pipe that ran down from the attic.

A long, white gown belonging to Fr. Eddie stretched from a coat hanger and the white rope, with the frickly ends, that the priest tightened before Mass time, lay draped over it.

The trunk fascinated me. Brown and rectangular in shape, it had a curved lid that fell down onto a black latch on its side. I shouldn't have opened it. I did. Elizabeth McEvoy's name was written on the inside panel. There before me lay the oddest collection of practically everything and anything you could imagine. A tin box with an assortment of buttons; big buttons, small buttons, black ones, green ones, red ones and a darning needle stuck in a small cushion. There was a gold chalice like the one Fr. Dolan used at Castletara Mass. Then there were the white tablecloths still wrapped in plastic coating sitting on top of an old and damp smelling patchwork quilt. And the small red clock.

It no longer worked despite my shaking it. There were three candles, long white ones and one had been cracked in its middle showing the white chord that ran through its wax. A sprig of holly, whose berries had long since dried up and crinkled, lay on top of the black and white photos of serious looking and holy men.

Probably Fr. John or maybe even the Bishop who'd gone to Perth in Australia, I thought to myself.

Then there were the books. An array of books of all shapes and sizes. Big books, small books, fat ones, thin ones. Books in hard-backed covers about Greek and Roman mythology and a book about Red Indian herbal cures and a big fat one on Irish myths and legends and folklore. I picked it out and opened it up.

It had Edward Brady's name neatly printed in ink on its inside cover. I flicked through it and came to the page about the pooka. It said he was a November spirit and that he came in many shapes; sometimes a horse or an ass or a bull or even a goat. I flicked over a few pages and came to the story about the man whose herd of cows had been bewitched and were barely able to move about the fields and some, instead of milk, were now giving blood. The poor man was distraught. No one could figure it out or help him. It bet all.

Anyway an ould hag arrived one day and told him it was the work of the fairies and that for a silver sixpence she'd get them milking for him again. The first thing he had to do was nail horseshoes to the outhouse door to ward off the fairies.

Things got no better, however, and didn't your man and the hag sit up one night out in the fields to keep watch over the cows. And then it happened. His neighbour, a young farming woman herself, came gliding across the field in the moonlight, in a long flowing flowery dress, muttering all kinds of incantations to herself. She knelt down beside one of the cows and took on the form of a hare and sucked the cow dry and then moved on to the next one.

A cold shudder ran all the way down me spine and I shut the book quickly and pegged it back into the trunk. Bad cess to it.

The ball banged against the galvanise outside. Bruno barked. I turned to go, dizzy now, but cast my eyes back on the big pile of books again. I picked another one out, a book about Minoan and Mycenaen art. I couldn't pronounce the words. It was written by a fella called Higgins but had far too many big words for my liking. It had colour photos of gold chalices and the like.

"Show off", I muttered to myself and then pegged it back in. The Great Hunger was an ojous big book written by Cecil somebody and it told the story of the poor Irish people and how they had no spuds and how a million of them died in the fields from starvation and tonnes more had gone to live in America, where there was plenty of work and dollars and spuds too no doubt.

In the centre were black and white pictures mostly portraits of English people. I looked at him, Sir Robert Peel, "the English Prime Minister" it said. It got me vexed. The cheek of them English hoors. Imagine with not a single spud in the country to be ate at the time and their Prime Minister is a lad called Peel!

They probably did it for badness I thought to myself, just to rub it in for the Oirish.

"Yous have a famine and yous have no spuds and your country is run by a fella called Peel", I could hear them laughing. I couldn't get over it.

McGunker and Dad were right.

Rule Britannia my arse, there's not a country in the world but they hadn't landed in and treated the people like shite and them supposed to be gentlemen themselves speaking proper English all the time.

And meanwhile the other poor oul divils had only sticks and stones to fight back with and with no spuds in their bellies most likely, hadn't even the energy to do that much pegging at all.

Anyway I flicked the pages over and there she was, Queen Victoria herself and some eegit called Raleigh, throwing his coat over an oirish puddle so as she wouldn't get her feet wet. Me mind buzzed with the thickness. She had an umbrella over her head and a gathering of poorly dressed Irish childer cheered in the background, probably hoping that she had a bag of spuds apiece for them.

I doubted it and on the next page I was proved right. There she was again, arm in arm this time, with some big fella with a moustache and them strolling through her dining room in Dublin Castle, with big chandelier yokes hanging overhead from the ceiling and rows of rich looking people, standing with their hands behind their backs and them bowing their heads as she passed. The long drapelike curtains were pulled so as she wouldn't have to look outside at the poor Irish childer gawking in at her and them wondering would they get any spuds.

She'd probably consider them oul-fashioned whelps and ill-reared pups, I thought to myself. I turned the page......

"Mightil, Mightil, Mightil", I heard Nanna call. I'd noticed before that when something was wrong and if Dad was calling me from a distance, my name sounded more Mightil than Michael. It was this way now.

"Mightil, Mightil, where are ya gasun?"

I dropped Queen Victoria and turned towards the door. It wouldn't open. The harder I pulled, the more I shunted, the tighter it got. I knew it had been snibbed on the outside. I pulled and twisted and rattled the knob for all I was worth. My heart pumped in desperation. I sweated.

"Mightil, Mightil, oh Gawd, where is he at all?"

I turned to the wee window over the scullery roof and saw her standing there by the hayshed. She leaned on her stick. I rapped the window with my knuckles like I'd often seen Mam do.

I rapped again and again harder and louder each time. Still she couldn't see or hear me. Thoughts raced through my head. Total panic. I was helpless. She'll have a heart attack if I don't answer soon and what'll happen then?

I grabbed hold of the doorknob and pulled with all my might, determined to bust all before me if need be. The snib couldn't take any more pressure now and it cracked off the doorpost. The little screw dropped to the ground. I legged it downstairs and out to where Nanna stood. "Michael, are you alright son, I could see the rest of them and couldn't see you and thought you were down with the cattle and that something had happened to……"

She paused to catch breath and leaned gingerly on her stick.

"…and I wasn't sure what to do……"

I put my arm on her shoulder and edged her back towards the house. She was alright now she promised. I made her tea and asked her would she have a tablet. She said she was fine but that she'd had a fright.

The boys knew nothing about the snib and looked at each other. I thought back to your wan in the book transforming herself into a hare and wondered had she been involved? They came home and Dad said we were all great gasuns as we hopped into bed, having said the prayers. He rushed off saying him and Peter Rooney had to go for a cure and that if we were good he'd arrange for Philip, Peter's youngest son, to call by the next day. We liked Philip. He was a few years older than James, ahead of him at the Teck. Philip supported Leeds United. He liked Giles and Lorimer and Mick Jones too. He'd told us so.

Dad said he was like the rest of the Rooneys, an intelligent buck and as daecent as the day was long. We were tired now and each turned his own way to sleep. I thought back to the panic I'd caused earlier that evening and asked God to keep an eye on Nanna and to make sure nothing bad would happen.

"Sacred Heart of Jesus, I trust in dee, Sacred Heart of Jesus, I trust in dee, Sacred Heart of Jesus I trust in dee".

Chapter 27

Anyway the weather got better and the days became even longer and Kevin was still scoring goals and we were the big ones in sixth class. Dad told us that if we were up early enough on Easter Sunday morning and looked into the sky, we'd see the sun dancing across it. It was God's way of showing the world that he could triumph over evil. The sun would hop about in celebration.

"What comes after 299,999?"

We looked at each other.

Mam took Nanna to the Doctor's surgery and we helped Dad to carry the big black double bed down the stairs and into her room. He tightened the rusty bolts with an even rustier pair of vice grips. We had to hurry. The bed faced down to the door leading into the kitchen. Later on Mam fixed on the bed sheets and blankets and then spread the big eider-down quilt that Dot Kelly had once patchworked for her.

It felt strange the first few nights lying awake and wanting to sleep and yet knowing Nanna wanted to talk. Now and again I'd ask James something about the teck.

"What's that you're saying?" she'd enquire, no doubt fearful of falling asleep and missing something.

We'd be up before her in the mornings and I'd steal over quietly beside her to make sure she was still breathing. Even the younger ones now knew to stay quiet and let Nanna have her sleep. Later Mam would bring her the tea and toast and tablets on the tray that had come from Athlone.

West Ham were having a great run in the cup and James was in his element. Their young striker, Alan Taylor, had kept them on course for Wembley, it said in the paper. In a way I was glad for James. Apart from one of the Lynchs, I didn't know another soul that supported the Hammers, as they were nicknamed. They were stylish and unfashionable all in the one go and rarely won anything. This could be their year, I felt.

As for Liverpool, I worried about Kevin and the rest of the team.

Bill Shankly had surprised everyone by retiring and the new manager Bob Paisley, no relation of Ian's, didn't seem to have the same approach. Besides he'd brought in new players like Phil Neal and Joey Jones and I wasn't sure we were going to be as good anymore. Bill Shankly signed Ray Kennedy from Arsenal before he left and now this Paisley fella had bought Terry McDermott from Newcastle and "was introducing" it said in the paper, "local talent like David Fairclough and Jimmy Case". PJ Lynch told me not to worry. Sure hadn't Paisley been there for years at Anfield and hadn't he and Shankly and Evans and Moran met for tae in the boot-room every morning and discussed football for hours. PJ had read this in a book somewhere and was sure that Paisley could be as good, if not better, than Shankly. I wasn't convinced. He smiled.

Besides PJ was an Arsenal man and was probably only trying to make me feel good because deep down he knew we were finished now and that Arsenal, with all the young Irish boys, like Chippy Brady and Stapleton and O'Leary coming through, were going to rule the roost for years to come.

Then Kevin Keegan said in his shoot column that the boys had every confidence in the new boss.

I felt cheated now.

Why hadn't Bill Shankly written back to me?

Was there any point in writing to Bob Paisley?

Remembering the pact I'd made with God over Philomena, I decided to put things on the long finger. The days became warmer and longer and every Saturday we'd get the tractor going and we'd dig and clean more muck off the back street. The sods rolled back like the pieces of carpet Anna Mae had sent from Athlone revealing a surface of stone beneath and often, after a shower of rain, I'd stand and look at it and vow never to let the muck or grass take over again. Though we were stripping away the passing of time we nonetheless found the work backbreaking and monotonous and only felt relief each time we'd filled another box-load of the stuff and were sure of a rest while it was being taken away to be emptied.

We knew Nanna wasn't well.

Anyway Dathlones called a few times and Lizzie too. Fr. Eddie studied away in the University. He'd come down from Dublin at the weekends and go back up on a Sunday evening. I found this up and down business to Dublin very confusing. Looking at the big map of Ireland on the school wall, it seemed more sensible to say that we travelled down to Dublin from Cavan and vice versa on the return journey. No one passed any remarks when I asked. It was the same with the North. The old people talked of going down the North and wasn't it a holy terror the way there was so much trouble down there. Then I asked Fr. Eddie about it. He said that when in Rome we should do as the Romans do and laughed. I was no further on.

There was so much change now.

We set the spuds below in the meadow alongside the bull's field ditch.

Eddie Fitzsummons had ploughed it for us and Dad borrowed a spud-dropper from big Tom McCaffrey. He and McGunker sat either side of it and dropped the spuds at three-second intervals. Now and then they'd stop and have a smoke.

When all was done and covered over and with the rich smell of clay on our hands and clothes, we headed up to the house for tae and bread and boiled eggs. Charlie Coyle came out to see for himself. The men talked about grubbing them later on and the importance of spraying against the blight. McGunker had barrels and a sprayer for the job. Bruno barked when we came out.

Dad cut posts from branches of the sally tree below in the corner and drove them into the ground with a crowbar and then nailed on three row of thorny wire.

Fr. Eddie said it looked like Colditz prison. That night we watched Steptoe on the telly.

Anyway Confirmation evening came and me and Mam went to Kill Chapel over beyond Drung. Us Castletara ones stayed together feeling a bit dwarfed by the bigger crowds from other schools. The Bishop was nice. He didn't give anyone a slap on the jaw like McGunker had predicted he would.

Mam wore a brown dress with a white collar. I felt a bit awkward in my blue blazer and brown trousers. Mam said to pass no remarks. We came home. Some of the others went to the White Horse Hotel in Cootehill. Nanna gave me two pound notes and told me not to drink till I was eighteen or more. I promised her I wouldn't. She shook my hand. I hopped the stairs two steps at a time and hung up my good clothes in Anna Mae's old wardrobe. I pulled on my old clothes and suddenly felt more secure and comfortable, glad it was all over, with no disrespect to the Bishop or the priests or the Holy Spirit or even God Almighty himself. Harry wanted to know did it hurt getting Confirmation. I sensed his anxiety. It was the same with the entrance exam to the Tech. I worried before, during and especially after it. Myself and Oliver and Sean and Andy queued up with piles of other boys and girls from national schools from all over Cavan and sat down in the canteen and opened our booklets on page one. The young lady walked round and talked and then told us to start. I found the questions straightforward enough but sweated nonetheless, thinking they were all trick ones and worried that some of the teachers that walked around between the tables, might think I was copying from the lad beside me if I dared lift my head to think for a moment. The young male teacher wore a brown jacket with leather patches on the elbows. I felt he was looking at me and thinking to himself, well there's the young Conarty buck that won't be going to St. Pat's now and won't be a priest like all the generations before him and isn't it an awful slab in the gob for Bean Uí Fiaich altogether and all the ould women that lit candles for him out there in Castletara chapel, the ungrateful whelp.

I left in a hurry and met Mam on the road. She too felt uncomfortable in our big yellow Austin 1800 motor car RID 550. She couldn't get used to the gear changes or the big bonnet that stretched out before her.

We came home and had tae and duck's tail cake as Dad called it. Mam had bought it in McDonnell's in Main St., the shop with a grocery and drapers and pub all under the one roof.

I sat down with Nanna. Her hands were warm. She smiled. Her rosary beads glittered like jewels in the half-dark of the room. "Sure won't it be grand, yourself and James together, like it should be, and sure pass no remarks Michael of what anyone says or thinks, even the likes of me. Do your best son". She closed her eyes again. "God knows I spent me whole life worrying about people around me and why did I bother?" I let go off her hand and placed it on the bedspread and slipped outside.

Bruno came with me. Harry called.

We walked through the fields till we came to the old house that stood on the hill beside Shantemon Lake. McGunker had told us about him, the RIC polisman, the Pealer who'd once lived there. "A rough man, with a shotgun, not to be trusted like all the polismen, even the bucks going today in their shiny blue uniforms", he'd said.

The green door hung perilously on one hinge now and cattle had tramped their dung into what was once someone's kitchen floor.

A couple of slates had slid their way down directly onto the doorstep and the rusted down pipe had broken away from the wall and lay among the nettles and briars. We came round by the lake and stopped for a while to spy on the swans that sailed so gracefully near the shore. Bruno barked.

On the road home we met RadioactiveKate. She began asking questions. Harry told her where we'd been. He had a habit of doing that, blabbing all out and this bugged me especially when I eyeballed him with a look that said shut the blazes up will ya and he couldn't pick up on it. She looked at me inquisitively "and you're not going to St. Pat's I hear and sure you surely won't be a priest now Michael will ya?"

I didn't answer.

"God it's a holy terror, God bless us what'll the Whitefathers think and poor Mrs. Brady and them all, it's an ojous blow". She paused and kept looking at me.

"Sure, like meself, I'm sure they all thought you'd be a priest; well you can't now, not if you're going to the Tech!"

She smiled a false grin. I got thick and turned to go. I stopped.

"Nanna says not to give a shite what people say or think and Daddy and McGunker say you're only a nosey oul hoor and a shit stirrer at the best of times and. ...and....and...." I couldn't think straight anymore. The look of horror etched on her face told me it was time to go.

"C'mon Harry", we strode off. Down the lane I began to feel bad. I knew I shouldn't have said what I'd said. It didn't seem right. Guilt set in. Talk about showing respect to your elders, huh!

Harry lagged behind. He didn't say anything. I roared at him to come on. I was thick with myself now or was I? Was I not just thick with the situation? Then I justified it. The cheek of her. No point in her looking at me horrified now. If she can't take it, then she shouldn't give it, I thought. I never butted into her business.

Harry wondered why I was talking to myself. I smiled and we

walked on. I thought to myself again. Imagine me asking her why she'd never married? It'd be a fret. She'd probably head straight to Peggy Dearg now and tell her she was right. That we're all ould-fashioned whelps for sure, that I'm only a pup, attacking her with such a mouthful. For the first time in my life, I didn't give a damn. In fact I didn't give a shite. I kicked a stone on ahead of me down the pass. Harry sauntered along. We met Annie Reilly coming from the shop with fags in one hand and a pound of Killashandra butter in the other. We liked Annie. Harry told her about the swans on the lake. She smiled and handing us a wine gum each told us to give her regards to Mrs. Brady.

Later Mam told us that when Mick Brady, her Dad, had died, that Annie and her sisters Maggie and Mollie had been fierce good to Nanna altogether. They'd even taken the childer for a walk down the fields the very evening he was dying. They were horrid good people.

"That was way back in 1936", she frowned.

"Mammy, Mammy, Michael gave out to…" Harry suddenly blurted, but distracted by the tap on the hall door, Phyllis didn't hear him and a dirty look and clenched fist ensured he wouldn't be reminding her.

It was Fr. Dolan. He sat at the kitchen table and crossed his legs. His black shoes were immaculately polished and he hadn't a hair on his head out of place. He broke a Marietta biscuit in two, the way he'd break the big round wafer on the altar, and proceeded to dip it into his tea. We stood gawking.

"These boys are getting horrid tall", he commented "and what age is the wee lassie now?" Mam was looking for a candle and didn't hear him. Eddie informed Fr. Con that Philomena was six since the previous October and would be seven before the following Halloween.

We asked him what he thought of West Ham winning the cup. He smiled.

McGunker

Later on he went up to Nanna's room and said prayers and then he went.

"He's horrid down to earth and doesn't pass a bit of remarks on anything", Mam told Dad. He was reading the Evening Press. That night they showed the highlights of United's promotional season from Division Two. They had Gordon Hill and Stevie Coppell and a big, burly striker named Pearson. I hated them. I could hear Martin Breslin and his "glory, glory, Man United". After all, they'd only won the second division championship under Tommy Docherty, no big deal I thought. There were far better teams in the first division, not just Liverpool, but Queen's Park Rangers too.

They weren't getting the same adulation as United. "Glory hunters", James called them.

"Most of the big ones in the tech support United because of Georgie Best from Belfast", he'd said. If only Best hadn't played for United.

"Is he a Catholic or an IRA man?" Harry enquired.

No one answered.

I lifted the old hard-backed English book from its place on the shelf and headed to bed. Nanna said the prayers. The kitchen light shone sufficiently for me to be able to read.

Merlyn Rees was on the telly giving out about the IRA. John Hume said he wanted unconditional peace for all sides.

The young boy's real name was actually Philip, but since he couldn't pronounce it, everyone simply called him Pip. Anyway both his parents were dead and he found himself wandering through a graveyard reading the names of dead infant children. Suddenly he was grabbed by a rough-looking man who threatened to kill him by cutting his throat. I closed the page and dropped the book onto the floor.

James had a cutting of Alan Taylor wearing a cap and holding aloft the F.A. Cup. He'd cut it from our Shoot magazine. "It's a horrid pity Bobby Moore joined Fulham", he whispered.

I grunted. "Do ya know Kevin Keegan calls himself yours truly nowadays, the little bollix?" he continued.

I pretended to be asleep.

"At least Bobby Moore lifted the World Cup, more than Keegan will ever do".

My eyes were heavy now and John Hume's and my brother's voices became more distant.

Chapter 28

Anyway it was much later during that very night when Nanna called and James heard her. He shook me. I didn't know whether I was awake or asleep. My mind said come on get up quick but my body proved more negative. By the time I got out on the cold linoed floor Mam and Dad had both arrived. I knew by their voices it was serious. They muttered silently. Mam held Nanna's hand. I followed Dad as he opened the back door and disappeared into the darkness to go for the doctor. Mam told us to head upstairs to bed and assured me everything would be alright. My head was heavy now and begged for the comfort of a soft pillow. My cold legs too wanted shelter and warmth. I promised myself I wouldn't sleep. I'd just lie there and stay warm and listen. James said nothing.

Nanna was having one of her turns. I knew he wouldn't sleep till all was well again and I shouldn't either.

It was bright outside when Dad pulled the blankets back and the look on his face told me what I didn't want to know. His lips didn't move. He left the room. James was long up. Anger beset me. Anger from within. Anger with myself. I dressed.

I felt like one of the boys in the garden the night before Jesus died. They too had been more interested in their comforts and I'd hated them for it. Now I felt guilty. Downstairs was quiet, eerily quiet. I looked at Mam. No words were spoken. Fr. Con arrived. The room door stayed shut. He shook hands with James. He looked at me then and stretched out his hand.

"Be good for your mother now lads and help out", he said. He went up to Nanna's room. The younger ones snored upstairs.

I wandered round in a daze. Someone had pulled the curtains. The kettle sang its usual tune. Mam and the priest whispered.

She'd felt for a good while it would happen sooner or later. Luckily the boys had heard her.

Dad got Dr. Hayes out. He'd given Nanna an injection to help her breathe more easily. He'd been looking at the tablets when Mam turned. Nanna's eyes had rolled back.

"Oh my God, she's dying", the doctor had said.

Mam looked at me. The whispering stopped. She bent her head and cried. Fr. Con held her hand. His compassionate look said there, there Phyllis don't be hard on yourself, there was nothing more you could do. He let go her hand slowly. Benny Hannigan the undertaker arrived. There was more whispering. Dad came in. "Sorry for your trouble, Jem". They talked. There were things to be organised. Phone calls to be made from the shop. Food to be ordered in. White sheets to be found. Fr. Con would ring Uncle Eddie above in Dublin. Then the neighbours arrived. Someone brought flowers. The clean up began. Annie Miney swept floors. Kathleen in the shop came in with groceries. Kathleen Clarke had two pounds of Lyons tea.

The younger ones came down. They sensed the silence, the eerie silence and aimless walking around and shuffling of feet that told them something was wrong. This only comes with death.

"Has Nanna didied?" Harry asked.

"Why did she didied?" No one answered.

Kathleen in the shop ruffled his blond hair. Philomena followed Mam and tugged on her dress. Annie Reilly came in like she did way back in 1936. The women hugged. Annie had sweets and took the younger ones outside. Bruno barked. The clean up continued. More flowers arrived. Orange ones, St. Anthony's lilies or were they St. Joseph's? Nanna liked them.

No one wanted to play football now. Mam and Dad whispered, beneath the stairs. More tea and toast. Lizzie arrived. There was uncontrollable sobbing. The women hugged again. The men lit fags. I left and ran up through the orchard and lay against the tree me and James had carved our names on once. My stomach rumbled and tears welled up in my eyes. Thoughts raced at a hundred miles an hour. Why had I slept? Why hadn't I held her hand? Why hadn't I said are you alright Nanna? Or I love you Nanna or even Goodbye Nanna? This was all my fault. She'd have been there for me. I pictured her apron and brown walking stick and round glasses and the wee bit of cabbage that sometimes got caught in her teeth and only became visible when she smiled. It was all my fault.

The rooster crowed, but only once and not three times. I felt some relief. More cars drove up and parked sideways in the garden. Doors opened and clapped shut again.

"Sorry for your trouble Phyllis".

"Too bad Jem, too bad, not unexpected, but too bad".

People sat with cups of tea and took sandwiches when offered or muttered "Ah sure I'm alright, ya needn't bother with the likes of me, sure haven't youse enough to be looking after". Then they ate the sandwiches. Ham sandwiches, egg sandwiches, cheese sandwiches. The women stood in the scullery waiting for kettles to boil. They chatted in low tones.

We went outside. The men moved Nanna upstairs to Fr. Eddie's room with its two windows, one looking out on our rocks and the other on Packie's Mass rock. Everything seemed brighter and whiter and cleaner now. There were chairs lined up around the room. Someone had put wallflowers in Anna Mae's china vase.

"Dow O Lord ill open our lips".

People rattled their rosary beads and looked at the floor. My throat swelled. I wanted to cry and couldn't. The Holy Mary echoed downstairs.

"To dee do we cry poor banished childer of eve, to dee do we send up our sighs, in this valley of tears".

Someone's morris minor was spinning in the grass outside. We could hear Eddie Fitzsummons.

"Houl on, houl on, don't rev her so much".

Nanna lay there quietly. I looked at her soft wrinkled face and wanted her eyelids to flicker and prove everyone wrong. I thought of the silvermints and the black polished shoes and the handbag with the silver clasp and the hens and Cissie Thunder and the Black and Tans and her brother falling on the road beside Crosserlough school and Charles Mitchell on the radio reading the news. Nanna didn't move. People dipped the green palm into the bowl of holy water and sprinkled it on her forehead. Some just used their fingers and traced the cross. Poor Nanna. I looked at my brothers. I looked at Philomena. No one spoke. Everyone hurt. Blank faces, white faces, watery looking eyes.

"May her soul and all the souls of the faithful departed, through the mercy of God, rest in peace, Amen".

Dathlones arrived. Derek showed us his book about Wolverhampton Wanderers. Anna Mae cried. She hugged us all. Tony ruffled everyone's hair. They'd brought sweets and Tayto crisps and bottles of whiskey and cooked hams and biscuits. Eamonn and Deckie and Adie wore suits and looked very grown up. Adie tanted us about Man United. More people came in. They shook hands. Car doors clapped outside. More prayers were said and more tae was wet and more sandwiches ate. Then there was more silence.

That evening Fr. Eddie came down from Dublin on the bus. Dad collected him. The people stood up and shook his hand. Roseanne held him by the arm. He looked thinner now and tired and hurt. He didn't cry. "Priests can't cry, they're not allowed to", Tommy whispered to Eddie. Harry showed him his big book with numbers in it. "Very nice, very good Harry". More people called. They all talked in clusters. Other priests called. White Fathers from Longford and student White Fathers from Blacklion. One of them had a pile of dandruff on his collar and Philomena wanted to tell him he had white stuff everywhere. Mrs. Boylan was very upset. She leaned on her stick just like Nanna used to. Mam talked to her in the parlour. Tears rolled down her cheeks. She stumbled forward as she left and balanced her shoulder against the wall. Her son, Tom linked her. She stopped at the foot of the stairs and unable to conquer them, lifted her hand and said "Goodbye Lizzie, goodbye". Mam and Tom walked her to the brown escort car. It took her a while to get in. She squeezed a hankie in her hand and looked back. We went to the shop, me and James and our three biggest cousins. Aiden Rehill didn't want to come.

Adie chatted. He was coming up for the "At home week", the annual carnival in Ballyhaze at the end of the summer. We told him we might be getting medals for the underage football if we could bate Redhills. Eamonn laughed.

Anyway on the way back up the pass a car stopped and Eddie Rehill hopped out and joined us. We liked Eddie. He was a horrid nice gasun with no airs nor graces Dad had always said.

Cars came and cars went the whole evening. Deckie handed out the blackjacks. Lorna refused. Our Tommy grabbed it. Then Eddie rattled the toilet door and a posh-looking woman came out and said "take your time, ya whelp ya, trotten when I was your age we'd have to go outside and do it behind the ditch". Anyway they got ready for the wake and we were sent to bed. Mam closed the door. She didn't tell us to stay quiet. She didn't have to. I pitied her now. This was her Mam, the mother who'd reared them all when their daddy had died. James said it was the eleventh of June and we should all say a Hail Mary for Nanna's soul. People's voices chorused downstairs. The next evening the hearse came. Benny Hannigan had bouquets of flowers. There were so many faces from so many places. Dad's ones from Crosskeys, the posh-looking and Yankee-sounding women from Athlone, more White Fathers, people from Crosserlough, Mam's relations, Barnaby Jones and his mother, piles of neighbours, Dr. Lorigan and a couple of nuns. People sobbed. A cow bawled on Packie's rocks. The new gravel that we'd put down only the week before crunched on the path. The hearse moved away. McGunker told Dad he'd keep an eye on things and that Roseanne and the other women would straighten everything up inside. Dad squeezed his arm. Lorna Hughes had flowers. Annalene wanted them too. Johnny McCormack rang the chapel bell like he always did and they carried Nanna's coffin, with Elizabeth Brady written on the gold plate, inside.

More people lined up and then shook hands and said they were sorry for the troubles. The two TDs wore long blue overcoats and clasped their hands. There was an ojous pile of priests. I prayed for Nanna and thought back to the day when she'd been calling out my name and me locked above in Ned's room. I wondered had she gone to heaven yet or did that happen after the funeral Mass. Outside the men smoked fags and Jemmy the chin went into McCormack's house. I looked back and saw the pile of clay neatly stacked beneath the big Celtic cross that told everyone in both Irish and English that John Brady had been the very first Bishop of Perth in Australia.

Jerry Melligan was fixing a puncture.

Anyway the very next morning Fr. Eddie said Nanna's Mass. He referred to her as Ma throughout. Fr. Comey was there and Fr. Con too and a pile of other priests. One of the TDs came back. The priest shook the smokey yoke and everyone stood up. The men carried Nanna's coffin, Daddy and Tony Hughes and Sean Rehill and Anthony Gorman. We all walked behind. Packie Brady took off his cap and so did Gerry Flood. I looked up at the coffin and pity filled me once more. Then terror. A fear gripped me. Supposing poor Nanna wasn't dead at all? Supposing she was alive inside and had just woken up from one of her big sleeps? What if she was tapping on the lid and trying to get out and couldn't be heard now because of Johnny McCormack ringing the bell and the people crunching on the gravel that covered the path leading up to her grave. I daren't open my mouth though. There'd be an ojous scene and I'd be dismissed as an ould-fashioned whelp with no respect for either the living or the dead. Besides deep down I knew Nanna was gone. I knew she was dead and wouldn't be coming back. There was no point in fooling myself. Tony Hughes ruffled James' hair and I caught Martin Lyons looking over at us and I thought back to when his brother Vincent had died and we'd all lined up at the side of the chapel as a mark of respect and some of the girls had seen a dead rat in the grass and screamed and Andy Traynor had wanted to lift it and then Mrs. Fay had shouted at us to have manners for the coffin coming out.

It was the same now. Everyone stood still with their hands clasped and no one dared smile or snigger. I looked away when they lowered Nanna's coffin. I heard Mam sniffling and wanted to hold her hand and tell her everything would be ok. After the prayers more people shook hands. Johnny McCormack's Friesian cows bawled in the field across the road. Some of the men lit pipes. The priests mingled. We came home. Roseanne and the others had cooked roast beef and spuds and vegetables. Someone opened a bottle of wine for the priests. Everyone agreed we were great childer. Deckie Hughes talked about Monaghan Co-op and the pub in Athlone. Dad gave us coke in the kitchen and told us we were all good gasuns and a credit. Roseanne lifted empty plates. An old priest lit up his cigar and asked Dad was he connected to Bishop Nicholas Conaty. "I've enough fecking problems", Dad said. Tony Hughes laughed. The priest didn't.

Some of the visitors left and the rest sat on in the parlour. The women held glasses of wine and sherry and the men drank whiskey and bottles of stout. People gave us money. Lorna Hughes was bored and wanted to go home. I felt anger filling up inside me again. How could they all sit and laugh and talk and drink and smoke and poor Nanna lying in a cold grave?

Mam went out to the kitchen and lit the gas ring beneath our big kettle. Herself followed her. Derek Hughes had stickers, football stickers, a big pile of them. He laid them across the table, the Wolves players first, Dougan and Richards and Parkin. We gawked; Trevor Brooking, Peter Cormack, Billy Bremner, Georgie Best, Trevor Hockey, Kevin Hector, Frank McClintock, Peter Shilton, Stuart Pearson. We kept on gawking.

Mam cowered by the cooker. I knew Herself was giving out. Probably about us being ould-fashioned pups going to the Teck and then getting the home place. Or maybe there hadn't been enough food or drink to go round for all the priests and the posh ones from the Apostolic Society. Or was it Dad being disrespectful to the old priest with the cigar when he enquired about the Bishop's connections?

Anyway it didn't matter. Mam wouldn't fight back. She stood there and took it all in. Dad came out with empty stout bottles and Herself turned. "Ah there ya are Jimmy, well that all went off the best and the weather kept up and it didn't rain and sure isn't this grand, grand altogether?"

Dad knew better. He glanced at Mam. I read his mind. I knew he'd like to tell Herself where to shove her weather and her Apostolic Society and to get to feck from about the place and quit domineering from now on or he'd deal with her the right way. But then Mam would only get more upset and say "leave it Jimmy, leave it, the quiet way is the best way".

Fr. Eddie appeared. He and Fr. Maurice were going for a walk. They'd be back for coffee at half-past seven. Lizzie walked them to the door. Tony Hughes smiled. He started imitating Tom Riordan and Batty Brennan. We laughed. He pulled on his overcoat and shook hands with us and gave James a fiver to go and buy sweets for everyone. He laughed again. "Right says he but she never wrote". Eddie asked him why he always said that and what it meant anyway. Tony ruffled his hair for him and clapped his hands in a fashion that said it was time to be off. He looked back, "Be good boys and none of youse come home a guard or a priest or your oul fella'll go clane mad altogether". Anna Mae hugged us and we all smelled of perfume. Francie Kelly said he'd be back after he'd strigged the cows. He and McGunker strolled down our meadow.

Then she heard it and froze to the spot. The chirping of Nanna's pullets below in the barn hurt Mam. She cried and said "oh God oh God". I gave her a hand to feed them and reassured her that they were grand. It wasn't as if she'd forgotten deliberately. After all she'd been trying to please and entertain everyone and now here she was blaming herself again because no one gave a bollocks about the poor chickens or so it seemed.

Dad insisted on Peter and Mrs. Rooney staying for another drink telling them they were daecent neighbours and he'd be vext if they left now. Peter took off his hat again.

I went up to where Nanna had been laid out. Everything had been transformed. The chairs were gone and the white sheets replaced and the crucifix and holy water and palm removed. Fr. Eddie's clock, pen and book on psychology sat neatly on the table. Nanna was gone and wasn't coming back.

"Turn them most gracious advocate
Thine eyes of mercy towards us…"

Anyway that night when all was done and the younger ones asleep, me and James sat listening to Horslips on Nanna's radio. Dad gave us more coke and told us again that we were good gasuns. "It's alright son, turn it up a bit if you want, just don't have it too loud!" James nodded. We ate Tayto. The men drank whiskey mixed with water and chatted and laughed but not in a disrespectful fashion. Now and again Francie Kelly threw his head back and laughed but only because Phil Kane or Uncle Jack had told him something funny.

Mickey O'Brien and Peter Rooney talked about the North and what might happen if Paisley got his way. Then they'd all join in together and talk about days gone by and things that were done and yarns that were told and boys that were hardy.

Barnaby Jones arrived and closed the door gently behind him. He rubbed his hands together. Mam got up. The men carried on talking. Mickey O'Brien looked at Barnaby. He joined the women and talked about the Legion of Mary meeting he'd just attended. And then Nanna's funeral. Wasn't it great to see the big turnout of priests and the Monsignor and the two Canons. And wasn't he off to Knock the following Sunday with all the other skewards as he called them and the handmaids too and sure wasn't everything grand, grand altogether.

He could only manage one bun on account of the feed of sandwiches they'd had at the Legion meeting.

And wasn't the Apostolic Society doing great work at the moment and sure wasn't poor Fr. Eddie right to go on to bed if he was tired.

He sat clasping his hands and now and then felt for the Pioneer badge that adorned his jacket. He looked over at the men and smiled. Dad poured more whiskey. Kelly flashed the fags.

"Bejeminey I had Reilly the vit out with a heifer this evening and he's not giving her much hope, hay and water for three days and no male says he, and sure her lying there this past while ating nothing at all, at all, on account of the red water".

"It's an ojous curse altogether the same red water", replied McGunker.

The smoke ris above them and now and again the ash would miss its target and sail to the floor.

Mam lifted the kettle and set about rinsing more teacups.

Roseanne got up to help her.

It was gone two in the morning when me and James headed for bed.

"Eternal rest grant to her dear Lord and let perpetual light shine upon her".

I could see Nanna's smile in the distance, a smile that told me not to be worrying.

Chapter 29

Anyway Fr. Eddie just kept on walking. Fast! We'd go with him occasionally and talk. About everything and anything. Football, American Presidents, World hunger, Norn Ireland, how it was long ago. Now and then he'd tell us stories. Things he'd seen and heard below in Templeport. Things he'd done above in Dublin. Books he'd read. People he'd met. The simple things of life impressed him most. Things people said to him and their outlook on life, whether African or Irish. Like the time he and McGunker and John the Yankee had been talking about the Kennedys and how many had felt that Senator Teddy Kennedy should've run against Nixon for the U.S. Presidency and kept the family name in politics, like his poor father would've wanted.

"Sure it's alright talking", McGunker had said. "Aisy for them to talk, not for Teddy and them pushing him all the time and his three brothers dead, two of them shot and his father heartbroken and his wife too fond of the wine and the bad car crash there'd been and then they wanted him to run for President. Put yourselves in his shoes, sure it'd be aisier to push water up a hill".

Fr. Eddie closed his eyes and laughed.

"Aisier to push water up a hill", he repeated.

He talked of life in Africa and more especially Tanzania and the great leader they had in President Julius Nyeree, a kind and gentle soul, a father figure that everyone looked up to and admired cos they knew he was fair, fair with everyone.

Unlike Idi Amin Dada who seemed to be an ojous whelp altogether. He ruled the neighbouring state of Uganda through fear, him and his S.I.B. They were his private army of spies and interrogators. The sort of whelps that roamed the country like the Black and Tans did here years before, accusing the people of being traitors and bating them up, especially in the middle of the night. Then their bodies would be found in a swamp in the morning and no one could pass any remarks. Anyway everyone was terrified now and many of them were fleeing the country as refugees and running into Tanzania. And sure weren't they coming to a land that was already struggling to feed its own and this was causing tension. That's the way it was and there was no sign of it getting any better either. Sure hadn't Idi Amin Dada even ordered the execution of one of his own ministers because he didn't act tough enough. Sooner or later he'd target the Church and what would happen then?

"Why do youse call him Dada?" James asked. "We don't", Uncle Eddie replied. "Sure that's his own title, Idi Amin Dada, President for life, Dada was his father's name, Dada Amin".

"That'd be a bit like me going round calling meself James Conarty Jimmy".

Fr. Eddie laughed again. He rubbed the crease in his forehead and walked on adjusting his glasses now and then when the sun became too strong. The road was dry and there was an ojous heat. Then he told us about Mount Killymanjaro with its snow peaks all year round and then the way everything stopped in its tracks when the rainy season came. Still the people didn't mind. Sure they'd be praying for rain. Drought was worse. Everything burnt and nothing grew for months and months. The rains brought new life to the plains and the people rejoiced. Tommy told him that when McGunker was thirsty, he'd say, "There's a horrid drute on me altogether". We sat beneath Kettoes bush. Fr. Eddie twisted his bony wrist and checked the time. He leaned back on his elbows and crossed his feet. James pulled a fistful of grass.

"Would Francie Kelly bate him?" Harry shouted.

We looked at each other.

"Bate who Harry, bate who?"

Fr. Eddie had his eyes closed again.

"Bate your man Dada Idi or whatever youse call him", Harry protested.

We lay back and laughed.

Harry was thick now and got up to go.

"Well he says he could bate Muhammad Ali and Joe Frazier together at the wan time so why don't youse ask him to go over and bate yer man?"

We all got up and stretched.

Fr. Eddie tried to diffuse the situation by pointing at an imaginary rabbit running in Hughie Smith's lane. "You missed him, you missed him".

We walked back through the plantin.

Our mouths were dry now with the drute.

I longed for a can of Crosskeys coca-cola.

"Pass no remarks of Kelly", our Eddie advised, "Sure he'd get it hard to bate Willie Whitelaw's granny".

Our spontaneous bout of laughter only frustrated Harry all the more and he sulked now.

"I'm only saying, I'm only saying, if yer man is such a big bully then something should be done about it". We kept walking.

Fr. Eddie talked about Kavanagh, Paddy Kavanagh. He'd met his sister beyond in Longford. Kavanagh was a poet and a writer and a farmer too. He loved working with the clay but he loved the words even more.

He'd write poetry sitting by the canal above in Dublin. A day would come when every student in Ireland would learn Kavanagh's poetry. Students might even come from abroad to study it, our Uncle predicted.

He half-closed his eyes again as we walked down Ned's brae.

"So, very nice, very good Harry…
Oh you are not lying in the wet clay
For it is a harvest evening now and we
Are piling up the ricks against the moonlight
And you smile up at us…eternally"

We ignored Mary Margaret's goats though it was hard. I wondered if Fr. Eddie was thinking of Nanna now but didn't like to ask him. There was more silence.

After all we'd only gone as far as Kettoe's bush and not on to the graveyard below, where her poor body lay.

I wondered too if Fr. Eddie knew something we didn't. Like what really happens when people die and do priests' mothers get a special entry pass into Heaven and would it be the same now for our poor Mam if only I'd change my mind and go to St. Pat's in September?

Roseanne smiled. McGunker was in the town, he'd be sorry he missed us. Fr. Eddie didn't want tae thanks all the same. She gave us mint sweets.

We headed on. Fr. Eddie stopped at the wee gate and looked across at Fairtown bog.

"Very nice, very good,
…Now I turn,
Away from the ricks, the sheds, the cabbage garden
The stones of the street,
The thrush song in the tree
The potato pits, the flaggers in the swamp;
From the country heart…"

We straggled on coming into view of our own spud stalks that rose a foot or so majestically above the drills beyond in the meadow. Eddie and Harry sauntered behind. Peggy Dearg had a big shovel in her hand scuffling the weeds that dared to peep up by the roadside. She turned in our direction. We hesitated. Instinct told us we were safe enough with Uncle Eddie and we wouldn't be ranted at or called ould-fashioned tramps today. She gave him money for a special intention and he said it was far too much. They stood together, arms folded in the middle of the road and talked. We edged forward. No one passed any remarks.

Prince Philip had a pair of binoculars in his hand. He smiled and tried to be funny. We edged further forward. "Gobshite", Tommy muttered. Fr. Eddie caught up.

Above the crossroads Peter Rooney dismounted his bike. His well-oiled clippers sat strapped to the carrier. He was on his way to the graveyard, to tend to the plot his young son had been buried in all those years before. "These are great gasuns Eddie", he informed our Uncle who naturally agreed that indeedn't we were. We left our goodbyes again. Mam had chicken and cabbage and brown bread ready for him when we got in. Our homemade chips sat steeping in water waiting to be fried.

That night he lit a Marlboro fag and told us more about Paddy Kavanagh and Mucker and Tarry Flynn. He quoted freely. The television was on but turned down low. James stared at Clint Eastwood. "Dirty Harry" they called him. A cop that took no shite from anybody and drove round in an ould battered car looking decidedly grumpy and disgusted with everything and everybody even when things were going his way.

Then he chatted about the Moonlight Players, the local drama production troop he'd been involved in with Mam and Sean and Mary Boylan and Packie Cahill and Francie Kelly and the Hannigans and Alo Prior. The crack they'd had rehearsing in the old schoolhouse above in Shantemon and how they'd gotten their name by looking through a hole in the roof and gawking out at the moon that shone down before them. And how they'd then moved to Jemmie Macs to practice and the rivalry there'd been between them and the O'Briens above in the Killygarry troop and how they'd won cups in the Town Hall in Cavan and beyond in Tubbercurry and below in Larne. Dirty Harry crashed his car and a gaping hole in his head had blood gushing from it. He passed no remarks. Uncle Eddie was quoting lines from Mungo's Mansion when Dad came in.

He looked across at us and waited till his brother-in-law was finished before clearing his throat and commencing

"To be or not to be, that is the question

Whether tis nobler in the mind to suffer…

Or to get to feck to bed boys

As quick as youse can…"

Uncle Eddie laughed. Mam lit the kettle. The very next day Nanna's memorial cards arrived. I know cos we were there. Mam struggled to cut through the thick brown cellotape that bound the small cardboard box together.

"Is it from Dathlones, is it?" Harry shouted excitedly.

"Can I've one, can I've one?" Philomena begged, thinking they were chocolates.

Mam lifted them out and showed us. The front cover had Mary on it standing still with her hands joined and a swirl of blue adorning the background. She opened it and inside was Nanna's picture. She was wearing her glasses and smiling and you could see that she had her good black coat on. Beneath that it read in small neat print:

Sacred Heart of Jesus

Have mercy on the soul of…

And then in bigger writing:

Elizabeth Brady

Corratubber, Cavan

Who died on 11th June 1975

Aged 81 years

R.I.P.

There were prayers on the other side.

Mam stared.

"Did Nanna send that from Heaven, did she?" Philomena enquired. We looked at each other. No one said anything,

Mam went to the window. We stood there. And that was that then. Confirmation that Nanna was dead and wouldn't be coming back to feed her hens or listen to Charles Mitchell, ever again.

"Oh Mary conceived without sin,

Pray for us who have recourse to thee".

Chapter 30

Later that summer McGunker said things and times were changing horrid quick. Too quick for his likening. He filled the copper spud sprayer with a mixture of Dithane 945 and water and took off again. We followed, getting our legs soaked by the dripping stalks that rebounded into our path. I thought of Patrick Kavanagh and wondered how they sprayed spuds below in County Monaghan. Anyway that evening we met Pat Shannon junior beyond on Ted's Hill for the very first time. He came across with Eamonn Boylan, his cousin, and the Bomber. His yankee accent bet all. It was a terror. I gawked at him initially. He seemed so much more maturer than us and sounded like a man of forty. But he wasn't. Pat Shannon junior was roughly the same age as our James, fourteen or so. Sure his mother, Mary and our Mam had been the best of friends before she'd gone to the States and married Pat Shannon senior, a Fermanagh man.

Anyway young Pat insisted on playing in goals. We picked sides and when his side attacked Pat roared "Hustle baby hustle!" We looked at each other. Pat knew of Clint Eastwood but didn't very much like him, he informed us as we lay down for a break. The air was still and the sun shone. He seemed to have a knowledge of our countryside and the people that inhabited it and wanted to talk about them. Like the time the young guard walked up to Ted Reilly after Castletara Mass and cautioned him for selling Easter Lillies. He whipped out his wee black notebook and asked Ted his name.

"Terence O'Raghallaigh", he responded.

"Howdeya spell that?" the young man enquired, with his pen poised for action.

"Gawd you're some boy alright, sure you're not fit be an Irishman never mind a guard", Ted informed him.

We knew Ted and the Boylans were friendly and understood that this act of Republican endeavour had obviously been relayed to Pat by some of his uncles. Then again he'd maybe heard about it in America such was the link between the Sinn Féiners and the Kennedys and Martin Luther King and even Muhammad Ali himself.

The Bomber picked at a scab on his knee.

"I'm writing down all the figures in the whole world and I'm up as far as four and five noughts, that's four hundred thousands", Harry announced.

"Gee, ya mean you've written down every single digit from zero to 400,000, way to go, gee", Pat looked at him in disbelief.

"He sure as hell has, ya sonofabitch", the Bomber replied bursting into laughter as he imitated Pat's Yankee brogue.

"Why don't ya call by sometime and have a few beers and we'll show ya, goddammit", he continued hysterically.

We looked at each other.

Though it was funny we felt awkward about what he'd just said and James barked an abrupt "Shaddup ya brit git" in an effort to appease our new found Yankee friend. We laughed.

The bomber got thick.

"I'm no brit git, I'm no brit and if ya ever…"

No one passed any remarks.

Bomber stumbled to his feet wiping his sweaty brow and beckoned at Bruno to go get the ball.

We all stretched. Game on again.

With the scores tied at fourteen apiece and next goal winning, the Conartys got a free kick just outside Ted Reilly's penalty area.

I floated the ball in just high enough. I knew James would get his head to it even in the crammed goalmouth. Everyone jumped and missed. Not so our Bruno, who ghosted in unnoticed at the far post and nodded the ball with his snout past an unsuspecting Pat Shannon.

Shure there was mayhem!

We tore after that dog in celebration. Pat protested. "He's an illegal player, goddammit, he's an illegal player, he can't assist".

Bruno couldn't have cared less and neither did we.

Anyway the protests continued, more vehemently now. The Bomber got into it and Eamonn too. Someone had to relent. A penalty kick was agreed upon to decide the outcome. We all stood around pushing and shoving. The shovers tried to create more room for out taker, James, the pushers were more intent on making it as uncomfortable as possible for him. Plenty of argy bargy.

Martin Brady smiled. Stalemate. More shoving. More pushing. Psychological warfare.

Pat came striding out authoritively. He cleared his throat and began:

"There can be no defense, there can be no offense either, goddammit, don't you guys understand the regulations?"

I didn't like it when he called us "guys". We looked at each other and dispersed awkwardly.

James' kick was low and hard and just inside Pat's right hand post. Pat took it like a man peeling off his gloves and shaking James by the hand. We turned to go.

"Ha-ho, it's hard to bate the Conartys", McGunker cheered inside the far hedge from where he'd been watching. He didn't mind us playing soccer so much, now. Shure wasn't his own relation, Chippy Brady, making a good living from it beyond at Arsenal.

He shook hands with Pat Shannon and told him he was welcome to Fairtown, the most famous townland in all of Western Europe.

"Why, the pleasures all mine", Pat replied.

They talked about a fella called Tip O'Neill, a Yankee T.D. I looked at him again now as he strode by McGunker's side and marvelled at his air of maturity. What must he think of us, I wondered quietly?

I needn't have bothered. Sure as the summer months passed Pat became one of the gang, accepted unconditionally by each of us in turn and more especially when he used the bollox word now and again. Even when he carved the date backwards on his Uncle Matt's big chestnut tree, we still passed no direct remarks assuming he knew what he was doing in the first place and fearful of causing offence in the process if we queried it.

7-15-75 his digits read and we looked at them now and again with growing concern. We said nothing. It was Uncle Eddie that pointed out to us the odd fact that the Yanks, unlike ourselves, stick the month in first and then the day's date after it.

And so that was that. Except that it was often better to pass no remarks and avoid attracting unwanted attention as Kelly might say.

Which is what we shoulda done the day the creamery boys came to deliver the rolled barley and Ennis' dairy meal and Kilmore 99 disinfectant. But we didn't, or rather we couldn't.

There we were kicking a ball at the gable end of the hayshed when the hardy pair of bucks leapt from the back of the lorry. Maybe they felt threatened by the sight of us five gasuns or maybe our reputation as ould-fashioned whelps had spread further afield than we'd imagined.

Anyway, wee fat Charlie, the mouthiest one spotted our Eddie in a pair of his father's old wellies and couldn't resist a dig.

"Are them wellies big enuf for ya?" he enquired, laughing as he yanked a meal bag onto his shoulder.

McGunker

Eddie stood his foot on the ball and looked at him.

"They're big enuf to fit in your gob if you want them, ya prick ya".

With that he legged it laughing. Wee fat Charlie tore after him but hadn't a hope. The rest of us laughed and the pair of boys got thicker. There was an uneasy silence as the other bags of meal were thrown off. The lorry headed down the lane. But Charlie just couldn't let it go; "Be Gawd, Peggy Dearg could be right boys, youse are ould-fashioned brats". He laughed loudly. Then he cheered.

Eddie was first to lift a stone. The rest of us followed. We knew the procedure by now and stood there like the firing squad we'd seen in Clint Eastwood's Mexican movie. We waited for them to pull up at the lower gate before turning to climb the hill. A moving target is always harder to hit, we knew that much. And so it proved. The lorry stalled.

We peppered them like an IRA hit squad. One shot, and Eddie was adamant it was mine, pierced the Perspex sheet that acted as a back window and the subsequent squeals from inside the cab told us we were in trouble. There was only one thing to do now and that was leg it, as far as we could. These were grown men after all. We took refuge out in the whins. Part of me wanted to laugh but most of me was scared shitless. It didn't help that Eddie repeated "Great shot, Michael, great shot!"

We sat there peeping, only occasionally daring to rise above the cover of the thorny whin bushes, with their glorious array of yellow flowering, to see what, if anything, was happening. Maybe we'd gone too far. Maybe they were hurt now or cut by the splintering Perspex that had exploded around them or maybe one of them had been struck by that deadliest of stones? Still we waited.

Wee fat Charlie got out and picked up a stone and muttered. He checked out the carnage and then got back in again swearing. The other fella revved up the engine and they slowly climbed the pass hill, cringing the gear stick occasionally till they got to the top, before horsing it on down towards Mineys.

We stood there like South American revolutionaries. "That'll teach the git to mock me about Dad's wellies", Eddie laughed again before complimenting me on my accuracy once more. I didn't need this sort of glory and so told him to shut his mouth. James said that if we all sang dumb then we'd be fine. And with that we headed back towards the hayshed. We'd be safe for another week or so woudn't we?

Mam came out. We hadn't thought of her. Had she seen us?

"Boys, boys, Pippy the Creamery manager is after ringing the shop to say there'll be no more meal delivered till youse have manners and stop throwing stones at them men".

We ate our rice somberly. Mam was in bad humour and that didn't happen too often. No one looked up. No one laughed or sniggered even. We knew we'd gone too far this time. Still we wondered. How had the pair of bucks gotten back to the creamery so quick? And if Pippy had rung the shop with a message then Kathleen would've delivered it and we hadn't seen her or Packie about. Perhaps Mam had seen the carry on of us and was implemting the "wait till your father gets home" approach and all we could do now was wait and hope for the best.

If only we'd passed no remarks. But sure Eddie was only ten and there was yer man, fully grown, running after him, all over an ould-fashioned remark passed about an even oulder-fashioned pair of wellies.

Anyway Dad came home that evening and no one passed any remarks and the following week the meal was delivered and yet again no one passed any remarks.

McGunker called in. He'd been in Donohoe's bar earlier that day when the English fisherman asked Paddy McGlorey had he lived, all his life in Ballyhaze?

"No, not yet", Paddy replied.

The other men laughed and laughed and laughed. The Englishman got thick and left the pub. McGunker drank one of our bottles of stout and laughed some more.

"No, not yet, boys oh boys McGlorey".

Dad laughed at McGunker laughing.

"Sure your man stood there like one of them dummies in Vera Brady's shop window not knowing what to make of McGlorey at all, at all. No, not yet!"

Later on during the night it spilt rain like never before and I thought of the Tanzanians out dancing and cheering cos the drought was over.

Chapter 31

Anyway Fr. Eddie kept on going till he got his degree above in UCD. We were looking at the photos below in the kitchen. There they were, the four of them. Him and his three sisters standing in front of a big flowery bush.

"Why are you wearing a black dress Uncle Eddie?" Harry enquired. Dad laughed. Our uncle smiled and then explained that it wasn't a dress he had on him at all at all but a graduation outfit that everyone had to hire before getting their scroll on the big day. Harry looked again.

"Will I ever have to wear one of them yokes?"

"That all depends Harry, show me your ledger, how are the numbers coming along?"

Uncle Eddie winked at the rest of us.

"So, very nice, very good Harry, four hundred and forty two thousand no hundreds and ninety nine, very very good Harry!"

Harry beamed.

Uncle Eddie closed over the ledger and informed him that he'd soon reach the half million mark. We looked at each other.

Then we went for a walk up past Mineys and he told us all about David Livingstone the Scotsman that travelled through the African jungle and discovered a huge waterfall on the Zambezi river and called it Victoria Falls after the Queen of England.

"Was she the one that caused all the spuds to rot and the Irish to die?" I interrupted him. "Ah now Michael, that's not true, no, not at all, the famine in this country was caused primarily by the blight and by an overdependence by the Irish on the spuds".

We passed the bull's feet or was it the horse's? I wondered. Cos an tSearraigh, Castletara, Cor an Tobair, Corratubber.

"So many millions to feed and only one crop grown at the time, sure they couldn't hope to survive, it wasn't practical".

We walked on. James pulled a stalk of grass.

"How come your man below in Monaghan didn't die then?" Harry protested.

"Which man, Harry, which man?" Uncle Eddie enquired impatiently. He scratched behind his ear and then flicked his wrist round to check the time. He swung at a passing fly.

"Your man that you're always talking about that wrote them poems and liked digging in the clay for spuds at the same time, Paddy something?"

Uncle Eddie smiled and ruffled Harry's hair.

"Ah very good Harry, very good, ah that was Patrick Kavanagh but sure the famine happened in the last century, the eighteen hundreds, though maybe some of his ancestors died in the great hunger".

I thought of your man's big book, Cecil somebody's, above in Ned's room trunk but kept my mouth shut.

"Begod Harry the way you're going with the figures and the poetry, you'll soon end up wearing a black dress yourself".

He closed his eyes and smiled and walked on in a dead straight line and we kept up with him. We could hear the pigs grunting and squealing as we came down the brae towards McCollums. A 35 tractor was driving a power shaft that wormed its way through a pighouse wall.

"That's a grand day Fr. Eddie, how are ya keeping?" the tall bearded man wanted to know. They shook hands.

"Ah Howard, good man, very good to meet you again Howard".

He looked at us and half smacked our Eddie, jokingly, across the back of the head.

"Are these the famous Conarty cowboys?"

We all shook hands with him.

He led us round the corner to the big old farmhouse. "So your mother and father are keeping well, that's good, that's really good".

Inside, Jack McCollum was reading the Celt and his wife, a much taller person, was steaming the spuds on their cooker. They all shook hands.

We stood there like goms.

The younger Mrs. McCollum was feeding a baby. Fr. Eddie insisted she didn't move. He knew her brothers well and enquired after them.

She told us her name was Catherine and probably because we were gawking so much turned the baby round on her lap, giving us a better view.

The men talked and talked.

First about the weather. And then Africa. And then your man Ian Smith beyond in Rhodesia and then Mugabe and Winnie Mandela and even Charlie Hockey. They laughed about Hall's Pictorial Weekly and Steptoe. The older Mrs. McCollum gave us Club orange. We kept staring at the baby. Trying to be sociable James asked was it a boy or a girl? Howard laughed and said the pink coloured dress was a bit of a giveaway. James blushed.

Then he asked us about Martin Breslin. "Why do yous call him the Bomber?" James explained.

The men talked more. Howard said the pig trade wasn't great but sure things could only get better. Then they talked about Justice Bridges and the Birmingham Six and oil prices and power sharing

McGunker

and how Catholics and Protestants pulled much better up here than down yonder and sure us only a few miles away from the troubles. Howard unbuttoned his blue coat and washed his hands at the sink. My eyes followed him. He was tall, very tall and very well built with curlish hair like Bomber Breslin's and he had a bearded face. He thought before he spoke and he smiled frequently. The baby cooed and her mother rubbed her on the back. Then she burped. Harry laughed. Anyway Howard liked the soccer and even knew about young Brady beyond at Arsenal. He joked that maybe he and Uncle Eddie were related. We told him that McGunker felt sure he was. Howard laughed more and proceeded to spread a chunk of butter over his steaming spuds. We got up to go. Jack and Mrs. McCollum came to the door. She handed our Uncle some money and he said it was far too much and then she informed him that Charles was doing the best and would be down at the weekend and she'd tell him Uncle Eddie had asked after him. We left our goodbyes.

The sun shone brightly now, as bright as it had done that whole long hot summer and then Uncle Eddie told us he was going back to Africa. We looked at each other.

"Why?" Tommy wanted to know.

"Yeh why?" Eddie junior echoed the sentiment. There was silence.

Our Uncle smiled. "Well boys, a man's gotta do what a man's gotta do, that's my job and there's lots to be done, simple as that".

. James told him that he'd heard Clint Eastwood say the exact same thing in a film of his lately.

"Sure stay for another while and we'll go for walks with ya and talk about things", Harry protested. "We'll not be ould-fashioned", I assured him. Uncle Eddie smiled again.

Then Peggy Dearg came flying up the brae in her Vauxhall Viva car. Her angry face seemed set to explode on spotting us, the ill-reared Conarty pups, but noticing Fr. Eddie amongst us, she beamed a huge smile instead and honked her car horn cheerfully. She was gone. We looked at each other.

"So, very nice, very good, up your big fat arse Peggy Dearg, see if I give a shit", I muttered. James glared at me as the younger boys laughed and Fr. Eddie just strolled on in our gate and passed no remarks at all, at all.

Then the bull man went flying up the pass in an ojous hurry altogether. Inside Mam had the cabbage and chicken ready. She pealed our spuds. Harry squeezed the last of the red sauce and Tommy protested. Harry laughed and then roared as Tommy kicked him under the table and tanted him about Pauline Reilly. Then he bawled. Dad roared. Silence. Fr. Eddie passed no remarks. Dad spoke.

"Get to feck out there and find something to do or go and gather a lock of frogs for the frog-man".

James found two 10:10:20 bags in the hayshed and we headed down to Fairtown bog and gathered frogs for the frog-man for the very first time. It was hot and sticky. I thought of your man, Livingstone, beyond in Africa looking for the waterfalls as we waded through the boggy water. Now and again we'd spot one and all surround him and make sure he was going nowhere. The evening got cooler. Midgets bit us. James said they were midgets. Tommy insisted they were called piss-miners. Kathleen Galligan and her nieces, Rosemary and Anne went past with two galvanised buckets. They were going up to the well and thought we were only joking when we told them we were gathering frogs for the the frog-man. We all stopped and listened.

Eddie Fitzsummon's 135 revved up on the far hill and the excitement of seeing the hay being cut sent us all scuttling out of the bog water and back up the fields.

"Wait for me, waited for me", Philomena panted. I looked at her and laughed. She'd proven herself more than handy at frog spotting but, like Harry, always insisted on someone else catching them. Tommy had said that they pissed into our hands with the excitement when they were caught. Dad turned the swats of hay the next evening with the hay-man he'd bought from the Costelloes. It was an ojous machine altogether except when the belts clogged up with the hay and Dad fecked it into hell and out of it.

Anyway Michael Reilly of Corravarry was tall, very tall and he wore a cap. He talked slowly and deliberately, a bit like John Wayne and always said that the man who made time made lots of it and for no one to ever panic.

"There'll be time when we're all dead and gone", he told us.

We liked Michael Reilly of Corravarry and his wife Eithne too. They were homely people. Warm people. Sure Eithne had once owned the shop at the foot of Castletara brae and, no doubt, was the sort of woman like Mrs. Edgeworth or Kathleen in the shop, that'd give ya six blackjack bars even if you only had the price of five of them. Very daecent. They were a terror.

Our Harry and their son Michael were fierce great and Harry started staying over now and again and so we tanted him even more about Pauline, Michael and Eithne's daughter.

They kept a nice batch of Friesian cows and a garden full of hens and ducks and drakes and a big white rooster and a dozen or so Friesian calves below in the meadow. Eithne had bees, loads and loads of them and though often tempted, we never interfered with them and so they never bothered us either. The parish priest called regularly for a feed and you couldn't blame him. Eithne could produce a fry that'd feed ten men. She baked her own brown bread too and could drive their A40 car better than any man in the country.

Michael drove round the hill with a good rev on his 185 tractor. The baler swallowed and chomped away to its hearts content. We gathered them into windrows and fought over who'd build them. Dad said the rain was coming and there was no time for fighting.

McGunker appeared. He lifted a handful of our hay. He wondered was it fit for baling. Eddie looked at him. "Ha-ho McGunker, hard work's not aisy and dry bread's not grazy, ha-ho!" McGunker laughed. Michael got down off the tractor slowly and went about readjusting the back end of his baler so as to get through the gap into the next field. He looked back. "There's another town conquered, as Hitler used to say". The men laughed. He baled more. Later on we came in for the tae. Mam had ham and lettuce and beetroot stuff for the men and fresh batch bread. They talked about the IRA ceasefire. We got banana sandwiches. I hated the way the sharp spikey ends of the hay got stuck under the skin and saw James trying to bite and then suck one out of his thumb. I knew how he felt.

The men talked more. About the weather and South Africa and whether the IRA would ever quit or would the Brits pull out of Norn Ireland first. And Lenny Murphy and Henry Kissinger. McGunker didn't like these sectarian killings, murdering a man simply cos he was a Catholic or a Protestant or even a Jew. "Imagine", he says, "killing one of the McCollums or the Braidens or the McClanes simply on account of the chapel they went to and forgetting that they were all horrid daecent neighbours that'd give anything ya wanted in the first place".

He shook his head. Michael Reilly agreed. "And visa-versa", and pointed out that none of them'd ever think of killing any of us either.

Dad picked his teeth with a matchstick.

"It's different down here boys, no one gives a shite and rightly so, but up yonder there's plenty at stake, we'll hardly ever see peace, not in our time anyhow". Mam poured more tea. James announced that the next President of America would've been a peanut farmer in his time. The men looked at him. "Well bejaysus I hope there's more money in the peanuts than there is in the bales", Michael replied. They laughed.

That night I dreamt about Bean Uí Fiaich in Castletara school.

"Armoured cars and tanks and guns
 Came to take away our sons

McGunker

But every man'll stand behind
The men behind the wire…"

Chapter 32

Anyway Fr. Eddie went back to Africa from Dublin airport and didn't seem to have a care in the world. "Very nice, very good, so that's really good now", he said. Herself bawled. Mammy was afraid some of us would get lost and never be seen again or be run over by an aeroplane or maybe even break something that wasn't ours. Tony Hughes wanted a drink. We all ate our Tayto and drank coca-cola. "Right says he but she never wrote", Tony laughed as we got up to go. He told the barman that he lived down beside the river Shannon and that he should drop in sometime. The barman looked at him. Tony laughed. "C'mon gasuns it's a long way home to Kaavaan". He put his arms round me and James' necks. "Here's my advice boys, go wherever yous want in life and do whatever yous want to do as long as none of yous…" he paused, "…ever come home a guard or a priest". Our cousin Aidey laughed. We left our goodbyes and drove home in the dark to Cavan. We checked our frogs in the barrel. Bomber arrived early next morning and said Eddie Fitzsummons was cutting his aunty Kathleen's hay. Bruno yelped. We kicked ball at the back of our hayshed. The ground was bare, brown and hard. None of us had any energy. Bomber informed us that he was getting a new Raleigh chopper. We looked at each other. We lay back on the grassy ditch and no one said anything.

McGunker

"It's a bike ya dummy, it's a bike, my Godd do ye not know what a chopper is?" he enquired in his best pleading Belfast accent. He scratched his head. No one passed any remarks.

A cloud mosied overhead and gave us temporary reprieve from the strong sunlight. The minutes passed.

"What do you call these yokes Breslin? Midgets or piss miners?" Tommy enquired, showing one that crawled up his arm. "They're a horrid fecking nuisance anyway". Martin looked at it.

"Och they're just insex", Bomber informed him. "Just insex".

No one passed any remarks for a while.

"What's sex?" Harry shouted.

There was silence.

We all laughed, no one louder than the Bomber.

"Harry, for Goddsakes, whaddya mean what's sex?" He stared at Harry now.

The rest of us stayed still.

It was an awkward stillness.

"You're always talking about sex", Harry informed him, "like the time up on the mountain road with the Yankees from America and now this".

"Now what?" Bomber pleaded.

Harry looked at the rest of us for support.

"Now what, Harry, now what?" Bomber insisted again, mopping the sweat from his brow. He jumped up and pranced about impatiently. Our eyes followed him.

"You're calling them piss miners insex, that's all", Harry protested.

"For Goddsakes Harry I'm only telling Tommy that whether you call them wee yokes piss miners or midgets, it doesn't matter,… they're all insex for Christsakes Harry".

"Oh", replied Harry.

Then there was more silence.

Bomber looked round at us.

I knew he sensed our ignorance. I just knew it.

"For Goddsakes boys don't tell me yous don't know what sex is, what's the matter with ye anyway? Yous never heard of a Raleigh chopper and now yous don't know what sex is for Christsakes".

James told him to shut to feck up or he'd teach him a thing or two himself. This statement caused even more tension.

Bomber got thick. We all got up. No one said anything for a minute or two.

"Smart know-all git", James muttered, "get to feck home to Belfast and make yourself useful ya prick ya, you and your Raleigh choppers, see if we give a shit about ya". More silence. We all laughed now, even Bomber.

"Naw, naw, James, don't get thick, I'm only saying…"

"You're only saying what? Ya little Belfast shit, see where it gets ya?" Bomber looked at our James.

There was more silence.

Then he stuck out his hand.

"Put it there James, no offence for Christsakes, yous are good to me". I could see the tears in Bomber's eyes. James shook his hand. Everyone calmed down.

The quiet way's the best way Mam had always told us and so it proved.

"Three and in", roared Tommy heading for the goals. Bruno barked in delight. Soon it got sweaty again and Mam arrived home from the town with ice-lollies.

"There ya are childer, how are you Martin? And how's Kathleen keeping?"

"Grand Phyllis, aye grand, thank ye", he replied.

We lay down again and kicked off our wellies. Everyone slurped. Bomber edged himself round on his arse impatiently.

"James, who's the greatest footballer ya ever saw?" Bomber enquired. He rolled up his ice-lolly paper. James looked at him.

He thought for a minute.

McGunker

"I dunno Martin, Pele maybe, yeh or Bobby Moore, Best's not bad if only he'd stop messing". We all had our say.

Keegan, Hector, Giles, Muller, Beckenbauer, Brady, Cryuff, Gunter Netzer, Bobby Charlton. Best maybe, nah it hadda be Pele.

James could remember seeing him play. Bomber had seen old clips on the telly. "Black, Brazillian and bloody magic", he squealed.

He'd even seen the save Banks had made from Pele's header on his brother's telly. His brother's name was Tom and he was gonna be a solicitor. "What's that?" Harry asked.

No one answered.

"Whatta save, whatta save, for Goddsakes, sure poor oul Pele couldn't believe it".

And then he showed us. The downward header with plenty of power and spin and yet he'd saved it, Banks had somehow saved it. James smiled.

"Is that the fella that crashed his car and lost an eye from Stoke City?" asked Eddie.

"Aye, aye, och, aye that's him alright", Bomber informed him, delightedly, as if losing your eye was something to be proud of.

"Has your man any childer?" wondered Harry.

"Who?"

"Your man, the black fella from Brazil, Pele, imagine if he had a son, sure he'd be some footballer wouldn't he?" Harry replied.

Tommy laughed. Harry got thick. We waited.

Then Bomber informed us that it all depended on Pele's wife. Now if she was good at soccer and most girls weren't, but anyway, if she was any good and if they had a son, then the chances were that he'd be brilliant too, just like his Da, Pele. But if Pele's wife was into gardening or camogie or music or something else like that, then the chances were he wouldn't be worth a shite. It all depended on his mother! We looked at each other.

"What if they had a daughter?" Eddie enquired next. Bomber laughed aloud.

"Sure girls are shite at soccer".

No one said anything. After all our Philomena was good enough in goals providing no one blasted it. We licked our lolly sticks and flicked them aside and then got up.

Then it happened.

Eddie wondered if the world's greatest footballer had yet to be born?

Bomber's eyes lit up.

"James, promise you won't get thick if I say something, will ye?" Bomber pleaded.

We looked at him, puzzled. Then we all sat down again.

"I've just had a thought", Bomber informed us.

"Ya better let it out or it'll die of loneliness", James laughed. Bomber smiled a wry smile.

"Promise ye won't bate me, will ye not?" he pleaded. James laughed.

"Go on, go on, tell us Bomber", pleaded Eddie.

He scratched his head and seemed to be composing himself before making a big announcement.

We didn't know what to expect.

"Imagine", he began, "Imagine if Pele had a daughter, a wee daughter, and then she was fully grown and Georgie Best got his hands on her and they had sex", he paused and looked at James, "and then nine months later a baby boy was born", he paused again, to draw his breath, "for Goddsakes boys, he'd be some footballer, he'd be world-class wouldn't he?"

Bomber stood there, eyes wide open and seemed delighted with himself. We looked at each other.

"Well, think about it boys, maybe your Eddie is right, maybe the world's greatest footballer hasn't yet even been born. But if Pele has a daughter and her and Georgie have a baby and it's a boy, then his Daddy is Georgie Best and his granddaddy is Pele and there'd be no stopping him, especially if he played for United!"

McGunker

We all laughed hysterically now at Bomber's theory. "You gobshite Breslin" muttered James as he got up to go. He'd heard enough.

"So that's what sex is", Harry announced. "It's all about Georgie Best making babies". He beamed a silly big grin from ear to ear. Even James smiled now.

Then Mam called us in for our fish fingers.

We strolled towards the back door.

Bomber hummed.

"Georgie Best
Superstar
He met Pele's daughter…
In a bar".

And that was that then till the Bomber arrived back the very next day on his brand new Raleigh chopper with its three gears and fancy saddle and our James told him it was only a hape of shite and that he'd seen far better contraptions beyond at Gerry Flood's house.

Bomber got thick and cycled off home up the brae. "Shower of ignorant hoors", he roared back at us. Then we fired stones at him.

"I'm telling Aunty Kathleen".

"Shite for you and Aunty Kathleen".

That night we gathered thirty-seven frogs for the frog-man and I washed out the rusty oul creamery can that McGunker had given us. I used Jeyes Fluid and thought I'd done a great job. I even dug a sod and threw in a fresh bucket of water. The very next morning Eddie found them all belly up and bloated. Frogs don't like Jeyes Fluid. Anyway eleven of them were mine so Eddie worked it out. I now owed me brothers and kid sister compensation for twenty-six dead frogs which would be deducted when we got paid for gathering frogs for the frog-man.

Chapter 33

Anyway Francie Kelly called in on his way home from the town. Mam was frying rashers and sausages on our ould blackened pan. Francie was as good humoured as ever. I knew he'd been drinking. Sure I could smell it on his breath.

"Bejeminey", he says, "I told them guards in the town that they'd never find yon buck, Lord Lucan, no bejeminey, not the way they were going about it, sure they might as well be pissing again the wind". Mam laughed. Then she buttered brown bread. Francie ate. He paused briefly.

"Sure he could be at the back of the mountain, bejeminey, for all we know". He dipped his bread into the greasy plate and swooshed it all around before slicing off a bit and popping it into his mouth. When all was gone he lit a fag and Mam topped up his mug. The smoke ris.

"Any word from McGunker lately boys?" he looked at us.

"He won't believe us that we're catching frogs for the frog-man", Harry informed him.

"Boys oh boys, the McGunker Conartys catching frogs, bejeminey, that's a good one". Francie sat back and laughed. He tipped the ash of his fag onto the floor. Dad came in. "Ha-ho". He handed James six penny bars and Mam a packet of peanuts. "What's the

McGunker

crack Kelly?" he asked as he poured him a whiskey. They laughed and talked. About Lord Lucan and getting the hay in and the state of the country. And Kerry football.

"Bejeminey, they're all the same if you ask me, them politicians".

Dick Emery was on the telly, dressed as a woman. "Ooh you are awful, yeh but I like you". He bashed another fella with his handbag. It rained a bit. Dad explained how canned laughter worked. You'd think people were laughing away but sure it was all recorded and then let loose when Dick Emery or Steptoe said something funny. It was the same for Benny Hill. "Bejeminey, so that's what canned laughter is and I hear they'll all be drinking the Guinness from cans very soon too". Francie shook his head. Then they talked more. About ould Guinness himself. Francie had read about him. Sure hadn't he started life as a Catholic like the rest of us and him gathering in the rent for the ould Protestant Archbishop and if he didn't go and change sides and become a Protestant himself because he figured he'd have a better chance in the economic world of British business and the like. And now some of his whelps of grandsons or great-grandsons wanted to put Guinness into cans and have the people drink it like childer would coca-cola from a tin. Francie shook his head. Dad poured more whiskey. "Bejeminey he was as cute as the Christian, ould Guinness alright, but sure look at the curse they're supposed to have on them as a result, bejeminey".

"You mean a curse like feck or bollox or shite?" Harry enquired. "Hey boy", Dad roared. Francie laughed.

Harry went back to his figures.

"McGunker always says that", Eddie pointed out.

"Says what, bejeminey?"

"He's always saying that such and such a person is as cute as the Christian and once he told me that I'd be a horse of a man only that I can't shite walking, like horses do", Eddie beamed.

Michael Conaty

The men laughed hysterically now and even Harry felt safe to join in.

And then Francie told us of the night that the Gripper Jackson bruck into Mooney's house back in the fifties and locked himself in the upper room when the local men came to batter him.

"Bejeminey, wasn't he the cute hoor to brake out the gable window and dother boys thinking they had him surrounded".

Dad opened two bottles of Smithwicks.

"Now boys get to bed", he motioned with his finger towards the door.

But he wasn't too serious, we knew that. He never was with the few jars in.

Besides the crack with Kelly was too good in that smoke-filled kitchen and we all wanted to hear more. His cap lay at the leg of our table. He'd cough and splutter and laugh in the middle of his stories but we didn't mind. Like the time when Philip Brady had been at Ellen Fargie's wake and sure didn't he go down in the middle of the night to her room and stick on the long black dress she used to wear and up he comes to the kitchen again and cleared the place of neighbours and relations. When word got out they all thought it was a terror. It was a fret. Francie struggled to contain himself through the fits of laughter and spluttering.

"Bejeminey, as long as there's meat on me bones, I'll never forget that one". We laughed till our bellies hurt.

Mam made more tea and buttered cream crackers for us. Flaky bits dropped to the floor. Then the chat got serious. About the troubles and the UVF and the way they'd killed the Miami showband and them only coming home from a concert below in Banbridge. And their own bomb going off early and killing two of them.

And sure the IRA'd be sure to retaliate now and some other poor ould divils would end up suffering too. It was a fret. Anyway it was near three in the morning when Dad and Kelly headed out to the car.

McGunker

"It'll soon be bright", he announced.

James whispered something to him about John Wayne and Francie reminded him not to pass any remarks for fear of attracting unwanted attention. We smiled and headed inside. Tired limbs ached now and heavy heads hit pillows. Mam cleared up downstairs. "Goodnite gasuns, say your prayers", she shouted.

That night I dreamt we were raiding Philip Brady's orchard and Ellen Fargie came in the lane in her long black dress and roared at us that we were only ould-fashioned whelps! We ran for all we were worth but she kept after us.

"Get up, get up quick boys, the frog-man's coming today", Dad roared, pulling back the curtains and blazing the room with warm sunlight. Harry opened his ledger.

"What comes after 499,999?" No one had time now.

We struggled to dress ourselves. Tommy and Eddie fought over a pair of socks. Mam had tea and Marietta biscuits ready. Out in the byre James unfurled the special net bags the frog-man had left for packing them in on the day he'd be collecting. We watched him impatiently. Tommy healed a barrel sideways and about forty hopped to their freedom. We cursed and then closed the doors and blocked any wee gaps with fistfuls of hay from an ould bale that lay in the corner. We set about recapturing them. "Poor wee frogs, it doesn't seem fair", said Philomena.

"Shite for them, bad enough catching the hoors below in the bog, without having to chase them again", I replied. And that was that then.

We filled them net bags and tied up the tops and left them lying sideways. They could hardly budge. Bits of legs and bloated bellies and soft green yellowy skin peered out at us. Eyes blinked. I wondered what Lorna Hughes would think of it. Anyway the frog-man came. He got out of his car and hoisted a bag onto the bonnet and proceeded to open it. "Don't let them out!" Harry roared. The frog-man looked at him. Then he measured one or two with a U-shaped yoke that he took from his back pocket. We stared. He put them back in.

"Sound so boys, seven hundred and seventy two you say, not bad, not bad at all for a first go gentlemen", he smiled at us.

"Hey, I'm a girl", Philomena announced. He smiled again and apologised and told her he felt sorry for her being so badly outnumbered. Philomena looked at him. Nothing was said. Then he took out his fancy calculator and made it all up. We watched him.

"Who's the treasurer?" he enquired. James stepped forward and he paid him in notes and coins. The rest of us stood there gawking.

"Same time, same place gentlemen, oh and the lady of course". He smiled at Philomena. And then he was gone. Eddie reminded me of the Jeyes Fluid and the frogs that I'd murdered and the compensation I'd now have to pay. We went inside. Mam was delighted.

"Now boys, don't waste it on blackjacks and the like; James you'll need longer trousers and Michael you've new books to get for the Teck and ..."

She lifted the earnings for safekeeping. Eddie persuaded her to part with ten pence apiece for the shop. Packie Brady laughed.

"Begod boys, there might be a recession and an oil crisis and plenty of inflation about, but yous Conartys are gonna dig your way out of it with all that frog money". He jingled the coins in his hand and pulled on his pipe. Out in the kitchen the Angelus bell rang and everything was still. We stood there muttering pretend prayers and didn't dare to look at each other. Kathleen threw two more sticks into an already blazing fire and the water pipes gurgled and moaned. She shut in the damper. We stood there. Packie talked. About Oliver Plunkett's head beyond in Drogheda. The poor man had it chopped off by the English after they'd hung and quartered him ages ago beyond in London.

Harry rubbed his throat.

"Would that be sore?" he enquired, looking at Packie.

"Well now, you'd hardly feel it if you'd been hung first me good man", Packie replied as he stuffed more tobacco down into his pipe. Kathleen handed him matches. Eileen and her friend giggled inside. And then McDonnell's bread van pulled up and Jack Rahill hopped out. He totally agreed with Packie. It was an ojous thing to do to any poor man and especially him, Oliver Plunkett, and him the Archbishop of Armagh and totally innocent of all charges relating to a French invasion.

But at least he was a saint now and his head safely back in Drogheda where it belonged and it carefully preserved in a big glass case above on the altar.

"How's it preserved Packie?" James wanted to know.

Packie couldn't be certain but he figured it must be some kind of fluid or other that kept him intact, Blessed Oliver Plunkett, Saint Oliver Plunkett, the man that died for his faith, a real martyr that man.

Anyway we doddled across the road and up Jim Costelloe's brae. Eddie wondered was he related to the Plunketts of Ballyhaze, to Felim the footballer?

Harry was more interested in how a man's head could be kept from rotting all this time in a glass case beyond in Drogheda. Tommy informed him that the fluid they used was made from frog's piss and that the frog-man got paid extra for squeezing the last drop out of them before cutting their throats. He stored it in jam-jars and sent it over every so often. James laughed. Philomena was disgusted. Anyway we picked the small white balls from the egg-tree hedge above Costelloes and fired them freely. Soon we'd be heading back to school and the new soccer season starting but none of us gave a dam. Not really. These were the days to enjoy. Days of freedom and divil may care. Days of fun.

"Who'll die first, Mammy or Daddy?" Harry enquired as he squeezed the juicy ball between his fingers. We looked at each other. "Can we serve Mammy in that fluidy frogs stuff?" he continued.

"You gob-shite", Eddie teased him. Motivating ourselves to get out and gather frogs for the frog-man was the hardest bit. Once we'd got started and had a few caught then we'd feel like staying at it all night. That's how it was that very evening. The strong sunlight had dimmed and a light breeze whipped up over the valley behind McGunker's. We chattered away. About Oliver Plunkett and Bomber Breslin and McGunker's horse, Bob. And Johnny Giles at Leeds.

Someone was whistling, a light whistle, the sort Jackie Fitch would be at as he mosied along in his car. We listened.

"Pass no remarks, it's Prince Philip", whispered James. "He's always doing that, peeping through hedges and listening, watch now and he'll say something smart". We waited.

"Hrrmph, begod boys yous'll soon have that bog emptied and the frogs'll be extinct". He grinned a silly grin. It felt strange. Normally, he wouldn't speak. We carried on spotting.

"Save it for your wife, ya prick ya", I muttered, low enough for him not to hear and loud enough for the boys to pick up. "Pity you're not half as ould-fashioned and funny with her, ya bollox".

We laughed in unison and carried on with the work. Prince Philip joined in thinking we were humoured by his thoughts on the potential extinction of the frog. His silly grin widened as he sauntered back up the field. Now and again he'd stop and look round and smile back at us.

Tommy gave him the thumbs up and muttered, "You're some tool alright, pity you're not extinct". Prince Philip waved back. We laughed.

Twenty-nine had been gathered as we headed for home. Bruno's ears cocked and he paused momentarily as Bredin's gun dog yelped in the field next door. Then he carried on trotting and passed no remarks. Philomena spotted two in the bull's field. Total thirty-one, James wrote it down in our notebook. He always did this. How many were caught and who caught how many. Now he was leading on seventy-one.

Chapter 34

Anyway Dad bought a cock-lifter for twenty pounds from Big Paddy Brady below in Ballyhaze. It was a steel yoke with five long hard prongs and could be reversed under cocks of hay and then lifted up by the tractor. That's why it was called a cock-lifter. We janted in the cocks of hay from the three-cornered field the next evening. Dad took his time. He had to. Every time he hit a hard ould bump the cock of hay seem destined to bobble and heal over. I thought of Michael Reilly, beyond in Corravarry. He was right. The man that made time had made plenty of it so there was no point in rushing. We built them in the lower corner of the shed the way McGunker had said and left loads of room for the bales.

"No bodder, horse on Jem", he told Dad as he pulled out. The steel prongs rattled and dragged the stones from the street. McGunker pitched the hay up and we pulled it back in. When he wasn't looking we'd heal each other over now and again in the soft hay. "Me brother John is half-ways across the Atlantic right now", he informed us, looking at his watch. Then he took off his hat and pulling a stained handkerchief from his pocket, wiped the sweat from his brow. I looked at the thick blue vein that ran under his arm and right up behind his elbow. He sat there with us, waiting. Now and again, we could hear the spluttering of our wee twenty tractor in the distance. The minutes passed. Eddie cracked a ball against the galvanise behind us and we all leapt. McGunker laughed.

"Boys oh boys, the McGunker Conartys, it's well for yous boys". He looked round at us and pulled on his fag. I felt for him now. I'm sure he'd have liked a few sons and daughters of his own. He wasn't getting any younger and wouldn't marry now, I knew that much. I sensed an emptiness within him. All that hard work and sweat and hardship, and for what? Someday he'd be too old to run his farm anymore and what'd happen then? He'd have no one to pass it on to. Roseanne was too old to marry either. John the Yankee had childer, three of them, beyond in America. I thought back to the day when we'd met one of them with his girlfriend and Bomber being ould-fashioned. I laughed to myself. Harry caught me.

"What's so funny Michael?" he wondered.

"Ah, nothing, nothing", I replied, getting up with the rest of them.

Maybe the nephew would come over and run McGunker's farm? I doubted it. It'd be an ojous change for him coming from the States with the hot weather and the people driving round in big floats of cars like Clint Eastwood's and them with big fancy supermarkets and restaurants like we'd seen on Kojak. Plus he'd never cope with the narrow roads we had over here and could ya imagine his girlfriend stuck behind Eddie Fitzsummon's tractor as she made her way to Dublin to buy herself new clothes and maybe perfume too. I stopped the daydreaming as Dad reversed back in. Dad was cautious. He strained his neck.

"That's her McGunker, the one we were looking for", laughed James.

McGunker smiled and spat into his hands. Mam brought the tae out. We dug into the bananna sandwiches. She had ham ones for the men and she pushed them aside. Then she knelt down slowly beside us and Philomena propped herself against her shoulder. A late evening wasp, doing his rounds, threatened to spoil things.

"Don't worry, I'll get the hoor", Tommy assured us. McGunker laughed. And then the grown-ups talked. About Roseanne's flu and the way it had lasted so long and wasn't it great she was coming out of it now and her brother John arriving the next day and the way he'd enjoy himself and sure they'd be over and then they could all head into Sean Boylans some of the nights.

Anyway the men lit fags and Mam topped up their mugs. And then they talked more and McGunker wondered was Dad wise selling sites above on the rocks and who'd be coming to live there and wouldn't it bring a horrid change to the country altogether and what if the newcomers, as he called them, turned out to be awkward and contrary, what'd happen then? Hard to know.

McGunker didn't like change. The only changes he'd make would be to turn the clock back to the way things were years ago when neighbours needed each other. "Sure that ould feckin EEC will be the ruination of us all yet", he protested. "They're getting horrid independent some of these young fellas", he reminded Dad. "I don't like it at all, at all". "Bejeminey, neither do I", mocked Eddie passing by.

"Go on and play ball and have manners you", Dad instructed.

The men lit two more fags. Silence. I could sense the tension now in Dad's face. He tried to justify what he was doing.

"Ah no, these young bucks are different, different altogether, sure they're working with the P and T, the phone crowd, and sure they're getting married and settling down and need to start somewhere in life".

McGunker winced.

"Sure I know all about them, didn't I meet your man and his woman beyond on the road and him pushing a pram, the gobshite, and bidding them the time of day, told him a big stack of a lad like himself should have no bodder digging holes for poles for a living. Well clare to God, he was mortified. Herself pointed out that himself didn't dig holes for poles for a living at all, that he was in fact a Tee wan technition with the phone crowd, a T.I.T. Begod, says I to meself, that makes ya a TIT so, and that's all you'll ever be".

Dad laughed.

The tension eased and McGunker got up and stretched himself. "I'd better get going, sister'll be rooting and fussing over there and I'll head on so, thanks for the feed Phyllis, good luck Jem".

He doddled down the bulls field and was only gone a few yards when he stopped to pick up a frog.

"Here boys, first man down gets him", he shouted. McGunker held it high. We dashed. James now had seventy-two.

We kicked ball for a while. Bruno yelped. Mam gathered up the bits and pieces and then headed towards the door. She stopped suddenly, distracted by someone's cheery call. Peter Rooney had specks of white on his face and hands. He handed Mam a bundle of rhubarb. They chatted. He'd been whitewashing that day. Before it got too dark we checked the frogs and closed in the hens. I thought of Nanna. "Chucky, chucky, chucky". Inside the Reverend Ian Paisley was roaring on the telly. He wanted nothing to do with Dublin and its Roman anti-Christ. We passed no remarks. Peter looked round at us when we spoke.

"These men are getting horrid tall", he announced. Mam washed Philomena.

"Ah deedn't they are and ould-fashioned too", Dad replied.

He told him about Eddie imitating Kelly outside and they both laughed.

Peter was happy. As happy as ever I'd seen him. Sure wasn't Patrick, his son, coming home from across the water and starting a new job with the County Council. Dad was glad and predicted that in no time at all he'd work his way up and be the top man there, such was his attitude and rearing. Peter beamed. He liked it when Dad praised his childer. Dad had great time for the Rooneys and the way they'd reared such a big family and more importantly the way they'd all

McGunker

turned out. "Begod if our own turn out half as friendly and capable Phyllis, then that'll do me, I can tell ya". Mam agreed.

It was the very next day, about noon, that it happened. I was there with Dad as he swept the street. Mam came running up the pass. She was agitated and sweating and red in the face and trembling, all in the one go. Something was wrong. It had to be. Something bad. I looked at him. His face said it all. What could it be? Sure, she'd only been gone a few minutes. Into the town to get the lock of groceries and a few slices of ham for John the Yankee coming over. Was it a crash? A puncture maybe? Did she hit something or someone by accident?

Mam stood there still trembling and then she bent over. I thought she'd be sick. She was only trying to catch her breath she assured us.

"Oh God Jimmy, oh God", she panted now. Dad put his hand on her shoulder and sent me in to get her a cuppa water. The boys were in the scullery fighting over a packet of raisins and I couldn't get through. I roared. They looked at me. Some of it dropped on the way back out. Now she was calmer.

No, she hadn't hit anyone and no it wasn't a puncture either.

There she'd been, driving down Costelloes brae and who'd come up and stopped her on the corner only Peggy Dearg in the Vauxhall. She'd plenty of room apparently but insisted on Mam reversing back up the brae and Mam couldn't do this. Mam wanted no trouble. She said to pass no remarks and to just come down and help her move the car. "I'll brake her fucking neck the bitch", Dad roared as he ploughed forward. He rolled up his sleeves. "No, no, no Jimmy please, don't, don't, don't", she started to cry. I caught Dad's arm. He was thick now, ris. Mam was right. Now was a bad time for him. I knew he could kill her or anyone else for that matter that upset our Mam in this way. He'd do something in the spur of the moment and maybe have cause to regret it later. I wrestled between calming him down and making sure she wouldn't have a heart attack over the whole thing. I could see both points of view. He was right to be thick. Peggy Dearg was a bitch to block the road like that and intimidate Mam the way only she could. I'd seen her before. Sure she'd done it to her own constantly. But now was a time to be calm and to rise above it all.

Me and Mam struck off together like we'd done yon day beyond in Drumalee when Tommy had been run down, below on the narrow road. We walked quickly. She begged me not to say or do anything. "The quiet way's the best Michael, just pass no remarks, don't be like your father", she pleaded. I agreed.

There she sat, RID 550, on Costelloe's brae corner. We got in. Mam got it started and I released the handbrake. She revved and revved and eventually got moving back up far enough to allow Peggy Dearg car to pass. It didn't. She drew near and I could see that she had a passenger on board; a woman. I looked at her now. She shocked me; the vitriolic look, the foam spewing from her mouth as she ranted and raved, the hatred etched on her cheeks and then the sniggering grin. Worst than that was the fact that she had Radioactive Kate sitting alongside her and she too was sniggering away at us. I eyeballed her. A look that told her plenty. A look that told her that I knew from the grown-ups that she was no better than her brother, who'd returned from England to run a farm and him only a double-crossing throat-cutting git that had forgotten the past, when their family and Mam's had been fierce friendly altogether. "Eaten bread's soon forgotten", McGunker had always said. He was right. Radioactive Kate stopped sniggering and looked downwards. She had to. She knew she was wrong. Peggy Dearg revved and revved and blew triumphantly on her horn. We sat there. Mam trembled. I wondered what would happen. If only someone would come along and witness this. But sure no one would believe it and since Peggy Dearg had the whole neighbourhood terrified of her, no one would want to hear it anyway. There I sat, caught between passing no remarks and wanting to fight back. It was pointless though. If only she'd drive on home, the bitch, and bring sly Radioactive Kate with her. But no, she persisted. Now and again, she spat. I thought of McGunker. "Fighting back against yon one will cost yous Conartys", he'd warned. "You're better off leaving her be, give her time and she'll destroy her own and drive them away when she has no one else to fight with, and then she'll wither and die like the rest of us, she'll win an odd battle surely, but'll lose the war eventually". Mam squeezed my hand and then gambled. She put the car in gear and moved forward away from yon evil bitch. We only went as far as Reilly's shop. Her face was white. Coming home the road she handed me a curly-wurly and pleaded for me not to tell Dad what had really happened.

Anyway we passed the spot where all hell had broken loose earlier. Mrs. Costelloe waved her dish cloth. Inside Dad wanted to know what had kept us? Mam filled the kettle. Dad looked at me inquisitively. I looked away, a look that told him I'd tell him all later, at milking time. I knew the score the way he did now. The next morning me and Martin Smith served Mass for Father Dolan. Peggy Dearg and Prince Philip sat in the very front row. They were first up for Holy Communion.

"The body o' Christ". I held out the plate. "Amen", she answered. I looked her straight in the eye but it was different now. She turned, serene and pious. Prince Philip did the same thing and straightened his tie after blessing himself. Outside in the car park Radioactive Kate smiled and said it was a grand morning. Mam spoke and passed no remarks. I looked her straight in the eye too and then she turned and walked away to her brother's car.

Chapter 35

Dad was off the next day, Monday. Young Harry Johnston was filling the petrol.

Though some of the bales were heavy, we preferred bringing them in than the cocks of hay. We could see more progress with every windrow opened in the fields and with every load drawn in on the cock-lifter. Besides it all seemed tidier. The whole thing was to build them straight and keep them tilted inwards. We took it in turns to go down for the loads. Dad hummed away…"Many young men of twenty said goodbye…" With no hood on the tractor days like this one were great. The soft breeze brought welcome relief from the sticky hayshed and I wondered how Mick Brady and indeed McGunker himself had managed in bygone days. Mam pealed our spuds. Her glasses steamed. A car pulled up outside. We leapt, thinking it was McGunker and Yankee John, his brother. Outside, the bullman requested a basin of water and soap and a towel. He looked at us and smiled. Pulling a pen from his inside pocket, he wrote down our Friesian cow's ear-tag number. We asked him questions, lots of questions. "Don't call me a bullman, I'm an artificial inseminator", he informed us. We looked at each other. "What team do ya support?" Eddie enquired as the bullman pulled on a plastic glove and proceeded to stick a long needle-like yoke up our Friesian cow's arse.

"I support me wife and family and that's as far as it goes", he replied.

James handed him the money and took the yellow docket in return. No, the bullman didn't want tae, he was under pressure and had lots more calls to make, thanks all the same. We followed him to his car. He looked at his list. John Joe Lyons was next. "What happens now?" asked Harry. He ticked off Jimmy Conaty, Corratubber and folded his notebook.

"What happens now?" he repeated. "Well, with a bit of luck, in nine months time, your Friesian will have a big bull calf and he'll be worth a few bob".

We trailed alongside as he backed up his car.

"Is it a bit like Georgie Best and Pele's daughter having sex?" Harry beamed.

The bullman looked at us, smiled and then drove off. We headed back. Harry laughed. Philomena informed him that he was an ould-fashioned pup. He couldn't care less.

"Georgie Best, superstar
He met Pele's daughter in a bar
Georgie Best, superstar
They now own a farm..."

He stopped as Charlie Breslin's car pulled up behind us and a big bronzed man, with brilliant white teeth, got out on our street. He wore a green jersey with a white shamrock crest. It was John Brady. We shook hands and led him inside. McGunker followed, listening to our tale.

"Boys oh boys, the McGunker Conartys are bulling cows now, boys oh boys".

Another man came too. We knew him to see. Inside, the grown-ups shook hands. I sensed their friendship. The third man was Jimmy too, Jimmy Murphy from the Bridge. The Murphys and McGunker's people were related. He reminded me of Peter Rooney.

Anyway, Mam put on our kettle and Dad poured four Crested Tens. He left the bottle on the table and nodded at James to fill a jugful of water.

They talked. About the weather and Roseanne's flu and his family beyond in the States and the Murphys below in the Bridge. John the Yank went through our names and ages. He never mentioned his own son or the girlfriend or the mountain or sex either. We liked him. He kept talking. No, he'd never heard of Kevin Keegan. Yanks preferred baseball and their own American football and a bit of golf too.

Now and then he'd turn round to the grown-ups to answer a question but kept coming back to us.

Yes, he'd seen Kennedy once, in the flesh. A fine, tall, thin, good-looking man with an ojous smile that all the women fell for. He'd been mowing his garden the day Kennedy was shot in Dallas, Texas.

"Gee, I'll never forget it", he told us.

The news had rocked America. People wept openly, not just the Irish, everyone, black and white, cried in the streets and sure what else could they do? He was gone now, gone forever.

Some liked the Kennedys and more didn't. Yet they'd had fierce hard luck altogether and now people talked about the Kennedy curse and maybe there was more to come.

"Goddammit, look at Bobby and sure it's only a matter of time before they get Teddy, those sons of bitches".

We agreed with him and said it was a terror altogether. He seemed pleasantly surprised that James had heard of the FBI and Sirhan Sirhan and the CIA and Oswald and no, he'd never met Muhammad Ali or Joe Frazier but wouldn't mind shaking either of their hands. We kept hopping the questions. He knew all about the troubles in Norn Ireland and John Hume and Bernadette Devlin and Merlyn Rees and Paisley and the collapse of the Sunningdale agreement and

Garret Fitzgerald ringing up Henry Kissinger for help. And the end of internment and Edward Heath and Brian Faulkner too. And no, there'd never be peace, not in his time anyway and the IRA ceasefire wouldn't hold and sure they had fierce support beyond in the States altogether. What else would Irish people do over there only support them?

Sure looking at the pictures on television and seeing Father Daly and him waving a white hankie and it doused in blood and him trying to save a young fella's life that day, bloody Sunday, and the Brits still firing at them, what else were the Yankees to think?

Sure it was the worst thing the Brits could ever have done. "Remember", he told us, "the same British troops were welcomed by the Catholics at first cos they'd been battered and oppressed and burnt out by the Loyalists and now, goddammit, if ever a young fella needed an excuse to join the IRA, he got it that day in Derry, January 30th, nineteen hundred and seventy two".

He paused then and drank some more of his whiskey. Our eyes followed him. "Is Georgie Best in the IRA?" Eddie asked him. "Does he help them plant car bombs? Cos when that happens the policemen have to shovel up the people's guts off the street", he informed him.

John the Yank had never heard tell of Georgie Best. We looked at each other.

Mam was leaving the men over in Fairtown and Dad got up to go out and milk. We shook hands with the American and he promised he'd be back and then we'd talk some more about the Kennedys and the Mafia and Muhammad Ali and Elvis Presley too. He handed James a five-dollar note and told him to trade it in Packie Brady's shop.

And then he was gone. Gone back to Fairtown, his birthplace, with McGunker his brother and Jimmy Murphy his friend. Later on we gathered fifty-eight frogs for the frog-man and came home tired. Mam and Dad were dressed up. They were meeting the Bradys in

Sean Boylan's bar and she worried that we'd act the brat or maybe break something. James assured her we wouldn't.

I could tell by the way he lifted the loose hairs from the collar of her brown dress, the one Anna Mae had sent her, that he was glad she was getting out and didn't want her worrying. The door closed and he pulled out the five-dollar note and warned us that anyone acting the bollox wouldn't be going to Packie's shop in the morning.

Anyway we watched the tail end of Hall's Pictorial Weekly with the men dressed up as nuns and everyone giving out about the Government and the state of the economy. Lying in bed later on, I thought of Kennedy and what it must've been like getting shot through the head like that and what his poor wife and childer made of it all. Maybe his people would've been better off staying at home all those years ago and not getting mixed up with the Mafia and the CIA and the FBI and their like. I thought of the hole in Kennedy's head and then changed things completely.

Tommy Smith hoofed a long ball out of defence and Peter Cormack nodded it down into my path. I looked up, just in time, to dodge Johnny Giles' tackle, a thundering one, and the crowd cheered. Billy Bremner came across but I evaded him too.

"Here, Michael, here", I could hear Stevie Heighway's call.

I released the ball down the wing and from Stevie's cross, John Toshack nodded it down and K.K. finished it into the bottom right corner. The Kop went wild. Kev pulled me aside and told me to watch Bremner and Giles and to keep out of their way. I nodded. He reminded me of what had happened yon day in the charity shield between him and Bremner and them throwing off their jersies in disgust.

"Don't worry son, I'll watch out for ya". Tommy Smith's words encouraged me and I smiled at him.

We headed back to the centre circle.

At the end of the game Johnny Giles shook hands and said "Nothing personal son, nothing personal". Jackie Charlton laughed.

McGunker

Downstairs Mam cut the last of Roseanne's soda bread as the postman arrived.

"Par Avion" it said on the front.

Uncle Eddie was fine and had settled in well and though the rainy season was coming, the poor people were still very hungry and sick. He needed a book on alternative medicine which could be got in the second-hand bookshop in Cavan and sent on to him. He reminded Mam of the time they'd won the drama cup beyond in Tubbercurry. She smiled to herself and folded his letter.

I opened the ledger slowly. Harry had stopped at 615,200. I closed it over again and passed no remarks.

Anyway Packie was reading a book about the Germans and one buck in particular called Martin Bormann. Seemingly he licked up to Hitler and made him feel like a genius. He'd even bought him a farm and an ojous big house altogether. He controlled the finances and lifted one German marc per month from eight million party members and Packie reckoned Fianna Fáil should do the same. Bormann told the Nazis not to buy anything in a Catholic shop. It bet all. "It's a good job your shop is here in Corratubber Packie or else them Nazis could burn ya out of it", said Tommy. Packie pulled on his pipe and laughed. Anyway he named his eldest son Adolf Martin Bormann and didn't he grow up, according to Packie, and become a Catholic priest in spite of his father, the bollox. He escaped when the war ended and was sentenced to death in absentia.

"What does that mean Packie?" I asked.

"Well. He's wanted dead or alive", he replied, "anyone seeing him can feel free to shoot". We looked at each other.

"They should ring up Francie Kelly or the IRA or Muhammad Ali or even Clint Eastwood", Harry suggested, "they'd be sure to get him". Packie laughed again before explaining the conversion rate from dollar to pound to our James and giving him back his change.

Outside he reminded us of the Fianna Fáil bazaar taking place the next night and gave James a green ticket for Dad. "Sure yous might come yourselves boys and sign up for the party?" he laughed.

"The Nazi party?" Eddie shouted back as we crossed over the road. Packie smiled.

Chapter 36

That evening we tackled the dunkel for the very first time on our own. We had two grapes, one of our own and the other one borrowed from McGunker. The dunkel was the pile of cow-shite that had piled up from the previous winter and spring when the cows had been in. Now we were drawing it out to the fields and dumping it in piles from our transport box which could be spread later when the aftergrass had been ate. The warm weather made things sticky and the smell was a terror. We took turns, me and James and Tommy. The one thing worse than this was trying to clean out the oul stable where the young weanlings had been housed all winter. They'd left behind them two foot of bedding; rushes and shite mainly. It rolled back into layers handy enough but was a divil to lift. The dirt got into our skin and clothes and the smell of it was a fret. Then the blisters appeared. I thought of Lorna Hughes below in Athlone.

Anyway Fianna Fáil had to cancel their bazaar because Maurice O'Doherty announced on the radio that Dev was dead. It was a fret. He'd been Taoiseach for twenty-one years and President for fourteen. It just bet all. We'd often heard Nanna talking about him but hadn't passed enough remarks. Now he was gone. We went down to Packie's anyway thinking there'd be a bit of crack. They had a sign up on the door. It read, "Bazaar cancelled, owing to the death of Eamonn de

Valera, founder of our nation". A crowd gathered regardless and the men huddled in groups and smoked fags and muttered. They looked to Packie for leadership. He offered up a decade of the rosary and finished it off with "May his soul and all the souls of the faithful departed, through the mercy of God, rest in peace, Amen". Packie had bottles of stout for the men that wanted a drink. McGunker said it was cheaper within in Sean Boylan's. Peter Rooney laughed and lit up a Woodbine.

Some of the Ballyhaze men were there and wanted to know what the local cumann should do? Packie looked at them. "What do yous want to do? Help dig his grave? Or go to the wake maybe?" No one replied.

McGunker laughed. He had no time for the young buck, "the Taoiseach", he called him, the lad everyone said wanted to be our next Fianna Fáil councillor. He got up to speak. "Whatever brains he has he's sitting on them", muttered someone behind us as the County Councillor elect paid tribute to Dev. McGunker had a few drinks in him now and laughed. "Boys oh boys, what would yon upstart know about constitutional politics?" he asked Peter Rooney. Peter shook his head and smiled. The small crowd clapped quietly when he had finished and he jumped down off Packie and Kathleen's pumphouse roof and adjusted his tie. I could see that he was wearing a green, white and gold Fianna Fáil badge. The men talked some more. We ate our penny bars. Kathleen poured us coke in the kitchen. She smiled and told us she couldn't give a shite either way. "Sure there's thousands starving beyond in Africa and not a word about them", she informed us, "anyway, as long as there's a bit to be ate and a body is able to ate it, then what more could we ask for?" We agreed.

Outside, the odd car passed by, on its way to Cootehill and seeing the crowd, slowed down. We headed up the hill for home. The papers and telly were full of it about Dev and I longed for Nanna to be around so as she could explain things properly to me. In her absence I turned to John Tully when we met him again at Kettoe's bush.

McGunker

And sure it so happened that Dev was a hero alright and had played his part in the '16 rebellion and had only been spared on account of the Yankee blood he'd had within him. His father was Spanish so that explained the funny sounding de Valera surname. John took off his hat and mopped the sweat from his brow. He was in no hurry and only liked talking history and giving his opinion, when I suggested that maybe he was in a rush and wanted to go and look at his bullocks. "Aw deed aye, sure it's good to talk", he told us. The evening sun disappeared behind Hughie Smith's of the mountain and a magpie twittered away in the trees. I thought back to the day when we'd sat there with Fr. Eddie after Nanna had died.

Anyway, hadn't Dev and Collins from Cork, the big fella, fought side by side with Boland and the others against the Brits and had taken the British Empire to its very knees. Then there were the talks, the peace talks beyond in London, that Dev himself had refused to go to and had sent Collins, against his will, instead. "Oh, he was cute, the same Dev alright, boys". He stuck back on his hat.

Sure the delegation couldn't get the thirty-two counties they'd wanted and had to settle for the twenty-six instead, twenty-three originally if they'd left in ourselves and counties Monaghan and Donegal too. "And thank God they didn't, things are bad enough down here boys, I'm sure you'll agree?" We did. Collins knew it wouldn't be enough but sure what could they do? "I've just signed me own fecking death warrant", he'd told his friends getting off the boat. "And do yous know something boys? He was right". We looked at each other.

Eddie Fitzsummons came up the hill on his tractor and normally we'd have taken a lift home. But John Tully was too interesting now and we just hadn't enough urge within us to part.

"What team do ya…?" "Shhh, shhh", James barked at Eddie and motioned at John to carry on. Anyway, sure Dev wasn't happy and then came the split, with the pro-treaty on one side and the anti-treaty on the other. Sure it bet all. The same boys that had earlier fought, side by side, tooth and nail, to get rid off the Brits after seven hundred years of occupancy, now turned the guns on each other. "That was our civil war boys, our civil war", he told us, "it'd be the same as if yous boys were divided and split in the years to come and trying to kill each other but sure that'll never happen boys, not to sons of Phyllis and Jem". We looked at each other. He continued, "Collins had played more than his part and had outsmarted and killed more Brits than Dev could ever have dreamt of and knew that half a loaf, or twenty-six counties, was better than no bread at all but then your wans, being anti-treaty, like the McEvoys, might see things differently boys, they might indeed and might even be right, I don't know to be honest, sure I'm only voicing an opinion boys, voicing an opinion". He opened the blue door and rolled up the window fearful of an oncoming shower. I told him we hadn't a clue about things but were willing to learn and begged him to carry on and tell us some more. He scratched his head and looked at his watch and then smiled, a wry smile, a smile that told us he'd come so far and that he'd better finish off his story now. Anyway, didn't they set up an ambush below in Co. Cork, his native county, and didn't Collins end up dead on the road, as dead as a doornail, with his brains blown out. It was just like poor Kennedy beyond in America, I thought to myself. "Was it an assassination so?" James asked him. "Well it's funny you know, young Conarty, they say that the shot that killed him was actually fired from behind, whether accidental or deliberate we'll never know, either way he was gone, just like Dev is now and we'll all be, some day". He cleared his throat and spat the contents out into the hedge behind us. "Pass no remarks me gasuns, I'm only telling yous what I know, merely voicing an opinion". And with that John Tully sat in and drove off and left his bullocks for another day. We kicked a plastic bottle on the road for home and only stopped once and that was to tant Mary Margaret's goats from the ditch. "I wouldn't mind assassinating yon big wan", James laughed, before concealing his stone at the sound of John Joe's new Vauxhall heading into Ned's brae. John Joe blew the horn and smiled as he passed, a smile that indicated he knew what we were up to and couldn't give a shite either way as he'd probably done worse, himself and Felim Dunne, when they'd been our ages not long since before. We walked on. "Imagine his poor father and brother died in the same year a lock of years ago", James informed us, "it must've been horrid hard on the mother and the rest of them, Mam says they're daecent oul divils the Lyons' and one of them is even getting married to McCreesh the footballer above in Armagh, and he's supposed to be famous and she's a beauty queen too".

Anyway McGunker's outside light was on now and Roseanne had a holy candle from Knock lit for Dev on the kitchen table. "Don't mention your man, Collins from Cork", James muttered to the rest of us as she turned to the dresser for sweets. We knew better. Roseanne showed us the Evening Press Dad had sent over. "Dev, an influential statesman", it said. I read on. Sure he'd even written our constitution under the watchful eye of the Archbishop, himself a native of Cootehill and had boldly declared us a Republic in 1949. Roseanne had been in the States at the time. "And that was his legacy and what he should be remembered for boys", she said.

Later that night I met Dad in the bathroom and asked him what a legacy was? He told me it was what a fella had left behind him and that in his own personal case, it'd be sweet feck all. He looked at me and laughed and then added more brylcream to his hands and, having mixed it a bit, slid it back through his hair before combing it out. And then he told me that it didn't matter whether we voted Fianna Fáil or Fine Gael, that they were out for themselves and all they could get. "Gobshites, the lot of them, and yon prick spouting shite from Packie's pumphouse last night, sure he wouldn't know his arse from his elbow". He rinsed his hands under the cold tap. "Coming in here to preach to the people, who the hell does he think he is? I'd rather listen to Benny Hill meself". He smiled again and winked at me. During the night someone painted "Up the IRA" on the road beyond at Drumalee. I know cos we saw it the next morning heading into Fagans for a roast chicken for the visitors coming.

They buried Dev and loads of important people turned up for the funeral and we saw it all on the telly and I wondered if him and our Nanna and the McEvoys and Michael Collins would talk if they ever met each other above in heaven.

Anyway they came in at half-eight or so, all of them dressed to the nines; McGunker, Roseanne, Yankee John, the Murphys, Francie Kelly and the Rooneys. Mam had been fussing and rooting all afternoon and had warned us not to touch the fancy place mats or Anna Mae's crystal glasses that she'd carefully wiped and positioned on our good sitting room table. Dad took their coats and told us to feck off outside with ourselves for a while.

We hadn't intended hitting Philip Brady's neatly kept orchard, it just happened. We wandered up Packie's rocks and came in the back way through the white-headed cows that lay chewing their cuds in the still of that autumn evening. The Volkswagen was gone and no one about, or so we thought.

His plum trees were laden, mostly purply-red with the odd green one interspersed that hadn't been hit by that warm summer's sun. It didn't feel right. Philip was so decent and friendly, always sure to buy a ticket or two, whatever the cause, and then liberally pour Cavan Coca Cola that would've been nurtured and brewed by Benny Costello himself within in the Mineral Waters. He had nearly as good a collection of biscuits and sweets as Mrs. Edgeworth beyond in the shop. He'd been to the States for a while and would sit there in his neat little kitchen and tell us the tales from this faraway land. Like the time he'd worked on the railways and had strolled in one morning at ten minutes past his starting time and his boss, a Yankee foreman, had pointed to his watch in frustration. "Ah sure as we say at home in Ireland, a good man's never late", Philip cheerfully informed him. The Yankee sacked him on the spot.

"What did ya do Philip?" James asked.

"What did I do? What did I do?" he repeated.

"Sure I went and got meself another job, that's what I did and kept me mouth shut, early or late, everyday afterwards".

We were just sneaking out round by the gable when we spotted Jaffa, as Dad had nicknamed him, and him busy filling diesel from Philip's tank.

We stopped in our tracks, fearful of being spotted and then darted back in behind the neatly trimmed hedgerow that circled the house. We held our breaths and watched. He finished his pumping and then carefully screwed back on the cap of his five-gallon drum, all the while checking around him. Jaffa was totally oblivious to our presence and us only a few yards away. It was too serious for laughing though; even the young ones could sense this now. No one moved. We watched as he pulled on his hood and then headed down through the meadow, keeping tight to the ditch, till he got to the road. Now and then he'd stop and change hands so as to lighten the load and in no time at all he was gone. Feeling safer we sneaked out, back the way we'd come in and over the rocks for home.

"The cheek of the hoor", James whispered to me, "ceilying away every second night of the week and making Philip feel he couldn't manage without him, and then… then nicking his diesel when he gets his back turned, by Jaysus we'll tell him tomorrow Michael, we will, we'll have to won't we?"

"What did ya say James, what did ya say?" Tommy wanted to know. The others looked round

"Shh, shh, nothing, I'll tell ya later, ok", he replied. We kept going.

The younger ones headed inside and we stood in the hayshed debating what we should do.

James was livid. "I'm telling poor oul Philip tomorrow, I don't give a shite, it's not fair on him, Jaffa shouldn't do that and we're eyewitnesses now Michael, whether we like it or not!" We finished off the last of our loot.

"Ok, so we'll tell him James, fair enough, we'll tell him, but will we mention the fact that we only saw what we saw cos we were nicking his plums at the time, sure we're no better ourselves, are we?"

James looked at me and then jumped, startled by Dad's call. "Boys, boys, are yous right?"

We agreed on the way in that we'd discuss it in bed and in the meantime we'd pass no remarks.

Chapter 37

The grown-ups had finished their eating and Mam was making fresh tea. We circled round John. Dad tried to disperse us. We peppered him with questions about Ali and Elvis and the Kennedys. He laughed, "One at a time, goddammit, one at a time". Eventually we got round to the Mafia and Yankee John gave us an insight we'd never forget. These families, their Godfathers, the importance of respect and honour and their dying allegiance to the Roman Catholic Church and the man himself, above. The Sicilians bet all, hardened men bound by codes, who'd come across to the States and wrapped it up for themselves by wiping out anyone that stood in their way, even the Irish.

Harry was hovering with intent. "Are you in the IRA or the Mafia or the British Army?" he asked. We laughed.

The Yank looked at him and smiled and then placed his big, bronzed hand on our little brother's thin white wrist. He whispered, "Well, even if I was son, I'd be bound by Omerta not to open my mouth". He winked at us and then supped a mouthful of whiskey before turning to Jimmy Murphy to discuss Pat Spillane's shooting technique. Later, when the younger ones had gone up to bed, James got his attention at the side of our table and quizzed him again about this Omerta stuff.

Anyway, it transpired that the Sicilians had a code of honour whereby no one witnessed anything, knew anything, and more importantly, said anything. "Omerta, the code of silence boys, hear no evil, see no evil, do ya get my drift?" He lifted his dark bushy eyebrows and smiled. And that was that then. No point in telling tales on Jaffa.

"We weren't there", James whispered in bed, "We saw nothing, we heard nothing and so we say nothing, ok?" I agreed before turning sideways to sleep. Silence. Omerta. It was best if we passed no remarks.

Dathlones arrived after dinnertime. We heard their car pulling up and we leapt out together. Tony Hughes looked as brown as any Yank. They'd been to Spain on an aeroplane and Anna Mae gave Mam a gold banglet and told her to mind it. They asked Harry about his numbers. "I'm up to nearly three quarters way, Eddie says", Harry beamed into his face. Tony smiled and ruffled his hair. Lorna's toe nails were painted and no she didn't want to see the new cow we'd just bought from Seamus Ruddy the dealer. They'd only come up for the Castletara night of the "At home" week below in Ballyhaze and Lorna was excited. Derek showed us his poster, a full sized picture of Wolverhampton Wanderers and warned Tommy not to crease it.

The "At home" week was held in the big tent alongside the school and the village was packed. James had been there before but this was my first time. The grown-ups drank in Donohoe's pub and then made their way back up to the wooden hutch and paid their way in. Everyone seemed happy and friendly and shook hands with the emigrants as they were called. I heard PJ Lynch and his brother Sean and some other fella talking about Arsenal and Brady in particular. I moved closer to listen. "Sure we were up on the North Bank the last Saturday in May and Brady skips past two of them, right in front of us, and floats her in with his left boot and didn't she curl away from the keeper and big Nelson the full back nodded her home, ah sure Brady's a terror, he's a genius altogether". PJ could see I was listening. "Ah, young Conarty, how's she cutting? Any word from Kevin Keegan?" He clapped me on the back. I moved back inside following James and the older boys. Big Tom from Monaghan sweated and sang above on the stage. Fast songs, ballads, slow sets… "The garden of Eden has vanished they say…" he tapped his boot on the stage… "But I know the lie of it still, just turn to the left at the bridge of Finea… and stop when halfway to Cootehill" The crowd waltzed. Aidey Hughes had his hands on the Slowey girl's shoulders and he winked at me as he passed. Derek wanted more money for coke but Tony was too busy acting the lad with Johnny Con to hear him. They laughed… "Ah sure she's the sort of whore that gets her ears cleaned out once a week for fear of missing something", said Tony.

I stood next to the strangers. The biggest fella had bushy hair and a red face. He was sweating. "There's going to be a wow tonight, there's going to be a wow, I can feel it in me bones" he kept shouting. Now and again he'd slurp more from his beer bottle. Big Tom winked at someone on the floor. I looked up at him in his shiny blue suit with the gold coloured buttons. One of the Quinn triplets said he was an ojous big farmer below in County Monaghan and made a fortune from the singing as well. He sweated a terror. The music stopped and he threw off his jacket. Everyone bought tickets for the raffle. Then there was the tea and the sangwidches beyond in the corner. The pushing started and then the shouting. The big bushy red-faced fella ended up outside on his arse in the grass. He'd been right, there would be a wow tonight, he'd started it and a small lad from Drung had sent him flying with a box. He got himself up and I could see the blood trickle from his nose. I felt sorry for him standing there alone now and not knowing whether to head back inside for more or simply go home. If only he'd stayed quiet, I told myself. "A shut mouth catches no flies", Dad always said. Anyway Paddy Walshe presented the football medals to the big lads and called out my name at the end. I felt a little bit awkward climbing the three steps up onto the stage. After all it wasn't as if I'd done very much to help the under fourteens bate the Redhills boys in the tournament final, I'd only come on for the last ten minutes or so and hadn't contributed very much either way. "There ya are son, well done", he smiled and shaking my hand, presented me with my first ever medal. "Thanks Paddy", I mumbled. "Thanks very much". He patted me on the back.

Big Tom battered out a few more songs and then we all stood still...

"Shina Fianna Fall
Ata fee gall ag Erne..."

I remembered the words from Bean Uí Fiaich's room. The grown-ups stood rigid and some of the men had their hands clasped behind their backs. Tony Hughes tried not to laugh. Outside it had started to rain, though not too heavily as we joined the queue with our cousin Eddie at Pat Cahill's van. I could see the buckets of chips he'd cut up in the corner and them soaking away in the water. The steam bet all as it poured out of the place and someone tried to grab the bottle of vinegar.

Big Tom's van edged its way out through the crowd. "Ha-Ho, Big Tom, ya bollox ya, you couldn't sing to save your life", shouted Tom Quinn as he banged his fist against the side of the van. Everyone laughed. The van stopped. Big Tom let the window down and growled. He reminded me a bit of Clint Eastwood himself. I could see the freckles on his big knuckly hands and the sweat that still poured down his red hairy chest. And then he smiled and grunted a wee laugh, a wee laugh that said ah sure it's well for yous lads having the crack and with that he was gone, on down through the village and back home to his farm below in Co. Monaghan.

We ended up at home very late. Tony and their childer stopped over in Ballyhaze. Anna Mae stayed with us. Dad opened a wee green bottle of white wine. "How do ya drink this shite?" he laughed. Anna Mae smiled and sipped from her glass. She talked of bygone days when she'd cycled to Bailieboro and then home again on her half-

McGunker

day. And the crack they'd had at the carnivals, her and the Cahills and Boylans and Mickey Costello of course. "Ah poor Mickey, he's beyond in Derby now, in England", she said. She'd been talking to the Greenan brothers, Andy and John.

Anyway Anna Mae adjusted her glasses in the same way Mam did and then got upset when Nanna's name came up. She pulled out a hankie and wiped herself. She talked. Nanna had had too hard a life but hadn't helped herself by being so strong-willed and independent. She'd fought the lone battle and it needn't have been that way at all. People were willing to help; she had great neighbours but always insisted on paying her way. Though admirable in one way it only made life tougher for herself. I thought back to her glasses and the polished shoes and the sunlight soap and the sadness squeezed me in the throat. Poor Nanna, she'd never been outside Cavan town much, never mind flying off to Spain.

Anna Mae had a lie-in that morning and coughed and spluttered when she got up. I knew it was the fags. Mam made toast and buttered it into a pile. We all grabbed. Anna Mae laughed; "Ah sure they're great gasuns God bless them". Tony arrived. He looked at his watch. They headed for Fairtown to leave their goodbyes as John Brady too was heading home that very evening, off up to Dublin and then across the Atlantic Ocean the next day to the land of Ali and Elvis and the Kennedys and the Mafia as well. We knew he'd be calling and so we hung round all day.

Bomber called with news of the caravan. Auntie Kathleen had heard it below in the shop. It had been towed out earlier that morning by the Vincent-d-Paul and a strange, old man by the name of TomFada now lived there it seemed. Everyone was to be wary of him, Bomber warned us. "Aye they say he's up to no good and no one knows where he's come from", he continued. We looked at each other.

"Three and in", called Eddie.

Bruno barked and tore off for the ball.

"Aye, I swear to God he's there alright boys and don't go near him, he's there all alone over near Kettoes and his name is TomFada and nobody wants him, aye and someone's even sent for the guards for Goddsakes", said Bomber. "Is he a mafia man?" asked Harry.

We all laughed and then got stuck into the game. Brooking versus Keegan versus Brady versus Hector versus Pearson and Georgie Best! It didn't last long. Charlie Breslin's car pulled up on the pass. McGunker got out first and then his big brother. They weren't staying long as their driver would be back in an hour.

We followed them in. "C'mon boys get out to feck quick and let us talk awhile in peace", Dad roared. Big John smiled and nodded at us to sit round him. Dad shook his head.

"Didya hear about yer man above at Kettoes?" asked Tommy.

"Yeh, sure I did", he replied, "The guy has to live somewhere I guess".

Dad poured crested tens. And yes the Yank was looking forward to getting home, it had been a good holiday alright and yet he was looking forward to getting back to his family.

James nudged him, "Tell us more about the Kennedys, John". He smiled at him.

"What is it with you guys and the Kennedys?" he asked, "you seem to think that the President was God Almighty himself". He thought for a moment or two and then went on to inform us, that in his opinion, the greatest Yankee President of them all had been Abraham Lincoln or Abe as they called him. He was the man famous for his Gettysburg cemetery address that had honoured the Civil war dead of America. He'd come from a very humble farming background and had had it rough in every sense of the word. He'd been their sixteenth President and his term was completed entirely in wartime and he'd even lost a young son in office and sure then his poor wife had gone mentally insane.

"What's that mean?" piped up Harry, taking a break from his figures. "Shh, shh, listen will ya?" I squealed. John smiled and was persuaded to continue his story. Even as a kid life had been tough for Abraham Lincoln. A kick from a horse had left him with a cast in his eye and he appeared lanky and awkward and not what you'd expect from a President at all. And despite all of this he'd worked shocking hard for peace between the peoples of the North and the South. Sure they respected him for this, most of them anyway, and even today loads of towns and roads have been named after him and a big pile of statues erected in his honour, such was his greatness. He'd come from an even humbler background than Kennedy and had had as good a vision, if not better, than himself. He'd wanted freedom and equality for all the people under the law and especially the blacks and fought hard for an end to their slavery. He'd been re-elected in eighteen hundred and sixty-four and had been assassinated the following year just like poor oul Kennedy, rest in peace. And that ended that. The car horn honked loudly outside. The grown-ups shook hands. McGunker led the way out and I could see a tear or two in his brother's eye as he hugged our Mam and Dad a goodbye. We followed the car out the lane. "Say hello to the Kennedys", Harry shouted, "and the Mafia and Muhammad Ali too", added Eddie. John Brady looked sideways and smiled.

During the night Ruddy's cow bawled and bawled. She was having her calf and the waterbag was out. Dad got the feet and tightened baler twines around them and then we pulled. She grunted in pain as the head came, all covered in slime and then the body slid handy enough till the back legs slowed things down momentarily. Slap! The calf landed in a bed of goo and shite and Dad widened its hind legs. "A bull boys, a bull calf and we'll have plenty of milk for the winter", he told us. We lifted him up to his mother, who between pants of agitation and excitement licked him totally clean and then, slowly but surely, he got to his feet and started to suck. Dad explained all about the beastings, the most nourishing of milk he'd have to himself for a few days till we got him onto a bucket and then Ruddy's cow could start earning her keep. She dropped her after-birth, the cleanings, when we'd gone back to bed. I know cos Dad lifted them in the morning with the grape and fired the jelly-like mass across our egg-tree hedge. Philomena thought it quite disgusting. I wondered what Lorna Hughes would make of it all below in Athlone.

Chapter 38

Anyway the door was closed as we trailed by and so we passed no remarks. His caravan looked plain enough and small too and we could see the bundle of sticks he'd obviously gathered on the mountain and shoved underneath. There was no one at Castletara school either when we got there though someone had scuffled the weeds and swept round the back in readiness for its re-opening. We found ourselves a busted orange ball out on Pe Smith's rocks and had a kickabout. I pulled myself up on the windowsill and gawked inside. Nothing had changed over the summer.

The big map of Éire hung in its usual place and all the wee guts of its western seaboard were still intact. I laughed to myself. We met Francie coming back from the shop.

"Bejeminey that's great boys, a bull calf for the Conartys, bejeminey there'll be no stopping yous now".

We lay back on Packie Tully's ditch and finished off the penny bars James had gotten us in the shop. We hadn't a care in the world. "Imagine Yankee John is up there somewhere right now", said Eddie as he pointed to the clear blue sky with its one fluffy white cloud. "What'd happen if the driver went up too far?" asked Harry, "would they all land up above in heaven with the McEvoys and yer man Dev and our Nanna?" We laughed. Harry got thick. He hated being laughed at. "It's alright for yous, it's alright for yous, yous are older than me, I'm only asking what'd happen, that's all", he protested. No one bothered answering him.

Anyway we picked ourselves up and headed into the hill. We could see Caitríona O'Brien and her mother Maggie ahead of us.

He stood with his back to us and I could see that he wore the same style of gallises as our Dad. TomFada was tall, about six foot tall with snow white hair and a cast in one eye. I thought of Abraham Lincoln but only for a second. We slowed our pace nervously. I'd visions of us having to run, maybe down Hughie Smith's lane, but how would Harry manage? This was TomFada after all, the most feared man in all of Ireland, a deadly suspect, now residing on the Shantemon mountain road.

Panicky thoughts raced through my mind. I could sense the same fear in my brothers' faces. Five of us, one of him, I reassured myself. But all he wanted was one of us maybe and it'd surely be Harry and what'd Mam do then? Sure, Dad would bate him but it'd be pointless then with Harry gone. Why hadn't we listened to Bomber? The seconds passed. He spoke first.

"Whadda bout ye lads?"

"Howya, how's she cutting?" Eddie replied.

James stood out in front like he always did. If TomFada or Tom anyone wanted any of us, then he'd have to come through our James first.

No one said anything till Harry coughed nervously and addressed him.

"Are you an IRA man?"

"No", he replied.

"Are ya in the Mafia?"

"No", he laughed.

"Shhh", ordered James.

"Didya ever see Ian Paisley?" asked Eddie.

McGunker

"Once or twice wee man, on the telly, but sure you'd hear him oftener", he laughed again.

"What about Willie Whitelaw?" Eddie continued.

"Only on the telly, me lad".

"Are ya married?"

"I was".

"Where are ya from?"

"Here at the moment, that's me house". He pointed to the caravan.

"It's got its own name, no fixed abode", he laughed heartily now.

I could see the two empty whiskey bottles that had been tucked in behind the wheel.

"Bomber says you're a dangerous man", said Tommy.

"Who's Bomber?" he asked.

We looked at each other.

"Bomber sounds dangerous enough himself", he continued.

Then he turned and headed inside, hopping the one step and came back out as quickly again and handed James a fistful of sweets.

"Call again me wee men, all the best now". We thanked him and left.

Eddie and Harry thought there was no one like him, this Tom-Fada fella that nobody wanted. Sure he'd even given us sweets.

We straggled on. James cautioned us. "He seems alright the poor oul divil and sure people don't even know him, but we'd better be careful, a stranger's a stranger and never forget it".

Mary Margaret's goats were nowhere to be seen. We met McGunker at McKiernan's lane. He was pushing his bike.

"Ha-Ho", Eddie shouted.

McGunker laughed. We could see that he was sweating. He threw down his jalopy, as he called it, and lay back on the ditch.

"From now on yous may call me McGunker O'Brady", he announced.

We looked at each other.

"Why's that?" James asked him.

"Well sure they're all putting O before their names nowadays and sure McGunker might as well too, and yous may become the McGunker O'Conartys when we're at it", he laughed.

"Sure some of the Reillys are O'Reillys and some of the Gormans O'Gormans and before long everyone'll have an O before themselves, so from now on we'll be known as the McGunker O'Bradys and the McGunker O'Conartys, it sounds horrid respectable don't yous think?" We agreed. "That's it then", he said.

Anyway we told him about meeting TomFada above at Kettoe's.

In McGunker's opinion there was piles of room on the planet for everyone and sure hadn't the mountain supported plenty of families before the Great Famine and hadn't that bollox of a landlord below in Ballyhaze driven them all off cos they couldn't pay the rents. He spat on the ground. "Bad cess to him anyway". He carried on telling us how it had been once.

And sure the tracks of the spud plots were still up there to be seen and no one, certainly none of the locals, had ever complained about a tigín before. Not till now anyway.

And sure 'twas all the newcomers' faults. Them coming in and trying to change things as if they owned the place and God only knowing who they were and where they'd come from themselves or what they'd been reared on. Sure it was a fret altogether to see grown men pushing prams on the roads and hanging out clothes on the line and them wearing oul tracksuits and sunglasses and going for walks with the women and the dogs up and down the hill every evening. You'd think it was Dublin you were in or New York City itself and sure it wasn't right at all at all and the next thing'd be the men would be having the babbies themselves. McGunker closed his eyes and laughed.

"Ah dear God what's the world coming to? I couldn't imagine Jem Conarty pushing a pram or walking a dog". We agreed.

"Never let that happen to the McGunker Conartys, do yous hear me boys?"

We assured him we wouldn't.

He stuck on his bicycle clips and crushed the butt of his fag into the road and with that he was gone.

"Good luck McGunker O'Brady," I shouted. He raised his right hand in salute.

Back home there was a crisis.

Mam had promised Dathlones we'd go down for a night before the schools'd re-open but sure who'd look after the things and do the milking and stuff?

Dad had thought of asking Batty but didn't like his attitude now and him being so independent that he wouldn't give the bollox the satisfaction of turning him down or maybe asking for payment for services rendered.

"Me and Michael'll stay and do it", James shouted.

Mam wondered. "Ah we'll see boys, we'll see, sure I know yous mean well but..."

"We'll manage the best and sure yous'll be back in a day or two", I pleaded with her, "and sure if anything goes wrong, we can give McGunker a shout".

Mam and Dad talked after the tea.

They'd go in the morning when the milking was done and sure it'd do me and James no harm at all, the bit of responsibility, and us willing as well. And they'd leave plenty of grub that we could heat up and sure cornflakes'd do us rightly if we were starving and sure they'd be back in a day or so, or maybe two, if Anna Mae insisted which was more than likely, knowing her, and sure even if she did they'd be home sooner or later anyway.

They drove off at eleven and Tommy stuck his two fingers out at us from the back window of RID 550 and James laughed. We came back inside and it suddenly reminded me of the times we'd stayed here together, me and James, with Nanna and the peace and the calm there'd always been with no one about.

First stop was the shop to break on the pound note Dad had pressed into James' hand below in the hayshed before telling him we were good gasuns and what it meant to our mother. Kathleen had a bundle of sticks in her arms as we crossed over together. She was troubled. Reilly the Vit had cut the horns off their red cow and now she was bleeding a terror. Packie had tried cobwebs, several of them, but the poor oul divil wouldn't stop and now he was gone up to Annie Miney for the cure. Surely we'd met him on the road or maybe he'd gone by Mary o' the rocks. "Is that the woman that died during the snow and her last words were mind me cats?" James asked her.

"Ah deedn't it is, poor oul Mary, above on the rocks all on her own but sure she wouldn't move till she died and then the men, your father included, had carried her down here wrapped in a blanket for the wake itself". We looked at each other.

Anyway Kathleen spread jam on two cuts of soda bread and we told her about the rest of them being gone down to Athlone.

"Make sure and get up to no divilment boys and don't go near the tractor and if there's anything the matter, make sure and call, do yous hear me now? We'll be here, me and Packie and keep well away from that TomFada fella above on the mountain", she warned us.

Packie was back, beyond in the shed and the bleeding had stopped. The red cow held her head sideways. "It's a prayer boys", he whispered, "and a good one be all accounts, so never be stuck especially if the cobwebs don't work". The cow moaned. Fresh red blood stained the walls. Packie tipped his pipe upside down on the pier and emptied the thick black goo that had accumulated, from inside. Then he scraped more out with his penknife, before proceeding to pack it up again with stringy tobacco. We doddled back up the hill for home.

Philip Rooney called in just as we finished the milking and him and James struck off for the football training below in Ballyhaze. The strong evening sun disappeared behind a cloud as I let the cows out and followed them down the Bull's field lane. Tails swished to brush away the flies that lingered about and Ruddy's cow bawled back at her calf. Back in the kitchen I rummaged through the press under the stairs for a forgotten about pack of chipsticks or blackjack bar.

I found a cutting from an old newspaper, one of Fr. Eddie's; he was always doing that, cutting out interesting articles about people and underlining sentences here and yonder.

Anyway wasn't Michael Meagher a Cavan man and a famous one at that, even though he'd been born in 1843 and shot stone dead, beyond in America, thirty-eight years later. Him and his brother John had emigrated and worked at different jobs before fighting in the Civil War. Uncle Eddie had underlined Civil War and drawn an arrow out to the side of the page where he'd then written "N.B. Gettysburg address, Lincoln". I thought of Yankee John Brady. The Meaghers had worked their way up the hard way and sure wasn't Michael elected Marshal of Wichita and wasn't everything going great till he tangled with an ojous whelp of a lad named Sylvester Powell. Sure he stole horses and drank whiskey and terrorised everyone and everything in sight. They crossed paths on New Year's Day 1877. Powell was drunk and stole someone's horse and didn't Meagher give chase. But didn't Powell steal up on him later on in the night and shoot him twice in the back. Meagher fought back cos he was Irish and tough and didn't he catch up with this Powell fella outside the pub and shoot him clean through the heart. He was stone dead before he hit the ground. And that should've been that except that poor oul Meagher didn't last much longer himself. Sure wasn't he shot by a fella called Talbot and didn't the townspeople carry him into the Barber's shop where he died. I looked at the heading again, "Michael Meagher, a famous Cavan man!" I folded up the cutting and shoved it back into the press and made do with a bowlful of cornflakes instead. The clock read ten to eight and I felt uneasy about being in the house by meself. Out in the byre Ruddy's calf chewed on a bit of hay and bawled. I headed for McGunker's.

Chapter 39

The cows were still below in the three cornered field and chomped away heartily on the fresh green overgrowth as I passed. Now and again I'd kick an imaginary ball and pretend to be Keegan or rise in the air and flick my head sideways to meet a Stevie Heighway cross. Anyway I caught two frogs as I skirted Ted's bog and knew I'd have to hold on to them till I'd get to McGunker's. He wasn't there. Neither was Roseanne. I decided to avail of the galvanised bucket that sat on their street. Turning it upside down I set about imprisoning my pair of croakers and placed a stone, that I'd plucked from the nearby wall on its top, in the dual hope that they wouldn't escape and that McGunker might realise there was something beneath it and would leave well enough alone till I'd get back the next day with a fertiliser bag. I turned to go. And I shoulda gone home but didn't.

Anyway I looked up Ned's brae. All was still. I felt drawn towards the mountain. I knew I shouldn't go, the wee voice in my head said so. After all there was no one at home and what would James be supposed to think when he'd get back from the football. I shoulda left him a note. And then I comforted myself with the notion that if McGunker and Roseanne had been at home in the first place sure I'd have been away for an hour or two anyway and he'd probably have passed no remarks.

Besides it wasn't as if Mam and Dad were to know and them below in Athlone, without a care in the world, having the crack with Tony Hughes and Anna Mae.

Half ways up the brae I changed my mind again and turned to go back. I looked over towards home. The cows were still grazing and all seemed grand in the last of that late evening sunlight. Then I decided I'd go as far as Ned's. No harm in it, sure there was no one about. I doddled on another bit to the top of the sailor's brae, as Mam called it, before stopping to gawk into the half darkness of Shantemon's undergrowth. All was calm. Not a stir, not even a rabbit or a young hare to be seen like ya would normally, just the carpet-like brownness of dead needles that covered Shantemon's floor. A wasp busied itself on the nearby cluster of briars. Dad always said they were dangerous hoors at this time of the year, dying to get rid off their sting before the cold winds of Autumn set in. I passed no remarks.

The sky darkened a bit. And then I heard it. The singing. It had to be TomFada and him singing the same tune Mam had played for us umpteen times on the rickety ould record-player that Dathlones had sent up. About them lads and lassies blowing up Nelson's pillar above in Dublin in the year of sixty-six. I listened and then edged my way cautiously forwards till he came into view and then duked down behind a whin-bush for fear of being spotted. I waited. The minutes passed. He'd stopped singing by now and stood on the flat of the road with his hands on his hips like John Wayne in the movies, waiting for the other fella to make the first move. There was silence.

"Whadda bout ye, young lad?"

I stood up and waved back.

"Will ye do me a favour wee mawn?" he shouted in a Bomber Breslin like accent. I didn't know what he wanted but moved forward anyway, safe in the knowledge that there was still plenty of distance between us.

"Will ye get me a few fags wee mawn and as many sweets as ye can eat for yourself and the rest of the wee uns with the change?" he asked.

He was waving something in his hand.

I moved a wee bit closer.

It was money alright. TomFada was staggery enough on his feet, a bit like the men when they'd had too much to drink. He smiled at me and suddenly I didn't feel threatened anymore. I walked on another bit and then froze again and thought about running back. I looked behind me fearful of someone creeping up. What would James do? I asked myself. What had Bomber said? I tried to remember. Confused again, I stalled.

"Alright wee mawn, I can see ye're scared, well don't be, I've never harmed a soul in me life. I'll just put this here pound note down on the road, right there wee mawn and maybe, when I'm gone back in, you'll pick it up and go to the shop and do as I've asked and remember the sweets, do ye hear me? As many as ye can eat wee fella!"

He turned and walked away. I paused. Should I stay or should I run? I couldn't very well risk offending him now by walking away and showing a distinct distrust in him, the poor ould divil. He had enough people doing that already and besides he probably even hadn't the energy himself to make it as far as Packie's shop and I knew from Dad that the urge for a fag could be an ojous thing altogether.

But then what if?

What if Bomber was right and TomFada was an ojous dangerous buck and this was a trap and the minute I'd bend down, he'd come tearing out after me and what'd happen then? It'd be a fret. I waited.

TomFada stepped up into his home and turned to look back at me.

"There's a good wee mawn, I wouldn't ask ye only I'm stuck", he pleaded. And that swung it for me.

"Never see anyone stuck", Dad had always told us, "no matter what race or creed he may be, never see him stuck". I moved forward again and could see that he'd placed a small stone on the pound note and before I knew it, I was stooping down to pick it up.

"Alright TomFada I'll get ya your fags and I'll be back I promise ya", I shouted as I turned to go. He didn't answer. I headed back over the road and turned for a peep. He'd heard me alright and stood there waving from the door, the door of no fixed abode.

I ran as quick as I could, mindful that enough time had been wasted already and found myself sweating as I came down by McGunker's. Inside, the light was now on and Roseanne busied herself with the kitchen curtains.

I slowed up and tiptoed a bit.

I hated sneaking past. A quick kind of a sidewards glance told me the frogs hadn't moved and I guessed that McGunker was now sitting down to watch the news. He always did that and if an IRA man had been shot or arrested he'd curse the newsman and all belonging to him into hell and out of it and then surely if the weatherman said there'd be rain coming in the next day, he'd feck him out of it too altogether and then Roseanne would frown and say "Now Brother". I looked at the pound note and leapt the ditch. My heart raced. Ruddy's cow was still picking away with the rest of them and only stopped momentarily as if to query my passing. I caught another frog at the foot of the Bull's field and carried him home before pegging him into the barrel and marking it down in the book. I checked the house. Great! James wasn't home. I headed on down the pass conscious now of the fact that there wasn't anyone else about to annoy me. True, I missed my brothers and Philomena but welcomed this time to myself and sure they'd be back soon enough and then it'd be business as usual again. Below in the shop Packie took his customary time and fidgeted about. I was fidgety too, I knew I was and hoped Packie wouldn't notice. Anyway he didn't. "Good luck Packie". Kathleen met me on the way home on Costelloe's brae. She smiled and stood to talk. About the nice evening there'd been but the way the days were cutting up a terror and the ojous hot summer we'd had altogether and the way the like of it would never be seen again.

"Are yous alright up there on your own you and James?" she enquired.

"We're grand" I assured her, eager to get away.

"Who's them fags for Michael?" she then asked.

I looked at the yellow packet in my hand and paused, "oh, em, em, McGunker, they're for McGunker, Kathleen, I have to go, he's waiting", I replied and then turned and took a few short steps before skipping away. "Michael", she shouted, "Michael, Michael, sure McGunker smokes Carrolls, always has, always will, them's Sweet Aftons ya have". I stopped dead in my tracks.

"Sure they'll do him rightly Kathleen", I shouted back, "I'd better tear on". I ran backwards now.

Kathleen stared at me. She had her hands on her hips. It was a look that said she knew I was up to something. And then I turned forwards. Terrified now and sweating again, I decided the best option was just to keep going. The hall light was on telling me James was home and that I'd missed him as Packie futhered about below in the shop. I glided through the scullery and our eyes met above in the kitchen. He stared me.

"Where the hell were you?" he snapped anxiously. And sure I just had to tell him. About catching the frogs and McGunker not being at home and then me hearing the singing above on the road and TomFada leaving the money and me getting him the fags below in the shop and the pile of pennybars and blackjacks and gobstoppers I'd gotten with the change and them all for ourselves! I emptied the pockets. James's eyes lit up as he quickly snapped at a bar and set about stripping it off its plastiky coating.

Anyway we set off for the mountain.

"As long as no one finds out, you'll be ok Michael", my big brother assured me as he chewed away on his bar. We cut in behind McGunker's and up through Mary Margaret's fields and out onto Ned's Brae. TomFada was whistling. We could hear him loud and clear. A small oil lamp, like the one Nanna used to have, lit up the inside and he stooped to rake the ashes of his little black stove. We waited. James coughed. He passed no remarks. I wondered had he heard us at all and so I tapped on the window pane and James coughed again and TomFada leapt nervously. We stood back a few foot. He peered out, cursing to himself, "feck off yous free state shites, can yous not…?" He held a poker in his hand but lowered it quickly on spotting us and smiled. "Och, me wee friends, whadda bout ye lads? Come in, come in, I'm wild sorry, I thought ye were the Free State pealers! C'mon in, c'mon in", he pleaded. He held his boney hand out. We looked at each other.

James went first. Inside was cosy enough. His cups and cutlery had been washed in a basin and left in a pile to dry on the table. It was like something Francie Kelly would've done and I thought back to the night we'd been with him when Jemmy, his brother, and the Bailieboro wans as he called them had visited him at Christmas time and Francie hadn't been expecting them and he rummaged about and lit the kettle and then roared "Bring up the baste, bejeminey". We all looked round and Betty, his niece, appeared with what was left of Francie's turkey in the doorway and we laughed. It was the same now. No fixed abode might just as well have been Francie's kitchen. A transistor radio with a wonky looking aerial lay propped on a shelf against a stack of dusty and old looking books, most of them hard backed it seemed. August 1975 read the calendar from Mullens Footwear shop, that had been thumbtacked to the wall and directly above it a picture of our Lord himself and him with outstretched hands. He had a sofa, a small one at that, and it done him as a bed at night-time he informed us. A bundle of sticks lay neatly stacked beneath his only comfort, that being the stove and a worn looking broom stood upright against the far inside corner and under it a black steel shovel with rusty specks. And that was it then. No fixed abode, home to TomFada, the man everyone wanted out, or so it would seem!

Chapter 40

Anyway he made tea and gave us a chocolate coated bun apiece and then he sat down and talked. He wanted to know if we were related to Conarty the Councillor, within in the town, or not? We weren't. Well not directly but maybe back through the generations, James informed him. He wasn't sure. A car drove by and slowed up a bit. TomFada peeped through his curtains. "Probably that wee prick of a guard again", he muttered.

"He's been here twice before today alone and him trying to get me to move on", he whispered. We looked at each other. "Aye, I laughed at him boys, it'll take a better mawn than ye to get me outta here, ya wee shitbag of a freestating pealer ye, I told him". The car drove off. He closed the curtain. TomFada laughed heartily now and we felt compelled to join in. Some of the bun fell into my tea but I passed no remarks. He started again.

"I'll tell ye what me wee men, that clob is living proof that ye don't have to have a brain to become a polisman down here boys; sure if you're five foot ten in the free state and if your Daddy is well in with the local T.D., then ye're away with it me boys. Solve a crime? Sure some of them wee shits couldn't solve a crossword puzzle".

He stood up again and banged his fist on the table and cheered and this frightened the life out of the both of us for a minute or two, as if we, as freestaters, could be just as guilty by association.

I looked over at James and he winked at me and then I sensed we'd be okay so long as we agreed with everything he said. We talked more. He had no problem with us, we were only childer, he informed us.

It was the polis and the Church that pissed him off the most, that along with the nosey do-gooders!

And now they were organising the mission, he told us, and an ould timer of a priest was coming in for the Mass and the Confession and the Benediction and the whole lot, and there they'd be, the hypakrits, all running to the rails every morning and evening and the same holyjoes had been going around that very day and them getting people to sign a petition to have him, TomFada, driven outta the parish.

"So much for free-state Christianity me wee men, sure Dr. Ian Paisley himself, as bad as he's supposed to be, wouldn't see me stuck, I can tell ye", he shouted. He banged his fist again. Both our cups leapt. We looked at each other. There then followed an awkward pause.

"That's a terror", I replied, meekly, trying to comfort him and distance ourselves, the Conartys, from all such dirty acts of slyness in the process. The clock read twenty five past ten as he reached for a bottle of stout and, having opened it with a gadget he'd taken from his inside pocket, TomFada slowly poured the contents into a long, thin glass that had a crack running down about half an inch from its top. The froth nestled neatly, just like it would for McGunker, and he waited a minute or two before toasting our good health and fortune and then he apologised sincerely for having no lemonade or coke so that we, in turn, could toast him, TomFada, back! We assured him it didn't matter.

He wiped away his bubbly moustache and then topped up the stout once again. We watched and we waited and we passed no remarks. And then he talked more. Lots more. About his own life and where it had taken him and how the drink had affected him and how he wished he could turn the clock back, and the things he'd seen and done in his seventy seven years to date on the planet. Things he'd said and mistakes he'd made and regrets he had. His wife had left him years earlier and he'd only seen his childer, who by now had childer of their own, once or twice in the last twenty five years. Anyway it didn't matter now. Soon he'd be going, he informed us, not just from the mountain but from this life itself too, altogether! We looked at each other.

"Och aye, it's a fact, me wee friends, I'll be going soon, wild soon, it's a fact, sure the wee woman told me herself". TomFada rattled his box of matches and then lit up one of Packie's Sweet Aftons. The smoke came down his nose.

"What wee woman?" James asked him. TomFada was thinking. He tipped the ash to the floor and then kicked it away again as if disgusted with himself for messing up his otherwise spotless floor in the first place.

"Ye don't have to be running to Mass and the Mission and the like me wee men to get close to the mawn above. Sure I haven't stood in a chapel in years and yet I know when the time comes, and it'll be soon, I'll get as good a deal from the Almighty as anyone else in the queue". He smiled. We agreed by nodding our heads but only to keep him happy. Sure we both knew it was horrid important to be going to Mass every Sunday and the Benediction with the smokey yoke that the priest used and the confessions too. Sure everyone did. And once I was going to tell the priest that I was guilty of day dreaming about Kevin Keegan scoring a diving header when he was preaching of a Sunday but thought I'd better not in case he'd tell Dad and then there'd be ructions altogether. And sure then Andy Traynor told me it wouldn't have mattered a damn cos the priest wasn't allowed to tell anyone your sins anyway, not even if you confessed to committing a murder, he'd still have to keep quiet about it. Anyway TomFada stubbed out his fag.

"Who's the wee woman ya mentioned TomFada?" James asked again. He looked at him and thought for a second. The lines in his forehead deepened again.

"Sure a sight of the people going to Mass aren't Christian at all, me wee men", he told us, "better off staying at home as heathens than running up the aisle as hypakrits, sure they're so heavenly they're no earthly addition". And then he proceeded to tell us that the daecentest man in County Cavan was John Maughan himself, the travelling man, the carpet man. A man that'd never see ya stuck for a fiver in your pocket or a heal of bread in your mouth and him as good a Christian as any you could meet, if not ten times better, than some of the bucks within in the Cathedral lepping about in their smart suits and ties and them shouting about all they were doing, a bit like the farasees you'd read about in the bible. I didn't understand.

TomFada lit another fag and, reaching over our heads, pulled an old book from the shelf. I could smell the sweat of him. It was a terror, but I passed no remarks.

He opened it up and read a few lines to himself. Then he snapped it shut and a sprinkling of dust dropped on to the table.

"This boy C.S. Lewis is a wild good writer me wee men, I've read most of his stuff, aye", he informed us. "He says a proud mawn can never see God cos he's wild busy looking down on everyone and everything else about him and when he's doing that he can't see what's above him wee men, and do ye know whose above him? Sure it's the mawn above himself, aye…God Almighty". We looked at each other. He scratched his head. "Aye, the free state me wee friends, too much pride and too much prejudish, excepting people like John Maughan of course and yerselves too, I'd imagine, be the looks of things, ye're not here judging me are ye? Wee men!" We shook our heads. Anyway I was just about to ask him what prejudish meant when he leapt again.

"Quick boys, ye better go now, I'm expecting a visitor, come back tomorrow night and we'll have a wee chat then", he whispered. He looked at his watch and seemed a bit flustered. We hopped up. James turned. "Who's the wee woman ya talked about TomFada?" I didn't understand. Was James teasing him? I wasn't sure. I looked at James. He looked anxious. TomFada sighed. Putting his big hand on my brother's shoulder he informed him that the wee woman was the Predicktor. He ushered us towards the door. "What's a predicktor?" enquired James as the caravan door opened and then flapped back into the darkness. We stepped down unsure of ourselves.

"The predicktor predickts things", whispered TomFada.

"What does that mean?" I whispered back in innocence. He paused.

"She's the voice of the future wee mawn, the voice of the future, she's been there boys and knows what's going to happen long before it does to any of us. It's all in her eyes you see, she's on her way now so hurry up and be off with ye and thanks again for the fags wee mawn, thank ye". I tried to mutter something back but my lips wouldn't move and anyway the door had by now closed again and TomFada was gone, back inside No Fixed Abode.

We walked in the silent and still darkness of Shantemon's night and I was fearful of someone or something bumping into us. We didn't scuffle our feet like we'd normally do or talk or laugh either, not till we were coming down Ned's brae. I kept thinking we'd be dragged off somewhere by someone unknown, never to be seen again and Dad and Mam would come home and be wondering why the cows hadn't been milked and they'd be bawling at the gate and the boys and Philomena would have no one to play soccer with again and it'd be on the RTE news and it'd be all my fault for wandering off in the first place and what if…?

Anyway we kept walking. James cleared his throat and spat. "That's a load of shite that predicktor stuff, pass no remarks of him Michael", he said. I agreed though I wasn't so sure. The light in the kitchen blinded us momentarily and I squinted at the Sacred Heart on the wall. I could see that he had that "tut tut, ye shouldn't have been out so late" look about him and I felt bad and couldn't concentrate when James started the prayers. I hated this confusion. Anyway we went to sleep but that whole night a small, white haired woman screeched round Shantemon Mountain in my dreams and I woke up shivering with the cold in the morning. I tried to blank her outta my mind but I couldn't and by the time they were home from Athlone I wasn't sure what to be afraid of most, the white haired predicktor or Kathleen below in the shop, who might tell on me about the Sweet Afton fags and then there'd be trouble and I wouldn't be needing your one to predickt things for me cos I'd be dead anyway if Jimmy Conarty found out. The hours went by and nothing happened and no one passed any remarks and I knew I'd be safe, at least till Dad went into the shop, which he did only once in the week anyway, and sure by then Kathleen might've totally forgot. Mam talked about DAthlones and the great time they'd had and the way Harry had kept so quiet by writing his figures and sure Tony had nearly gone and had himself a heart attack when he'd seen how far he'd gone, over 900,000.

"Be Jaysus you're some boy alright Harry", he'd said to him within in the kitchen behind Hughes Bar and Lounge. Anna Mae had sent up heavy shirts for the winter, ould ones of Aidey's. The sleeves were too long but sure she could stitch them back up for us and they'd do rightly. Mam held one up against James. He grunted.

"Did anyone call or did yous go anywhere boys?" Dad wanted to know after the tea. We looked at each other. "No", we both chorussed. Eddie smiled at me as if to say he knew we'd surely been up to something.

I looked away from him and picked up the Evening Press and read about Georgie Best being chased by the guards beyond in America. I thought of Pele and the daughter and when I pictured Bomber's curly hair and cheeky grin, I smiled to myself.

Chapter 41

Anyway Dad was going to Sean Boylans that Sunday night. It had been arranged and that was that. He was bringing me and James with him by way of a treat for stopping at home when they'd been below in Athlone. Tommy and Eddie protested. Harry wrote his figures and Philomena read a Scooby doo comic. Dad shaved. We listened.

"The young the old
 The brave and the bold".
Now and again he'd laugh to himself.
Then Mam talked to him and brushed the collar of his tag coat. He picked at something in his teeth. And then we were gone, the four boys and him, our Dad. Nothing was said. He parked the car alongside Oliver Young's menswear shop and led the way in. Who was standing inside the door only Capper?
They looked at each other.
Dad held out his hand and they shook.
"What'ya drinking?" Dad asked him. It was over. Tommy adjusted his glasses and no one called him names any more. We sat in the corner, the four of us, drinking the red lemonade that Gretta had placed in front of us and watching Dirty Harry Callaghan on the telly that nestled high above us beyond in the far corner. The

McGunker

Sweet Afton clock read five minutes past ten. Eddie enquired about the availability of Tayto crisps. Gretta smiled. "Coming up bucko, coming up".

The place was packed and I watched Dad as he mingled with the other men and laughed. This was his kinda pub and his kinda people, McGunker, Peter Rooney, Francie Kelly, Jackie Fitch, Murphy, Mickey O'Brien, Phil Kane and his brother Seamus. Everyone seemed friendly. Sean Boylan winked at us. He'd had the place painted or undercoated at least, and wanted it finished in good time for Christmas, which to be fair was still ages away. But he wondered when Johnny Greenan would be back?

"Didya specify which Christmas Sean?" Peter Rooney asked. The men laughed. Our Eddie came back from the toilet and he was laughing too. He wanted us out. One by one we followed him. Someone had written a verse on the inside of the wee toilet door.

"Here I sit broken hearted
Thought I shit
But only farted".
J.G, July 1975.

Sure we found it hilarious. "J.G must be Johnny Greenan", James informed us, "remember Sean said he was painting".

On the way back up the narrow hallway who did we meet only Capper? We stood in to let him pass. He looked at us. "What are yous drinking boys, Cavan Cola or red lemonade?" he asked.

We looked at each other.

"Ah we're ok thanks anyway", James replied. Back at our table Gretta handed in another bottle of red lemonade and four packets of tayto. She gestured towards someone. We looked round and Capper lifted his pint of Guinness and said "Good health lads". "Cheers", Eddie replied.

I suddenly had one of my flashbacks. I thought of TomFada beyond on Shantemon and him having nothing for me and James to toast him with and then a shiver ran down my spine as I pictured the white haired predicktor and her lepping and squealing her way round the mountain.

Tommy noticed my trance like appearance.

"Michael, Michael, what's up?" I snapped out of it.

"Nothing, aw nothing", I replied. Anyway someone leapt into Dirty Harry's blue, Ford Cortina looking car and he stood there watching him drive off in it, which wasn't like something he'd normally do. Your man only got a few yards and she blew up in flames.

Dirty Harry looked down at us and said, "A man's gotta know his limitations".

Jackie Fitch was lilting away and had probably never heard tell of Dirty Harry or could care less about him. The place went quiet. Sean Boylan dried a glass. Mickey O'Brien started telling a joke. Phil Kane called for husht.

Anyway it was about these two men and they were good friends and one of them had a stammer and the other fella had a short leg and they went everywhere together.

And one day the stammerer said,

"Do, do, do, yo you kno know some something? I, I, I have a, a, go, gooo, good cure for, for you, your, shor, short leg prob, problem".

McGunker was laughing already.

"Shusht will ya", Mickey's son Barry ordered. He had a smile on his face, a suppressed smile that seemed to blend in with his rugged features and curly hair. We liked Barry.

Mickey carried on.

"Why, why, why don don't ya, ya wa, walk with the shor, short leg on, on the foo, foot, footpath and the goo, good one on, on, on the ro, ro, road and no, nobody'll no, no, notice?"

And sure your man with the short leg thought this was a great idea and off he went down the street, whistling away to his heart's content and him walking level for the first time in his life. And sure everything was going grand, Mickey O'Brien informed us, till a bus came along at the other end of the street and wiped your man clean out. Anyway an ambulance came and took him to the hospital. The stammerer felt bad and so he bought a bunch of flowers and went to visit his friend. Eventually he found him stretched out in a bed covered from head to toe in plaster of paris. They looked at each other. The stammerer looked awkward cos it had been his idea in the first place. And then your man announced,

"Do you know something, I've a great cure for your stammer".

"Wha, wha, what is, is it?" his friend asked.

"Keep your fecking mouth shut".

The place erupted. Eddie Murphy slapped O'Brien on the back and McGunker shouted "One for the road". The men cheered. Sean Boylan looked anxious now.

"Ah boys c'mon, it's nearly two o'clock in the morning and dem hoors of guards'll be round soon", he protested.

Ould Mickey Brady from Shankill stood up and announced…

"I'd better be going boys, Agnes is expecting..", he paused for a second and everyone looked. "..expecting Mickey home".

The men all laughed again. Sean Boylan smiled. The smoke by now was a terror. I rubbed my eyes and wanted, just like my brothers, to get out and get home.

Then Eddie found a butt of a crayon somewhere and headed back towards the toilet. We followed him and all crammed in. Derby County, champions of the world, he scrawled beneath the verse we'd read earlier. We all took turns. West Ham won the cup! Kevin Keegan rules! Arsenal are magic! Eddie took the crayon again and added Shite for Man United and the Bomber Breslin!

We left laughing and met McGunker and the other men in the narrow hallway.

"Ha-Ho it's the McGunker Conartys", he announced. "Boys oh boys, the McGunker Conartys". Sean Boylan closed the door out quietly after us. Everyone from Castletara, ourselves included, piled into RID 550. I looked across at the surgical hospital through the back window and wondered were they all asleep and hoped the noise wouldn't waken some poor sick soul. A light fog had descended by the time we reached Lismagratty. "Good luck Murphy", Dad called as Eddie hopped out. He slapped his hand on the roof and we headed off home with Kelly. His lane seemed stranger and darker than usual. "Bejeminey, I bet ya the Bailieboro wans were here and I missed them, well feck it anyway", he muttered, getting out. Dad laughed.

We blessed ourselves going up past Castletara Chapel and I thought of poor Nanna lying within in the graveyard. Thinking of her and trying to remember what Uncle Eddie had said about Paddy Kavanagh's dead mother meant we were up at Hughie Smith's lane before it dawned on me that we'd be going past TomFadas. Tommy and Eddie were asleep. I glanced. His light was off.

"Any word from your man?" Dad asked McGunker.

"No, no, though I see he's still there Jem", he replied.

"Ah deedn't they could leave the poor oul divil alone", Dad muttered, "Sure what harm is he doing?"

He switched the engine off and rolled the car down past the gable end of the shed so as not to waken Roseanne.

They talked for a while and then McGunker got out. "Goodnight Jem, goodnight boys".

Dad carried Eddie in his arms up the stairs and pegged him into the bed.

"Not so ould fashioned now are ya?" he laughed.

"Don't forget the prayers boys", he reminded us. The smell of fag smoke from my shirt sleeve was a terror. It was so late and cold now and I wanted to go to sleep and knew I should but sure I couldn't. Not with lively thoughts of the predicktor racing through my head and flashbacks to Castletara graveyard. I tried to think of something nice. We were heading into the last week of the holidays and with Bomber coming to his Auntie Kathleens tomorrow there'd bound to be a bit of crack. Still I heard her cackling! The frogman was coming for the frogs on Wednesday and we'd be getting a pile of money.

McGunker

I twisted and turned. The rest were asleep. I thought of Howard McCollum's piggery and wondered would he sell me a pet pig? I'd go for a sow pig and when she'd grow up she'd have her own pigs and then there'd be no need to gather frogs anymore and we'd all be rich, rich beyond our wildest dreams.

Still I lay there worrying. What if the predicktor knew what lay in store for us Conartys? And what if she told TomFada and he told us and it was all bad and what'd happen then? I twisted again. It was no good. Eventually Kevin Keegan came to my assistance and I nodded off. We're playing Manchester City at Anfield, a goal down and only minutes remaining and then Kevin gets fouled in the penalty area and it's a penalty and he gets up covered in muck and dirt and wipes the ball in his jersey and throws it at me. "Go on, son, you can do it, I know you can", he winks at me.

I place the ball and step back seven steps and look at the ref. "Ready when you are son", he says to me.

The Kop are staring with hands clasped. There's silence, an eerie silence. Such expectancy. I look round and can't believe it. So much distraction. Packie Brady is waving an "Up Fianna Fáil" banner. He smiles at me. PJ Lynch is there too and he's grinning, a grin that says he loves Arsenal but wants me to score all the same. Joe Corrigan fills the City net and he's looking impatient. He spreads his gloved hands and claps them together. "C'mon", he roars. I can't move, not yet. I look round again and hear a familiar voice.

"Michael, Michael, she's yours if you score". And there's Howard McCollum draped in a Liverpool flag and him holding up a pet pig for all the world to see. I look at him. He's standing there smiling beside Eddie Fitzsummons who's trying to light his pipe and next to them is McGunker and he shouts, "Go on McGunker Conarty". I stare at them. My knees shake and I'm not so sure I can do it.

"C'mon son, we haven't all night", barks the referee.

Anyway I run forward and hit it with all my might, just as Kev had shown me in training, and guess what? I miss it. The ball ends up in the crowd. There's a few seconds stunned silence and then the Kop roars, "Ahh, feck it anyway!" There's no time for the kickout now and it's all my fault. I can't look at anyone. Kevin comes running towards me and puts his arm round my shoulder. "Don't worry about it Michael", he says. I smile. "My grandfather's oirish, did I ever tell ya?" he says next. We look at each other. And then Georgie Best steps out with Miss World and they walk over the pitch towards us and she's picking her steps cos of the fact that she's wearing fancy high heels and Georgie looks at me and says "Hey Michael, has Pele got a daughter?" Kevin pulls me forward. "Do what your mother'd do and that's pass no remarks of him, Michael", he whispers in my ear.

Still I can't resist a look back at the pair of them. Georgie's still smiling. "Ha, ya missed a penalty at Anfield Conarty and do ye know what? Bomber Breslin's gonna love this, ha ha ha", he teases me. And Miss World just stands there grinning.

Chapter 42

Anyway Fitches dog, Bonzo, died the very next day at half past twelve. I know cos we were there above at the crossroads or at least not too far from it when it happened. It was an accident, everyone agreed. Sure how was poor Aussie Kelly to see him lying there and him stretched out in the midday sun on the middle of the road with not a care in the world to annoy him. It was the back wheel of the tanker that got him. We'd met Bomber and were heading back in Boylan's lane to go to Shantemon lake, with nothing specific in mind. Bomber had a new watch, a digital one at that, with a fancy silver wrist band. We gawked at it. "Top of the range boys, aye, top of the range", he'd just said. By the time we'd run back up the lane and reached the scene of the carnage I estimated that two minutes had elapsed since hearing Bonzo's last yelp. Bomber's watch read 12:32.

Bonzo lay there with his tongue sticking out. A little bit of blood trickled from his ear. Tommy nudged him in the arse with the tip of his right wellie. We waited. No movement, nothing. Bonzo was dead alright and Aussie was horrid upset. We stood there. Then Annie appeared and we decided to run. I don't know why. Maybe it was instinct. It just seemed the natural thing to do. We'd done it before on countless occasions and now was no different. We ran like hell. Then we stopped. Bomber laughed. "Aye, poor Bonzo, the dopey hoor, that'll teach him to take a wee nap on a busy junction, aye on the middle of a public road for Gawdsakes, boys".

We all laughed now even though we knew we shouldn't. It didn't feel right. After all we'd grown up with and accustomed to Bonzo and now he was gone. "Gone to that great big kennel in the sky", as Bomber had put it.

Anyway we walked on hoping that Eamonn Boylan was down from Dublin but he wasn't. Bomber informed Matt of Bonzo's tragic passing and wondered whether we should all stand for a minute's silence. Matt smiled. "Ya cheeky wee hoor ya Breslin, here lift that yard brush and make yourself useful, instead of giving your guff", Matt shouted, trying to be serious and finding it impossible not to laugh. We went through the fields at Ellens and reached Shantemon lake and then indulged in our favourite pastime, stone throwing! We fired away aimlessly. I could feel the sweat on the soles of my feet and begrudged Bomber his swanky new runners and the watch too.

"Mind the swans", Harry roared, "they could be the childer of Lir that Uncle Eddie told us about". We looked at each other. And then we kept on firing. Boredom set in and we doddled on round by the lake. It was only a matter of time I felt, before TomFada's name came up and sure enough it did. "Aye, I hear he's not right in the head boys, out on the road at night roaring and shouting, och aye, like a madman, shouting about the future and end-times, whatever the fuck that is, for Gawdsakes boys!" Bomber informed us.

"Och he's dangerous alright and the sooner he's locked up the better, aye". We were lying up against the lone cock of hay that stood on Dunne's hill overlooking the still waters of Shantemon lake. Everyone had their own bit of grass to chew on. "Och, he's strange alright", Bomber continued. James looked over at me and I looked back at him and neither of us passed any remarks. OMERTA. The sun shone down and we could've stayed there the whole day and we probably would've done if it hadn't been for the strange and sudden smell of smoke that engulfed us. The six of us leapt. Dunne's cock of hay was on fire and our Tommy and Eddie were laughing. We ran. We kept on running like we always did. Looking back I could see the flames raging now and the cock of hay disintegrating. "Yous pair of hoors", James roared. Bomber was in stitches. I understood. It was like a re-run of Bonzo's death. The harm was done and there was no point in hanging around. James was like a bull and couldn't see the funny side of it. He leapt around punching the air. "It's alright talking, it's alright talking, Dunne's not stupid and he'll know rightly it was us, and I'll get blamed as usual…and you will as well Michael, so I don't know what you're grinning about, ya stupid bollox ya", he roared.

He stormed on ahead. "Why, why…?", Harry began. We looked back at the smouldering pile. Anyway it transpired that the pair of boys had found a box of matches the night beforehand within in Sean Boylans and had waited till now to test them. We wandered around aimlessly through the neighbouring fields and eventually James cooled down sufficiently to double back and meet us.

Nothing was said.

We fleeced the crab apple tree at Petie McKiernans and headed back for the crossroads. Bomber began humming.

"Felim Dunne
Superstar
His cock-o-hay
Looks like a
Black jack bar!"

Harry struggled to keep up. The heel of his wellie was hurting him a terror and he was afraid to take it off in case the skin would peal in the process. "Why aren't yous going home be the fields?", he pleaded.

This was our normal route but since a couple of hours had by now elapsed since Bonzo's passing, we felt it safe enough to go back to the scene and see how things were.

There wasn't a stir.

Bomber plucked a dandelion and placed it on the road. We looked at him. He grinned.

"Bonzo Miney
Superstar
That's what ya get
For sleeping on the tar".

We tried not to laugh and it was just as well. The sight of Jackie coming down from the garden with a shovel on his shoulder changed our mood entirely. We all knew what that dog had meant to him. He turned the corner and it was the first time we'd ever met Jackie and him not to be lilting. We stood there numbed. "Howya lads", he gestured. He walked in. No one said anything. There was nothing to say. Even Bomber was speechless. Anyway Mam had the rice made when we got in. "Well boys, any news? What are yous up to today?", she enquired handing us out the dishes. Her glasses were steamed up again. "Aw this and that, not much...you know yourself Mam", James replied. But she didn't and we could only hope she never would and what she didn't know wouldn't harm her. I looked at Harry and wondered...

Anyway the row was inevitable.

Bomber wanted football. We needed frogs for the frogman on Wednesday. One by one we headed away. He called us peasants when Eddie tanted him and he stormed off in a huff, frothing as only he could. Mam was at the clothes line and came over to try and diffuse the situation. "Shite for him, let him go, the spoilt prick", James instructed. Still she followed. "Martin, Martin, don't mind them", she pleaded. Bomber kept going.

"Peggy Dearg is right, aye, yer only a shower of tramps... and, and she's putting a curse on ye, aye, and she's right", he shouted back, "aye see what happens then".

"Go on ya prick ya", James roared.

Then we traded more insults.

McGunker

"And, and your cousin is gay", he boomed. We looked at each other.

"Aye, gay, do ye hear me? I heard all about him in Brady Brothers last night, aye, he's gay alright, a right homo if ever there was one", he droned in his Belfast accent. Mam gave up and wheeled back and when she was safely out of firing range, we traded stones.

"Get back to Belfast ya brit git ya Breslin", I roared.

The boys laughed. Harry dropped his frog bag. "What's, what's gay?" he asked. No one answered.

The truth of the matter was we didn't know what gay meant. Obviously Bomber did and this only irritated us older ones.

"Ould-fashioned wee fat cunt", muttered Tommy.

Heading down the meadow we could hear him loud and clear above on the pass.

"Frogs! Frogs! For Gawdsakes boys, I ask ye, frogs?" We passed no remarks.

Then he quit, for a while anyway.

"Glory, glory Man United, glory, glory…" James smiled. It was a smile of resignation. We knew this moment would pass and that he'd be back and that all would be forgotten and that we'd carry on as usual like we always did. We could say what we liked about Bomber and he about us. The fact remained; he liked us and we liked him.

Anyway we caught forty one between us which wasn't bad, before the drizzle came to dampen our spirits.

We knew from experience that this was the best time of the evening to catch them but the escapades of earlier in the day had caught up with us leaving tired limbs aching to get home. Besides Steptoe was on and we rarely missed it.

We trudged through the bog field. Bruno followed. Harry struggled to keep up and we stopped once or twice to wait for him.

"Wha, wha, what's gay again boys…are we gay?"

We looked at each other. Silence.

"C'mon we'll miss Steptoe", Eddie shouted as he tore on ahead.

James entered the details into our frog-book and poured in a half bucket of water. The very next day Mam picked up a few odds and ends within in Maurice Brady's for us going back to school. I know cos we were all there standing behind her and Dad had warned us to have manners or he'd break someone's neck when he'd get home from Smith's garage that evening. Eddie hummed…

"Bomber Breslin
Superstar
Thinks he's great
In Brady's bar".
We grinned at each other.
Mam picked out the vests.
Maurice Brady passed no remarks.

Chapter 43

Anyway Wednesday came and we kept ten pence apiece outta the frogman's money. James gave Mam the rest. She looked at us proudly and her top lip quivered.

"Your father's right childer, yous are good gasuns", she told us and before Philomena could protest, she smoothed her hair and said "and you're the best wee frog-spotter in Ireland". Our little sister beamed. We headed for Packies. We always did. The two younger ones struggled to keep up, not so much Philomena as Harry.

"Hey, hey, wait for us", she pleaded.

Jack Rahill filled his wooden bread tray and whistled. He smiled when he saw us coming across.

"Ha ho Jack, ya boy ya", Eddie greeted. Jack laughed.

Inside, Packie was counting the coppers as he called them. The wireless was on.

"Ah bad cess to them anyway", he muttered. We thought it was someone from Fine Gael. "Are ya…?" and that was as far as James got.

"Whisht, whisht will ya gasun, sit down there and listen and ya might learn something", Packie insisted.

He handed out penny sweets to keep us quiet. Jack Rahill sat too. He winked at us. And no, it was no one from Fine Gael. The men on the radio were talking about the Fethard Boycott that had happened way back in 1957, long before any of us were born. It was horrid interesting. Anyway wasn't there a Protestant woman and wasn't she married to a Catholic man below in County Wexford and that's how it all started. And your woman didn't want their childer going to a Catholic school and the priest put them under horrid pressure to send them. But sure your woman didn't pass any remarks. "That was her right and privilege", Packie interjected. He coughed. We looked at each other. Jack Rahill smiled.

Anyway she was so troubled that she moved up to the North and then on to Scotland. And then the Catholics refused to buy anything in the Protestant shops below in Wexford and none of them sent their childer to the music teacher who was a Protestant too and the Catholic teacher left the Protestant school and the cleaner, who was a Catholic too, refused to clean the Protestant church and the bell ringer quit as well. It was an ojous mess altogether. "Sure it bet all, it was a fret", Packie stated as we waited for the Angeleus bell. He stopped. The men took off their caps and muttered quietly to themselves and we muttered quietly too, pretending to pray, and doing our damndest not to laugh. When all was done, Packie put the sliced pans and batches from McDonnell's bakery under his counter leaving one or two of each for show on the top.

"Poor oul Dev, the lord a mercy on him", Packie started. He took off his cap and put it on again.

"Sure only for Dev, it woulda been a terror altogether, sure he knew the Catholics were wrong, the priests and the Bishops together and didn't he try to make them see sense and eventually they did and on this very date eighteen years ago today, didn't it all end when the parish priest went into the Protestant shop to buy something". We looked at each other. "What did he buy Packie?" James asked.

"Who?" he replied.

"The priest in the shop Packie, what did he buy?"

"Ah, a package of fags or something me gasun, it doesn't right matter, the main thing was the boycott was over and sure only for Dev, the Lord a mercy on him, it'd still be going on". Jack Rahill got up to go as Luke Costelloe's tractor pulled in on the street.

"Don't you be going marrying a wee Protestant lad, me lassie, do ya hear me now?" Jack said to Philomena as he passed by. Philomena sulked. She didn't like being teased about boys, Protestant or otherwise. We finished our business with Packie and offered Luke a sweet or two. He wasn't too bothered about them but thanked us all the same. We piled out and stood there on the street as the Royals car came into view. Prince Philip looked straight ahead in his nice suit and tie. He had to, herself was with him in the front and she looked like a bull. Maybe it was us? Anyway who's sitting erect in the back seat of the car, smirking away, only the bould Bomber himself.

It was the ultimate act of betrayal. He waved at us. We instinctively stuck up our fingers. Peggy Dearg shook her head in disgust.

"Never again lads, never again", James muttered, as we crossed the Cootehill road. Bruno followed.

We knew Mam had been crying. We could always tell. It was her sniffle and red eyes that gave her away. No one said anything.

"Well childer, I'd say yous are hungry, gimme a minute". She went to the scullery. I picked up Uncle Eddie's par avion letter and read it by the window…

"Dear Phyl and Jimmy and children, every good wish. I sent two letters recently. The last I got from you arrived in July. It can take a letter over a month to come. Letters go to Ireland much quicker. I remember in 1952 (23 years ago) we got a wireless, the first one we ever had. Joe Miney and Charley Bredin dug a hole and put up the aerial pole. Uncle Fr. John came up that evening and was delighted. He said he would get one. That was the first radio (1952) he had seen since 1940 when his old one went out of order in Staghall. It was 14th Sept 1947 that Cavan won the All Ireland in the Polo Grounds USA.

Willie Doonan's mother was from Templeport. It was in September 1953 that Joe Miney and Johnny Conn went to England. Johnny didn't like it much and came home after a few months.

I remember the cold room or coal room at home in 1935. Ma went down and shouted at Da that there was a rat! I saw a rat dropping a small chicken and running away. Da came down and lifted the chicken. It was dead.

When Da was in hospital in Dun Laoghaire I was with Fr. John in Castleraghan. I was about 6½ yrs. Fr. John was going to see him so I wrote a letter to Da.

Fr. John showed me my letter after Da died. I had written: To Da Brady, did the chickens come out of the eggs? (It must have been a hen hatching in Corratubber).

Then Fr. John suddenly stopped talking and when I looked up at him he was crying."

Mam came up from the scullery and I flicked the letter sideways. "C'mon boys some of yous set the table there, will yous?", she asked. James obliged.

I went back to the window.

"...It was in September 1954 that Mary our housekeeper was working for Larry Boylan in a house this side of Belturbet. Ma and me used to go there often and Larry visited us too. Ma knew him well long ago in Crosserlough. He told us that he was never treated different by any of the Protestant police and that they had nothing against the Catholics. One day they got a report that the Catholics in Crossmaglen were rioting and throwing stones. They were told to go there at once and arrest them. But they did not want to, so they took the wrong road on purpose, and arrived in Crossmaglen when all was over and it peaceful. It was in Sept 1950 John Brady (Yankee) went back to U.S. He used to cycle everywhere. He called to our house to say goodbye. Mick Lyons was with him. It was 1st October I started in Courthouse. It was Owen Roe week and Ma and Mrs. Miney walked into Breffney Park. I did not really like the Courthouse or town hall. I felt a stranger in Corratubber on account of the fact of being away so long.

I'm sure the boys are getting big and Philomena too. Tell them to keep reading and keep Harry at the figures!

Every good wish

Ed

P.S. I miss Ma and I know you do too."

I looked round. Our Ma was pounding the spuds. I looked at her and wanted to ask was she alright and couldn't. We all sat down. Her Ma was only dead a wee while and her Da a lifetime. I pictured the dead chicken and wanted to cry. No one passed any remarks.

Anyway TomFada left Castletara on the last Friday in August of 1975. I know cos me and James stood there looking at the empty rectangular site and the pale green grass that hadn't seen sunlight that whole summer. I thought of our Nanna and didn't like this idea of old people going away without ever saying goodbye. There was nothing left, not even an empty whiskey or stout bottle or any of the twigs he used to gather from the mountain and store beneath the doorway of no fixed abode. We looked at each other. Silence. All the time I kept thinking he'd leap out from the ditch behind us and shout "whadda bout ye, wee mawn?" I pictured his crinkly face. Nothing happened. James scuffled a few stones. Still nothing was said. An empty Sweet Afton box fluttered in the breeze that whistled through yon whitethorn bush. It was all that was left of him. I couldn't help but think now of John Tully and the story behind Kettoe's bush and then we turned to go. We had questions, lots of them, as we headed on down the brae.

Where had he gone?

Was he dead?

Had he been arrested?

Was it something to do with the Predicktor?

Was it our fault?

Would McGunker know anything?

Why hadn't we gone back to see him after yon night?
More silence.
We came to the foot of the brae.
"Ha-ho, if it isn't the McGunker Conartys, Gawd boys, yous look as if yous lost an election or something", McGunker laughed.
We smiled.
"Any news from Bomber?" he enquired.
We shrugged our shoulders.
Roseanne appeared with the Crunchie bars.
We stood there, the four of us, engaging in small talk about the weather and going back to school and the like.
"TomFada's gone", James announced.
McGunker and Roseanne looked at each other. "We know", Roseanne replied eventually. She took off her glasses and folded them neatly. "Sure didn't Brother help him pack before the wee lorry towed him away late in the night". We looked at each other.
"Now boys, we know yous got on well with him, the poor oul divil and Gawd knows he caused us no trouble either, but it's best if yous put him behind yous no and pass no remarks", McGunker instructed.
"Where did he go?" James asked.
"Is he alright?" I added.
McGunker produced an envelope, a brown one with sellotape stuck to the back.
"He didn't say boys, he didn't say but he did leave a message for yous and said to say thanks and that he'd always be looking out for yous".
With that McGunker handed over the envelope. James began to rip at it.
"No, no leave it till later boys, it's none of our business", Roseanne interrupted.
James stopped and folding the brown envelope, tucked it neatly into his arse pocket. Nothing was said.

Roseanne put back on her glasses. "It's best forget about him now boys", she told us. "After all yous'll be heading back to school next week and there'll be plenty of work to be done and here boys, there's a little something from Brother and I for all that yous did for us all summer". And with that James was handed his second envelope of the day.

We looked at each other.

We knew it was money, it had to be, especially when McGunker said "put that in with your frog earnings and give it to your mother and help her out, Gawd knows there's enough of yous in it". He smiled.

We shook hands, said thanks and left goodbye.

Turning round, a bit over the road, I could see McGunker and Roseanne still standing there, she with her hands clasped and him lighting a fag. I thought of the Walton childer and the two ould sisters that looked out for them. We had a lot in common. Not just friendship I knew but kinship as well. McGunker and Roseanne treated us like family, their family.

Anyway, we ripped open the envelope crossing our bog field. Six crisp pound notes, one apiece. We couldn't believe it. A small fortune. Temptation only lasts a few seconds. We'd get a bigger kick seeing the look in Mam's eyes when we'd hand it over and Dad standing there saying "Ah the poor ould divils, aren't they shocking daecent, that's McGunker for ya and Roseanne too".

. I can't speak for James but I know my heart fluttered in the goodwill of that moment. He shoved all back into the envelope and stuffed it down again. We kept climbing.

Anyway it was under the plum tree on the Bull's field ditch that we opened TomFada's envelope. The white paper had been folded neatly and when we opened it out, the list, written in scrawly black writing, seemed to go on forever.

"The Predicktor says…" it began.

"Kevin Keegan'll come to Castletara but first he must go to Germany.

Keep an eye on Peggy Dearg, in fact keep both of them on her.

The Pope'll be shot, but not for a while.

Every tree on Shantemon'll be flattened someday.

Elvis Presley'll die, sooner than yous think. Big Tom won't, he'll go on forever.

There'll be women Presidents, but no women priests.

Bruno'll go someday soon and never be seen again. There's no point in looking for him.

Stop throwing stones.

Don't trust the people in uniform record their voices.

Ten IRA men'll die of starvation so have a black flag ready.

There'll come a big man to Castletara and he'll be the best ever. Call him Peter.

Have manners.

Charlie Byrd'll be the main man.

Harry'll reach his target soon".

We flicked the sheet over. On the back was a heading. "Good News" was underlined.

"There'll be another boy and then a girl in the Conarty house. Wait and see."

We looked at each other.

And then we saw it. The word "Warning" stood out above all the others. It too had been underlined.

"Watch out for the woman with the black hair. She'll come among yous and try to divide you up. She'll wear blue hats and have a pale complexion. Watch out for the words she'll write but never sign. Stick together boys, stick together and your sisters too.

Now burn these predictions and say nothing till yous hear more."

We looked at each other.

Anyway, me and James arrived home and amidst the usual mayhem of the evening tea, handed over the envelope, Roseanne's one. Mam fingered the crisp notes gingerly. "Glory be to God", she said before sitting down and adjusting her glasses. "That bates all", said Dad. We thanked the Lord for our food and for McGunker and Roseanne Brady.

It was only when the younger ones had sat down to watch Laurel and Hardy that James winked at me.

We burned that white paper at the back of the hayshed with matches that James had borrowed from Dad's tag-coat pocket. The evening wind took what was left of the ashened script away towards Shantemon. And that was to be that, we both agreed. Omerta.

It was later on that night when it happened. I know cos we were all there at the time in our front room. Harry had been quiet and no one had passed any remarks.

"What comes after all the nines?" he suddenly shouted.

"Whaddya mean all the nines?" Eddie replied.

Harry held up his ledger.

"You know, when you get to 999 comma 999, then what comes after that?"

We looked at each other.

Anyway.

THE END

ISBN 1-41206196-2